m.su

"IT'S GOING TO TAKE ME SOME TIME TO GET USED TO YOUR HONESTY."

Rachel almost laughed. She was not being honest. She was letting this conversation continue because she did not want Wyatt to guess that every word he spoke, everything he did, every glance he gave her threatened to unsettle her completely.

"No, K. C. hasn't been out to *The Ohio Star* since last week."

"Are you sure?"

"I just said I'd be honest with you, didn't I? Do you think I'd lie about something as important as that child is to you?"

"No."

"Then believe me, honey, when I tell you that K. C. hasn't been back to *The Ohio Star* this week."

"Don't say that!"

"What?"

"Don't call her K. C. here! And don't call me honey."

"Could you get into trouble?" he asked, so abruptly serious that she was astonished.

"No . . . Yes . . . River's Haven Community has a certain level of formality that we all are supposed to respect."

"I'll try to remember that." He cupped her elbows and smiled as he bent to kiss her. . . .

BEARLY READ BOOKS
by the 1000's
16441 S.E. Powell
Portland, Oregon 97236
(503) 667-9660

Dear Romance Readers,

In July 1999, we launched the Ballad line with four new series, and each month we present both new and continuing stories set everywhere from medieval England to the American West—the kind of passionate, romantic stories you love best, written by the most gifted authors. At the back of each book, we tell you when you can find subsequent books in the series that have captured your heart.

First up this month is **Moonlight on Water,** the second book in the fabulous new *Haven* series by beloved author Jo Ann Ferguson. Will a young woman leave her familiar community behind for a steamboat's dashing captain? Next, talented Annette Blair takes us back to Regency England to meet **An Undeniable Rogue,** the first irresistible hero in her new series *The Rogues Club.* Marrying a fallen friend's sister is a simple matter of honor for one dashing rake newly returned from the war, until he meets the wildly tempting—and very pregnant—woman in question.

The MacInness Legacy continues with new author Sandy Moffett's **Call Down the Night,** as the second of three sisters separated at birth discovers her gift of second sight may lead her to a strange heritage—and keep her from the man she loves. Finally, talented Susan Grace begins the new series *Reluctant Heroes* with **The Prodigal Son** as one of the infamous Lady Cat's twin sons masquerades as the other—and finds himself falling for his brother's beloved . . .

These are stories we know you'll love! Why not try them all this month?

Kate Duffy
Editorial Director

Haven

MOONLIGHT ON WATER

Jo Ann Ferguson

ZEBRA BOOKS
Kensington Publishing Corp.
http://www.kensingtonbooks.com

ZEBRA BOOKS are published by

Kensington Publishing Corp.
850 Third Avenue
New York, NY 10022

Copyright 2002 by Jo Ann Ferguson

All rights reserved. No part of this book may be reproduced in any form or by any means without the prior written consent of the Publisher, excepting brief quotes used in reviews.

If you purchased this book without a cover you should be aware that this book is stolen property. It was reported as "unsold and destroyed" to the Publisher and neither the Author nor the Publisher has received any payment for this "stripped book."

All Kensington titles, imprints, and distributed lines are available at special quantity discounts for bulk purchases for sales promotion, premiums, fund-raising, educational or institutional use.

Special book excerpts or customized printings can also be created to fit specific needs. For details, write or phone the office of the Kensington Special Sales Manager: Kensington Publishing Corp., 850 Third Avenue, New York, NY 10022. Attn. Special Sales Department. Phone: 1-800-221-2647.

Zebra and the Z logo Reg. U.S. Pat. & TM Off.

First Printing: July 2002
10 9 8 7 6 5 4 3 2 1

Printed in the United States of America

For Barbara Ward
who knows that some children grow in our hearts

**Also look for these Zebra romances
by Jo Ann Ferguson**

His Unexpected Bride
A Kiss For Papa
A Guardian's Angel
His Lady Midnight
A Highland Folly
A Kiss for Mama
Faithfully Yours
A Christmas Bride
Lady Captain
Sweet Temptations
The Captain's Pearl
Anything for You
An Unexpected Husband
Her Only Hero
Mistletoe Kittens
An Offer of Marriage
Lord Radcliffe's Season
No Price Too High
The Jewel Palace
O'Neal's Daughter
The Convenient Arrangement
Just Her Type
Destiny's Kiss
Raven Quest
A Model Marriage
Rhyme and Reason
Spellbound Hearts
The Counterfeit Count
A Winter Kiss
A Phantom Affair
Miss Charity's Kiss
Valentine Love
The Wolfe Wager
An Undomesticated Wife
A Mother's Joy
The Smithfield Bargain
The Fortune Hunter

Haven Trilogy:
Twice Blessed

Shadow of the Bastille Trilogy:
A Daughter's Destiny
A Brother's Honor
A Sister's Quest

And writing as Rebecca North
A June Betrothal

One

River's Haven Community
Indiana
1876

The Assembly of Elders enjoyed drama. Rachel Browning had seen examples of that, time after time, when they had been asked to rule on a request by the residents of the River's Haven Community.

As the trio of men and one woman filed back into the simple room that was filled with enough backless wooden benches to allow seating for all members of the Community, they sat at a table set between two tall windows. On the wall behind them, on either side of a clock, were the American flag and a picture of President Grant. Those were the only items of decoration in the otherwise plain room. The men's black coats and the woman's simple dress were as undecorated.

Only one man wore a beard, the eldest man, who sat in the middle. Mr. Carpenter was one of the founders of the River's Haven Community.

The man on his left, Mr. Johnson, was also a founder. Miss Stokes, the woman on his right, had been the third founder. Recently, Mr. Foley had joined the Assembly of Elders, the first person chosen by the Community to do so in the seven years since River's Haven's establishment near the banks of the Ohio River.

Rachel had been amused in the past by the show of sagacity and ritual. Today she wished they would just announce what they had decided during their hour of deliberations in the small room beyond this one.

"Don't fidget," her older brother muttered, not taking his gaze from the front of the room.

Rachel did not reply. Merrill sat as motionless as the bench beneath him. His hair was black like hers, but his intense eyes were a much lighter shade than her brown ones. In his sedate black frock coat and gray trousers, he resembled the trio of men sitting at the table.

She folded her hands on her skirt that reached no farther than her knees. When she had first arrived in River's Haven Community, she had tugged endlessly at the hem, which was as high as she had worn when she was a child. But in the past few years she had learned to appreciate the shorter skirt and the pantalets beneath it. Her work took her everywhere in the Community, from the sheepfold to the weaving rooms and the metal shop, and it was made easier because of this sensible outfit. As the person in charge of the Community's finances, she was responsible for making the various industries profitable.

Glancing at the clock, Rachel was glad to see that there was still almost an hour before the youngest children would be released from their play. The older children had chores to do, but during the time before supper the ones as young as Kitty Cat were allowed to be with one of their parents.

She watched the Assembly of Elders as they whispered together. Were they still debating the reason that had brought her here today? Rachel's request to the Assembly of Elders had been on behalf of Katherine Mulligan, who preferred the name Kitty Cat. Over three months had passed since Rachel had brought the little girl here from the orphan train that had stopped in the nearby village of Haven. Rachel guessed the little girl was almost seven years old. Kitty Cat knew she had been born on Independence Day, but she did not know which year.

"Miss Browning," said Mr. Carpenter, "we have reached our decision."

She nodded. No one but Mr. Carpenter was allowed to speak during the meeting unless he asked a direct question.

He tugged on his beard, glanced at the others at the table with him, then looked back at her. If some silent message had been passed among the Assembly of Elders, she was not privy to it.

"Miss Browning, we have reviewed your request for Miss Katherine Mulligan to be granted permission to go to Haven to visit the children she traveled with on the orphan train." He paused, and Rachel held her breath.

Kitty Cat had brought more joy to Rachel's life than seemed possible. This chance to see her friends from the orphan train was so important to Kitty Cat, who had been pining for the other children. Kitty Cat spoke of them endlessly, especially two of the older boys named Sean O'Dell and Brendan Rafferty. The little girl had pleaded, over and over, for the chance to visit them and discover if they were happy with their new families. Kitty Cat was content living at River's Haven, but she had spoken over and over of needing to be certain that her friends were happy, too.

"After much discussion," said Mr. Carpenter, "we wish to inform you that your request is denied."

"Denied?" Rachel asked, shocked.

Beside her, Merrill ordered, "Hush, Rachel!" He stood and took her arm, pulling her to her feet.

She yanked her arm out of his grip. Since Merrill had brought them to River's Haven, she had accepted each of the edicts from the Assembly of Elders, even the ones she had believed were ridiculous. *This* she could not accept, not without an explanation of why the Assembly of Elders was about to break a little girl's already well-patched heart.

"Why are you denying Kit—" She halted herself, knowing that the Elders did not approve of nicknames. All the adults in the Community were supposed to address each other as miss or mister. "Why are you denying Katherine the chance to go into Haven for a single day to visit her friends? Such a visit will do no harm to River's Haven, and it'll do much good for Katherine."

"There's no room for debate, Miss Browning. The Elders are in unanimous agreement about this."

"But why?" She ignored her brother's tug on her arm. She could not leave until she understood why they had made this absurd decision.

"It isn't our way to encourage our children to create friendships with those beyond River's Haven." Mr. Carpenter frowned. "You should know that by now, Miss Browning. You have been living here almost three years."

"But she isn't *creating* a friendship. These children are already her friends. She traveled with them from New York City on the orphan train." She edged around the bench and took a step toward the table. Hearing the sharp intakes of breath from both in front of her and from behind her, where Merrill was standing, she halted. She clasped her hands in front of her as she begged, "Please reconsider. It is only one visit, and she'll be so relieved to know that her friends are all right in their new homes."

"The decision was unanimous, Miss Browning." Mr. Carpenter continued to stare at her as if he believed he could daunt her with his gaze.

"Rachel," warned her brother in a near whisper. He took her arm again. This time, when she tried to shake off his hand, his grip tightened. She looked at him, but his eyes were focused on the table where the Assembly of Elders sat as he added in a louder voice, "Forgive my sister for her outburst. She cares so deeply for Katherine Mulligan that I fear she has let her emotions overtake her, making her forget the ways of this Community. She appreciates the Assembly of Elders taking this time to consider her request." He jabbed her with his elbow. "Don't you, Rachel?"

Rachel nodded, although she seethed inside. How could the Assembly of Elders—and her brother—be so short-sighted? Kitty Cat would be completely happy here if she had this single chance to see her friends.

Merrill steered her toward the back of the room. She did not protest. It was useless. The Assembly of Elders had made their decision, and they would not be talked into reconsidering, no matter how many facts she offered them.

"Kitty Cat is going to be terribly upset," Rachel said as they walked out of the building that was dwarfed by the common house where all currently single and childless members of the Community lived. For the married couples and those with small children, there were small cottages on either side of the massive building and the stables. When the final wing of the huge brick building was completed, all members of the Community would be able to live within the common house.

"She must learn to live with River's Haven's rules." Merrill paused on the walk and faced her. "As you must, Rachel. Another outburst like that one, and you will cause the Assembly of Elders to ask us to leave."

"I was simply expressing my opinion." She did not lower her gaze from his angry eyes. "You know that everyone in River's Haven is encouraged to offer opinions."

"But not as you did. You questioned the authority of the Assembly of Elders."

She shook her head. "I most certainly did not. I only requested that I be given an explanation for their decision. That was not unreasonable."

Merrill strode toward the common house, then turned

and walked back to her. Jabbing a finger at her, he said, "Bringing that child here was a mistake."

"She needed a home, and we have a home here. The Assembly of Elders has said so often that we should reach out to those who need River's Haven and will embrace its principles."

"When are *you* going to embrace our principles?" he fired back.

"I already do."

"Do you? You haven't agreed to any marriage arrangement offered to you."

Rachel hoped her bonnet concealed her flush from anyone who might walk by. "Merrill, I would prefer to speak of this in private."

"Why?" His eyes narrowed. "The arrangement of compound marriage here still bothers you, doesn't it?"

She looked around and saw others of the Community on the stone walks through the green grass. She must choose her words with care, for she wanted to keep from hurting anyone. This Community, in spite of what Merrill seemed to believe, had become her home. She did not want to be banished from River's Haven because she spoke words that ridiculed the teachings of the Assembly of Elders, especially the tenet of compound marriage, which was a keystone of the Community.

Mr. Carpenter had taught that having a marriage last for only a year before it was dissolved so that the husband and wife might seek other mates, if they wished, had a twofold purpose. It dismissed the idea of the family unit of only a husband and a wife and their children. Instead, the family was the whole of the Community, but it was a very formal family. Only those related by blood and within a marriage used given names.

In addition, this arrangement protected a woman from dying from endless sessions of pregnancy and childbirth. If a woman wished to take some time between husbands and births, then she could without being ostracized. This second part of compound marriage was what had appealed to Rachel after having her mother and two cousins die in childbirth. Too many women contracted childbirth fever and were lost, some along with their children. She wished there was another way to save those women, but River's Haven's compound marriage was the only solution she had discovered yet.

And she loved children, which was why she had hurried to the nearby village of Haven as soon as she heard of the orphan train's arrival. From the first moment she had seen Kitty Cat among the other children, Rachel had welcomed the little girl into her heart. Kitty Cat had been as eager for a family, and she was happy . . . except when she was anxious about her friends.

"Rachel, why won't you answer me?" demanded her brother. "Or do you fear answering?"

"Don't be absurd." She smiled, although she had never felt less like doing so. "You know the answer is simple to why I haven't married. I haven't found the right man to marry yet."

He snorted. "You had best do so soon, or the Assembly of Elders will do so for you."

"I know." She began to walk again toward her cottage. It was time to end this conversation before Merrill suggested another person who might be the best first husband for her. Pausing, she looked back to add, "Thank you, Merrill, for coming with me this afternoon."

"Think about what I've said," he called to her before striding in the opposite direction.

That would be an easy request to obey. She had thought of little else in the past month, ever since Merrill had first brought up the subject of having a man share the cottage where she and Kitty Cat lived. His subtle hints had dissolved into blatant orders.

Rachel hurried to the front door of her light blue cottage.

The door was a bright red that she had painted herself. Those who lived in the cottages were allowed to paint them any color they wished, although each of the rooms in the common house were identical.

Her smile returned when she entered her home. She and Merrill had brought only a few things with them when they came to River's Haven. He had not wanted to take anything, but Rachel treasured these few connections with the past. Save for a rag doll that she had given Kitty Cat, a small metal pot that held colorful and odd-shaped stones found by the river, and the guitar that her father had taught her to play were the only things that were truly hers. Everything else Merrill had sold or given away.

There had been those who pleaded with her to stay in the small Ohio town where she had been born, but, after so recently suffering her father's passing within a year of her mother's death, she did not want to lose all her family. So she had come with Merrill, hoping, as he did, that they would find a new family at River's Haven.

Merrill had found that family quickly when he married his first wife, Susan Tyler. She had three other sisters living in River's Haven. Her youngest, Carol, had become Merrill's second wife eighteen months later.

Rachel had tried to make a life for herself here, too. She discovered that her skills with numbers could be put to good use in helping manage the financial business of the Community. The position, which she could never have aspired to in the world beyond River's Haven, gave her a great deal of satisfaction. Since their arrival, she had let herself believe that contentment in a job well done was the same as being happy. She had been mistaken, for, although her days had been filled with the hubbub of the Community, each night she slept in silence in her narrow room in the common house.

When Mr. Atlee, who brought paperwork from the metal shop, came back from the village of Haven with news of an orphan train coming from New York City, Rachel had decided to build herself a family with one of the orphans. The approval from the Assembly of Elders for her to bring a child to join the Community had come swiftly, and she had gone to Haven. There, she had met Katherine Mulligan, her very dear Kitty Cat.

Rachel sighed as she untied her simple bonnet and put it on the table. She walked along the short hallway that led to the two bedrooms that were even smaller than the ones in the common house. Kitty Cat's had a narrow bed and several hooks for the little girl's clothes. In the middle of the bed, waiting for Kitty Cat's return, was her precious rag doll.

On the other side of the hallway was Rachel's bedroom. It contained a double bed and a single chest of drawers. A writing table with a bench was set to one side, and there was a washstand beneath the window. Her beloved guitar, which Kitty Cat loved to hear her play, leaned against the headboard. A rag rug on the floor added the only color to the room, but the view through the open window was so glorious that she never noticed how plain the room was.

She loved to stand by the window and watch the wide river slip between the banks. The Ohio River, which was framed by trees on both sides, could be bright blue or a ferocious gray, depending on the weather. Boats followed its currents or fought their way upriver. In the winter, when the leaves had fallen, she could see a small farm on the Kentucky side of the river. The people there followed the same patterns as the residents of River's Haven, but the river separated them completely. The closest bridge was more than a day south.

Today she did not linger to enjoy the view. She dropped to sit on the bed. The iron springs creaked, but she paid no attention.

How was she going to tell Kitty Cat that her request had been denied?

"Rachel!" Kitty Cat's voice rang through the cottage. "Rachel, are you here?"

Knowing that she could not lie to the little girl, Rachel stood and went into the front room. A smile tugged at her lips when she saw how dusty Kitty Cat's bright red curls were. Dirt was painted across the child's freckled cheeks. One stocking was drooping over her high shoes, and the other had been ripped across the knee.

"What have you been up to?" Rachel asked as she held out her arms.

Kitty Cat hugged her enthusiastically. "I've been learning to play baseball."

She was about to remark that baseball was a boy's game, but she bit back her comment. Here in River's Haven all the children were supposed to be raised without the social bigotry beyond its borders. A girl could play ball, and a boy might sit and enjoy a doll, if that was what the child wished.

"Kitty Cat, I have something to tell you."

Her voice must have given away her dismay, because Kitty Cat's smile vanished and tears boiled up into her large brown eyes. The little girl gulped back a sob when Rachel took her by the hand and sat on the well-worn sofa, sinking deeply into the cushions.

"Did you speak to the Assembly of Elders?" whispered the little girl.

"Yes," Rachel said as softly. "They said they don't want you to go to Haven now."

Kitty Cat burst into tears. Sobbing, she pressed her face against Rachel's knees. Rachel held the little girl while she wept. She leaned her head against Kitty Cat's unruly red curls, knowing that she had broken this most precious promise. She was unsure if she could persuade the little girl to trust her again.

When Rachel drew her up to sit beside her, the little girl regarded Rachel with large watery eyes. She looked away, but not before she saw the pain on Kitty Cat's face. She wanted to keep the little girl from seeing hers.

She took Kitty Cat's hand and grimaced when she felt the dampness. Kitty Cat had been using the back of it to wipe her nose again.

Too distressed to chastise her, Rachel said, "I am so sorry, Kitty Cat. I will ask again in a few weeks at the regular Community meeting. Then, they might agree."

"A few weeks? How many?"

"Three or four."

"Four? That's a month, isn't it?"

Rachel nodded, knowing that it would be useless to try to fool the little girl. Kitty Cat, despite her life on the streets of the slums of New York City—or maybe because of it—learned with a speed that astonished Rachel. Already she was excelling in school, passing her peers. The teacher had hinted that Kitty Cat might be older than six, but Rachel had pretended not to hear. As soon as a child celebrated his or her seventh birthday, that child was supposed to go live in the children's section of the common house. Rachel had only just found Kitty Cat. She did not want to turn her over to the matrons in the children's dormitory so soon.

"A month is *so* long," Kitty cried. "Sean may have forgotten all about me!"

"He won't forget about you. Just as you won't forget about him." She took the little girl by the shoulders and looked directly into Kitty Cat's brown eyes. "I promise you that I will ask the Assembly of Elders as soon as *three* weeks have passed. All right?"

Kitty Cat stared at her, then nodded reluctantly.

"Would you like to sleep in here with me tonight? I will tell you a story, and then you can tell me one." She smiled, hoping Kitty Cat would eagerly agree as she always did. Rachel loved the times when, cuddled together under the quilt, they laughed and pretended to be frightened as they took turns telling each other silly and scary stories.

Kitty Cat shook her head as she wiped another pair of tears from her dark eyes.

Rachel smoothed the child's red curls back and kissed Kitty Cat on the forehead. She would find a way to make this up to the little girl, even if she had to petition the Assembly of Elders every month for the rest of the year. She hoped that would be enough to satisfy the little girl.

The next day, when Kitty Cat did not come home from playing with the other children, Rachel knew it had not been.

Two

Wyatt Colton set two cases of supplies on the counter in Haven's general store. The blond woman behind the nicked counter quickly calculated his order. Beside her was the list of parts he had asked her to get from Louisville.

A long list . . . and a long shot at getting *The Ohio Star* back to work. The side-wheeler had barely made it to the pier in the Ohio River below the bluffs where this village sat. He and his partner, Horace Appleby, were the only ones left aboard. The rest of the crew had hitched a ride on another steamboat to Cincinnati.

Captain Hancock had wanted to scuttle *The Ohio Star* in a cove nearly a mile up the river. Instead, he had agreed to give Wyatt and Horace the chance Wyatt had not guessed he would get for another decade. His crewmates had called him every kind of a fool. He had told them that they would be sorry they missed out on this opportunity.

The opportunity to own his own side-wheeler. He could make his living on the river—if he and Horace could get the boat running again. In the meantime, he was stuck on the shore here in Haven. Maybe he should have put in on the other side of the river. Then the parts could have come overland from Louisville. It was too late now. *The Ohio Star* was not going anywhere until the boiler and one of the side-wheels could be repaired. The boards along the prow had to be replaced, for they had been shattered when *The Ohio Star* hit that sandbar. As long as the river stayed quiet, the boat should not sink before they could fix it. But he knew how fickle the river could be, for any strong storm could have it frothing like eggs being beaten into a meringue.

Once those basic repairs were completed, they could get back out onto the river and return to Louisville where the rest of the work on the boat would be done. The first thing he needed to get when they arrived in Louisville was a real gangplank, because the boat's was now sunk somewhere in the river. One narrow board connected the boat to the pier. Another led to the shore, but he did not trust the boards to stay in place, even though he had nailed one end of each plank to the deck.

His lips tightened beneath his mustache. If the captain had not been drunk, the boat would never have ended up on that sandbar, tearing up the wheel and straining the boiler so much that a crack burst along one side. It was good that the crack had appeared. Otherwise, the whole boiler might have blown, and he would have been on his way to the Pearly Gates instead of this small town.

Pearly Gates? More likely, if the boiler had exploded, he would have been face-to-face with Beelzebub while negotiating his way through the underworld.

He must have chuckled aloud, because the woman behind the counter looked up and smiled.

"Don't mind me, ma'am," he said. "Just a silly thought wandering through my head."

"I hope you can keep that good humor when you see how much these provisions and parts are going to cost you." She handed him both slips.

Wyatt whistled under his breath. He had not guessed it would be *this* much just to patch the boiler and fix the paddles on the wheel. The total must be close to what it would cost to buy a whole new boat. Horace and he had pooled what money they had, becoming equal partners, but it was clear they were going to have to cut corners to get this boat back to Louisville.

"If you'd like to reconsider . . ." She offered him another smile, this one sympathetic.

"Thanks, but no. I need those parts if I ever hope to push *The Ohio Star* back from the pier."

"Maybe I can get you a discount because you're ordering so much at once."

"I'd appreciate every penny you can shave off this price."

"Let me send a telegram to check on what can be done. As soon as I get an answer, I'll let you know." Looking past him, she motioned to a brown-haired boy who was sweeping up at the back of the store. The boy must be nine or ten years old. "Sean, will you run this order down to the telegraph office? Tell Kenny to ask the folks in Louisville to give me their best price for Mr. Colton's order; then you can go and play ball with your friends until supper. Be home to eat when it gets dark."

"Yes, Emma!" He put the broom against the wall, obviously eager to get out into the last of the day's sunshine.

Wyatt watched Sean race out. When he had been the lad's age, he would have hated being cooped up in a store. He had spent all his free time on the Cincinnati docks, talking to anyone who would answer his questions and learning everything he could about the steamboats that came up and down the river. A lot of things had changed as he grew, but his love of the river and the boats upon it had not.

"I'll send Sean to let you know when I get an answer on these parts," Emma said. "Are you staying on your boat?"

"Yes, ma'am." He did not add that he could not imagine sleeping anyplace that did not let him feel the motion of the river under him. "I can pay for these supplies now. Do you want a deposit on the other order?"

She shook her head, pushing a loose strand back out of her eyes. "I appreciate you paying for your provisions, but there is no sense in paying for the parts until we see what sort of price they will give you. Once you have that, you can decide how much of that you wish to order."

"Makes sense." He reached into his pocket and counted out what he needed to pay for the supplies. It *did* make sense, but he did not like the idea that they might not be able to get the parts they needed to make the boat river-worthy again. "I hear I can get wood from Noah Sawyer."

She smiled. "He has a wood lot just outside the village. I'll let him know you want to talk to him about some boards."

"Thanks very much, ma'am, but you don't have to go to that trouble on my behalf."

" 'Tis no trouble."

"You have enough to do here without traipsing out of town to deliver a message for me."

With a laugh, she said, "Mr. Colton, Noah Sawyer is my husband. I'll be glad to give him the message over supper."

"Sawyer is your husband?" He frowned, baffled. "But the sign says this is Delancy's General Store."

"You'll find that folks in Haven like to watch their pennies, too, Mr. Colton. I didn't see any reason to repaint the sign simply because Noah and I got married a couple months ago."

He chuckled, but he had to wonder about a town and the menfolk in it when they let their women run stores and keep their maiden names on the businesses. Out on the river, men did the work and women . . . Well, women had their place when a man was ashore for a night or two.

Setting the two cases of supplies on his shoulder, Wyatt bid Emma Sawyer a good afternoon. He left the store and headed toward the river. Haven reminded him of any of a dozen towns along the Ohio. It had a church and a Grange

Hall and a courthouse in an arc around the village green, and a general store and a livery and a train station along the main street. Hearing shouts, he looked back to see a bunch of kids playing on the green.

A very cozy scene . . . and one that made him shudder. He was not tempted by this town and its bucolic life. A man like him would suffocate in the conventionality of Haven. His life was along the ever-changing river, not in this town that looked the same day after day.

He tipped his cap to a woman he passed, keeping the cases balanced on his shoulder. She gave him a smile, surprising him. He had not guessed a woman in this town would have any interest in a river rat like him. Maybe she was looking for a way out of Haven. It would not be with him. The only mistress he wanted was the one he had—*The Ohio Star.*

The town was built above the river. When he had seen where water had gouged out a path high along the hillsides, he had guessed the town had been situated up here to avoid the spring floods. This spring's had been especially appalling along this section of the river.

Wyatt smiled when he saw *The Ohio Star* bobbing like a cork next to the pier. The white boat was almost forty feet long and about half as wide. Two lower levels of deck were separated by stairs at both the bow and the stern. Railings along all three decks were shadowed by the rooms built in the center of the boat and the smokestacks that rose high above the uppermost deck. The starboard paddlewheel was hidden, as was its twin on the far side of the boat, beneath a wooden casing that was painted with the boat's name. *The Ohio Star* was lettered in red in a half circle above and below a blue star that was as tall as Wyatt and set in the middle of the cover.

He knew the boat looked just like others along the river, but this one was his and Horace's. All they had to do was find a way to pay for those parts and get the boat repaired.

Then he would be back on the river, and he and Horace would be masters of this steamboat.

Laughter came from the boat. Not Horace's, but another voice. Higher and unquestionably sweeter. A child's voice.

Balancing the cases with care, Wyatt walked across the narrow plank. He set the cases on the deck and heard the laugh again. Who was on the boat? If one or more of the village kids had decided to sneak on board, he would toss them off along with a warning not to return. *The Ohio Star* was damaged enough without curious kids poking their noses into everything.

When he heard a deeper laugh, he frowned. He recognized the laugh that rumbled like faint thunder. Horace! Was Horace talking to some kid? Or *was* it a kid? That light laugh might belong to a young woman. And Horace getting involved with some gal could mean them being run out of town before they could get the parts to fix the boat.

Coming around the storage room that was set in the middle of the bottom deck, Wyatt saw his partner perched on a crate. Horace was talking to a little red-haired lass who was sitting cross-legged on the deck as if *The Ohio Star* had been her home since her first breath.

Horace Appleby might be thirty or fifty or a hundred. His face was weathered by years of sun reflecting off the water, but he was as spry as a lad. His hair could have been blond or white. Wyatt was not sure. Dressed in black twill trousers, Horace made a stiff sound as he moved. Not from his joints, but from the heavy material that was edged with copper rivets. Suspenders climbing up over his light blue cotton shirt outlined his narrow chest. On his feet were boots as scuffed as Wyatt's. It was the same outfit he wore every day, washing it out in the river whenever he felt the need to.

Wyatt discovered that he was being stared at. By that girl who had the reddest hair he had ever seen. It was almost the color of the red letters on the sidewheel . . . or the color the words had been when freshly painted. Freckles were scattered like brown sugar across her nose and cheeks. Beneath red lashes, her brown eyes were appraising him with an astute regard that seemed far too old for her tender years.

He recognized that expression, although he had not expected to see it on such a young face in a town like Haven. It reminded him of a frightened, cornered animal. She was trying to figure out if he was a potential friend or an enemy, and she wanted to be prepared either way.

"Howdy, Wyatt," Horace called, motioning for him to come closer. "We have company."

"So I can see." He looked again at the little girl who was holding a rag doll with hair as scarlet as hers. "Who are you?"

The little girl leaned her elbows on her knees as she swung the doll in front of her. "I'm Katherine Mulligan, and this is Shirley."

"Well, Katherine—"

Her nose wrinkled. "I don't like being called Katherine."

"What do you like to be called?" He glanced at Horace and smiled. This child spoke her mind. No wonder, Horace had not told her to go ashore. Horace liked kids, which was why he had more than a dozen of his own in various towns along the river. Most of them were grown, and several were working along the Ohio and the Mississippi. The youngest one—at least the youngest one Wyatt knew about—was about the age of this kid.

"Kitty Cat."

"Kitty Cat?" Wyatt repeated.

Horace chuckled. "Ain't it the perfect name for her? I found her tiptoeing about the boat, as quiet as a cat."

"I wanted to see the boat," Kitty Cat said. "It's a pretty boat."

"It is that." Wyatt rested his shoulder against the wall of the boiler room.

"I've never been on a boat before."

"Never?"

She shook her head and leaned her doll on the white pinafore she wore over her simple green dress. "Never."

"You've lived on the river for all these years—"

She held up three fingers on each hand. "I'm six years old."

He smiled. "So why have you lived here for six years and never been out on the river?"

"I just got here a few months ago."

"Then your parents must be extra worried about you. It's late. You should go home before they think you've disappeared."

She continued to stare at him as she said, "I don't have any parents. Not anymore."

"Someone must be anxious about you."

Kitty Cat lowered her eyes. "Rachel will be."

"Who is Rachel?" Now the chatty kid was being as tight-lipped as a sinner when a minister was calling.

"I was placed out with her when I came on the orphan train to Haven."

"Orphan train?" asked Horace, frowning. "Someone sent you away? That's plum awful."

"I'd heard," Wyatt said, "when we delivered some supplies to Haven two weeks ago, that some kids arrived here on an orphan train a few months back." He arched a brow. "So I guess you haven't been in Haven for long."

At a low rumble, the little girl put her hand over her stomach and grinned.

"Hungry?" asked Horace.

"Yes. Shirley and I are hungry."

Standing, he held out his hand. "I don't think we've got any food for your doll, but I do believe there's enough gravy, beef, and biscuits in the saloon if you want to share our supper."

"Up the stairs there," Wyatt said. As the little girl ran toward the steps, bouncing her doll on every skip, he added, "Horace, her name may be Kitty Cat, but she's not an abandoned kitten. Someone must be getting downright anxious about where she is. Folks in Haven might not be too pleased to find out that we let her stay here."

Horace waved his hand and chuckled. "I'll take her home as soon as she puts something in that grumbling stomach. I may have to give that Rachel a piece of my mind for letting a kid like Kitty Cat roam around the river when she doesn't know how to swim."

"Don't give away any pieces of your mind. We're going to need all our wits to figure out a way to get the parts to fix *The Ohio Star*."

"Expensive?"

When Wyatt told him what he had learned at the general store, Horace's smile vanished. It did not return as they climbed the stairs to the upper deck.

Light from the full moon rippled on the water, creating a creamy path from the Ohio shore to the Kentucky one on the other side of the river. The boat strained against the ropes holding it as if it wanted to escape back into the river and be on its way. The moonlight was not strong enough for Rachel to see what name was painted on the wood covering the side-wheel, although a big star was visible in the center.

Sean O'Dell had seen Kitty Cat heading in this direction after they had spoken in the village. Whatever had possessed Kitty Cat to come down to the river and this boat?

Rachel's heart twisted painfully. Maybe Kitty Cat had not run away just to see her friends. Maybe she wanted to flee River's Haven forever.

Gathering up her long black skirt, she inched down the hill toward the boat. She always changed into more conventional clothes when she came into Haven, because she had seen how the dresses at River's Haven made people in the village uneasy. She hated these skirts, for they were bulky and confining and had a tendency to catch on every stalk of grass. Every time she put on this skirt and the white blouse beneath a black bolero jacket, she appreciated the sensible clothing she usually wore.

She paused when a man carrying a lantern appeared out of the shadows on the steamboat. She hesitated. Merrill would be furious to learn that she was here speaking to a stranger without anyone else from River's Haven with her. How many times had he told her that outsiders could cause trouble for her and the Community? Outsiders did not understand—or had no interest in understanding—River's Haven. They were happy with their assumptions, no matter how inaccurate they might be.

But Merrill would have been even more outraged if she had asked him to come with her to retrieve Kitty Cat. Her brother had made his feelings about Kitty Cat very clear after the ruling by the Assembly of Elders. By this hour, he was with *his* friends or calling on Miss Page, who had completed her year with her most recent husband just two weeks ago.

Helga Page was not a woman who would want to be alone for any length of time. In any Community other than River's Haven, she would have been labeled as trouble. She was a flirt and clearly on the outlook for her next husband while she was with her current one. She had had a different one each year since Rachel had come to River's Haven, and it seemed Merrill was in line to be the next.

Rachel pushed that uneasy thought out of her head. She had to find Kitty Cat now. She tried to see onto the boat, but the only person in sight was the man. Something about his self-assured stride across the deck drew her attention back to him.

"Are you going to stand there and gawk all night?" the man shouted as he set the lantern down and rested his arms on the railing.

In the light from the lantern she could see how his dark hair twisted across his forehead beneath his hat. Its floppy brim could not cloak the strong angle of his chin or his aquiline nose. He wore a coat of the same gray as his eyes. Unbuttoned, it flapped open to reveal a dusty shirt and trousers that ended in his scuffed boots. Hardened muscles told her this was a man accustomed to a grueling life on the river.

When she raised her eyes to his face again, she flushed at his smile. It broadened as his gaze moved along her in a slow perusal that made her aware of every tangle in her hair and each wrinkle in the skirt that brushed the tops of her shoes. He tipped his hat in her direction, and she had the strange feeling that he meant the everyday motion to be a challenge.

Rachel looked away, berating herself for being so forward. Admiring a handsome man who was bronzed by the sun upon the river was silly. Letting him eye her as if she were something for sale at the general store was even more stupid.

"Well?" he called. "Are you going to stand there or come aboard?"

"I shouldn't."

"Why not? We can go on shouting so everyone in the county can hear our conversation, or you can come aboard and tell me what brought you down here to the river at this late hour."

Rachel wiped her hands on the heavy black fabric of her skirt. He was right. Bellowing out her questions would not get her any answers.

She let her feet slide down the rest of the hill. When

she saw that the only way aboard was across a slender board, she called, "I need to ask you a question."

"Come aboard." He motioned with his head, then smiled as if he could read her uneasy thoughts.

That smile vexed her. She put one foot on the board and found it was steadier than she had feared. Even if she fell off it, the water was not deep here. She hurried across before her courage failed her.

The heels of her shoes striking the deck echoed strangely. When the man turned, the knowing smile was again on his lips. She hoped he would be able to help her find Kitty Cat right away. Then she could head back to River's Haven.

"You must be Rachel," he said.

She smiled. If he knew her name, he must have spoken with Kitty Cat. "Yes. Rachel Browning. Is Kitty Cat still here?"

He nodded and hooked a thumb toward the deck above them. "She's having supper with my partner up in the saloon."

"Saloon? You took that little girl to a *saloon?*"

"Calm down. That's the name of where we eat."

She took a steadying breath. She was acting like a shrew, but she was worried about Kitty Cat. "I thought the dining room on a boat was called a mess."

"On a ship, it's a mess. On a riverboat, it's the saloon."

"Oh."

He smiled, his eyes crinkling into lines that suggested he smiled often. "Anything else I can help you learn?"

"About the boat?"

"Or whatever you wish."

Hoping that she had misunderstood his suggestive answer, she hurried to say, "I must ask you to bring Kitty Cat to me immediately, so I can take her home."

"It won't hurt to let the kid finish her supper, will it?"

"She should come home now."

"Rachel—"

"You should address me as Miss Browning."

"Why?"

She was not going to spend the evening teaching him his manners. "If you will bring Kitty Cat to me, I shall leave you to your business."

"Kitty Cat *is* my business at the moment."

"Yours?"

"Everything on *The Ohio Star* is my business, and she is on *The Ohio Star*." He eyed her up and down, and a rakish smile tugged at his mustache. "So are you. Why don't you come up and have supper with us? I suspect you've been searching high and low for the kid and missed your own supper."

Rachel hesitated. Perhaps the man was trying to make up for his crude comments. "I should take Kitty Cat home without delay."

"All right. Suit yourself, but I'm going to go and get my supper. You can wait here until Kitty Cat is done with hers and I'm done with mine."

Rachel frowned. The man was not being gracious. Nor was he being kind. She could not leave the little girl with such a rogue.

"All right," she said, using his words. "I will accept your invitation, Mr.—"

"Colton, but you can call me Wyatt." He gave her another grin that dared her to slap it from his face.

"Mr. Colton, I would like to see Kitty Cat now."

"Say please."

"What?"

He arched a brow. "I thought a lady always said please. If you aren't a lady"—he ran a finger along her jacket sleeve—"that would be all right, too."

"Mr. Colton!" She edged back a step and bumped into a wall. She looked over her shoulder to discover there must be a room in the middle of this deck. When he moved toward her, she said, "Please!"

"Now that isn't a very nice please."

"It wasn't intended to be." She put her hand over her mouth, shocked at her own impertinence. She was being as outspoken as when she had questioned the Assembly of Elders. Her expectation that she had learned her lesson then and would now curtail her impetuosity seemed to be misguided.

"Well, well." Mr. Colton put a hand on the wall and grinned. "The kid's name may be Kitty Cat, but I can see who has the claws."

"Mr. Colton, would you *please* show me the way to where Kitty Cat is?"

He held out his crooked arm. "This way."

Rachel hesitated again. She might speak up boldly, but she never had been comfortable around strangers. Especially this strange man who seemed to be able to irritate her with every word he spoke and every glance he fired in her direction.

"Do you want to go or stay here?" Mr. Colton asked. "My supper is getting cold, Rachel."

She put her hand gingerly on his arm. As she had expected, his shirt sleeves were tight against hard muscles. "Mr. Colton, I think it would be much easier for all involved if you would address me as Miss Browning."

"I don't always like to take the easy way."

With a motion as grand as if they stood in an elegant ballroom, he turned her toward the stairs that were just wide enough for the two of them. She put her foot on the first riser and wobbled.

"Steady there," he said, pulling his arm from beneath her hand and putting it around her waist. "You'll get your river legs under you in a few minutes."

"I am fine."

"Yes, I believe you are."

Rachel thought curses she would not speak aloud. This man had a patter as smooth as a planed board. Every word she spoke, he found a way to twist and toss back at her. The very best thing she could do would be to collect Kitty Cat and be on her way back to River's Haven before anyone discovered they both were gone.

How would she explain all of this to her overprotective brother if he noticed she and Kitty Cat were not in the cottage? She glanced at Mr. Colton. How would she explain *him*?

Three

Rachel was astonished to see simple curtains in the rooms that took up most of the upper decks. Only a small room at the front of the uppermost deck had no curtains. It had a big wheel at the center. She guessed that was from where the boat was piloted and an unobstructed view would be necessary.

Mr. Colton opened a door about halfway to the back of the boat and announced, "Get out your best manners, Horace. We've got company."

Who was Horace? She did not ask that as she grasped the door frame when the boat rocked beneath her. It was not a fierce motion, but she never had been off solid ground before. Stumbling in Mr. Colton's view would be embarrassing.

The room was far more spacious than she had expected. It must be almost twice the size of the front room in her cottage. A cast-iron stove sat at the far end, its stovepipe snaking out through a hole in the wall. A trio of rocking chairs were set beneath a large window that gave a view of the back of the boat. She could not imagine Mr. Colton sitting there and complacently rocking. Beneath her feet as she entered the room was a braided rug. One section had pulled apart, and she could see where hasty stitches had drawn it back together again.

Delicious aromas filled the room, aromas that reminded

her of her family's small farmhouse when she had been a child. She could almost believe that if she closed her eyes the spicy scent would carry her back to that time and place.

"Rachel!" Kitty Cat jumped up from a bench on one side of a table that was big enough for a dozen to sit at. Waving as if she feared Rachel could not see her, she called, "Over here!"

Fighting her unsteady feet, Rachel went to the table and gathered the little girl up in her arms. She hugged her tightly even as she said, "You have scared at least a year off my life, Kitty Cat. How could you go off like that and not tell me or anyone else where you were going?"

"No one else cares."

"But *I* do!" She wished Mr. Colton and the older man who had been sitting across the table from Kitty Cat were not listening to this conversation. "Kitty Cat, you must never go off without telling me first where you are going. Not ever again."

Squirming to get away, Kitty Cat pointed to the older man. "That's Mr. Horace. He cooked supper tonight. It's good." She grinned. "And he's funny."

The older man nodded toward her. " 'Tis a pleasure . . ."

"She's Rachel," Mr. Colton said as he walked past the table, heading toward the far side of the room.

"Rachel Browning," she added with a glower in his direction.

Horace—or was it *Mister* Horace as Kitty Cat called him?—smiled, but said, " 'Tis a pleasure, Miss Rachel. Can I get you some grub?"

"Pardon me?" she asked.

Kitty Cat tugged on her sleeve. "He means supper, Rachel. I told you that Mr. Horace is funny."

"Yes." She glanced at Horace and nodded. "Thank you. I'd like that."

She heard a thunk behind her and saw Mr. Colton setting

a chair at one end of the table. He motioned for her to sit. She hesitated again when she saw it was the only one, other than the rocking chairs, in the room.

"I don't want to take your chair, Mr. Colton."

She realized she had said the wrong thing again when he answered in a clipped voice, "You're not taking it. I'm offering it. You can sit or stand as you wish. I'm going to eat, and I don't like to eat on my feet. Either both of you ladies sit down so we men can sit, or go back outside and wait until we're done."

Kitty Cat giggled.

Despite his sharp retort, Mr. Colton did not sit until she did. Then he threw one leg over the bench and the top of Kitty Cat's head, making the little girl giggle more as he sat beside her.

Between herself and Kitty Cat, Rachel noticed with a pulse of dismay. Then she told herself not to be silly. These two men had treated the little girl with obvious kindness, and they had kept her here so anyone looking for her could find her.

The man who had been introduced to her only as Horace brought two heaping plates to the table. He set one in front of Mr. Colton and the other in front of her. Intriguing aromas flowed upward on the steam, but she looked at it in dismay.

"If you don't clean your plate," Mr. Colton said, "you won't get any dessert."

She raised her gaze to find him regarding her with far less amusement than in his voice. His eyes were, she realized, a shade somewhere between blue and silver, combining both but not exactly either color. One side of his mustache quirked, and she suspected he was trying to exasperate her again. She must not allow him to get the better of her once more.

"Before I attempt to eat all this," she replied, "I need to know what's for dessert."

Horace chortled as he sat down again. "She's a quick one, Wyatt. You need to watch out for her." Leaning toward her, he added, "Pumpkin pie."

"That is what smells so good."

"Clean your plate," said Mr. Colton, "and you can find out if it tastes as good as it smells."

"All right." She picked up her plate and slid half the food onto his plate.

As gravy spilled over the sides of his plate, he stared at her in disbelief. "Why did you do that?"

"You told me I needed to clean my plate, and I shall, although, as I said, I can't eat it all."

Horace slapped the table and laughed. More gravy splattered off Mr. Colton's plate when the table trembled. Kitty Cat wore a tentative smile while she looked from Rachel to Mr. Colton. Rachel gave Kitty Cat a broad smile. The little girl relaxed and began to eat again as heartily as if she had to finish off a plate as overflowing as Mr. Colton's.

"You should come to call more often," Horace said. "This is the best laugh I've had since *The Ohio Star* struck that sandbar."

"Sandbar?" Rachel asked, abruptly dismayed. "This boat is damaged?"

"It isn't going to sink, if that's what's making you turn as pale as death. Calm down and eat up," ordered Mr. Colton, putting his hand over hers as she gripped the table and started to stand. "And sit down!"

Rachel dropped back to her chair. She could obey that command, but calming down was impossible when Mr. Colton's work-hardened hand surrounded her fingers. A very peculiar sensation rushed through her, a pleasurable sensation of holding onto something that sizzled. She pulled her hand from beneath his, and the feeling vanished. *He* had caused this? She had to get Kitty Cat and herself out of here as soon as was politely possible. She must not have any feelings—not even these odd ones—for a man who did not belong to the River's Haven Community.

Mr. Colton grimaced and looked away. When he took his fork in one hand and tapped the fingers on the other against the table impatiently, she clenched her hands on the arms of the chair. He might as well have spoken the insult he obviously was thinking. His distaste with making the mistake of touching her could not be any clearer.

"Maybe Shirley and I can come back tomorrow," Kitty Cat said, "and see the rest of the boat, Mr. Horace."

"You know that won't be possible," Rachel said, trying to keep a lighthearted smile in place. "Tomorrow you have your ciphering class with Miss Hanson."

Horace chuckled. "Maybe some other day, then."

Putting down her fork before she had taken a single bite, Rachel said, "I'm afraid that's not possible. We prefer that the children remain close to the Community."

"I saw kids playing all over Haven this afternoon," Mr. Colton said.

"Maybe in Haven, but I'm speaking about River's Haven."

"River's Haven?"

She recoiled from the venom in his eyes. It was nothing like the teasing provocation she had seen on the deck below. Any hint of humor had vanished into this fury that was aimed directly at her.

"River's Haven?" he repeated tightly. "You two are from *there?*"

"Yes."

"Why do you live *there?*"

She looked at Kitty Cat, who was listening avidly, then said, "I'd prefer not to speak of that now."

"Ashamed?" he fired back.

"Wyatt," growled his partner, "give Miss Rachel a chance to eat before everything is cold."

Nothing, Rachel decided, could be icier than the chill

in Mr. Colton's eyes. She was not ashamed of where she lived and the people she lived with, and she would not allow anyone to disparage River's Haven within Kitty Cat's earshot just now. The little girl needed to become more comfortable in the Community before she faced the prejudice outside it.

"It might be better if we left now," she said.

Horace shook his head. "You said you'd stay for dessert, Miss Rachel."

"Please," seconded Kitty Cat. "I've never had pumpkin pie. I want to see what it tastes like."

Rachel suspected that Kitty Cat had learned the very way to persuade her to agree. The little girl seldom spoke of the deprivation and horrors of living in the city slums, but Rachel did not have to hear the stories. Her own imagination could supply enough appalling details. Since Kitty Cat had come to live with her, Rachel had tried to give the child as many different experiences as possible to make up for the ones Kitty Cat had missed out in the first six years of her life. But not in a hundred years would she have guessed Kitty Cat had never eaten a piece of pumpkin pie.

"All right," she said softly. "We can stay for dessert as long as it's all right with both of our hosts."

"It's just fine," Horace answered too fast for Mr. Colton to interrupt him. "Do you want to hear, Kitty Cat, about the time I came face-to-face with a real live gator down in a bayou of Louisiana? A gator that was twice the size of this table?"

As he began to relate a story that might be true or could have just as well been a tall tale, Rachel picked up her fork again. She was aware of Mr. Colton watching her closely. Did he think that she would do something outrageous or strange? She had not guessed a man who had been up and down the Ohio River would have the same provincial prejudices shared by too many of the folks who lived near River's Haven.

She was hungrier than she had guessed. The food was even more delicious than it smelled, and she wished she had not pushed so much off her plate and onto Mr. Colton's. When she noticed how he made his food disappear just as quickly, she had an unsettling thought.

In a near whisper as Kitty Cat slipped off the bench to help Horace get the pie and more plates, Rachel said, "If we're eating what should have been your dinner—"

"You worry too much," Mr. Colton retorted.

"But you weren't expecting company."

"Horace always makes too much. He's used to cooking for a whole crew."

She looked around. "Where is everyone else?"

"Gone."

"Gone? What happened to them?" Her eyes widened.

He laughed tersely. "You clearly have a lurid imagination, Rachel. We didn't toss them into the river. When the boat was run aground, they decided to look for work somewhere else. Horace and I are the only ones aboard now. We're working to repair *The Ohio Star*. If we can make her river-worthy again, we'll have our own boat to take along the Ohio and Wabash or even the Mississippi and Missouri if we choose."

"It sounds like a wonderful life."

"The very best." He smiled, and she wondered if he was being honest . . . finally. His annoyance had been sincere, but she had not been so sure about his smiles. "Haven't you ever wanted to see what was beyond the next horizon?"

"I did enjoy our journey from Ohio."

"Overland?"

"Yes. This is the first time I've been on the river."

"Really?"

"Real—" She frowned. "You don't need to taunt me at every turn."

"I wouldn't if you didn't make it so easy to do so."

"But aren't you the man who said he didn't always take the easy way?"

His gray eyes narrowed. "I'm honored."

"Honored? Why?"

"That you have paid such close attention to each word I've spoken."

"Don't flatter yourself."

He waved his fork to dismiss her words. "So you've never traveled along the river?"

"No." She smiled as Kitty Cat put a stack of plates on the table and then climbed into her lap. "I don't need to travel when I have what I want right here." She gave Kitty Cat a hug.

Horace set the pie on the table and went back to the stove for the coffeepot. As he placed that next to the pie, he said, "Some folks need to settle down and some need to keep looking for what they want."

"You're philosophical tonight," Mr. Colton said.

"Pumpkin pie always makes me philosophical."

Rachel laughed. When they all looked at her, she put her hand over her mouth. Had Horace meant that seriously?

Horace cut two pieces of pie and put them in front of her. Then he winked at her. Handing a fork to Kitty Cat, he said, "Try it, young lady." He held out another fork to Rachel. "Both of you."

Kitty Cat did not wait for a second urging. She dug into the golden-brown pie and took a big bite. With her mouth full, she mumbled something that might have been that the pie was delicious.

Taking a bite, Rachel said, "I agree with Kitty Cat. This is wonderful. Do you share your recipes?"

"When I can get another in return."

"I have one for a blueberry—"

Mr. Colton snorted. "I feel as if I'm at a church social with the old ladies."

Horace laughed. "No old lady—or anyone else—makes a better pumpkin pie than I do." He poured cups of coffee before sitting at the table.

"I have to agree," Rachel said. She put her arm around Kitty Cat, who, as soon as she finished her pie, cuddled against Rachel. "And the coffee is wonderful, too."

"A recipe I learned down in New Orleans." He chuckled. "Have you ever been there, Miss Rachel?" He answered before she could, "Probably not. You should go there. They have some of the best coffee in the world."

Once he started, he continued to go from one story to the next about adventures he had had and people he had met in New Orleans and other towns along the Mississippi. She laughed at his jokes, which seemed to make him more determined to entertain them. Even Mr. Colton chuckled at Horace's stories, surprising her, because she would have guessed that the two men had known each other for a long time if they were partners.

Rachel looked down and saw that Kitty Cat was asleep, the rag doll nestled in her arms. The little girl was seldom without the doll she had named Shirley. Rachel wondered if Kitty Cat had ever had a doll before Rachel gave her this one. She glanced at the rocking chairs, thinking of how nice it would be to hold Kitty Cat in one of them. It amazed her to realize she could not recall seeing a single rocking chair in River's Haven.

"Looks like that little one is all adventured out." Horace stood and carried some of the dirty dishes to a galvanized tub beside the stove.

"I would be glad to help with cleaning up," Rachel said.

"No need. You've got a long walk ahead of you. I suspect you're going to be carrying that child all the way."

She smiled, resisting the temptation to give Horace a hug for being so kind. "Thank you for a delicious meal."

"It was nice to have some company other than our own."

Mr. Colton stood when she did. "C'mon. I'll see you

off the boat." He picked up the lantern and motioned toward the door.

Bidding Horace a goodbye, Rachel lifted Kitty Cat into her arms. The doll fell to the deck. With a smile, Horace set it atop the sleeping girl. Thanking him again, Rachel followed Mr. Colton out onto the deck. The night was loud with the songs of frogs and insects that nearly drowned out the water's hushed whisper against the boat. As he held the lantern high so she could pick her way along the deck, bugs swirled around it.

"Careful," he murmured when they reached the stairs. He put out his arm to halt her. "Let me take her down the steps for you."

"Thank you." She was not going to be too proud to accept his help. Her feet were steadier on the deck, but she did not trust them to carry her down the stairs while she was holding Kitty Cat.

He set down the lantern and held out his arms. That odd stirring exploded through her again, even though he had not touched her. She stared at his hands, broad and open. If she stepped forward and they closed around her, how would they feel? Gentle like his smile now when he gazed at Kitty Cat, or rough like his voice when he retorted to a comment she made?

She placed the little girl into his arms, drawing her hands out from beneath Kitty Cat. She could not silence her gasp when her skin brushed his. When her gaze was caught by his shadowed eyes, she could not tear it away. He took a step toward her, then paused as he broke the connection between them to look down at the little girl.

"Get the lantern," he ordered, his voice taut. "I don't want to trip going down the steps."

"Yes . . . Yes." The answer was sufficient, but, as she reached for the lantern, it seemed as if she should have said more. What? She could not guess.

Holding the lantern up high, she brushed away bugs as

she walked with him down the stairs. She clutched the railing so she would not fall. She was relieved when she reached the bottom. Turning, she watched Mr. Colton put Kitty Cat on her feet. The little girl yawned broadly, then grinned up at him. He smiled back at her.

Taking Kitty Cat by the hand, Rachel held out the lantern to him and said, "Thank you."

"My pleasure, I assure you."

She was about to smile, then saw his amusement. What a cur! He was enjoying every chance to tease her. She started to retort, but she could not throw Mr. Colton's sparse courtesy back into his face by disagreeing with him about everything.

As his gaze swept along her, his smile vanished. It was replaced by an intense expression that urged her to step back. She tried to move her feet, but they refused to budge. When he hung the lantern on a brad on the wall, he walked toward her until the toes of his boots nearly brushed the hem of her gown.

His motion freed her feet, and she edged back as she said, "I'm sorry that we intruded."

"You haven't been too much of a bother."

"Then why are you acting as if you'd rather welcome a bear onto your boat than us?"

He gripped her chin between two fingers and leaned toward her. Shocked, she stared up at him. His voice was perfectly controlled as he said, "In a few moments, you'll be gone from my life, Rachel Browning, except for the few times I may see you in Haven. We'll be strangers. We *are* strangers, and I want to keep it that way."

"I agree."

"Do you?" His finger stroked her cheek, and that amazing buzz surged through her once more. "Then why do you look at me with those doe eyes suggesting that you'd like to get much more friendly with me?"

"You're deluding yourself."

"Am I?" He tipped up her face and brushed her lips with a quick kiss.

She jumped back in shock. "Are you out of your mind?"

"You're not the first to ask that, Rachel."

"*Miss* Browning!"

With a laugh, he bent and shook Kitty Cat's hand seriously while the little girl stared at him. "Thank you for calling, young lady." He looked back at Rachel. "See? I do have manners."

"Then I suggest you recall that they don't wear out with practice." Turning Kitty Cat toward the plank back to shore, she said, "Good evening, Mr. Colton."

"Good-bye, Rachel."

She did not want to let him have the last word, but staying longer to argue would be foolish. Then he might discover how utterly he had threatened her hard-fought façade of serenity with his antics . . . and his kiss.

Four

"Rachel, I must speak with you right away."

Rachel looked up from her desk as she heard Eve Hanson's voice. The gray-haired woman's motherly face was deeply wrinkled with worry. When Miss Hanson came into the room that Rachel used as the accounting office for River's Haven, she closed the door behind her. That astonished Rachel. Doors were usually left open, because the Community viewed itself as a family that should have no secrets.

"Sit down, Miss Hanson." Rachel shut the account book she had been working on and stood. Coming around her desk, she put her hand on Miss Hanson's trembling arm. She guided Miss Hanson to one of the chairs along the whitewashed wall.

"I shouldn't sit here," Miss Hanson said. "These chairs are for the Assembly of Elders."

"They aren't using them just now." Rachel poured a glass of water from the pitcher set on the wide windowsill. Handing it to Miss Hanson, she asked, "What is wrong?"

"She's gone again."

"She?" Rachel closed her eyes and let her breath sift out in a deep sigh. "I assume you mean Kit—Katherine."

"She never came to play with the other children this afternoon." Miss Hanson drained the glass and put it back on the desk. Wringing her hands, she rose, then paced in front of Rachel's desk. "I thought she might be here with you. As soon as I could leave someone else with the children, I came here. But she isn't here."

"No."

"Do you know where she might be?"

Rachel nodded. "I'm *sure* I know where she is."

It had been only three days since Kitty Cat had scurried away to visit Sean O'Dell in Haven and had found her way onto *The Ohio Star*. That evening, on the walk back to River's Haven, Rachel had again asked Kitty Cat not to leave the Community without telling her. The little girl had agreed. It was not like Kitty Cat to break a promise.

Excusing herself after asking Miss Hanson not to speak of Kitty Cat's absence to anyone else, Rachel rushed to her cottage. She was not surprised to see a piece of paper leaning against the vase of flowers in the center of the table. On it were two words that she guessed were meant to be "Sean" and "Mr. Horace," although they were spelled "shan" and "misterhors" in Kitty Cat's still-scrawling printing. Kitty Cat had kept her promise to let Rachel know if she left the Community.

Rachel did not chide herself for failing to realize that she should have asked for Kitty Cat to promise not to leave. Instead, she hastily redressed in the black dress that she wore when she went to Haven. The day was warm, and, as she crossed the common area, sweat rolled along her back.

"Where are you off to, Rachel?" called a familiar voice.

She turned to see her brother walking toward her. With him was Miss Page. The blonde was extraordinarily beautiful, tall and slender but with voluptuous curves. Merrill's eyes glittered with joyful anticipation each time he spoke Miss Page's name, so Rachel expected an announcement would be forthcoming as soon as the Assembly of Elders approved the match.

Was wanting their marriage authorized why Merrill had

insisted that Rachel not press her request on behalf of Kitty Cat with the Assembly of Elders? He did not want to upset them in any way, so they would reject the petition for marriage. She could not fault him, if that were so. He seemed smitten with Miss Page.

"You're in such a hurry, Miss Browning," Miss Page murmured as their path intersected Rachel's.

Merrill laughed. "Rachel is *always* in a hurry. I'm surprised you haven't noticed her running hither and yon about the Community as she collects information to keep River's Haven's books balanced."

"I had no reason to notice her . . . before." She gave him a warm smile.

Merrill's affection for Miss Page must be returned. That pleased Rachel, because she liked to see her brother happy. Unlike her, he had been miserable in their Ohio home before their parents died, and he had wanted to come to River's Haven as soon as their father was buried.

"So where are you bound, Rachel?" he asked.

"I have some errands to run in Haven."

"I guessed that by the way you are dressed." He smiled. "You look overly warm."

She wiped sweat from her forehead, then straightened her bonnet. "It feels as if it is going to rain." She laughed. "Or should I say as if it *should* rain?"

"The sooner the better," came a reply from behind her.

Rachel turned to see Calvin Foley, who was widely regarded as the best-looking man in the River's Haven Community. His hair beneath his tall black hat was the gold of spun sunshine, and his features were even, enticing one's eyes to linger on his strong chin or his full mouth. It was rumored that he had left a well-to-do family to come here and find a home with those who shared Mr. Carpenter's ideas. Even in a simple coat of black and an unadorned waistcoat that matched what Merrill wore, he possessed an aura of wealth and power. He showed no sense of arrogance, but the strength of his will refused to be ignored.

"You know Mr. Foley, of course." Merrill's smile appeared to be very genuine, although Rachel noticed how he moved a bit closer to Miss Page. Was he afraid that Miss Page would set her cap on Mr. Foley instead? Since he had finished his year-long match with Miss Turnbull, Mr. Foley's name had been mentioned in connection with several women. He had his choice among the Community as a member of the Assembly of Elders, so Merrill might be wise to be concerned.

"Of course." She gave Mr. Foley a smile she hoped did not look false. Somehow, she had to find a way to slip away from this conversation. Every moment that passed might be the very one that revealed how Kitty Cat had run away again. "How are you this afternoon, Mr. Foley?"

"Too warm." He chuckled. "Did I hear that you're going into Haven?"

"Yes."

"If your errand can wait until the morning, I'd be glad to offer you a ride with me."

"Thank you, but unfortunately this errand can't wait."

He tipped his hat to her and said, "Another day, perhaps."

"Thank you." She was not sure what else to say when she must take care with every word. No one had mentioned the little girl, and she wanted to put an end to her part in this conversation before someone did. "Good afternoon."

Slipping away was easier than she had guessed, because Mr. Foley began talking to her brother about some of the horses that were in the common stables. Miss Page seemed captivated by every word each man spoke.

Rachel lifted her skirts out of the dust on the road. After the spring's heavy rains, the weather had been dry. She hoped storms would come soon to ease the heat. Not the rough storms that sometimes struck the river valley, but gentle, healing rain that would give the crops a good soaking.

She passed several farmhouses on the road. No one was visible in front of any of them, and she guessed everyone was working in the fields or hiding from the sun. She adjusted the black bonnet that seemed to encase her head like an oven. The straw bonnet she wore at River's Haven was much cooler.

Perspiration was gliding along her bonnet ribbons as she reached the bridge over the creek just outside of Haven. She hurried across it. The boards had not yet weathered. Mr. Sawyer had recently replaced the bridge, which had washed out in the floods earlier this spring.

The village was a welcome sight. When she saw a sign being hammered over the door of a building next door to the Grange Hall, she smiled. HAVEN PUBLIC LIBRARY was lettered across it. She had not guessed that the village was getting a library. Would the residents of River's Haven be allowed to borrow books, too? She would have to find out—after she discovered where Kitty Cat was and impressed on the little girl the need to remain in the Community.

Rachel looked both ways along the main street, then rushed across it to Delancy's General Store. A train must have recently arrived, because the street was filled with carts and people going in every direction in a hurry.

She climbed up onto the porch and went into the store, pausing just beyond the doorway to let her eyes adjust to the dim light within. Slowly the interior of the store emerged from the shadows. Two women were talking at the back of the store. She recognized one as Alice Underhill, her dark blouse dusted with chalk, who was the schoolmistress in Haven. The other woman was as easily identifiable. Emma Sawyer, who ran the store. Mrs. Sawyer's silhouette was not as slender as it had been the first time Rachel had met her, for Mrs. Sawyer was already showing signs of her pregnancy.

Rachel lowered her eyes. It would be expected that she give Mrs. Sawyer congratulations on the impending birth. She could not. Her mother and cousins had had this happy glow when they received news of the coming child . . . and then they had died.

Both women turned as Rachel walked toward where they stood beside a pair of rocking chairs. Again that twinge struck her. She must speak to the steward in the woodworking shop in River's Haven about having a rocker made for her cottage. Rocking Kitty Cat to sleep would be so wonderful. Reminding herself that she should not be thinking of such a thing now when the little girl was missing, she greeted the two women.

Miss Underhill gave her a terse "good afternoon," then bid Mrs. Sawyer a good day. The glare that the schoolteacher fired in her direction told Rachel that Miss Underhill did not want to be in the company of someone from River's Haven. Rachel should be accustomed by now to the insult, but each time it hurt. If those who were frightened by the Community would come out to see how peaceful and prosperous it was, maybe they would set aside their prejudices.

"Miss Browning, right?" asked Mrs. Sawyer.

"You have a good memory."

"It's important when one is running a store." Mrs. Sawyer smiled.

"Is Sean here?"

"He just ran down to the train station for me. Do you want to wait?"

"No. I'm looking for Kitty Cat."

"Again?" The shopkeeper's face became abruptly serious. "Is she lost?"

"Not exactly lost. She left me a note that she was going to visit Sean."

"She can write that well at her young age?"

Rachel chuckled. Her shoulders relaxed, and pain burst from the tension easing across them. "Her message was clear enough for me to guess this was where she was bound. When Sean gets back, will you ask him if he's seen her? I'll keep looking around the village."

"Don't take this the wrong way, Miss Browning, but—"

"You are wondering if Kitty Cat keeps running away because she doesn't want to be at River's Haven." She sighed. "She loves living at River's Haven, except for not being able to see your Sean and her other friend, Brendan Rafferty."

"Could she have gone to Mr. Jennings's farm to visit the Rafferty children?"

She shook her head. "Her message was that she was coming to see Sean. She's been talking nonstop about the village ever since she came here a few days ago. I'll look around and see if I can find her." She thanked Mrs. Sawyer before rushing back out onto the street.

The glint off the river below caught Rachel's eye. Kitty Cat had been talking about the village *and* the steamboat. Could she have gone there again, even though Rachel had asked her not to? "Misterhors" had been the second word on the page left on the kitchen table.

Why was she hesitating? Was she so intimidated by Mr. Colton that she did not dare to go to his steamboat again? She frowned at the very idea. The man was a rogue, but she had met rogues before. They usually were mostly bluster, and if one ignored them they got bored and went on their way to bother other people.

Gathering up her cumbersome skirts, Rachel hurried past the railroad station and down the hill toward the river. She heard a carriage behind her. As she stepped to the side of the road, she heard a shout of warning. She turned and saw a hooded buggy speeding too quickly for safety. Was it out of control? She was about to jump out of its way. Then she saw a small, redheaded form in the middle of the road where a ball was rolling to a stop.

"Kitty Cat!" she screamed in horror. As she raced back up the hill, she stepped on her hem, nearly stumbling. Fabric tore, and a flash of hot pain scored her ankle. She did not slow as she yanked the little girl out from in front of the approaching wagon. The ball flew up into the air and under the carriage. It bounced away into some high grass.

"Rachel, that hurts!"

She squatted before Kitty Cat. "I didn't want you to be run over by that carriage."

"Carriage?" Excitement fired Kitty Cat's voice as she whirled to stare after the vehicle, which was spraying dirt behind it in a brown cloud.

Rachel stood and drew Kitty Cat out of the dust. "You need to be more careful when you're in Haven. It isn't like our Community where no vehicles are allowed near the walkways."

Sean rushed up, his brown hair falling into his eyes and the ball in one hand. He wiped dirt from his clothes as he shouted, "Wow! That was close! Kitty Cat, have you forgotten how fast a carriage can go?" He scowled at her. "You never were so silly when we lived in New York City."

"I forgot," said the little girl. "I wanted to catch the ball before it rolled all the way into the river."

"But you could have been killed," Rachel scolded. "Sean is right. You need to be more careful."

She hung her head. "Rachel, I am sorry."

"Just don't forget again."

"I won't."

"Good." She smiled at Sean. "Thank you for shouting your warning! If I hadn't heard you, I wouldn't have gotten up the hill in time." She shifted, taking weight off her left foot. She shook it, hoping the heated pain stabbing it would vanish before she began the walk back to River's Haven.

"Are you all right?" asked a man from behind Rachel.

She turned. Her smile wavered when her eyes met Mr. Colton's gray ones. "Yes, we are fine."

"I would readily agree." His gaze wandered along her as if he had never seen her before.

"Thank you for asking, Mr. Colton," she said in the same cool tone.

He was dressed in the work clothes she had seen him wear the last time she visited the boat. Oil stains drew her eyes to his strong arms and muscular legs. He pushed a broad-brimmed hat back on his head and greeted the children.

"Let's go, Kitty Cat." Rachel took a single step, then winced.

"Are you hurt?" Mr. Colton asked.

She clenched her hands, and the little girl yelped. Releasing Kitty Cat's fingers, she said, "I twisted my left foot when I rushed to save Kitty Cat from that carriage."

"And tore your dress."

"My dress?"

He looped a single finger in the torn seam at her waist. "Here."

"What are you doing?" She tried to step back as she pushed that probing finger away, but halted when more pain swirled up her leg.

"You ripped your dress." He gave her a rakish grin. "Just wanted to point out where."

The little girl piped up, "Rachel doesn't like long skirts. She says they just cause women to get hurt."

"Excuse me?" Mr. Colton asked.

"At River's Haven," Kitty Cat answered before Rachel could, "ladies wear sensible clothing. The skirt Rachel wears there comes only to here." She slashed her hand across the black skirt at knee level.

"Is that so?"

" 'Tis so. That way she—"

Rachel put her hand on Kitty Cat's shoulder. "I think that's enough."

Mr. Colton smiled. "Enough to give me a very good idea of what the female clothing at River's Haven looks like. Seems to me that I should pay a visit out there one of these days."

"I thought you were too busy with your steamboat for anything else."

"Retract those claws." He grinned when Sean and Kitty Cat giggled. "Lad, is there a doctor in Haven?"

"It's nothing to bother Doc Bamburger about," Rachel argued. If she said the Assembly of Elders would be furious if she went to an outsider doctor, Mr. Colton would start another argument. She did not feel up to trading words with him now. She glanced up at Haven, wishing there was a way she could have the doctor look at it without the Assembly of Elders knowing. Clenching her teeth to hold back her groan, she added, "Sean, will you let Mrs. Sawyer know that I've found Kitty Cat?"

"Sure." The lad took two steps up the hill, then paused to ask, "Can Kitty Cat come back to help decorate the wagon for the Fourth of July parade?"

"Please, please, please, please," begged the little girl, tugging on Rachel's skirt with each word.

Rachel bit her lip as the motion sent more agony along her leg. Lifting Kitty Cat's hand off her skirt, she said, "I can't promise, but I'll ask."

Sean's face fell, and Kitty Cat stamped her foot, but it was Mr. Colton who asked, "Why do you have to ask anyone? I thought Kitty Cat lived with you."

"The Assembly of Elders makes those decisions in River's Haven."

"You can't leave the Community without getting their say-so?"

"Don't be silly. Of course we can leave. It's just that the children shouldn't be wandering about the countryside on a whim."

"Nor should they be prisoners."

"I assure you, Mr. Colton, no one is a prisoner at River's Haven. I—" She could not halt this groan as another savage streak of pain surged up her left leg.

Mr. Colton frowned. "You can't walk all the way back to River's Haven when you can't take a single step."

"I'm sure it's just twisted. I'll rest it for a few minutes, and I'll be fine."

"Good. Come down to *The Ohio Star* and sit while you rest it."

"*The Ohio Star*? Thank you, but I think not. Kitty Cat and I must be getting back to River's Haven, so I'll go back up the hill and sit on a bench by the train station. At least that takes me in the right direction." She did not want to admit that she was unsure if she could walk as far as the riverboat. Looking around in dismay, she asked, "Where did that child go now?"

"To *The Ohio Star*." He hooked a thumb in the direction of the river.

Rachel wanted to moan when she saw the little girl's skirts bouncing down the hill toward the riverboat. No doubt, as soon as she had heard Mr. Colton mention the boat, she had taken off to visit it again.

"She seems determined to keep you on your toes." He chuckled as Rachel hobbled a single step. "Or off them. Let me help."

"Thank you, Mr. Colton, but—"

"Wyatt."

"Pardon me?"

"My name is Wyatt." He put his arm around her waist. "If I'm going to call you Rachel, you should call me Wyatt."

"I didn't realize you were back to using my given name."

"I never stopped using it."

Rachel was tempted to fire back another comment, but she had to concentrate on putting the least possible pressure on her left foot. If Wyatt had not helped, she doubted she could have made a trio of steps without collapsing. This was another debt she owed him . . . another debt she could never explain to her brother.

Five

Rachel paused when she and Wyatt reached the gang-plank. It was too narrow for the two of them to walk side by side.

She said, "I can wait here if you'd be so kind as to tell Kitty Cat to come ashore."

"I'd be glad to be so kind."

When he put an arm beneath her knees and lifted her as if she weighed no more than a drop of river water, she gasped. "Mr. Colton!"

"Wyatt, if *you* would be so kind."

She hardly knew the man, and she already found his superior smile irritating beyond endurance. She pushed her exasperation aside. Without his help, she could not get aboard the boat, and standing here on the shore and shouting for Kitty Cat would be humiliating.

"As you wish," she said as he stepped onto the gang-plank.

"I doubt you say those words very often." He chuckled.

Rachel smiled, but weakly. In the past week, she had spoken those words far too often during conversations with her brother. Arguing with Merrill had gained her as little as being stubborn would now.

She tried to relax, for Wyatt's arms were amazingly gentle. She leaned against him, glad that she did not have to take another step. Once she saw what the damage was to her ankle, she would figure out a way to get back to River's Haven.

Kitty Cat came running as Wyatt crossed to the deck of the riverboat. "Why are you carrying Rachel?"

"She hurt her foot saving you, K. C."

As the little girl began to apologize, Rachel asked, "What did you call her?"

"K. C. for Kitty Cat." He winked at Kitty Cat, but the youngster did not lose her frightened expression. "She's going to be all right."

"Are you sure?" asked Kitty Cat.

"Sure as I'm standing here."

When he lowered her toward the deck, Rachel let her knees fold and dropped onto a bench. She leaned back against the railing and closed her eyes for a moment.

"See?" Wyatt asked. "She's going to be fine, K. C."

"I like that name!" the little girl shouted as she spun about on her toes, dancing along the deck. "K. C., K. C., that's me."

"A nickname for a nickname?" asked Rachel.

"Why not?" Wyatt smiled.

"I . . . I . . ."

"Even you, proper as you try to be with that child, can't come up with any reason why not."

"I'm not thinking too clearly just now." She shifted her left leg, stretching it out in front of her. "Ouch."

"You may have done more than twist it," he said, abruptly serious. "You should have the doctor examine it. Wait here, and I'll find him."

She cried, "No!"

He paused and faced her. "Are you afraid of doctors?"

"Of course not."

"Then why won't you have him check your ankle? If it's a matter of money—"

"It isn't."

"Then what?" Before she could answer, he scowled.

"It's another of those damn rules at River's Haven, isn't it?"

"Watch your language in front of Kitty Cat."

His smile returned as he patted the little girl on the head. "I'm sure she's heard that word before."

"Rachel says I shouldn't say damn or—"

"Kitty Cat!" she gasped, frowning at Wyatt. "You don't need to encourage her to misbehave. I think we should leave."

Bowing, he motioned toward the plank. "Be my guest."

She drew in her feet to stand. Her heel caught between two boards on the deck, and she moaned as pain flashed up her leg.

"Are you done being foolish?" he asked.

"If you wouldn't keep—"

"Encouraging you to misbehave?"

Rachel looked away from his smile, because the concern in his eyes had not changed even when he was amused—or furious.

Wiping his hands on his shirt, he knelt in front of her. He took the hem of her skirt and began to raise it.

She turned on the bench, pulling her skirt out of his grip. Another groan bubbled from her lips as she moved her left leg, but she would not sit there and let this man act so outrageously.

Wyatt sat back on his heels. "Why the sudden modesty?"

"I'm not in the habit of allowing strangers to draw up my skirts."

He snorted a laugh. "You don't have to tell me that. You look as prim as a nun. However, you're used to showing off your legs if you wear your skirts only to here." He put a hand on her right knee.

Something blistering riveted her. Not from her ankle, but from where his fingers had settled on her skirt. A soft sound came from her lips. Not a gasp, but neither was it a moan, for this heat created a buzzing sensation along her, making her aware of every bit of her . . . and of his hand.

Her fingers trembled as she lifted his hand off her leg. She struggled to keep her voice from doing the same while she said, "The skirts at River's Haven are shorter than what's worn in Haven, but we wear pantalets beneath them. Our legs aren't revealed for everyone to ogle."

"That's a shame."

"I am not surprised you think so."

He chuckled. "Outspoken, aren't you?"

Wyatt's smile faded when Rachel grimaced in reply, and he knew she was hurting more than she wanted him to guess. She was wasting her strength trying to hide her pain, because the lines gouged into her face revealed the truth.

He had been horrified to look up from his work on the deck to see a carriage bearing down on a woman and a young child. When he had recognized both Rachel and K. C., he had rushed up the bluff to make sure they had not been hurt. He had not expected that the local sheriff would allow anyone to drive like that in the village. Maybe Sheriff Parker was busy somewhere else.

"Rachel, the only other female on the boat is a little girl who's now looking for Horace up on the deck over our heads, if the sound of her footsteps are any clue. Your ankle should be checked. You refuse to let the doctor in Haven do that. If you've got any ideas on how examining your ankle can be accomplished without me moving your skirt aside, I'd be glad to hear them."

Her eyes, which were dimming with anguish, looked down into his. His hand rose toward her cheek, but he lowered it before he could touch her. Having sympathy for her was one thing. Getting mixed up with her was something completely different.

Since her first visit to *The Ohio Star*, he had had trouble staying focused on anything but the memory of her snapping eyes and guileless laugh. Horace had bellowed at him more than once to keep his mind on his work while they worked on the boiler or the broken paddlewheel. When he had dropped a hammer into the river yesterday, it had taken him half the morning to retrieve it.

All because he kept thinking about pretty Rachel Browning who treated a man so coolly that she tempted him to consider ways to melt the reserve she tried to keep in place between them. Pretty Rachel Browning who wore her skirts no lower than her knees. Images of her slender legs draped over his arm threatened to lead him into a most complicated direction. He would be right pleased to see those legs as his hands slid up them, but she would not give him the opportunity. She was the sort of woman who would want a man to settle down and stay with her. He was the sort of man who did not want to stay anywhere.

Her voice was soft and unsteady when she said, "All right. If you must move aside my skirt . . ."

"I must." He reached for her skirt.

"No, I think it'd be better if I did."

Before he could take the hem again, she drew her skirt up her outstretched left leg. He stared as the toes of her black shoes appeared, then the rest of her shoe that reached halfway up her calf. Above it, a single handbreadth of lace was revealed. Breathing was suddenly a chore as his gaze wandered from her simple shoes to that lace that teased him to discover how much more was still hidden.

"Is that far enough?" she asked in the same faint voice.

He nodded, not sure he could speak. What was wrong with him? He had been in taverns and brothels along these rivers since he was not much older than K. C., and he had seen harlots showing off far more than this. He had become accustomed to their easy lack of inhibition as well as his own. So why was he now acting like a lad with his first woman?

"What's going on here?" asked Horace as he walked toward them.

His partner's voice freed Wyatt from his mesmerism with the leg in front of him. He cursed silently. He should not get all off-kilter about a leg hidden in enough lace to keep anyone from guessing its real shape. The problem was that he knew its shape after her leg had rested on his arm.

"Rachel twisted her ankle saving K. C. from a carriage that nearly ran the kid down. I'm checking it."

"I can see that," Horace said. "It looks as if you've got everything well in hand."

Rachel's face became an explosion of red as Wyatt growled, "Horace, watch yourself."

"Miss Rachel," Horace hurried to say, "I didn't mean to insult you in any way."

"I know that," she replied, each word sounding more breathless than the one before and making Wyatt wonder how badly she had hurt herself. "You've been very nice to both Kitty Cat and me." The look she gave Wyatt suggested that she would not say the same about him.

Wyatt shook his head, clearing it of the stupid thoughts of having this woman soft and willing and warm in his arms. She was prickly and disagreeable and cold as the ice that gathered at the river's edge on winter mornings. Maybe that was how the men liked their women in that strange group out at River's Haven, but not Wyatt Colton.

He cupped Rachel's left foot in his hand, moving it to rest on his thigh. Beads of sweat appeared on her forehead beneath her drab bonnet.

"Sorry," he muttered.

"I know that," she said as she had to Horace.

"Can I do anything to help?" his partner asked.

"I'll let you know in a moment." He looked up at Rachel again. She was biting her lower lip. "I'm going to unbutton your shoe now. It may hurt."

She nodded. "All right."

"You don't have to bear it in silence."

"I know." She drew in a shuddering breath. "Please be quick."

Without a buttonhook, the tiny, stiff buttons on her shoe were uncooperative. K. C. sat on the bench and put her arms around Rachel. The little girl's bonnet dropped back over her shoulders. Leaning her head on K. C.'s curls, Rachel said nothing as he worked to remove her shoe.

He drew off her shoe and grimaced as he touched her already-swelling ankle. "Did you really expect to walk back to River's Haven on this?"

Rachel leaned forward to examine it. She was pleased when Wyatt moved aside. She was hurting too much to argue further with him. "I had no idea it was this bad."

Kitty Cat slipped off the bench and sat cross-legged on the deck next to Wyatt. "We need some leeches," she said with as much authority as if she were a grizzled doctor instead of a little girl.

"I'm afraid we're fresh out of leeches," Wyatt said, ruffling her hair. "Horace, would you get some of those rags we were using in the boiler room?" When Rachel started to protest, he gave her a cockeyed grin and added, "The ones without dirt and rust on them."

"Right away."

As Horace went to get the rags, Wyatt asked, "Do you want something to ease that pain? I think there's some wine up in the saloon."

"That might not be a bad idea."

Kitty Cat jumped to her feet and offered to retrieve the bottle. When Wyatt told her where to find the wine, she rushed up the stairs.

He looked back at Rachel. "I thought you'd refuse a drink."

"Why?"

"I figured you had some sort of rule at River's Haven

that prohibited anything that wasn't on some approved list."

"You have the wrong idea about our lives at River's Haven."

"I don't think so. I think you have so many detestable rules out there that neither you nor K. C. can be penned in by them."

"Me?"

He did not answer as he turned to take some rags from Horace. Gently he wound several of them around her ankle, taking care not to touch the swelling. She was amazed how comfortable the binding felt, for it seemed to enclose the pain and keep it from surging up her leg.

"That's the best I can do for now," Wyatt said as he tied the top rag in place.

"Thank you." She brushed her skirt back down over her leg and slowly drew on her shoe. It would not close around her ankle, but she could not walk barefoot back to River's Haven.

"You should have it looked at by your doctor out at River's Haven."

"We don't have one."

"What happened? Did he smarten up and leave?"

Frowning, she tied a rag around the top of her shoe to hold it in place. Gingerly she rose, holding on to the railing to steady herself.

"I think it's time we left," she said, scowling at him.

"Go ahead. Don't let us keep you here."

"Wyatt," muttered Horace, "she's hurt."

"Her head as well as her ankle because she's not thinking straight," he replied as he stood. "Are you sure you didn't get brushed by that carriage, honey?"

It was not easy to maintain her pose of outrage when every inch of her ached as if the carriage really had struck her. "I would need more than a knock in the head to want to stay here." She raised her voice. "Kitty Cat, let's go."

"She's getting the wine for you," Wyatt said, wiping his hands on his trousers.

Horace cleared his throat. "I'll find her, Miss Rachel."

"Thank you."

She gripped the railing as she slid her left foot forward a step. Her smile at her accomplishment of that single step vanished when she tried to move her right foot. That put all her weight on her left ankle. She wobbled and collapsed.

Strong arms caught her before she could hit the deck. She moaned as the pain returned, doubly strong. Those arms lifted her up, and she looked at Wyatt's frown, which was too close as he leaned her against his chest again. Knowing that she might be inviting more trouble on herself, she still could not keep her head from resting on his shoulder.

The aromas of sweat and bay rum flavored every breath she took. His shirt beneath her cheek was coarse, but it was not as rough as his unshaven cheek. His ebony hair, which was in need of a cut, brushed her face as he shifted her in his arms. Beneath her fingers on his chest, his heart's steady rhythm accelerated when her other hand slid around his shoulders.

She raised her gaze to meet his. Raw emotions that she should not be viewing shone in his eyes. Was it his pulse or hers that was racing now? She could not tell.

"Are you satisfied yet?" he asked in a near whisper.

"Excuse me?"

"With proving that you're foolish?"

She swallowed hard. If he had had any idea that she had heard an invitation in his question that he had not intended, he would laugh loud enough to be heard up in the village.

As quietly as he had spoken, she said, "I don't think I'm the only foolish one."

"That's true." He grinned at her. "Here I am holding you in my arms, and all I'm doing is chattering like a squirrel."

When he bent toward her, she put her hand up to halt him. It took every bit of her strength not to pull it back so his lips could find hers.

Softly he said, "You look frightened, Rachel."

"I'm afraid you've lost your mind."

He laughed. "Is that all you're afraid of?" He set her back on the bench and leaned forward to rest his hands on the railing behind her. "I think you're scared of *me.*"

"Why should I be scared of you?" She tried to look past him. Horace should have found Kitty Cat by now.

When Wyatt's strong fingers brushed her cheek, she stared up at him. In a rough whisper, he said, "I think you're afraid of me doing this."

"No." She would not let him guess how his very touch threatened her composure. Then . . . She was not sure what he might do then, but she doubted if she should bait him enough to find out.

"Or are you afraid of me doing this?" He ran a single fingertip across her lips.

She gripped the edge of the bench as quivers raced outward from his touch. Fighting to keep her voice steady, she said, "No."

"Then maybe you're afraid of me doing this. . . ." His finger coursed beneath her chin. When she trembled at the onslaught of sensation, he smiled. "Or maybe you're afraid I *won't* do this."

"Won't do—?"

Her question vanished beneath his mouth over hers. When he explored her lips slowly, as if he wished to sample a single inch at a time, her fingers uncurled from the bench and slipped up to curve along his back. His muscles were firm and urged her to be more bold. When his tongue stroked hers, her fingers clenched on his shirt.

Lost in the thrill of his bold kiss, she was not sure when he had moved to sit beside her on the bench. His arm cradled her against him as it had when he had lifted her off her aching ankle.

"That's what I suspect you're afraid I won't do," he whispered as he caressed her cheek.

"How could you know unless . . . ?" She blushed as she realized she was begging him for another kiss.

When she inched away, he laughed and drew her back to him. "How can I know until I try these delicious lips again? Is that what you were going to ask me?" His gaze stroked her face. "You could prove to be quite a temptress, Rachel."

"You have proven to be intolerable." She arched her shoulders. As soon as he released her, she felt bereft. She could not understand how she could want to be in his arms and yearn to escape at the same time. What baffled her most was that she longed for more of Wyatt Colton's kisses.

Instead of the insolent smile she had expected, he was serious. "Intolerable wasn't what I intended to be." The grin she had anticipated returned as he added, "Nor did I intend to kiss you today."

"We can pretend this never happened."

His finger stroked her cheek gently. "I don't think that's possible."

"No?" she asked. When he put his arm around her waist, bringing her closer again, she whispered, "This is crazy, Wyatt."

"It is, isn't it?" He traced her lips with his tongue and smiled when she quivered.

She was not sure what else he would have said because he looked past her. Turning, she saw Kitty Cat proudly carrying a black tray with a wine bottle and glasses on it. Horace followed close behind, his hands outstretched to catch anything that fell off.

While Wyatt took the bottle and poured wine into a glass, Rachel tried to collect herself. It was all for naught, she realized, when he handed her the glass and his gaze held hers again. She tried not to think what he might have said if they had not been interrupted, but she was very certain of what he would have done. She tried not to think what she would have done when he pulled her back into his arms and against his lips, but she could imagine nothing else. And *that* frightened her.

When Wyatt saw the coffee and pastry, relief limb-ened Horace that a Chinese serving lass all his knight... the tea and Wyatt's knuckles and the glass and the curb... gold. Imagine she shook her thick, withering eager love medicine, and not have often deal on are you... were only reached helping, drinkt now, they can figure how to think what, such that little drink were bit the when... her lies, the turners and comfort ample the ready, had might with but me. And our head out ask not...

Six

"This is quite a predicament," Wyatt said as he put the empty bottle onto the tray. "You can't walk back on that foot."

Rachel nodded, then wished she had not. Her head was light, although her left ankle was weighted with pain. She should not have agreed to let Horace refill her glass. She needed all her wits to figure a way out of this dilemma. "I think that much is obvious."

He frowned. "You could hire a carriage at the livery."

"I don't have the money to do that."

When Wyatt looked at Horace, the older man drew out one of his pockets and said, "They all are just as empty at the moment. You borrowed five dollars to get even the few parts we ordered from Louisville."

"What sort of parts?" Rachel asked, handing Kitty Cat her glass to set next to the bottle.

"Parts for the boiler that cracked when the boat hit that sandbar." Horace gave Kitty Cat a smile as she picked up the tray and turned toward Wyatt.

"Metal parts?" asked Rachel, struggling to make her mind work.

He nodded.

"You didn't need to send all the way to Louisville for them. There's a metal shop at River's Haven."

Wyatt finished the last of his wine and gave the little

girl the glass to put on the tray. "Rachel, we're not interested in gewgaws. We need real parts that will fit in this boiler."

"The metal shop at River's Haven doesn't make—as you put it so delicately—gewgaws. The craftsmen are very skilled and have been doing work for the railroad for more than a year now. If they can make parts for the steam engines in a locomotive, I'm sure they can make ones for the boiler of a steamboat. How different can they be?"

"She has you there," Horace said. He chuckled. "Again."

Wyatt waved him to silence. "They've been making parts for the railroad?"

"Yes." She did not nod again, afraid her head would drift off her shoulders.

He went through a doorway shadowed beneath the stairs. When he came out, he asked, "Can they make parts like these?"

Rachel took the small pieces of metal and turned them over and over in her hand. "Yes, they can make these. These parts are simple. Threaded screws and bolts present a bit more of a problem."

"How soon can you have them made?"

"It depends on how many parts you need." She dropped the pieces to her lap and pressed her hand to her aching head. "Can we talk about this some other time?"

Wyatt reached to pick up the parts. When his hand brushed her leg, she shivered with the sensation she could not control. She shifted away. Pain shot up her leg again, warning her not to forget her ankle. Gathering up the pieces of metal, she handed them to Horace.

The older man said, "She's right. As bad as that leg was twisted, she can't be thinking very straight just now."

Rachel wanted to give Horace a grateful hug. He was right about her head being all ajumble, although her befuddlement was not caused by either her leg or the wine. It came from Wyatt's beguiling touch.

Grasping the rail behind her, she struggled to her feet. She nodded her thanks when Horace put his other hand under her elbow. Kitty Cat rushed to her side and put her arm around Rachel's waist.

"We really should be going back to River's Haven," Rachel murmured.

"How?" asked Wyatt.

Horace jabbed him with an elbow. "She ain't too heavy, Wyatt, and you were bemoaning the fact that you'd get weak when there weren't any crates to stack on the deck."

"What a silly idea!" Her laugh was stilted. "If you'll help me up the hill to the train station, someone will surely come by and give us a ride."

"At this hour?" Wyatt pointed toward the first stars peeking through the twilight.

"Maybe there's a meeting at the church or the Grange Hall tonight."

"And if there isn't? Are you going to sit there all night with K. C.?"

"It's going to be plenty warm enough tonight." She kept her chin high so he could not guess how she dreaded the thought of sitting on a hard bench while her ankle throbbed. "And it doesn't look like rain."

Wyatt shook his head. "There's no way in he—no way in perdition," he corrected when Horace scowled at him, "that I'm going to leave you and the kid sitting in front of the station when we've got plenty of empty rooms here on the boat."

"No! We can't stay *here!*" Before Wyatt's brows could lower in another fierce frown, she added, "I could go to Reverend Faulkner. He'll help us."

"Reverend Faulkner!" Horace smiled, obviously relieved. "That's just the answer!"

"K. C., c'mon," Wyatt said. "We're going to make a call on the preacher."

As he swept Rachel up in his arms without warning,

she said, "I'd wager those are words you never thought you'd say."

Horace roared another laugh. "You have that right, Miss Rachel." Without a pause, he said, "I'll clean up here, Wyatt, so we can get a good start in the morning."

Wyatt grunted something before carrying Rachel toward the board to the shore. Kitty Cat bounced across it, and he followed with more care.

Climbing the hill, he said, "It would be easier to carry you if you weren't as stiff as a corpse."

She was tempted to retort, but forced herself to relax against him as she had before. All she had to do was keep her own wayward thoughts from wandering too far and leading her into trouble. When she leaned her cheek against his shoulder, she had to fight her own longing to reach up and tease the hair brushing his collar.

"Better," he murmured.

Again she did not answer. She did not want to get into a discussion of how much better being in his arms was. As she listened to his heartbeat, she watched Kitty Cat skipping ahead of them along the quiet street. The buildings on either side of the street were dark, save for a window or two. She hoped no one was sitting on a porch and able to see Wyatt toting her toward the green.

The minister's house was set to the right of the church. The white church glowed in the light of the waning moon. Lamps were lit in the parsonage's front windows.

"Knock on the door, K. C.," Wyatt ordered.

She did, and the door opened almost immediately. A short man with graying hair motioned for them to enter. His somber coat and backward collar identified him as the minister.

Rachel had no chance to look around the dusky foyer before Wyatt carried her into a room on the right. The dark red upholstery on the furniture showed signs of long use, but the rosewood arms and legs glistened with care. Several tables and a piano nearly filled the room to overflowing. On top of them, books and papers and knickknacks threatened to tumble in the slightest breeze.

Wyatt placed her on her feet. She started to thank him, but agony ripped along her leg. The room contracted into darkness as she struggled to hold onto her senses. A soft voice, as lush as sun-warmed moss, urged her to sit. She did so with the help of a hand beneath her elbow.

"Are you all right?"

At the question, she blinked and focused on Wyatt's face, which was shockingly close to her. The shadow of every whisker emphasized his straight lips and the firm line of his chin. Wanting to tell him that he should not be leaning over her like this—it simply was not polite—she rested her head against the knobby antimacassar on the back of the chair.

"I'm none the worse for wear, thank you," she whispered, closing her eyes and trying to will away the pain.

"You look like hell." Hearing a throaty laugh, she opened her eyes as he added, "Sorry, Reverend."

The minister appeared on her other side. "Can I get you something, Miss Browning?"

"I didn't realize that you recognized me," she said.

"I've made it part of my duties to keep an eye on all the children who came off the orphan train and the people who took them in." Reverend Faulkner's smile was kind and concerned at the same time. "It's important to me—and to the Children's Aid Society, which placed them out here—that the children are happy and make a good adjustment to their new homes. I've paid calls on many of the children, and I'm happy to report that, for the most part, they're doing even better than I had dared to hope."

She sat straighter. "If you could share some of the stories of your calls with Kit—with Katherine, I'm sure she'd be delighted to hear how her friends are faring." Stroking the little girl's tangled curls, she smiled when Kitty Cat began asking questions too rapidly for Reverend Faulkner to answer.

"Shall we do that over a cup of tea? A bit of brandy?"

"Nothing for me, thank you, although Kitty Cat and Wy—Mr. Colton might like something."

"I should be going," Wyatt said, obviously ill at ease. Was it because he was in a minister's house or because he was ashore?

Reverend Faulkner smiled at the little girl. "I believe Mrs. Faulkner has at least one piece of strawberry rhubarb pie left in the kitchen."

Kitty Cat turned to go toward the back of the house, then paused. "Wyatt, tell Horace I said goodbye."

"Why don't you tell him that the next time you call?"

"Wyatt!" Rachel gasped. "I asked you before not to encourage her to misbehave."

"I don't think she needs any encouragement." He winked at Kitty Cat. "And I'm sure you'll be back to *The Ohio Star* soon."

Rachel did not want to quarrel in front of the minister. Instead she let Reverend Faulkner ask about her ankle and how she had hurt it. As he lauded her bravery, Kitty Cat returned with a pie plate in her hand. The minister sat her and the pie plate next to him on the sofa.

When he motioned for Wyatt to bring the chair next to the window closer to where they were sitting, Wyatt considered repeating that he needed to return to his boat. He opened his mouth to say that, but paused when he looked at Rachel's gray face. She winced when he dragged the chair forward, so he picked it up and set it next to hers.

"So you need a way to get back to River's Haven," said Reverend Faulkner when Rachel finished her story. "That you're here must mean that you can't help her, Mr. Colton."

"Other than carrying her out there, which doesn't sound like the best idea, my only transport is *The Ohio Star*."

"Which isn't ready to leave the pier, I assume."

"No." He smiled. "If you've got a buggy, Reverend, I can drive her out there before it gets much darker."

"Mrs. Faulkner is using our buggy while she visits her sister a ways up the river."

"That can't be the only buggy in town."

The minister chuckled and picked up a pipe he must have been smoking when they arrived. "No, it isn't. And, if you'll look out the window behind you, you'll see a buckboard in front of the courthouse. It's Samuel Jennings's."

"Mr. Jennings?" Kitty Cat jumped to her feet. "Is Brendan Rafferty with him?"

"I don't know. Samuel came into town this evening to attend the meeting about plans for a library in Haven." He smiled and added, as smoke curled around him, "Why don't you go over there, young lady, and see if he's willing to give you and Miss Browning a ride back to River's Haven?"

"That's too much to ask of him!" Rachel gasped. "I have never met Mr. Jennings."

Kitty Cat ran out of the room.

Reverend Faulkner smiled as the front door slammed. "You're right about Katherine, Miss Browning. It would do that youngster a world of good to hear about how her friends have settled into their new lives. Samuel Jennings's farm is on Nanny Goat Hill Road, which isn't too far from River's Haven. He's a good man, and he'll be glad to help you." The minister turned to focus his eyes on Wyatt. "That's the way we do things here in Haven. When we need help, we seek out one another without hesitation."

Was Reverend Faulkner trying to tell him something with that steady gaze? If so, Wyatt could not guess what it might be. Rubbing his hands on his trousers, he noticed for the first time the oil stains on the trousers. He glanced at his palms. The oil was dry, so it would not smear on the minister's nice furniture or . . .

His eyes riveted on the handprint on Rachel's blouse beneath her short jacket. Right where he had been holding her when he carried her here. Then he noticed the dark blotch climbing up the back of that coat. It was nearly lost in the black wool, but when she leaned forward to speak to the minister, the undeniable smudge left by his hand sweeping along her back glistened in the lamplight.

He stifled a laugh. Not too successfully, he realized, when Rachel looked over her shoulder at him. He was tempted to run his finger along that streak, but a glance at the minister made him recall his manners. He almost chuckled again. The very manners Rachel believed he did not have.

But it was not Reverend Faulkner's presence that halted him from teasing her. Pain had stolen the sparkle from her eyes, and her pallor warned him that her ankle was hurting even worse. If she had shown some sense and stayed aboard *The Ohio Star* tonight, she could have rested it in his quarters.

When he envisioned her leg propped up in his bed and her hair falling in a luxurious stream across his pillow, he kept his curse silent. Other women had tried to persuade him to give up his free life and stay ashore. They had failed. Rachel would be glad to see him gone . . . and yet she lingered in his mind.

Wyatt was glad when the front door opened and freed him from those bewitching fantasies. The man who entered was not as tall as he was. His black hair fell forward over his green eyes and a pair of gold-rimmed glasses. The man's boots were scuffed from hard work, but his clothes were clean and neatly pressed. He had, Wyatt saw, his arm around K. C.'s shoulders, and the little girl was looking up at him with the widest smile Wyatt had seen on her face.

They laughed together as they paused in the parlor door-way.

Something unpleasant struck Wyatt like a blow to the gut. He had no time to figure out what it might be because Reverend Faulkner was introducing Rachel to the man who was, as Wyatt had guessed, Samuel Jennings.

"I hear that you need a ride to River's Haven," Jennings said in a voice that hinted at years of education. "I'll be glad to take you out there so I can have a chance to talk more with this young lady." He put his hand on K. C.'s curls. "Brendan had me confused for days before I figured out that Kitty Cat wasn't a real cat." He turned to Wyatt and held out his hand. "Samuel Jennings."

"Wyatt Colton." He shook Jennings's hand.

"You're the fellow with the boat getting fixed down on the river, right?"

"News travels fast in Haven."

Jennings laughed. "Not a lot happens in small towns, so the arrival of your paddleboat was an exciting event. At least for Sean O'Dell, who rode out to my farm to tell Brendan and his sisters about it."

"Sisters?"

Reverend Faulkner interjected quietly, "There are three Rafferty children at Jennings's farm."

"You must have a generous wife if she's willing to take on the work of three children," Wyatt said.

The man's smile tightened. "I'm not married."

Curiosity pinched Wyatt, but he did not press. The com-ment should not have brought such coldness to Jennings's voice. Maybe his wife had died. But her death would create sorrow, not this frosty anger.

Shrugging aside a puzzle that was not his to solve, he looked back at Rachel. She was grasping the arms of the chair. Before she could push herself to her feet—this woman did not have the sense God gave a goose!—he picked her up again and settled her soft curves against his chest.

"Is your wagon out front?" he asked, to halt Rachel from scolding him for not asking her permission before lifting her out of the chair.

Jennings stepped back into the foyer. "Yes. Bring her this way."

With Reverend Faulkner and K. C. following, Wyatt carried Rachel out to the simple wagon that was parked by the church steps. He wished it was not so close. The light breeze was sending a single tendril of her hair up against his cheek, and he wanted to let it tease him a while longer. Its clean aroma was exhilarating.

"Rachel?" he asked quietly.

She looked up at him. "Yes?"

Fascinated by the warmth in her eyes, he forgot what he was going to say. He just wanted to look into her eyes again. Just? That was not *all* he wanted. He wanted her hair free and loose on his pillow and her arms around him as he delved deeply into her to revel in every bit of her warmth.

"What is it, Wyatt?" she asked.

"Send for the doctor if your ankle hasn't improved by the end of the week."

"I said I would."

Her sharp tone again shattered his daydreams of making love with her all night. Setting her on the seat of the buckboard, he reached to lift K. C. in. That irritating thud in his gut returned while he watched Jennings swing the little girl up into the back of the wagon.

Wyatt stepped back as Jennings climbed onto the seat beside Rachel. Jennings was a man who would catch a woman's eye, and he seemed to have caught Rachel's, for she gave him a warm smile. Wyatt cursed again under his breath, not caring that he stood in the shadow of the church's steeple. Jealousy was something he should not be feeling. Why should he care that Rachel was ready to flirt with this farmer? One kiss had warned him how easy it would be to get his life tangled up with hers, and he did not need to end up with ties to the shore if those ties were part of the River's Haven Community.

He said nothing as the wagon turned and headed out of Haven and toward the road leading along the river. He should be thinking good riddance when it drove out of sight, but that pinch of regret remained.

"The church is sponsoring a social," Reverend Faulkner said in a matter-of-fact voice, "to celebrate the exercises the children do each year at the end of school and the centennial of our country's founding. It'll be on the Fourth of July. I thought it would be nice to have the children from River's Haven participate as well as their parents. It could bring the folks in the village and River's Haven together as they were at the barn raising out at Sawyer's farm earlier this spring. It's good for folks to see each other instead of just listening to rumors." With his hands clasped behind him, Reverend Faulkner rocked back and forth on his feet as he watched the buckboard vanish into the darkness. "That's in just a few weeks, Mr. Colton. Surely you won't have all the repairs made on your boat by then."

"No, although I wish I could say that we'll be on the river and heading for Louisville by then." He tore his gaze from the road to look at the minister.

"You might want to consider coming to the social." He smiled. "It doesn't take much more than a couple of weeks for a twisted ankle to heal, you know."

"So I've heard."

"When I twisted mine a few years ago, the doctor suggested that I get some exercise for it as soon as the pain was gone. That took about two weeks, and then he wanted me to exercise it every day." He climbed back onto the porch and sat on a rocker. "Dancing isn't a difficult exercise for a young lady."

Leaning against the pole holding up the porch roof, Wyatt laughed. "You're wasting your time preaching, Reverend. You should be playing Cupid for the folks around here."

"I do. Regularly." He pointed his pipe toward the far side of the green. "There go Miss Underhill and her beau. I suspect the town will be looking for a new teacher soon."

"Don't take this the wrong way, Reverend, but this life in Haven isn't one I want."

"I know."

"So you're wasting your time trying to match me up with one of the gals here."

"I wouldn't waste my time or yours." The minister laughed. "I'm just suggesting that you shouldn't waste your time either."

Wyatt stepped down off the porch. "Good night, Reverend."

"Two weeks, and her ankle should be healed, Mr. Colton."

He did not answer. What could he say? That two weeks was not enough time . . . and that two weeks was too long? Not enough time to seduce Rachel and too long to be stuck in this backwater town. He strode toward his boat, determined to get the repairs done before that wily minister had him betrothed and wed to a woman who already was too enticing for *his* own good.

Seven

Rachel scratched out another line in the accounts book. She had never made so many mistakes. Usually her math was without errors. Today she doubted if she could add one and one together correctly.

She wished she could blame her lack of concentration on her ankle, but it was healing quickly. After almost a week, she could walk on it as long as she was careful.

No, thoughts of her ankle were not intruding on her work. It was her concerns for Kitty Cat. The little girl had not left River's Haven since the day Rachel had trailed her a second time into the village of Haven. Or so Rachel thought, although she was not sure about that. Kitty Cat could easily get to Mr. Jennings's farm to see the Rafferty boy and be back at River's Haven before she was missed.

The little girl was happier than Rachel had ever seen her. Was Kitty Cat deciding that she wanted to stay at River's Haven, or was the youngster up to some mischief?

And Kitty Cat was not her only problem. Rachel was plagued by thoughts of Wyatt Colton as well. No, she would not let him intrude on her work again. He must be busy on his boat, and she should be busy here.

Bending over the account book, Rachel tried to see where she had made her mistake. She picked up the invoice sheets that had come from the tool shop and from the weavers. They listed the work done during the past week and the billing for costs and supplies. Setting the pages back down, she rose from her desk, still being cautious about her ankle. She went over to the window and sat on the wide sill, looking at where the children were playing five stories below.

Kitty Cat was tossing a baseball with one of the boys. A broad smile brightened her face.

Rachel went back to her desk to continue her work. Maybe she was worrying for no reason. Kitty Cat had said she wanted to be sure her friends were well settled with their new families. Both Sean and Mr. Jennings had assured her that was so. Now the little girl could turn her mind to her life here at River's Haven.

When footsteps stopped in front of her door, Rachel looked up in irritation. Immediately, she stifled the harsh words that had burst into her head. She could not become so caught up in her fretting that she was short-tempered with one of the members of the Community.

Mr. Atlee regarded her with shock, warning her that her irritation had been on her face. He was a squat man with light brown hair, light brown eyes, and light brown skin. She had never heard him speak a cross word to anyone about anything.

"Miss Browning," he said quietly, "there's a gentleman here asking to see you."

"Who is it?" she asked as she folded her arms on the desk.

He glanced uneasily over his shoulder. "A stranger. No one who's come to River's Haven before. He said his name is Wyatt Colton, and that he was Katherine's friend." He paused before adding in a near whisper of despair, "How could that be? He's an outsider, Miss Browning."

"We have other callers from outside the Community."

"They come to see the Assembly of Elders."

She stood and smiled as if she were completely at ease with the idea of Wyatt Colton here at River's Haven. If he wanted to continue the argument that Kitty Cat should be allowed to visit *The Ohio Star*, she must put him to rights straightaway.

"Mr. Atlee, would you tell him that I'll meet him in the Community parlor?"

"Shall I have some refreshments sent in?"

"No. I doubt Mr. Colton will be staying long enough for that."

Mr. Atlee stepped aside as she came out into the hallway. When she walked toward the closest staircase, he went in the opposite direction. Where was Wyatt waiting? The main door to the common house was in this direction.

She chuckled to herself. The huge building with all its wings was disconcerting to the residents of the Community. For an outsider, it must be a bewildering maze.

Running her fingers along the mahogany paneling that covered the lower half of the wall, she tried to calm her frantic heartbeat. A week had passed since she had last spoken with Wyatt, but even when she worried about Kitty Cat, her thoughts had drifted to how his lips had seared hers and how his eyes twinkled as his mouth lowered toward hers.

Rachel greeted each person she passed as she went down to the ground floor. The stairwell was open from the first landing all the way to a skylight in the roof. More than once she had been tempted to bring her work out of her office to sit on one of the risers while sunshine cascaded around her.

The ground floor's hallway was as massive as the common house itself. It arched up more than twenty feet above her head. Intricate moldings marched along the walls and across the ceiling, reminding her of pictures she had seen of ancient cathedrals in Europe. This corridor always gave her the same sense of awe. Along the walls, at a height perfect to be read, was a listing of the doctrines guiding the River's Haven Community. Most were simple and commonplace—being kind to others and being willing to work hard for the betterment of everyone.

The Community Hall was as large as the Grange Hall in Haven. Everyone in River's Haven could gather here to listen to the Assembly of Elders, as they did once a month. Several small rooms opened off the great space. Each one was labeled with its name in a brass plaque over the half-moon window atop the door. The Community parlor was the nearest and smallest. With just three sofas and an equal number of chairs, it was cozy in comparison with the Community Hall. It was decorated in soft shades of navy blue and yellow.

Rachel paused in the doorway and stared at the man who was looking at the books on the shelves flanking the tall window. *This* was Wyatt Colton? This man who was dressed in what her mother had called "his going-to-church best"? The light gray coat he wore over darker gray trousers was double-breasted. His white shirt closed at his collar with a narrow black tie. He held a black top hat with a silver band that glistened as brightly as his shoes beneath pristine white spats. He could have been a fashion-plate, so she was surprised when she realized she preferred him in his work clothes that revealed his strong muscles instead of encasing them in dignified wool.

She wondered why he was dressed so. He obviously wanted to impress someone, but who?

"Good afternoon, Wyatt," Rachel said when she found her voice. "I'm sorry I've kept you waiting. I'm very busy this afternoon. I was told you wish to speak to me."

"Good afternoon." He dropped his hat on a nearby table along with his pose of being a gentleman caller. His eyes glistened as they narrowed and swept along her. A slow smile tilted his lips.

She looked down, realizing that he had never seen her

in a River's Haven dress. Other than the short skirt, the navy dress could have been worn by any woman in Haven. Her pantalets of the same color hid any hint of ankle, and the lace at their hem covered her shoes in an odd copy of his spats.

When his gaze rose, she could not halt herself from reaching up to touch her hair, which was in a loose net balanced on her shoulders. She had worn it in a tight bun each time she had seen him before. As she did with her clothes, she appreciated the comfort of this hairstyle favored in River's Haven.

"You're walking much better," Wyatt continued. "Why don't you walk back to the door?"

"What?" she asked, startled.

"I like watching you walk." He grinned. "Both toward me and away."

"May I remind you that you aren't on your boat?"

He smiled tightly. "I'll use my best 'going ashore' manners, Rachel. I should do this, shouldn't I?" He took her hand, and, with a bow as fine as any she had ever seen, he raised it to his lips and pressed a kiss to her skin.

She never had understood what was meant by the term "making one's head spin" until now. The courteous kiss was like one other men had given her, but none of those had delighted her like this. As he raised his head, she let herself become lost in his eyes.

He pressed her fingers to his face. They slipped from beneath his palm to stroke his smooth cheek. How would his freshly shaven skin feel against her if he kissed her mouth?

Several voices came from the Community Hall, and Rachel pulled back, shocked at how easily she had let him enchant her . . . and how much she wanted to linger within his touch's spell.

"We should—I mean—" Heavens, she was stuttering like a naughty child caught in the midst of mischief.

Wyatt ran his finger along her jaw. "If you want me to continue acting like a gentleman, I can spend the next ten minutes telling you how lovely you are, but I thought you'd rather talk business."

Never had he been so wrong about what she wanted, but, as he glanced uneasily at the door, she realized that he was not comfortable here. She had seen other outsiders act ill at ease in the common house. She would not have guessed that Wyatt Colton would be unsettled by the River's Haven Community. Then she recalled his disgust—there was no kinder word for it—when she had first spoken of living here. For a man who seemed to live by his own rules, making them up as he needed them, the very idea of a community like this one must be an abomination.

"Will you sit down, Wyatt?" When he arched a brow and smiled, Rachel added, "Please."

As he sat on a chair, he said, "I trust you got the oil stains out of your jacket."

Blast this man! He was the one who was uncomfortable, but he was doing everything he could to make *her* blush. If he thought he would unnerve her so much that she would say or do something foolish so he could tease her more, he would quickly learn his mistake.

"Yes," she replied. "The laundry here is very skilled. They're accustomed to the task of removing stains left by work in the shops here."

"That's lucky for you."

"Isn't it?"

"I see you aren't going to waste your 'going ashore' manners on me." His smile wavered at her sarcasm.

"I'm sorry." She sighed. She was lashing out at him when he was teasing her in an effort to put both of them more at ease. "I was in the midst of trying to track down some mistakes I'd made in the calculations I was doing, and I fear I'm cantankerous when the numbers don't add up."

"And I'm sorry for intruding on your work. I don't like to leave a job half done either."

She gasped at the apology she had not expected from him. But she barely knew this intriguing man, so why should she believe that she would know how he might act? When he did not pounce on her reaction, she relaxed against the sofa where she sat facing him. She discovered that was a mistake, for without her vexation between her and his charming smile, her thoughts drifted again to the memory of his broad hands and warm lips.

"That's quite the outfit," Wyatt said.

She again glanced at her navy dress. "It suits me during the hours of working on the financial reports for the Assembly of Elders or when I go from shop to shop. But I doubt that you came all the way out here to discuss my clothes."

"You're right." He pulled his chair closer to her. He leaned forward and lowered his voice. "What in blazes is a smart woman like you doing here? These places are for folks who can't think for themselves. You've proven that you can."

"This is my home. My brother and I have lived here almost three years."

He whistled lowly. "I'm surprised you could put up with this for that long."

"This is my home."

"So you said."

Folding her hands on her lap, she said, "I assume you came here to find out about getting parts made for *The Ohio Star*."

"That, and to make sure you were all right."

"Our shop can make most parts." It was easier to speak of work because then she could tear her gaze away from the silver fire in his eyes.

"For how much? You said Horace and I were fools to

send to Louisville for parts for *The Ohio Star* when we could get them from River's Haven for much less."

"For less, yes. It'd depend on what you wanted and the shop's schedule. You should speak with Mr. Dow. He'll be able to tell you if he can do the work you need on your timetable."

"I'd thought you'd make sure he did the work for me in lickety-split time."

"So I could be rid of you?" She laughed. "You seem to think that I have nothing but you on my mind."

"Maybe because you've been clogging up my mind too much since you barged onto my steamboat."

"You invited me on!"

"I should have known better." His smile grew wider. "You're a hard woman to get out of a man's head, Rachel."

She glanced toward the door to the Community Hall as she came to her feet. "You shouldn't be speaking so here. Others might hear and get the wrong idea."

"I don't see any reason not to be honest here," he said, standing. "This is your home. You're honest on the boat that's my home, so why shouldn't I be honest in your home?"

"But you're an outsider."

"Thank goodness." He went to the shelves and pulled down a pair of books. "Are all of these books about the tenets you follow here?"

"I'm not sure. I have my own books in my cottage."

"I thought everyone in River's Haven lived in this big mansion."

"There isn't room for all the residents until the new wing is finished. Kit—Katherine and I live in one of the cottages on the other side of the common area."

"Are you going to let K. C. come into Haven to work with the other kids on the parade?"

"I told you that I'd have to obtain permission from the Assembly of Elders."

"Have you asked them?"

"Not yet."

"Why not?"

She frowned. "That's none of your business, Wyatt."

"Why not?"

"Because she isn't your responsibility. She's mine."

"She isn't a responsibility. She's a little girl. Kids need some freedom, or they'll find it on their own."

"The voice of experience."

He stepped closer to her. This time she did not back away, instead holding her ground so that he would see how seriously she took her obligations to Kitty Cat.

"On this, honey—"

"Don't call me that."

"I won't if you'll listen to me."

She knew arguing was worthless, so she nodded.

"I do have experience in being a kid," he said when she remained silent. "My family tried to tie me down too much, and I fought to escape in every way I could. I found my escape on the river. That's fine for a boy, but you've got to make sure K. C. doesn't try to copy me and Horace. The river's no place for a girl unless she's willing to lift her skirts for any man who has the money."

"I'd never allow her to do that."

"As long as she'll heed you, but living in a place like this is sure to confuse her." He fingered the hem of her skirt. "After all, no one would have to lift these skirts too far."

Again sounds came from the Community Hall. Rachel knew she must put an end to this before anyone came close enough to eavesdrop. "I'll check with Mr. Dow for you tomorrow. As soon as I have some information, I'll send it to *The Ohio Star*. Good afternoon, Wyatt."

"Wait!" he called as she turned to leave. He reached out and took her arm.

Rachel pulled back, but he refused to release her. "I

must ask you to take your hand off me." She would not let him compel her to forget *her* manners.

He drew her closer to the chair. His eyes sparked with irritation. "Not until you're willing to act sensibly!"

"Me? I'm not the one who's manhandling someone."

"You couldn't."

"I assure you that I—"

"You aren't a man." His hand on her arm gentled. "A fact that I noticed right away."

"I'm sure you did. Let me go!"

Wyatt smiled at Rachel's command, but took her other arm. Standing face-to-face, he enjoyed a leisurely perusal of her. His first shock at her odd outfit had faded, and now he could admire how the mother-of-pearl buttons along the navy front accented her intriguing form. She did not need frills and jewelry.

But he needed to kiss her. Slowly he slid her hands up his chest while he drew her closer. Her eyes grew wide, then softened as her lips parted in an invitation he could not ignore, no matter how many members of this strange community were watching. With a groan that came from deep in his gut, he captured her mouth, feasting on every flavor it offered.

Her arms rose to his shoulders, and he pulled her tighter to him. When his lips traced a dazzling path along her neck, she trembled but pressed even nearer. Her ragged breath brushed his ear, and he was sure he had never wanted anything more than he wanted her at this moment. Guiding her mouth back to his, he tasted its sweetness with a hunger he was finding more and more difficult to govern. And why did he want to stifle this yearning for her? She was everything he should want in a woman—lusciously beautiful and sensual as well as tied to the shore as he was to his boat. She would not be begging to come and share his life on *The Ohio Star*.

All thoughts vanished from his head as he slowly glided

his hands up her back, pressing her soft breasts against him. Then he let his fingers amble lower as he held her hips tight to his.

Suddenly she stiffened, and he heard what she had. Footsteps coming closer to this room. Blast! He had to get her away from this place where there were too many people. Maybe in her cottage while K. C. was busy elsewhere.

He smiled as he lifted his mouth from hers. Sending the kid into Haven to work on the decorations for Independence Day would be the very answer to two problems. He could have Rachel to himself away from the little girl and all the rest of the folks here.

A soft denial bubbled from her lips, and he looked down to see diffused pleasure in her eyes. She brushed hair back from his forehead with trembling fingers. He could not resist taking her hand and running his tongue across her palm and up her longest finger.

Wyatt was not surprised when Rachel pulled her hand away and walked across the room to put the books back on the shelves. Even though his pulse pounded through him with the fury of wind-driven rain against *The Ohio Star*'s bow, he had heard those footsteps coming directly toward the room.

"Miss Browning?" came a voice from the doorway. "Oh, I didn't realize your guest was still here."

He turned to see a woman, a pair of decades older than Rachel. She was dressed in a dark gray dress, and her face was blank of any emotion.

"I assume you are Mr. Colton," she said.

"Yes, ma'am," he replied with the courtesy he knew Rachel doubted he possessed. He glanced at Rachel, but she was looking at the older woman.

"I'm Miss Hanson, Miss Browning's friend," said the woman in the doorway. "I trust you'll understand why it's important that Miss Browning not receive an outsider alone." She smiled at Rachel. "Mr. Atlee was sidetracked and failed to deliver the message to me that Mr. Colton was visiting."

Rachel's cheeks turned a charming pink. His hand tingled with the longing to touch that warm color, but he did not move.

"You may sit there, Mr. Colton." Miss Hanson pointed to the sofa.

Wyatt made no attempt to hide his smile. Miss Hanson spoke even more bluntly than Rachel. If all the women in River's Haven shared this trait, he could not figure out why the men had not fled in both directions along the river.

Miss Hanson smiled. "Miss Browning, you may sit there as well while Mr. Colton finishes up his call."

Rachel sat at the opposite end of the sofa, as far from him as she could. A single glance in her direction told him that she was putting space between them because she did not trust herself to sit closer to him. He could not keep from imagining her in one of those small cottages, welcoming him into her bed as the sun burnished her bare skin that lovely pink.

"Mr. Colton," said Miss Hanson as she sat in the chair that he had been using, "I assume you came here to allow Miss Browning to speak of her gratitude at your help when she hurt her leg."

"She expressed her gratitude at the time," he replied. "I'm here to discuss business with her."

"Business? What sort of business, Mr. Colton?"

Rachel hurried to answer before Wyatt could. If she let him take control of this conversation as she had let him take control of her senses, she was unsure what the result might be. "Mr. Colton and his partner are repairing a steamboat, and he's seeking the services of our metal shop to replace some broken parts."

"Ah, I see." Miss Hanson's smile returned. "River's Haven is fortunate to have Miss Browning's skills with business. She is, I believe, quite unique."

Wyatt grinned. "I would—"

"Not so unique," Rachel said, interrupting Wyatt before he could try to wheedle his way into Miss Hanson's good graces. "Mrs. Sawyer runs the store in Haven. What she does isn't so different from what I do."

"That's true," he agreed, his amusement drifting up into his fascinating eyes.

"I'll get the information you need from Mr. Dow and send it to you tomorrow." Rachel stood.

"An approximate price is all I need." Wyatt came to his feet, too.

His broad shoulders seemed to fill the room, and she went to a nearby table where paper and ink waited as she said, "All right. Give me a moment, and I'll give you a good idea of what the cost will be."

As she scribbled some figures on a piece of paper and double-checked them to make sure she was not in error, she heard Wyatt say, "It's been a pleasure to meet you, Miss Hanson."

"I may see you again when you come back here to work with the metal shop." Miss Hanson glanced at Rachel before heaving herself to her feet. "I see Miss Stokes in the Community Hall. I must speak with her posthaste about an important matter. If you need me, Miss Browning, please call."

Wyatt laughed quietly in Miss Hanson's wake. "In other words, if I fail to be the gentleman, she will swoop down on me like an avenging hawk."

Rather than respond to his comment, Rachel closed the bottle of ink. "If you'll bring the parts you need replaced here as soon as you can, the metal shop should be able to begin work on them by the beginning of next week." She handed him the piece of paper. "If you're willing to pay this much."

His brows rose, and he whistled. "This is half of what the parts would have cost in Louisville."

"With the cost of shipping—"

"Before the shipping." He chuckled. "You could be charging more, but don't start raising your prices before you finish this job for me."

"I'll let Mr. Dow know to expect you to bring the broken parts in—"

"Tomorrow."

She started to the door, then realized he had positioned himself so she would have to crawl over the sofa to get past him. Pausing, she asked, "Will you be honest with me about something?"

"I'm always honest." He lifted a strand of hair off her shoulder. "I'll be honest and tell you that I like when you wear your hair like this."

She frowned. "Wyatt, please listen to what I'm saying."

"I am. I told you I was being honest, right?"

Deciding that she needed to ask him outright, because he would continue to parry words with her as long as she gave him the opportunity, she asked, "Has Kitty Cat been back to your boat this week?"

"No." He became serious. "Has she run away again?"

"I don't think so."

"You don't *think* so?"

"No one has noticed her being gone, but she's giddy with happiness."

"And you don't think she could be happy if she was here all the time?"

"I have to consider that as a possibility."

His smile returned, but its edge was not as hard. "It's going to take me some time to get used to your honesty."

She almost laughed. She was not being honest. She was letting this conversation continue because she did not want him to guess that every word he spoke, everything he did, every glance he gave her threatened to unsettle her completely.

"No, K. C. hasn't been out to *The Ohio Star* since last week."

"Are you sure?"

"I just said I'd be honest with you, didn't I? Do you think I'd lie about something as important as that child is to you?"

"No."

"Then believe me, honey, when I tell you that K. C. hasn't been back to *The Ohio Star* this week."

"Don't say that!"

"What?"

"Don't call her K. C. here! And don't call me honey."

"Could you get into trouble?" he asked, so abruptly serious that she was astonished.

"No . . . Yes . . . River's Haven Community has a certain level of formality that we all are supposed to respect."

"I'll try to remember that." He cupped her elbows and smiled.

When he bent to kiss her, she forced herself to turn her head away, so his lips found her hair instead of her mouth. As much as she wanted his kiss, she knew how easily he wooed her good sense from her. She must avoid further temptation.

"Don't play coy with me, Rachel," he whispered. "Not when I want to kiss you so much."

"I'm not being coy!"

"Then why don't you want me to kiss you? You sure enjoyed it a few minutes ago."

"I don't know what I want."

"I know exactly what I want!" he growled.

He grasped her chin and found her lips again. Although she should move away, she let the pleasure of his surprisingly gentle kiss enthrall her. She had thought this kiss would be as honed as his words. She swept her arms up his back, captured anew by the joy that weakened her determination to keep him away.

Was she mad? Miss Hanson—or someone else—could enter at any moment.

It took all her willpower to push him away. "We aren't thinking this through. Otherwise we'd know this is just making things more difficult."

Wyatt snaked his arm around her waist and jerked her back against him. Squeezing her chin between his thumb and forefinger, he put his lips near hers as he whispered, his mustache brushing her mouth on each word, "Aren't thinking this through? Maybe you aren't, but I think of how exciting it is to hold you like this, Rachel. I think of how lonely it is in my quarters and how delectable you'd be in my bed." He crushed her lips beneath his. Before she could push him away—or draw him nearer—he released her and said, "I'll bring those parts out tomorrow as soon as Horace wrestles the last few out of the boiler."

Rachel blinked, trying to focus her mind on something other than his kiss. Her voice was as wobbly as her knees when she said, "That will give me time to check how long it'll take the metal shop to make the new parts for you."

"Just don't let them make new parts for you."

"Excuse me."

"I like *your* parts just the way they are." With a wink, he walked out of the room, leaving her to try to figure out how she was going to stay out of his arms when he came back tomorrow.

Eight

His hands curved along her face, and she held her mouth up for his kiss. As he leaned her back against the sofa, she whispered his name. His eyes glowed like two stars in a midnight sky. When he reached for the top button on her collar, she—

Rachel came awake with a shriek when the bed bounced.

"Did I surprise you, Rachel?" asked Kitty Cat, curling up next to her like her namesake.

"Yes." She laughed shakily. The dream of being in Wyatt's arms dissipated into nothingness as quickly as river fog on a sunny morning. Putting her arm around Kitty Cat and her rag doll, she said, "You're up early. Usually *I* have to shake *you* out of bed."

"Today's the day you said you'd ask the Elders about me going to help Sean with his panorama for the Centennial Day parade."

"Panorama?" She smiled and leaned back into the pillows with Kitty Cat's head against her breast. "That's a big word for a little girl."

"What does it mean?"

"You don't know?"

She shook her head.

Rachel laughed in spite of herself. "Then why are you so eager to go into Haven?"

"So I can see Sean and Maeve and Brendan and Megan and Lottie and Jack and—"

"Now I understand," she said before Kitty Cat could list the name of every child who had come with her on the orphan train. "I've got an appointment to speak with Mr. Foley this afternoon."

Kitty Cat's nose wrinkled.

"What's wrong?" asked Rachel.

"He smells funny."

Again she laughed. "That's because he stores his clothing in camphor to keep the bugs out."

"The smell makes my eyes water."

Pulling back the covers, she motioned for Kitty Cat to get out of the bed. The mantel clock chimed seven times. "It's so late! Why didn't you wake me earlier? You're going to be late, and Mrs. Hanson will be distressed."

"You usually wake me," the little girl said with a hint of impatience at having to remind Rachel of that fact. "Why were you such a sleepyhead this morning?"

"I was having a nice dream."

"What about?"

"Oh, all kinds of things." She gave the child a push toward the door. "Go and get dressed."

"If I hurry, can we sing before we leave?" Kitty Cat ran her fingers along the strings of the guitar. "We haven't sung in a very, very, very long time, Rachel."

She laughed. "We sang together last week."

"That's a very, very, very long time ago."

"Go and get dressed, or there won't be time even for talking this morning."

As Kitty Cat scampered out, Rachel sighed and stood. She went to the window that gave her a view of the river. Turning on her heel, she walked to where her work dress waited. Wyatt may have invaded her dreams, but she must not let him become more a part of her waking life. If she gambled her heart on a man who lived on a steamboat that never stayed anywhere for long, she was sure to be left unhappy . . . again.

Other than the fact that it was on the second floor instead of on the fifth and had hanging by the window a painting of some section of the river, Mr. Foley's office could have been Rachel's. He had the same simple desk and chairs, another example of the equality in the Community.

"Miss Browning!" he exclaimed in answer to her call of his name through his open door. "This is a very, very pleasant surprise. I hadn't guessed that Mr. Browning had already spoken to you."

"About what?"

His smile faltered, but it came back as he said, "Something he wanted to tell you himself. But if you didn't come here to discuss that, what's your reason for calling today?"

Merrill must have spoken to Mr. Foley about his plans to marry Miss Page and received approval from the Assembly of Elders. She wanted to cheer. While he was concerned about his new wife, Merrill would not be chiding her for trying to make Kitty Cat happy.

The very thought broadened her smile as she said, "Mr. Foley, I came to ask you a favor."

"Then come in and do so." When she started to sit on one of the chairs, he laughed. "The air's fresh and filled with the aroma of the flowers, so let's sit on the window-sill."

"All right." She was astonished by his suggestion, but it was a good one. Sitting on the wide sill, she looked out to see several children racing across the common area. Their laughter floated toward her.

Was she wrong to ask for Kitty Cat to be allowed to participate in the Haven celebrations? Allowing the little girl to retain her friendships in Haven was prolonging her adjustment to the River's Haven Community. She shook the thought from her head. That was Merrill speaking, not herself.

When Mr. Foley sat beside her after flipping out the back of his gray frock coat, he asked, "What's this favor you need, Miss Browning?"

"Mr. Foley, would you ask the Elders to consider allowing Katherine to be a part of the holiday decorating in Haven for the Fourth of July?"

"You know that the matter has already been discussed." He scowled.

"If she has this chance, she might be more willing to bid that part of her life farewell."

With a sigh, he shook his head. "Even if I take your request to the other Elders, I don't want to get your hopes high about what answer you may receive."

"I understand that, but will you ask them?"

He folded her hands between his. "Why do you want to put yourself and the child through this again? It'll only bring you both heartache."

"It's important to her, so it's important to me."

"And, so therefore, it will be important to *me.*"

Rachel leaned back from him. Although he was not moving closer, the intensity in his voice made it seem as if he were. She looked away from his fervent gaze. The door to the hallway was closed! That was a violation of the rules in River's Haven. Or was it? She was certain she had been told that when an unmarried woman was in a room with a man who was not her husband or blood relative, all doors must be left open.

She heard the children shouting in the midst of their game and told herself that she was being silly. Mr. Foley had closed the door to give her privacy to make her request, and he had asked her to sit here in view of anyone who might pass by.

Knowing that she must answer him, she said, "Thank you for caring so much about Katherine."

"She matters deeply to you."

"Yes."

He sighed. "I fear you're letting yourself in for a disappointment, but I'll ask the other Elders to consider your request."

"I truly appreciate that, Mr. Foley."

He smiled as he squeezed her fingers. "I'd be less than a gentleman not to help you ease that child's sad heart."

Rachel started to return his smile, then paused when he stroked her hand. Slowly she eased her fingers out of his. As he reached for them again, she stood, hoping her motion looked less like she was trying to escape and more like she had finished the business she had come to discuss with him. Thanking him again and bidding him a good morning, she opened the door and went out into the hallway.

She did not slow as she walked toward the stairs that led to the section of the building where her office was. Putting her hand on the banister, she paused when an idea burst into her head. Was she mad even to consider going to get an ally in Haven? Reverend Faulkner's offer to help make sure that Kitty Cat was happy and settled in her new life might not extend to helping Rachel persuade the Assembly of Elders to allow this excursion.

But she would never know unless she asked.

The once-familiar ache of homesickness became a cramp as Rachel looked about the simple, comfortable room. Like in the parlor across the foyer where she had sat only a week ago, tatted doilies topped the marble-topped tables that were covered with books and photographs. A horsehair sofa was set next to the larger window, and she imagined sitting there on a wintry afternoon while she read one of the books.

When she had been in Reverend Faulkner's house last time, her ankle had hurt so much that she had not paid much attention to her surroundings. She crossed the worn carpet and winced. Her ankle was protesting the long walk from River's Haven.

A door opened at the far end of the room, and Reverend Faulkner looked in. His eyes widened. Straightening his black frock coat, he entered, saying, "Miss Browning, when Mrs. Faulkner told me you were calling, I almost accused her of being in error."

"I realize you didn't expect to see me calling again so soon."

"How's your ankle?"

"Much better. It should be all well soon." She smiled so he would not guess that she was being overly optimistic. "I do have two reasons for calling."

"Please sit."

She selected the tufted green chair that could not be seen from outside the window, and the minister drew up a wooden chair so they faced each other across a table. When he glanced past her, she wondered if he suspected how she did not want to chance having anyone see her here.

"I wish to thank you for arranging for Kitty Cat—Katherine—"

Reverend Faulkner laughed. "You might as well call her Kitty Cat. Sean always does when he speaks of her."

"It isn't the way in River's Haven to use nicknames."

"I see." He became serious again.

"But I do wish to thank you for arranging for us to get back to River's Haven last week."

"My pleasure."

She wondered how the words could sound so innocuous when the minister spoke them, but the same words from Wyatt undid her resolve to keep away from his too eager gaze. Drat! Thoughts of him intruded at the most inopportune times. Even though she had tried to halt herself, she had looked about in hopes of seeing him as she walked through Haven.

Focusing on the problem that had brought her here, Rachel quickly explained her dilemma. She chose her words carefully, for nothing she said must, in any way, sound derogatory toward the Assembly of Elders. She would be in enough trouble just for coming here. Compounding it by insulting the Assembly of Elders could see her and Kitty Cat banished from River's Haven.

"I hadn't expected you to come to me for help, Miss Browning," the minister said when she finished. "The River's Haven Community sticks pretty much to themselves and deals with such matters privately."

"But I'm not sure they can help me."

"Cannot or will not?"

Instead of answering his question, she said, "If you were to speak to the Assembly of Elders about the importance of having all the children in the county, not just the ones in the village, participate in the Centennial celebration, your words might be heeded far better than mine."

"It *is* of great importance, Miss Browning. None of us, save a babe in arms, shall live to see the celebration of the country's two hundredth anniversary."

"Will you share that fact with the Assembly of Elders? I know Mr. Carpenter has previously heeded your suggestions on issues that concern both the Haven and the River's Haven Community."

Reverend Faulkner sighed. "Those issues weren't as potentially volatile as this."

She wanted to disagree, but the minister was right. The Assembly of Elders was protective of the Community's children. Too protective of Kitty Cat, she believed, for the other children had been given more freedom than the little girl.

"But I'll contact Mr. Carpenter," he continued. "I trust you'd prefer that I don't mention your call here."

"I don't want you to lie." The very idea of a minister being false bothered her.

His somber expression lightened. "There are ways of telling most of the truth that don't require lying."

Thanking him, Rachel bid him a good day. Her steps, even on her aching ankle, were much lighter as she walked out of the parsonage and across the green toward the river road. When Sean and several younger children ran up to her, she listened to their merry chatter about all the tidings they wanted her to share with Kitty Cat. The children off the orphan train remained connected tightly together with the bonds forged through their horrible struggle to survive in New York City and being placed out with strangers.

Songs from birds and the shrill insect sounds were her only companions once Rachel left the village. Beneath the increasingly hot sunshine, the road wandered between white farmhouses and red barns and fences that were weathered gray-brown. Pulling up a piece of tufted grass, she ran her finger along it and watched the seeds scatter onto the road. She smiled as she thought of picking buttercups when she took a walk with Kitty Cat on a warm summer afternoon. Holding the blossoms up under her own chin, she would show Kitty Cat how they reflected the sun to show how much she liked butter. It was a silly game, but the little girl had never had a chance to enjoy them in the city slums.

The common area was deserted, and Rachel guessed everyone was looking for a cool place to spend what was certain to be an oppressive afternoon. She quickly changed into the clothes she wore in the Community. Glad to be rid of the heavy petticoats that had clung to her more with each step, she opened all the windows in the cottage to let in any hint of a breeze.

She was crossing the common area on her way to her office when she saw Wyatt strolling toward the common house. He must have sensed her gaze, for he looked over his shoulder. He smiled as he walked toward her. She watched every motion he made, for each was as graceful as if he moved to a melody she could not hear. Today he had dispensed with his fancy clothes. As he came closer, she saw the oil on his clothes was matched by a shiny splotch across his forehead where he must have wiped away sweat. He was carrying a small burlap bag.

"Good afternoon, Rachel," he said.

Her heart did a somersault as his voice caressed her name the way she wished he would caress her. Clasping her hands behind her back before she could throw her arms around him and kiss him, she smiled.

"Horace must have gotten all the broken parts out of the boiler." She continued walking in the direction of the common house. The metal shop was around the back of it on the side opposite the stables.

"Most of them." He put his hand under the bag and jiggled it. "I swear almost every moving part connected to that boiler is in this bag. Captain Hancock should have blown his own head of steam before the boiler blew."

"Who is Captain Hancock?"

"The man who was in charge of *The Ohio Star* when she went up on the sandbar."

"I thought you or Horace had piloted the boat."

He shook his head. "If one of us had been in the pilot-house, *The Ohio Star* wouldn't be needing all these repairs now. From what I've seen, I'd guess that Horace can pilot a whale through a keyhole."

"That might be a bit of an exaggeration." She laughed.

"A riverman's prerogative."

"How many fish tales have you told me, Wyatt?"

He reached out to take her arm, but halted as he glanced over his shoulder at the common house. "That blasted monolith just sits there, lurking like a channel change in the river to catch anyone who doesn't watch out."

"I have often thought that might be why it is as big as it is."

His brow furrowed. "You don't like it either, do you?"

"How can one like or not like a *building?*" She pointed to her left. "The metal shop is that way. I need to get back to my work."

"Back? Where have you been?"

"About my business, if you must know the truth." She gave him a cool smile. "Everything within the borders of River's Haven is my business, just as everything on *The Ohio Star* is yours."

He motioned in the direction she had pointed. "Then tend to business. Show me the metal shop, honey."

"Wyatt, I told you not to call me that here."

"I heard you, and I'll try not to call you that here again, although it's difficult when your lips are as sweet as honey."

Rachel turned to walk away. This man refused to see sense in any form. She faltered when he said to her back, "I want to apologize."

"You? Apologize?" She faced him.

"It has been known to happen," he said, walking to her.

She glanced away, for she was not prepared to confront either the longing in his eyes or the need it brought to life within her. "I should apologize to you as well. I should have believed you when you spoke about Kit—about her going to *The Ohio Star*. I don't make a habit of calling visitors to River's Haven liars to their faces."

His roguish grin returned to match the twinkle in his eyes. "Do you make it a habit of calling visitors to River's Haven liars behind their backs?"

Rachel stared at him, then laughed. "I guess I deserved that."

"You deserve more than that." His smile warmed, and that enchantment he spun threatened to engulf her again. And she was tempted to let it. A single glance from him, and she had to fight not to press up against him, drawing his mouth to hers.

Rachel said nothing, and she was surprised when Wyatt was silent, too, while they walked toward the metal shop. As they approached it, the odors of heated metal and the clang of the tools reached out to guide them into the shop.

The shop was longer than the stable. Even though there were windows every couple of feet along the walls, the interior was dim. Dirt strained any light that tried to reach inside. The floor, tables, and every flat surface were littered with filings and ruined pieces of whatever the shopworkers had been trying to make. Machines that reached nearly to the roof obscured the workers.

"There are women working in here!" Wyatt gasped from beside her.

She laughed. "I thought you would have realized by now that we don't do things like everyone else. I handle the finances, and these ladies run machinery."

"It's not—"

"Natural?" she asked.

"I was going to say, it's not a bad idea to teach everyone to work the machines." He grinned. "You're as prickly as a porcupine about this Community, aren't you?"

"Only because I've had to defend it too often. In my position, I meet a lot of people who do business with River's Haven, but with about as much pleasure as if they were doing business with the devil."

He laughed. "I've done business with the devil, and it's not like this."

Rachel wanted to ask him what he meant, but bit back her question when Mr. Dow rushed over to greet them. The man looked as if he had been stretched through one of his machines, for he was the tallest man in the metal shop and not much wider than Kitty Cat. His canvas apron had several pockets that were filled to overflowing with tools, measuring devices, and slips of paper.

Mr. Dow barely waited for her to introduce him to Wyatt before he held his hand out for the bag. "What do you have in there, son?"

Wyatt opened the bag and laid the broken parts on a nearby table. Dow mumbled to himself as he examined each piece, and Wyatt watched Rachel, who was waiting with a patience he had not guessed she had. He listened when she answered several questions for Dow. She had not been bragging when she had said that she was deeply involved with the work done at River's Haven. Picking up a piece of paper, she shook bits of metal and dust off it. She found a bottle of ink and began to make notes as Dow continued to appraise each piece.

She was smiling when she looked up. "I've got good news for you, Mr. Colton."

He was momentarily startled by what she called him, then remembered what she had said about formality in the Community. It seemed ludicrous to him, but it apparently worked for these people.

"And what good news is that, *Miss* Browning?" he asked in the most innocuous voice he could manage.

Her eyes glittered with laughter that she did not free as she held out the page to him. "I'm happy to be able to tell you that Mr. Dow believes he can do the job for even less than I estimated. Nearly ten dollars less."

He tore his gaze from her smile to look at Dow who was gathering up the pieces to take to his workers. Knowing he should not risk a good thing, he had to ask, "You can make all those parts in the same grade metal for *this* price?"

"All our work at the River's Haven Community is of the highest quality," Dow said in a tone that suggested he was the schoolmaster about to rein in a much younger Wyatt.

"He didn't mean any insult," Rachel said quickly. "I

guess I'm so accustomed to the question, Mr. Dow, that I forget you don't hear it from our other customers."

He harrumphed and walked away.

Wyatt shook his head. "I apparently said the wrong thing."

"The very worst thing." When she put her hand on his arm and steered him toward the door, he realized he had disparaged Dow even more than he had guessed. Her laugh sounded as young as K. C.'s giggle when they stepped out of the shop. "Mr. Dow is very, very proud of the work that comes out of his metal shop."

"I guess I was luckier than I'd imagined when I tied up *The Ohio Star* in Haven."

"You were." She paused on the walkway and said, "Now I must leave you here and go to my office to finish up some work."

"Where is it?"

She pointed to the uppermost floor. "The fourth window from the left."

He whistled with awe. "You must have quite a view of the river from up there."

"It's nice, but the best one is from the bedroom window in my cottage."

"Your bedroom? Care to let me take a gander?"

Color soared up her face as if she had come in contact with the sun. "Wyatt, please remember where you are."

"I remember quite well. Otherwise, do you think I would have let you go so long without a kiss?"

He could not mistake the pleasure and the craving in her eyes as she said, "I appreciate your restraint."

"You've got no idea how much restraint, hon—Miss Browning." He laughed when she did. Good, he liked seeing her happy, because there was something so scintillating about her smile. "Which cottage is yours?"

"The one with the red door."

"Red door?" He laughed harder, even as he took note

of which one it was. The cottage was closer to the riverbank than he had expected. If he stole along the shore
from his boat and climbed up the bank, he could slip into
her house without anyone in the Community—but K. C.—
being the wiser. And if he was lucky, even the little girl
would not know of his call on Rachel on a starlit night
when he could persuade her to forget about all the restrictions of River's Haven and surrender to her passions.

"What's wrong with a red door?" she asked.

"Don't you know that a red door along the river means
the same as a red light?" When she gave him a puzzled
frown, he explained, "That's like putting out a sign that
you're running a brothel."

"A brothel?" She chuckled. "Not likely. Wyatt, I'll send
you a message when the parts are ready."

"Before you go . . ." He took her hand, shifting so that
no one could see that he held it. She glanced around, but
he put his finger under her chin and tipped her face back
toward him. "There's a social being held in Haven for the
Fourth of July." He smiled. "Reverend Faulkner tells me
it is to celebrate the Centennial as well as the children in
the school finishing their term. He wants to invite the kids
from the River's Haven school, too."

"I haven't gotten permission yet for Kitty Cat to work
on the parade decorations, so I doubt if the Assembly of
Elders would be willing to let the students from River's
Haven participate in the exercises in Haven."

"I wasn't mentioning it because of the children. I was
asking if *you* wanted to go."

"With you?"

"That's usually how it works when a man asks a woman
to a social event."

"Why are you asking me?"

"I could tell you that Reverend Faulkner suggested that
I ask you."

"He did?"

"The good reverend said it'd help your ankle get some needed exercise so it will heal."

"Wyatt," she said, with a pleading look on her face, "you know I should tell you no right now."

"I know, but you haven't."

She dampened her lips with her tongue, which he wished was touching him. "Let me think about it."

He tossed caution aside and let his hands frame her face. "No, don't think about it. Then you'll think of all the reasons why you shouldn't go to it with me. Say yes now, because of the only reason you *should* go to it with me." His thumb followed the same path her tongue had. "Say yes, honey."

"You're putting me in a difficult position."

"It isn't my intention to put you in a difficult position." He chuckled. "I have a few other positions—very pleasant ones—I'd like to have you in."

"You're a rascal, Wyatt Colton."

"I readily admit that, so why don't you admit just as readily that you want to go with me to the social?"

"I do want to go with you," she answered in a husky whisper that sent a tightening quiver all along him.

"Then come with me."

"I should—"

"You should do what you want to do for once. You work hard for this Community. It's time it let you have a night to kick up your heels."

Happiness blossomed in her eyes. "Yes, I should."

"Then it's settled."

"Wyatt," she gasped, "I didn't—"

He put his finger to her lips. "Let me know when the parts will be ready, and get your prettiest bonnet ready to wear to the social." As his thumb stroked her lower lip, he whispered, "In the meantime, I'll try not to let my lips envy my thumb too much."

He bid her a good day and walked away before she could

give him another reason why she should obey the stifling rules that she so obviously found as chafing as K. C. did. As he passed the end of the common house, he looked back over his shoulder. She was standing just where she had been when he headed back toward the river.

All alone.

As he stared across the empty river, Wyatt was sure that walking away from her had been the most difficult thing he had ever done. If he could convince her to succumb to the need he had seen in her eyes and felt in her innocent touch, she would not be spending too many more nights alone while he and Horace finished the repairs on the boat.

He was insane to want her. She was one of the fools at River's Haven. Yet he wanted her in his bed.

Was he mad? He had made a vow a long time ago never to get mixed up heart deep with some woman. It was just inviting trouble. If he had not known that before, he was learning that now. He must keep her out of his heart, but that did not mean he had to keep her out of his bed. He began to whistle again as he strode along the riverbank. He *had* been lucky when he tied up the steamboat to the Haven pier, and he was going to enjoy every bit of this good fortune as long as he was here.

Nine

While drying the dishes, Rachel sang a song she had
heard Kitty Cat sharing with her friends earlier in the day.
It was a nonsense song, but the words suited Rachel's
mood. Agreeing to go to the Centennial social with Wyatt
yesterday might have been the silliest thing she had ever
done. No matter. She was going to enjoy the anticipation.

She put the final dish back onto the shelf over the table.
The last social gathering at River's Haven had been only
days after Kitty Cat had been placed out with her, and
Rachel had not wanted to leave the little girl alone. She
had gone to the barn raising at the Sawyer farm after the
spring flood, but, if there had been any dancing there, Merrill had insisted that they leave before it began. Going to
Haven to the Centennial social would make up for missing
those two chances to swirl about to music.

The front door opened, and she smiled as her brother
walked in. She wanted to run to him and share her joyous
news. She must be careful how she let him know of Wyatt's
invitation. Merrill always treated her as if she were still a
child who tagged after him wherever he went, wanting to
share whatever mischief he might find. He had not been
pleased with how often she had to leave River's Haven to
do the Community's business. So she teased him that he
should not be so old-fashioned when the rest of the Community accepted her role in it.

Merrill was smiling even more broadly than she was. He pulled out a chair by the table and sat.

"You look to be in an uncommonly cheerful mood this morning, Merrill," Rachel said as she poured a cup of coffee from the pot on the stove and set it in front of him.

"That's because I am an uncommonly happy man."

She sat beside him. "Can it be that you're bringing me the tidings I've been expecting to hear all week?"

"Probably."

"So you finally had the courage to ask Miss Page to be your next wife?" She laughed when he gave her a playful frown. Pushing the sugar bowl toward him, she added, "I know this is what you had hoped for."

He stirred two spoonfuls of sugar into his cup, but did not take a taste. "It is."

"Tell me what she said when you asked her." She leaned her elbow on the table and rested her chin on her hand. "I'm sure she wasn't surprised."

"No, and she was very pleased. Now that the Assembly of Elders has approved—"

"Already?"

He continued to stir his coffee, paying no attention to what he was doing. "I asked Miss Page to marry me a few days ago. I didn't want to tell anyone until the marriage was approved."

"Not even your sister?"

"No, because I didn't want you to be disappointed if the marriage wasn't approved." He grimaced when coffee splashed out onto the table.

Rachel stood and went to get the wet rag she had been using to wash the dishes. As she dabbed up the spilled coffee, she was glad of the chance to get her thoughts in order before she answered Merrill. She did not want to ask him if he had feared that she might go to the Assembly of Elders and ask them to keep the wedding from being held. That petition was the right of every resident of River's

Haven, although she had never heard of it happening. She might not like Miss Page, but Merrill did, and that was what mattered.

After putting the cloth back into the bucket by the stove, she sat again. "Merrill, I'm happy it has worked out just as you'd hoped."

"It has. I thought we could have a double wedding, Rachel."

"Double wedding? You and Miss Page and who else?"

"Miss Page and me." He smiled. "And Mr. Foley and you."

"Mr. Foley?" She stared at him in shock. Gripping the edge of the table, she tried to think of something else to say.

He stood and squeezed her shoulders. "He asked me a couple of days ago to give him my permission for him to call on you and arrange for your marriage."

Rachel came to her feet again as she remembered how Mr. Foley had expected that she had had a conversation with Merrill about something important. Had he greeted her in his office with the anticipation that she had come to accept his proposal?

Calvin Foley was a handsome man and well respected in the Community. In addition, he was one of the smartest people at River's Haven. She found his conversation interesting and his ideas challenging. She would enjoy discussing most topics with him. The only problem was that she did not love him. As she imagined him holding her as Wyatt had, she hugged her arms to herself to keep her shudder hidden.

"What do you say?" Merrill asked excitedly.

"I don't think this is a good idea."

His smile dropped into a frown. "How can you say that?" He flung out his hands. "Rachel, Mr. Foley is on the Assembly of Elders, and he wants to spend the next year with *you.* You should be jumping for joy at the honor he's doing our family."

"Our family? I want to get married because I fall in love, not because of the prestige it'll bring to the Browning family."

"Don't be silly, Rachel! Any other woman in River's Haven would be happy to have this opportunity."

"Then let any other woman become his wife." Before he could explode with the anger turning his face crimson, she said, "I didn't mean that as it sounded." She sighed. "Merrill, you've married twice now because you fell in love. Now you'll have Helga Page as your wife, and nobody can doubt that you adore her."

"I gave him my permission to call on you," he said as if she had not spoken. "Will you turn him from your door?"

"Of course not, Merrill. Mr. Foley is a very pleasant man, so I'd welcome a visit from him. I just think he should turn his attentions to a woman who would be thrilled to have them."

He grasped her shoulders. "Give the man a chance. Let him call on you, and see what happens. It's amazing how one can fall in love when one least expects to. I never thought I'd fall in love with the youngest Miss Tyler after being married to her older sister for a year. But one day, I found I couldn't think of anyone but Miss Carol Tyler."

"But you loved Miss Susan Tyler."

"I did, but she was no longer my wife. It was time for me to love only the youngest Miss Tyler."

"How did you do that?" She stepped away from him. "How did you let go of the love you had for Miss Susan Tyler and discover the love you had for Miss Carol Tyler and then let that go, too, so you could ask Miss Page to marry you?"

His frown deepened, gouging lines in his forehead. "Rachel, you shouldn't be asking questions like this. You know what Mr. Carpenter has taught us."

"That we all are a family and that we should all be willing to open our hearts to each other."

"And that lesson tells you everything you need to do. That's what I have done, and that's what Mr. Foley is doing for you. Now you must realize that and let yourself love him in return."

She found herself agreeing to allow one call. As Merrill went out the door, a bounce in his step, she wanted to shout after him that he had not told her anything she had not already discovered for herself. Love did come at the most unexpected times and places and for the most unlikely people. She was learning that . . . as she was falling in love with Wyatt Colton.

Wyatt sang a song he had heard K. C. sharing with Horace when she slipped aboard *The Ohio Star* about an hour ago. It was a nonsense song, but the words suited Wyatt's mood. He was on the boat that soon would belong to him and Horace. The parts he needed to repair the boat were being made at River's Haven . . . and the Fourth of July social would give him a chance to hold pretty Rachel without the chaperones of River's Haven peering at them.

"Oh, it's you singing," Horace said as he entered the pilothouse, bringing another puff of the heavy, hot air with him. Even by the river at day's end, the air was still and thick. "I thought someone was strangling a crow."

Wyatt laughed. "Have you listened to *your* singing?"

"Yep, and it's unique." He struck a pose with one hand in the air. "I've heard it described as someone strangling a cat in heat."

"That's a fair description." He gave the brass in the center of the wheel a last buff and stood. It was getting too dark to see much up here without lighting a lamp. Leaving it unlit as long as they could might save them a few pennies to help pay for the parts. Somewhere, Horace had found a few dollars to buy more food. Wyatt was not sure where Horace had dug up the money, but he was grateful to have something to eat while the repairs took longer than he had figured. "What brings you up here? I thought you'd be chatting with K. C. in the boiler room."

"Too hot, even without the boiler running. She's sitting on the stern and fishing."

"Fishing? She can sit still that long?"

His exuberant laugh filled the small pilothouse. "Just don't plan on having fish for supper. She's dangling her feet in the water and wiggling her toes, so I doubt many fish will come close enough to be hooked."

Wyatt went to look out the window that gave him a view of the stern. Sure enough, he could see the glow of the moonlight on red curls. K. C.'s bonnet had fallen down her back and hung by its ribbons, but she did not seem to notice. She batted away bugs as she held her fishing pole—a stick with a string tied to one end—steady. Beside her, her rag doll was lying on the deck.

"I hope she knows enough not to fall in," Wyatt said. "You know you can't swim more than two strokes although why you've never learned is something I never figured out. It's too hot to be in stuck in wet clothes tonight. They'd never dry." He dropped the soiled cloths in the pail he had carried with him.

"Don't worry. Miss Rachel is watching her."

"Rachel? She's here?"

When Horace let loose another laugh, Wyatt knew he had walked right into the trap his partner had set for him. Then Wyatt grinned. Why did he think he was hiding his yearning for Rachel from his partner? He and Horace had been working the river as a team for nearly ten years. There were not many secrets left between them.

"Why are you standing around up here with me when

you could be down there with her?" Horace frowned in mock dismay. "Didn't I teach you anything about women, Wyatt? Let her wait alone, and some other man'll come along and turn her head."

"Rachel seems to have her head secured on very well. She's not about to let some smooth talker turn her head."

"No?" He hooked his thumb toward the stairs leading down to the lower decks. "K. C. told me something real quietly about wanting to leave the cottage before some guy named Foley came to call on Miss Rachel. The kid's all upset about him coming to live with them in their cottage, but she didn't want Miss Rachel to know. From what K. C. says, he's some high-muck-a-muck in the River's Haven Community."

Wyatt swore. When Horace chuckled again, Wyatt repeated the curse more vehemently before saying, "This isn't a jest. You know they've got those strange ideas of marriage out there at River's Haven."

"You think she's already married to this Foley?"

"Who knows?" He threw open the door and pushed past Horace. "But I intend to find out. Right now."

The sound of Horace's laugh followed Wyatt down the stairs, diminishing only when he reached the bottom deck. He was glad that someone was getting a kick out of this. Maybe K. C. was confused. Or maybe she was right. He swore again.

His steps slowed when he came around the back of the boiler room. He paused in the deeper shadows by the side-wheel.

Ahead of him, Rachel, who wore a trim navy gown, was kneeling beside K. C. The two of them were laughing together as Rachel tried to show the little girl how to cast her line more than an inch away from the stern. The day's last light could not dim the joy in Rachel's eyes each time she looked down at K. C. When she stroked K. C.'s hair, her fingers were so gentle the little girl did not seem to notice.

K. C. suddenly gave Rachel a hug, and they laughed again at some jest he could not hear.

Something he could not describe uncurled with serrated claws in his gut. He had been glad to escape the house where he had grown up and find a life for himself on the river. Yet as he watched Rachel and K. C. he missed, for the first time, that special intimacy shared only by those who called themselves a family. And, for the first time, he wanted it for himself.

He shook his head to dislodge these thoughts. Was he out of his mind? He had chafed at the restrictions he had hated before he left home. Why would he willingly take on that yoke again?

Rachel must have sensed him behind her because she looked over her shoulder. The merriment in her eyes deepened into the desire he knew too well, for it refused to leave him be, taunting him day and night to sate it with her. Even when he was cutting boards to repair the paddle and fitting them into place, he thought of her and how he wished he was holding her pliant body instead of the plank.

She might have said something in greeting, or he could have simply imagined it. A thundering throb echoed through his head, matching the pace of his pulse.

The connection between them was broken when K. C. jumped up and ran to him, holding out her fishing pole, which had a flapping fish hooked on the end of the line.

"Look!" she squealed.

Wyatt smiled as he squatted in front of K. C. "I'm impressed. You're quite the fisherman."

"Rachel helped me." She dimpled. "Rachel knows all sorts of fun things."

"Does she?" He slowly stood as he gazed over the little girl's head, catching Rachel's eyes again. "Maybe she'll teach me a few."

"Can we eat this fish?" K. C. asked.

"Take it up and have Horace gut it for you."

"Gut?"

He laughed and dragged his gaze from Rachel's again. "Maybe you'd like it better if I asked you to ask him to clean the fish."

"Clean? It was in the water."

Rachel laughed and said, "Take it up to Horace, Kitty Cat. He'll get it fixed for you to eat."

"You'll eat some, too, won't you?" She slipped her hand through Rachel's.

"Save Wyatt and me a bite or two." As K. C. gathered up her doll and skipped along the deck, Rachel added, "I'm sorry she's bothering you again. I came after her as soon as I discovered she wasn't where she was supposed to be."

Wyatt rested his shoulder against the cover of the side-wheel. He did not want her to guess how startled he was at her perception of the strain beneath his laugh. "She isn't what's bothering me. What she told Horace is."

"Told Horace? About what?" Her lips tightened. "Did she mention something that happened to her at River's Haven before she took off this time? I know she's had a couple of arguments with a boy who's several years older than she is, but—"

He put his fingers on her lips, wondering if this would be the last time he touched them. "It's no kid that's got her upset. She told Horace that she's worried about someone named Foley moving in with you and her."

Rachel's face blanched. She whirled away, her dark skirts flowing around her ankles. Gripping the railing, she gazed across the river that was dappled by star glow.

"Say something, Rachel," he said as he went to stand behind her. He did not touch her. If he did, he was unsure if he could halt himself from making love with her. If she was already another man's wife . . . His hands fisted, and he swallowed the oath he did not want to speak in her hearing.

"I don't have anything much to say," she whispered, not looking at him.

"So K. C. has the story wrong?"

She shook her head. "Not entirely."

"Rachel, you said you'd always be honest with me. Be honest with me tonight."

Rachel's nails dug into the wooden railing as she heard Wyatt's exasperation. She had tried not to think how she would tell him about the plans Merrill and Mr. Foley had devised. Maybe, in some part of her heart, she had known Kitty Cat would reveal the truth as soon as she reached *The Ohio Star*, saving Rachel from having to speak of it first.

Turning to face him, she said, "My brother, Merrill, has given Mr. Foley his permission to call on me."

"Which means?"

"You don't know what it means when a man calls on a woman?"

His lips quirked, but his eyes remained piercing with fury. "I wasn't sure if it had the same meaning at River's Haven. You've got a lot of strange customs."

"This is one custom that's the same within the Community as outside it." She closed her eyes as she whispered, "I told Merrill that Mr. Foley could call, but I promised nothing else."

"But your brother expects more to come of this than one call."

She smiled wryly and saw Wyatt's amazement. His face eased from his scowl when she said, "It's a compromise that keeps me from having to agree to a double wedding with Merrill and his third wife."

"It sounds as if he has it all planned out."

"Making plans are different from—"

"Making love?" His fingers coursed along the ribbons beneath her chin.

"That wasn't what I was going to say." She closed her eyes and let the delight of his touch flow over her.

His laugh was hushed and as heated as the evening air. "I didn't think you were, honey."

"Can we talk of something else?" She eased away from him while she could. Her feet protested, but she forced them to move her along the rail.

"Such as?"

"I don't know. The weather or politics or the Centennial Exposition in Philadelphia."

He slipped his hand in hers as Kitty Cat had. "How about a stroll along the shore before you leave?"

"Now?" she asked. "It must be past nine o'clock."

"Are you afraid of the dark?"

She laughed and forced her shoulders to relax. "Do you always need to make your invitations a challenge I can't resist?"

"You've resisted most of my invitations, honey. But let's go and get some fresh air before you and K. C. leave."

Rachel knew she should say no, but as she looked from his hand to his smile she could not. Tomorrow night, Mr. Foley would be calling. She was unsure when she would be able to see Wyatt again, other than when he came to pick up the parts from the metal shop.

They crossed the gangplank, and her long skirt and petticoats became damp with the evening dew on the high grass, even though she held them up. Her other hand was on Wyatt's arm. His fingers over hers held it snugly in place. Did he think she wanted to pull it away? She needed to treasure every moment she could tonight.

As they strolled, she listened to his tales of life on the river. She laughed when he spoke of his and Horace's mishaps. She had never given thought to how the steamboats went up and down the falls near Louisville. After hearing his tales of impatient captains who would bypass the locks and take their boats down over the falls, sometimes with disastrous results for their poorly secured cargo, she found herself telling him about some of the problems she had had with people who hired River's Haven's services. She had never guessed she could feel so comfortable with Wyatt.

The shore became rocky, and Rachel paused, drawing her hand off his arm. "I don't think it would be wise to continue in this direction. I don't fancy another twisted ankle."

"Nor do I." He held out his hand. "I guess we should return to *The Ohio Star*."

Rachel put her hand in his. When they turned, she stared at the distant lights on the steamboat. "I had no idea we'd walked so far."

"I hope you aren't so tired that I have to offer to carry you back."

"No, I'm not tired at all." That was the truth. She was so exhilarated that she believed she could dance back to the boat.

When his warm fingers stroked her palm, his touch seared through her like a shock from a telegraph. His hand moved in a tender exploration along her neck to rest on her shoulder.

"I'm glad to hear that, honey." He smiled.

"You really shouldn't get in the habit of calling me that," she whispered as he bent to press his lips to her neck.

"I can't give up all my bad habits," he murmured, then ran his tongue along the crescent of her ear. When she put her arms around his shoulders to keep him close, he added, "I'd like to help you discover some very good habits."

"Good?" She moaned as his breath swirled into her ear while he kissed the soft skin behind it.

"Very good."

Her own breath caught on the jagged edge of her craving

when his finger toyed with the button that closed her collar. Gently he traced a path from the top button to the next lower one, and the next . . . and the next.

"Very good?" she whispered as she drew his mouth to hers.

"Very, very, very good."

His lips claimed hers as his finger slowly climbed her breast. She clutched his shoulders, unable to do more as a powerful, mind-emptying frenzy whirled around her. In languid circles, as if he wanted to explore every bit, he let his finger rise to its tip.

When her knees sagged against him, he knelt, drawing her down with him as he continued to kiss her. Her arms around his shoulders brought him with her when he leaned her back in the thick grass.

She opened her eyes to see him regarding her with a hunger she understood so well. In the weak starlight, his strong face was shadowed, but she had re-created it so often in her dreams. His hard body pressed against her as his fingers roamed across her face. A single fingertip stroked her cheek before slipping along her neck.

"Rachel!" The cry in Kitty Cat's voice had a desperate edge.

Rachel sat as Wyatt came to his knees. She abruptly noticed the dew that had soaked her dress.Coming to her feet, she called, "I'll be right there, Kitty Cat!"

Wyatt stood and put his hands on her shoulders, drawing her back against him. "I assume you want to go and comfort her."

"She sounds very upset."

"If I called to you in that tone, would you come running to me?"

She closed her eyes as she put her arms atop the ones he wrapped around her. "Don't ask me questions I can't answer."

"Can't or don't want to?"

"Both." She pushed his arms aside as she heard Kitty Cat calling her name again. If someone from River's Haven happened to be nearby and heard as well . . . "Wyatt, I must go. I'm sure Kitty Cat is anxious to get back to River's Haven, so she can ask me to bring her to visit *The Ohio Star* again."

"She's a smart little girl."

"Smarter than we are."

He nodded as he stepped to where he could face her. Putting his hands on either side of her face, he whispered, "You're right. I'd better take you back to the boat before I make love to you as I want to do."

Stepping away again was the hardest thing she had ever done. "Wyatt, will you make one promise and keep it?"

"If I can." As they walked back toward the boat, he did not take her hand. She wondered if he felt as alone as she did without that physical link.

"Will you stop allowing Kitty Cat aboard your boat? If you refuse to let her aboard, she may stop coming here."

"Is that what you want? What you *really* want?"

"It's the best choice for Kitty Cat. She needs to make herself a real home at River's Haven."

"Even if she wants to be free?"

"When she last was free, she nearly starved to death." She paused, then asked, "Wyatt, have you thought what will happen when *The Ohio Star* is repaired and you leave Haven? She'll be despondent."

He walked away from her. When she heard him curse under his breath, she knew his anger was focused on himself. He faced her again and said, "All right. I swear to you I'd never do anything that might hurt K. C. . . . or you. If she comes back here, I'll send her home to you."

"There's no need for you to swear to anything. I trust you to keep your word."

"And what about you? Are you going to stay away, too?"

"My life is in River's Haven. Yours is here."

"Some parts of our lives are meant to be shared. Stay with me tonight."

As he spoke, he walked to her. She welcomed his lips eagerly . . . for what must be the last time. For too many long hours last night, she had sat by the window in her room and stared out at the moonlight bleaching the ripples in the river. All her thoughts had been of him. He had become a precious dream that never could come true.

He drew back and frowned. "That tasted like a kiss goodbye."

"It should be. Wyatt, it might be better if we ended this here and now."

"You agreed to go to the Centennial social with me."

"I should have told you no when you asked me."

His voice grew hard. "So are you telling me no now? Without any other explanation? You're just going to hide behind the excuse that you'll upset everyone at River's Haven by spending an innocent evening with me." He caught her face in his hands and forced it up so her eyes locked with his. "Or is there another reason? A reason that you don't want to say because you hate to lie?"

"There's no other reason."

"Not even Foley?"

She shook her head. "Mr. Foley has nothing to do with this."

"It sounds as if he soon will think he does."

"What he thinks isn't the issue." She clenched her hands, wishing she could speak the words coming from her heart. "Maybe it would have been better if you'd just kept on hating me as you did when I first stepped aboard your boat."

"I never hated you, Rachel." His arm slid around her waist. "I wanted you from the moment I saw you."

"Until you realized where I was from." She pushed away from him. "I'd be a fool to tangle my life with yours, so

I won't. And you'd be a fool to entangle your life with mine now."

"Because of your new suitor, Foley?"

"Partly, but mostly because of what you are and what I am."

"I'm a man who is willing to take a chance, and you're a woman who is afraid of her own feelings."

"It's not that."

"Then what is it?"

Kitty Cat's voice rang along the shore again.

"I must go," Rachel said.

He caught her arm, halting her. "Not until you give me an explanation. You owe me that much."

"All right." She raised her chin, not in defiance, but to keep tears from flooding from her eyes. "I want what you're offering me, Wyatt. I want it with every bit of my being."

"Then—"

She put her fingers to his lips as he had to hers on the boat. "Let me finish. I want it. I want you, but for more than a single night."

"It wouldn't have to be just one night. We'll be here in Haven for a while longer."

"And then you'll leave Haven . . . and me." Her voice broke as she whispered, "I don't want to be left alone again."

"Again?"

She did not answer. Her heart was breaking with pain. She did not want to resurrect the sorrows of the past, the sorrows she had come to River's Haven to forget.

She left him standing there as she gathered up her skirts and ran. She might be able to escape his arms, but she feared she was leaving behind her heart. Maybe that was for the best, because then she would never have to suffer heartache again. She could be the sister Merrill wished her to be and marry the man he wished her to marry and live the life she should have at River's Haven.

And forget about this one chance for true happiness.

Ten

Rachel steadied Kitty Cat, who was lurching more on every step. When the little girl paused to yawn widely, Rachel took her by the hand.

"You're going to fall asleep while Miss Hanson reads you a story tomorrow, Kitty Cat," she said as she took the doll before Kitty Cat could drop it again.

"Not if the story has a fish in it," the little girl argued, but in a voice heavy with fatigue. "My fish tasted so good."

"I bet it did."

"Why didn't you stay and have a bite?"

She hated lying to the child, so she said, "Wyatt is probably very hungry after working on *The Ohio Star* all day. He can enjoy my share."

"Horace says they're going to take the boat to Louisville as soon as the parts are ready. Can we go with them, Rachel? Horace says there's nothing like being on a boat when it's underway."

"We'll see. It might be better if we don't talk about it."

"Why?"

"We don't want to jinx the repairs, do we?"

She was uncertain if Kitty Cat understood the word "jinx," but the little girl nodded solemnly. Kitty Cat put her finger to her lips and said, "Shh!"

Rachel winced. Her own lips were still warm from

Wyatt's finger and his mouth. Even the most common-place motion had been infused with memories of him. She winced again, for if he kept his promise, that would be all she had of him.

She was glad Kitty Cat was too tired to notice her re-action. She had gotten Wyatt's promise to send Kitty Cat home if she went to *The Ohio Star* again, and now it was time to get Kitty Cat's.

Quietly, she said, "Kitty Cat, you know I told you before that you shouldn't leave River's Haven without telling me."

"I didn't. I left you a note."

She glanced at the common house. Its silhouette blocked a large portion of the sky. Every window seemed to have a light shining through it, and she hoped nobody chanced to see her and Kitty Cat.

"I know you didn't leave without telling me, and I'm proud of you for letting me know." Rachel smiled even though Kitty Cat could not see her expression in the dark. She hoped the smile would add a cheerful tone to what she had to say. "But now, I need you to promise that you won't leave River's Haven unless I'm with you."

"Why?"

Opening the door to their cottage, Rachel said as she lit a lamp, "The repairs on *The Ohio Star* are delicate, and you shouldn't go there unless I go as well."

Kitty Cat rubbed her eyes, which were filling with tears. "I thought Horace and Wyatt liked me."

"They do."

"Did Wyatt ask you to tell me this? Is that what you were talking about during your walk?" She yawned so hard that Rachel could see all her teeth.

"They do like you. Promise me, Kitty Cat, that you'll stay within the grounds of the Community unless I'm with you."

"Sean wants me to help with decorating for the Centennial."

"I know, and I'll be talking to the Assembly of Elders about that."

"Last time—"

"This isn't last time. This is *this* time, and you have to help me convince the Assembly of Elders that this time is different. You can do that by making the promise not to leave River's Haven without me."

Kitty Cat pouted, but said, "I promise to stay here unless you go with me. It's a stupid promise, Rachel."

"I know, but it may help when I go to the Assembly of Elders this time." She chuckled and turned the little girl toward the hall between the bedrooms. "And now it's time for you to go to sleep."

For once, the child did not ask for a story or a song before going to bed. She cuddled into her pillow, holding her doll close, and went right to sleep, almost before the covers were drawn up.

Closing Kitty Cat's door partway behind her, Rachel untied her bonnet, then set it on the peg by the front door. She was drawing the pins out of her closely bound hair when the door opened. Hope exploded through her. Had Wyatt followed them here?

She turned, faltering when she saw her brother standing in the doorway like an avenging angel. He eyed her, and his frown grew more furious.

"What's wrong, Merrill?" she asked.

He strode to her and bellowed, "How can you be so stupid?"

"Stupid? What are you talking about?"

"Rachel, I thought you knew the consequences of breaking our rules."

"Please lower your voice. Kitty Cat is asleep."

"Katherine! The child's name is Katherine."

Although she was tempted to let him change the subject,

she said, "You aren't here to argue about what I call her. What's wrong, Merrill?"

"You!" he retorted, but more quietly. "You and your sudden bout of stupidity."

"If you're going to stand there and repeat insults to me, you might as well go." Rachel frowned. "I'm too tired to argue with you, Merrill."

"Is that your excuse for failing to think clearly?"

"About what?"

He wagged a finger in her direction as if she were no older than Kitty Cat. "You have let that riverboat rogue woo you into what could have been scandal if I hadn't seen you." He began to pace from one side of the small room to the other.

Rachel sank to sit on the sofa as she choked, "You were in Haven?" If her brother had witnessed Wyatt holding her by the river . . . Merrill was right. She could be banished from River's Haven. Then she would lose both Wyatt and the family she had here.

"Yes. I saw you coming up the hill from the river near where Colton keeps his boat." He paused and looked at her. "What were you thinking?"

"I was thinking I should keep Kit—Katherine out of trouble. She went there to go fishing, and I brought her home."

"You went there to keep her out of trouble?"

"I just said that."

"So you could find trouble of your own?"

Coming to her feet, she said quietly, "I appreciate your concern on my behalf, but it's misplaced. I haven't done anything to create trouble. I asked Mr. Colton—" She almost choked on the formal name when such a short time ago she had whispered Wyatt's name while he was sending shivers of delight through her. "I asked him to send Katherine back here immediately if she went to *The Ohio Star* again."

"Maybe, if it's becoming too much of a chore for you to keep an eye on the child, it'd be for the best if she went to live with the other children her age."

"She isn't seven yet!"

"How do you know that?"

"Her birthday is coming up, and if she were already seven that would mean she would be turning eight. She's too little to be turning eight."

He sniffed in disagreement. "You have no idea how tall she should be. Who knows what she had to eat before she came out here? How many times have you said that she's growing like a dandelion?"

"She *is* growing, but I can't believe that she's already seven." She put her hand on the back of the chair by the table. "For heaven's sake, Merrill, she just left an orphanage. She needs a chance to live in a regular home."

"*This* is our regular home, and all children of her age should be living in the children's area. You have to face that fact."

"And I have. I understand that she'll be going to live with the other children when she turns seven. Until then, she stays here with me."

"Mr. Foley isn't pleased with the fact that you've got a child who isn't yours."

Good! she wanted to shout, but said, "He knew about her when he asked if he could call on me. Why is he upset now? If he's changed his mind—"

"He hasn't!"

Rachel flinched at her brother's sharp answer. Hearing bare footsteps behind her, she turned to see Kitty Cat standing in the hallway that separated the two bedrooms. The little girl was still yawning. How much had she heard?

"May I have a drink of water?" Kitty Cat asked.

With a sigh, Rachel guessed that once again Kitty Cat had been oblivious to a heated conversation. After getting a glass, she ladled water from the bucket on the stove. She handed it to the little girl and sent Kitty Cat back to bed.

Merrill barely waited for the squeak of Kitty Cat's bedroom door closing before he said, "I trust when Mr. Foley calls tomorrow evening, you won't allow that child to interrupt."

"Let me worry about that. Good night, Merrill."

"Rachel—"

She faced him and put her hands on her waist. "I need to get some sleep. I have a long day's work tomorrow, because it's my day to help in the barns in addition to my regular work. If I'm going to be receiving Mr. Foley tomorrow night, I shouldn't be yawning like Kitty Cat was."

"Katherine!"

"Good night, Merrill," she repeated, not wanting to give him a chance to start the argument anew.

He grumbled something that might have been good night and stormed out the front door.

She went to make sure it was securely closed. Leaning her cheek against the wood, she wondered why her brother seemed to be doing everything he could to make her rebel against his dictates.

She yawned almost as widely as Kitty Cat had and blew out the lamp. Such questions were for tomorrow. Right now she only wanted to sleep and dream that she was once more in Wyatt's arms.

Rachel looked around the front room of the cottage. Not even a hint of a breeze teased the muslin curtains, and the flowers in the vase on the table were beginning to droop. She could sympathize with them. Even her best dress, which was a light green cotton, was too hot. She wished she could be with Kitty Cat and the other children who had gone to splash in the shallows of the fire pond not far from the common house. The pond, which was there to provide water in the case of a fire, was not very deep even in the middle, so it was perfect for the younger children.

The door opened. For the first time, she wished that the Community did not believe that anyone should feel free to walk in anywhere at any time. The door had a lock on it, left over from when these cottages had belonged to someone else. To use it would break one of Community's most basic tenets. They were all family and should treat each other with informality.

Mr. Foley smiled as he entered. Not a hint of perspiration marred his brow or dampened his collar. He looked as dapper as always.

She wanted to ask him how he managed to stay cool amid this heat. Instead she said, "Good evening, Mr. Foley."

"It's a very good evening now, Miss Browning." He smiled as he set his hat on the table.

She fought not to flinch at the motion that seemed too intimate. He already was acting as if he lived within these walls. Picking up his hat, she hung it on one of the pegs by the door. A foolish idea, she realized, when she turned to see him smiling broadly while he looked at his hat next to her bonnet.

"I made lemonade, if you'd like some," Rachel said. Anything to keep herself from having to look directly at him. She could sense his gaze taking note of every motion she made. Mr. Foley always took in everything that was happening around him. That had never bothered her until this evening.

"Yes. In the parlor?"

"Yes." She poured two glasses, dabbing a cloth at what her quaking hands had spilled.

As she carried the glasses into the parlor, the lemonade sloshed like the river in a squall. She handed Mr. Foley a glass and then realized it must be as sticky as her fingers.

It was too late to clean them now, so she sat facing Mr. Foley.

Something flickered through his eyes, and she suspected he was irritated that she had not chosen to sit beside him on the sofa. She did not want to insult him. She simply wanted to avoid any suggestion that she wished to wed him.

Needing to say something to end the silence, Rachel asked, "Did you hear the news that the railroad has increased its orders for next month?"

"I didn't call to discuss River's Haven business."

"No, but I thought you'd like to know."

"Mr. Browning tells me that you're an excellent cook. He said that no one in River's Haven can make a better cake."

She set her glass on the table and then wished she had continued to hold on to it. Now she wanted to wring her hands. Even more, she wanted to jump to her feet and run from the room. Hiding until Mr. Foley left was a tempting thought.

"Merrill has always had a sweet tooth," she answered. "I believe he'd eat river mud if it was covered in chocolate."

The front door opened, and laughter rushed into the room before Kitty Cat bounced in. Each footprint dampened the floor, and more water dripped from the little girl's hair. She ran to Rachel and grinned.

"It was such fun, Rachel."

"I'm glad."

"Miss Hanson let us splash as much as we wanted."

She smiled. "So I see. Go in and get dried off."

As the little girl ran back toward her bedroom, Rachel was not certain what expression she would discover on Mr. Foley's face. She was surprised when she saw no emotion on it. Was he too angry to let her see, or were his thoughts elsewhere?

"Forgive her interruption," Rachel said. "She's been playing with the other children."

"The ones here instead of the ones in Haven?"

Rachel raised her hands and shrugged, although her shoulders were stiff. "You must realize that Katherine is doing her best. Our ways aren't what she knew in New York City. There, she answered to no adult, and she depended completely on the other children."

"You've given the Assembly of Elders that excuse before."

" 'Tis no excuse. It's the truth. She's becoming more comfortable here with each passing day." She smiled. "As a child, she can't embrace the tenets of the Community with the ease of the adults who join."

"She must learn."

"She will. I appreciate your continuing interest in her."

That answer widened his eyes, and she knew he was astonished at her apparent assumption that his comments suggested concern for Kitty Cat.

"I didn't call to discuss the child," he said.

"I know." The words tasted bitter on her lips.

"Your brother and Miss Page plan to marry as soon as possible, and he's very eager to have it be a double wedding." He smiled. "As I am."

"You've overwhelmed me."

"Surely since your brother spoke to you of my intentions, you've given them thought."

"Constantly." *Save when I am in Wyatt's arms,* she added silently.

"Then you must have decided upon an answer."

"Mr. Foley, may I be blunt?"

His smile faltered, but he said, "Of course."

"I barely know you, other than the fine work you've done as a member of the Assembly of Elders. I can't make such an important decision without being sure it's the right one."

"The Assembly of Elders would give their approval. I'm sure of that."

She kept her own smile in place. Did he think her completely witless? There was no question of the Assembly of Elders approving Mr. Foley's request to marry. He was one of the Elders!

"You misunderstand me, Mr. Foley," she said, trying to keep her voice from becoming taut with vexation. "I fear that I can't make such an important decision in the short time before my brother plans to marry Miss Page. After all, they've been courting for almost a month now."

"Closer to three weeks."

"But you're asking me to make up my mind after a single evening." She came to her feet, and he stood quickly. "I can't do that, Mr. Foley. I'm sorry, but I don't think it would be for the best for any of us."

"*Any* of us?"

"Katherine Mulligan must be considered as well. She's not yet seven years old." Clasping her hands, she hoped he did not see how they tightened to bleach her knuckles as they did every time she thought of having Kitty Cat leave to go to live with the other children.

What she had believed, before Kitty Cat came into her life, to be a rational way to bring up the next generation of River's Haven's residents now seemed absurd. She and Kitty Cat needed each other. Kitty Cat depended on her to take care of her and help her learn what she needed to know. In return, the little girl had found her way into Rachel's heart.

As Wyatt was doing.

Was she as crazy as Merrill had called her? She must not think of Wyatt when Mr. Foley was standing in her parlor.

"Rachel?" called Kitty Cat from behind her.

She turned to see the little girl now wearing an unadorned nightgown that was soaked where her red hair fell down her back. Going to the child, she asked, "What are you doing up still?"

"You didn't read me a story yet."

"Tonight . . ." She glanced over her shoulder. As she had guessed, Mr. Foley was wearing a displeased frown. "Go in and get the book you borrowed from the Community library. I'll be in as soon as I can. Until then, look at the pictures."

"And then, when you come in, I can tell *you* a story about them?"

Rachel wanted to thank the little girl, but she could not speak such words when Mr. Foley was privy to them. Kitty Cat's suggestion of devising a story for Rachel announced quite clearly that the child intended to stay awake until Rachel came to bid her good night. Not keeping the little girl awake too late was the perfect excuse to put a close to this uncomfortable call.

"Yes," she replied. "Now go to bed while I finish speaking with Mr. Foley."

Kitty Cat grinned and waved to both Rachel and Mr. Foley. "Don't be long. I already know the story I'm going to tell you."

Straightening as Kitty Cat disappeared along the hall, Rachel turned slowly to face Mr. Foley. His smile had returned, and she doubted if he had noticed her looking at him when he was frowning.

"A charming child," he said.

"She's a good little girl. Inquisitive, it's true."

"A sign of intelligence, which is something we hope for the next generation here at River's Haven. Such a child must be allowed to explore and learn."

Rachel smiled. "I agree. May I ask you a favor, Mr. Foley?"

"Most certainly. Friends do favors for friends. True?"

"True." She hoped the abrupt queasiness would stay in her stomach and not embarrass her, for she guessed what he would ask in return for the favor she needed. Yet, if she did not ask, Kitty Cat might get in such trouble that she was taken from Rachel even before her upcoming birthday. Losing the child would be as painful as when she had lost her father. "Mr. Foley, as I told you before, the Centennial celebration is coming soon. The children of Haven have asked if the children of River's Haven might join them in making decorations for the Fourth of July celebration in Haven."

"And you asked if Katherine might be allowed to participate." He frowned. "Is this the same invitation that Reverend Faulkner has extended?"

"Yes."

"It isn't . . ." He halted himself and smiled. "On second thought, I can see ways in which it's a commendable idea. I shall broach it without delay with the Assembly of Elders."

Rachel smiled back. "Thank you, Mr. Foley."

He raised his hands in a magnanimous gesture. "Save your thanks for when I return to take you for a carriage ride after dinner tomorrow evening. Is that agreeable?"

This, she knew, was the price of his favor. She could not tell him no. Not only was it considered a great honor to welcome an Elder into one's home, but she had promised Kitty Cat she would make the day of decorating Haven possible. She heard herself saying rather faintly, "It's agreeable, Mr. Foley, but not tomorrow. I have barn work tomorrow."

He chuckled. "I understand. Working outside in this heat will leave you no energy to receive a guest. The evening after that, then."

As she assented, she hoped that Kitty Cat would enjoy her visit to Haven, for Rachel doubted if she would enjoy Mr. Foley's next visit.

Eleven

Rachel sat back on her heels and wiped her forehead. Today was even hotter and muggier than last night. She glanced toward the west. Clouds were building there. Would a storm reach River's Haven and cool the air? Other clouds had gathered yesterday, but no rain had fallen. Yesterday, she had been in her office, which was much cooler than sitting on the hot ground.

Miss Stanley was insistent that the fence around the new pasture for the sheep be finished today. Rachel was not sure why, because the sheep would not be moved here for another two weeks. Arguing with Miss Stanley was fruitless and took too much effort on a hot day.

Picking up another nail, she tried to grip the hammer steadily in her left hand. Her right one was too sore to hold it because of blisters raised by the work. She was accustomed to working with paper and figures. She hoped she would be able to write tomorrow. Aiming the hammer at the nail, she barely missed her finger, and she heard a too-familiar laugh behind her. She looked over her shoulder and saw Wyatt squatting behind her.

Her heart clamored against her breastbone as if it were trying to escape and go to him. She slanted toward him, wanting his arms around her. Before he could pull her to him, she picked up her cup of nails and moved a bit farther along the fence. Not that it did any good. Even if she traveled all the way to distant China, she still would be unable to resist his powerful masculine aura that lured her to him.

"What are you doing here?" she asked, hoping her voice was not trembling.

"Checking on the progress of the parts your metal shop is making for us," Wyatt answered.

"I told you that I'd let you know when they were ready."

He chuckled. "I thought it'd be much more fun to come out and check for myself. Besides, until the parts are finished, work is at a standstill on *The Ohio Star*. I can polish the brasses only so long, and I don't want to hear any more of Horace's bellyachin' about being stuck on shore."

Awkwardly hammering in the nail to hold the board more securely, Rachel said, "That doesn't sound like Horace. He's always seemed pretty even tempered."

"The heat's enough to get anyone riled. I don't remember many Junes as hot as this one."

"I'll be glad when a storm washes away this heat."

"Don't be so sure of that. The storms can be bad when it stays hot this long. I'd wager your common house is the tallest thing in the whole county. Lightning may head right for it."

"Wyatt, I really don't have time to chat about the weather now." She reached for another nail, even though she wanted to reach for him. "I need to finish this fence."

"How much of it have you built?"

"Everything from here to that corner of the barn." She pointed to a spot about one hundred feet away.

"Today?" He plucked the hammer from her left hand and then grabbed her right hand. When he twisted it up so he could see the blisters on her palm, he demanded, "Can't you do anything in moderation?"

"What do you mean?"

"You know what I mean!" He raised her hand toward

her face. "You aren't accustomed to this kind of work. You shouldn't be doing it now."

She held out her other hand for the hammer, pretending she did not see the blisters bubbling up on that hand as well. "It's my turn to share in the work in the stables."

"Who's doing your regular work?"

"No one."

He laughed tersely. "So you're doing someone else's work, and nobody is lifting a finger to help with yours. It's a great system you have here, honey."

"It works for us. You can't tell me that you and Horace keep track of exactly how much work each of you does, so that neither of you has more work than the other."

"You've made your point. C'mon." He put his fingers around her wrist and tugged her to her feet. Gathering up the box of nails and the hammer, he said, "Anyone with any sense would know when it's time to call it a good day's work and quit."

"But I'm not finished, and you aren't the one to tell me what to do."

"Look at that sky." He hooked a thumb toward the western horizon where the clouds were turning a malignant gray. "I'm not telling you what to do. I'm suggesting you get inside before that storm sends you scurrying." He began to walk away.

Rachel started to call him back, so she could continue her work. The distant rumble of thunder silenced her. She hurried after Wyatt. She walked even faster when a flash of lightning reflected off the river.

"The cottage with the red door, right?" Wyatt asked as she caught up with him.

"Yes. Last cottage on the right."

When thunder sounded again, closer, she increased her pace again. She glanced toward the common house. Windows were being pulled shut. She needed to do the same thing in the cottage.

She winced when she opened the door. Even the simplest motion sent pain across her skin. Holding the door open, she gestured for Wyatt to come in.

"Don't just stand there," she ordered. "It's going to rain."

"So I noticed. But this is a momentous moment, honey. I never thought I'd be invited into your cottage with its red door."

"Will you stop being absurd?"

"Not likely." He stepped in and took the door from her, closing it. "So this is what's behind your red door." He laughed. "Not much like a brothel."

"I'll have to take your word for it."

"If your voice got any colder, honey, you could turn the coming rain to snow."

"Wyatt, if you'd step aside, I can get the windows closed before the rain arrives."

"Sit down. I'll get the windows." He held up his finger as she started to protest. When she stepped back before he could touch it to her lips, he asked, "Just the windows here?"

"And one in each of the bedrooms. I should get those."

He laughed again, but the humor was gone from the sound. "I'm not about to peek at all your private things, if that's what you're worried about. Sit down, and I'll tend to it."

Rachel nodded, relieved that she could cradle her burning hands in her lap and not touch the window frames that were sharp with bits of chipping paint. Sitting on the sofa, she leaned back and closed her eyes. Wyatt's steps were out of place in her house. Or were they? She had imagined this exact sound within her dreams.

Thunder cracked, and she flinched but did not sit up. Every muscle ached from her hard work. On the morrow, she would have to find a way to write without breaking these accursed blisters.

When her right hand was carefully cupped on a broad palm, she opened her eyes to find Wyatt kneeling in front of her. She watched as he swaddled her right hand in a warm, damp cloth.

"Ouch!" she gasped.

"Too hot?" He looked up at her, concern mixing with the sympathy in his eyes.

"No. Some of the blisters must have broken."

"You *are* a foolish woman. Injuring yourself won't do you or River's Haven any good."

She laughed. "I can assure you that it wasn't my intention to injure myself."

"If you weren't so stubborn—" He glanced toward the window as lightning flashed down in a pitchfork to strike somewhere along the hills edging the river. "I'll get K. C., if you tell me where she is."

Thunder thudded against the cottage like an impatient giant's fist as Rachel answered, "At this time of afternoon, she's with the other young children. Miss Hanson will watch over her. If the storm lasts for very long, Miss Hanson may have all the children eat together in the common house."

"All the children? Are they still in school?"

"They play together before dinner." She added nothing more. If she spoke of how Kitty Cat would be going to live in the common house with the other children after her seventh birthday, Wyatt was sure to give her a dozen arguments about why that was a stupid custom. She did not feel like arguing with him just now . . . especially when she would want to agree.

He picked up another warm cloth and draped it over her left hand. "You need to get these hands better if you're going to play that guitar in the other room. You do play it, don't you?"

"Not often lately, or so Kitty Cat complains. I haven't had time with all the work I've been given."

He wound the cloth around her hand. "Those blisters are going to hurt when someone grabs your hand to spin you about when we square-dance at the social."

"I told you that I shouldn't go with you to the social."

"Shouldn't isn't the same as wouldn't."

"You aren't going to let this go, are you?"

"No." He grinned.

"Even after the social is over?"

"There will be other events that come up around the Fourth of July celebrations." His smile widened. "So will you attend the Centennial social with me, or must I keep asking you?"

She tried not to let her eager heart answer for her. "I suspect you'll keep asking at times that are sure to create trouble for me."

"If that's what I must do."

"Why are you so insistent about this?"

"Because I hate to see you staying in this place for the rest of your life. If I can persuade you to take another look at the world beyond River's Haven, maybe you'll learn that remaining here is a mistake."

"This is my home."

"Just as the farm in Ohio was your home. You left that. You can leave here. Start by letting me escort you and K. C. to the social."

"Kitty Cat? You want Kitty Cat to go to the social with us?"

"Of course not, but I thought you might be more willing to change your mind if I included K. C. in the plans." He sat beside her on the sofa and ran his bent finger along her cheek. "What do you say, honey?"

"If I say no, you'll ask Kitty Cat directly, won't you?"

"No."

"No?" Now she was the one astounded.

He gave her a cockeyed grin. "I don't want to hurt the

kid. She's been hurt enough already, and she's going to be hurt more when you marry Foley."

"I haven't decided if I'm going to marry him."

"Are you still considering it?"

"Yes."

"Just because your brother told you to?"

"Yes."

He laughed and shook his head. "I guess I should be used to your honesty by now."

"You expected me to lie?"

"You're like no other woman I've ever met," he said softly. His long fingers curved along her shoulder. When she looked from them to his smile, he edged closer. She tried to move away, but his hand on her tightened. "Rachel," he continued in the same husky whisper, "I don't want to steal you away from River's Haven. You can tell your brother and Foley that."

"Steal me away?"

"Marry you."

She lowered her eyes, embarrassed that he would speak so openly of things she had thought of only in her dreams. "That's just as well, for I have no wish to marry."

"Why not?" He lifted the cloths off her hands and tossed them onto the table. "If you're going to stay here, your Assembly of Elders is sure to find you a husband. If not Foley, there will be someone else ready to marry you. I don't want you to get the idea that the someone else is me."

Pulling away and standing, she snapped, "I don't want to marry anyone. Especially not you."

Wyatt grabbed Rachel's arm and whirled her to face him. Shock shone in her eyes, and he knew his mouth was twisted with fury. He pulled her to him, so tightly that he could enjoy every inch of her soft curves beneath her gown's thin fabric.

"Good, because I don't want to marry you. I want *this* from you." His mouth covered hers.

An explosion, as powerful as the storm above them, coursed through him. When she curved her arms up around him, he caught her elbows and held her hands away, taking care not to touch her ravaged palms. As eagerly as if he had never kissed her before, his lips explored hers. When he drew her back down to the sofa, leaning over her so he could delight in her so close to him, she did not resist. Why would she? The soft eagerness in her eyes had told him that he was doing exactly as she longed for him to do.

With a strangled gasp, Rachel sat up, moving away.

His hand against her cheek gently turned her face back toward him. "What's wrong?"

"You know what's wrong. No matter how much I wish otherwise, while I'm considering marrying Mr. Foley, I shouldn't share these delicious kisses with you."

"You aren't married to him yet." He pressed his lips to her neck, and she quivered.

"No." She drew away again. "I can't let you seduce me into doing something that could persuade Merrill that I can't be trusted to make my own decisions."

"Honey, you're *deciding* to be with me here."

She shook her head, and her soft hair brushed his face. He wanted to pull it around him so he could breathe in the very essence of her. "You don't understand."

"You're right. I don't understand why we're talking when we could—"

"Stop." She raised her hands between them.

Did she realize that he would not draw them away, for that would hurt her? Did she realize how desperately he longed to press her back onto the sofa and make love with her?

"Rachel . . ."

She put the tip of one finger to his lips. When she winced, he knew even that slight motion had brought her pain. Before he could scold her for being silly, she said, "If Merrill decides that I'm unable to make reasonable decisions, he'll insist I marry Mr. Foley right away."

"He can't force you to marry Foley."

"You wouldn't say that if you really understood."

He seized her shoulders, keeping her from standing. "Tell me. Tell me the truth, so I can understand why you'd acquiesce to his demands."

She put her hands out to push him aside. A soft whimper burst from her lips. Instantly, he grasped her wrists, holding her hands up away from both of them.

"Tell me, honey," he said. "Tell me so I know what's scaring you so much."

"This is scaring me. This longing for you that I can't control."

"Because you're supposed to marry Foley?"

She shook her head. "This has nothing to do with him."

"Then what is it?"

"Kitty Cat."

"What on earth does the kid have to do with this?"

She raised her earth-brown eyes to meet his gaze. In them, he could see her craving for his kisses and caresses. He did not need a mirror to know that the same yearning shone from his.

"Everything, Wyatt. This wanting you—an outsider to River's Haven—is wrong!"

"That's your Assembly of Elders preaching, not you."

"But it's wrong!"

"Are you going to repeat it enough so you'll believe it?"

She looked away.

"Rachel, answer me," he ordered softly.

She flinched as rain struck the window. He looked past her. He had forgotten all about the storm as he fought the tempest trying to control his every thought.

"Once the rain is past," she said, "you should leave."

"Why?"

"I've told you why." She came to her feet.

He stood and put his hands on her shoulders. "You haven't told me anything. All I know is that you're frightened. What are you frightened of?"

"Of losing Kitty Cat."

"Why would you lose her?"

"Merrill thinks I'm more concerned about Kitty Cat than I am about the Community."

"Of course you are."

She closed her eyes and took a deep breath. "But it's not supposed to be that way. We are all supposed to care about each other in River's Haven."

Going over to the table, he swore as he picked up the cloths and threw them back at the bucket of warm water by the stove.

"Wyatt, try to understand."

"I would if you'd explain."

Tears filled her eyes but did not overflow on her cheeks. "If I lose Kitty Cat, I'll be all alone."

"You have your brother and the whole Community here and the village of Haven."

"If I lose Kitty Cat, I'll be all alone," she repeated. "You're going to leave as soon as *The Ohio Star* is repaired. You've got your life on the river. My life is here with Kitty Cat."

"But I thought she's only been with you for three or four months."

"In that time, she's filled my heart with such joy that I can't begin to describe it."

Something twinged in him. Envy? That was ludicrous! He was glad the kid and Rachel had found each other. They needed each other, just as he needed his free life on *The Ohio Star*. So why did her words refuse to stop resonating in his head—*She has filled my heart?* Why did that ache of longing and loss resound within him like thunder?

She gazed at him with those soft eyes and those delicious lips, and he wondered why he was fighting the truth. He wanted her to want him. He wanted there to be a place in her heart for him, so she would be waiting here, happy with her life of raising K. C., whenever he passed this section of the Ohio. Rachel would be here, eager and loving and responsive to his touch.

There was a broken-down pier in the river below River's Haven. He imagined her standing there, the wind sifting through her hair as his fingers longed to do. As *The Ohio Star* rounded the bend, he would see her waiting for him and the passion that would be hotter than the fire in the boat's boiler.

But would she be willing? She had said she did not want to marry anyone in this community—or anyone else. That suited him perfectly, just as she fit within his arms perfectly. No marriage, no ties, just a shared need that would be satisfied each time he held her. Would she be willing to agree to such an arrangement?

"Rachel—"

The door opened, and K. C. rushed in along with windswept rain. As Wyatt closed the door, the little girl shook water from her hair and ran to hug Rachel. K. C. gave Rachel a quick squeeze before turning to throw her arms around his waist. Words exploded out of the little girl as she tried to tell him about everything she had done since she last saw him.

He listened to K. C. but watched as Rachel sank down to the sofa. As K. C. looked at Rachel's blisters and cooed as if she were the mother and Rachel the child, he said nothing. The arrangement he wanted to offer Rachel could bring them both what they wanted. He could not ask her when the child was here and listening, but he would ask her at the social. It could be the perfect setup, for she would not lose the child and he would not lose her. All he had to do was convince her to agree.

Twelve

The morning of Merrill's latest wedding ceremony dawned as hot as midday. Fog clung to the river, warning that the day ahead would be so humid drawing a single breath would be a challenge.

Rachel took one look in the mirror and gave up any attempt to arrange her hair. She tied it back with a ribbon, letting it fall down her back. The wisps about her face curled as tightly as Kitty Cat's hair.

Smoothing her brown skirt that was edged with dark brown velvet, she smiled. The skirt was split to reveal the cranberry plaid petticoat beneath it. The same fabric decorated the lapels of the close-fitting jacket she had closed with velvet-covered buttons over her favorite white blouse.

Going out to the main room where her brother was pacing, she laughed. "Merrill, you look as nervous as a bridegroom at his first wedding."

"It never gets easier." He gave her a grin. "Miss Page wants everything to be perfect."

"It will be." She straightened his bow tie that was the same black as his double-breasted coat and trousers. She handed him his gloves, laughing again when she saw how his fingers trembled. "Would you like something to drink before the ceremony? Miss Page wouldn't be pleased if you swooned in front of your guests."

"Maybe that's a good idea."

"I believe there's some wine in the cupboard. Pour a glass to settle yourself down." When shouts came from outside the cottage, she saw people gathering in the middle of the common area. She gave her brother a kiss on the cheek before adding, "It sounds as if your guests are waiting for you."

"I shouldn't keep them waiting."

"Or your bride either."

He chuckled and picked up his silk top hat.

"You look beautiful!" cried Kitty Cat from behind her.

Rachel turned and smiled. For once, the little girl's gold hair ribbon on the top of her head was not askew, and her white stockings beneath her lacy dress had no holes. The gold sash around the light green dress that was hemmed with wide white lace still had its perfect bow at the back.

"You look beautiful, too, Kitty Cat."

The little girl twirled about, nearly tipping off her toes. Catching her and steadying her, Rachel said, "Try to keep this beautiful until at least the wedding ceremony is over."

"What's it like?"

"Haven't you been to a wedding before this?"

Kitty Cat shook her head. "Never. What do I have to do?"

"You and I have to be quiet like all the other guests." She tied the ribbons of her brown velvet bonnet under her chin. "Merrill and Miss Page will repeat their vows to love each other during their marriage. Then they'll kiss to seal the promise of their marriage."

"Kiss?" Her nose wrinkled. "That's disgusting."

"You may think differently when you're old enough to marry. You'll like when your sweetheart kisses you."

"Like you like kissing Wyatt?"

Rachel gasped and looked up, hoping that Merrill had left the cottage. He was standing only an arm's length away, and his frown was fearsome. He had heard every incriminating word Kitty Cat had said.

"Rachel?" asked the little girl. "Are you all right? You look sick."

"I'm fine." She came to her feet and gave the little girl a gentle shove toward the door. Not taking her gaze from her brother's fury, she said, "Go out to the common area and find two chairs for us."

Kitty Cat glanced at Merrill and faltered. "Rachel, I can—"

"Go! Now!"

The little girl rushed out of the cottage. Through the window, Rachel could see her running across the grass toward where the guests were talking and laughing. She wished she could flee with Kitty Cat, but she looked back at her brother, trying to steel herself for the explosion she knew was coming.

He stepped past her and closed the door. She understood why when his voice rang off the low ceiling as he demanded, "Is it true? Have you been kissing Colton?"

She would not lie. "Yes."

"How could you break every principle we live by?"

"I haven't. A single kiss—"

"So it's been just one kiss?"

Rachel stepped back as the door opened and a man called, "C'mon, Browning. You don't want to be late for your own wedding, do you? Might give your bride the idea you aren't interested any longer and she should be looking for someone else."

Merrill stiffened, warning that the jesting words bothered him. Maybe he did not believe that Miss Page would be any more faithful to him than she had been to her previous husbands. He glanced at Rachel, and she wondered if he was trying to shift his anger onto someone else. Fury darkened his eyes, and his mouth worked, but he said nothing as he walked out of the cottage with his friend.

She dropped to a seat at the table. Holding her face in her hands, she shuddered. How could she have been so stupid? Merrill would not allow her to do anything to get them banished from River's Haven. For the first time, she wondered what he might do to prevent that.

Rachel sat rigid through the wedding. She kept trying to relax her shoulders because she wanted to keep folks from getting the idea that she did not approve of her brother marrying Helga Page. Keeping her arm around Kitty Cat, she listened as Mr. Carpenter led Merrill and Miss Page through their vows. They were similar to what would be spoken in any church, but there was no mention of "until death do you part." Instead they pledged for one year from this day to be true to each other and love each other as a family within the family of the Community. A kiss sealed the promise, and flower petals were tossed on the newlyweds as they walked back down the aisle, hand in hand.

She waited for Merrill to look in her direction, but he did not. She blinked back hot tears. He had been angry with her before, but he never had shut her out of his life like this.

Kitty Cat tugged on Rachel's dress. A thread snapped.

"Be careful!" Rachel cried.

The little girl's smile crumbled, warning Rachel that her voice had been too sharp. The people around them stared. Taking Kitty Cat's hand, Rachel edged past the other guests, excusing herself as she mumbled something about making sure the food was perfect for her brother and his bride.

"I'm sorry, Kitty Cat," she said when they were walking across the grass toward the river. The food would be served closer to the water where it would be cooler and the children could swim in the cove. "I shouldn't have yelled at you."

"Is something wrong?"

"How can anything be wrong when we're at a wedding?"

Kitty Cat frowned again, and Rachel guessed her good humor had sounded too forced.

"Come and help me arrange the tables," Rachel said.

This time, as they walked down the steep riverbank, the little girl smiled.

Rachel was also smiling by the time they had taken linen towels off the many dishes that had been set on the tables. Shooing away flies, she listened to the musicians tuning up. The Community boasted a ten-piece orchestra and a marching band twice that size. She was not certain why there was a marching band, because the only place they performed was in the common area.

As the members of the Community swarmed over the food like another cluster of flies, she looked for her brother and Miss Page. Helga, she must remember to call her now that Miss Page had married Merrill.

"Congratulations!" she said when she found them among the crowd around the tables. "May your year together be everything you hope for."

Merrill's eyes were still dark with anger, but he kissed her on the cheek. "I hope you've taken inspiration from this ceremony, Rachel."

"Weddings are always inspiring." She glanced through the crowd, not wanting to chance Mr. Foley overhearing her and getting the idea she had decided to marry him.

She saw him at the far end of the long collection of tables. He was spooning food onto a plate held by Miss Turnbull, his ex-wife. She was nearly as tall as he was, and her luxurious blond hair surrounded a face that was the match for Mr. Foley's strikingly good looks. No one had been surprised when they had announced their plans to marry. Rachel recalled that they had been sitting with Miss Turnbull's family at the wedding.

"My weddings," cooed Miss Page, bringing Rachel's attention back to her newest sister-in-law, "are always inspiring." She kissed Merrill lustily.

Rachel hushed Kitty Cat, who was making a disgusted sound. When Merrill laughed and tweaked the child's nose, Rachel was astonished and pleased. She hoped her brother's good mood would last past his wedding day, and he would be more accepting of Kitty Cat.

The musicians began playing, and Rachel twirled Kitty Cat about until the little girl was laughing so hard she could barely stand. As the adults danced, many of the children frolicked at the water's edge. They shouted and splashed each other and anyone who came too close.

The joyous voices along the river bottom faded as a man appeared at the top of the riverbank. A hush spread across the guests as if the fog were returning. They turned as one when the man shouted Rachel's name.

Merrill swore under his breath and stamped to Rachel. Taking her by the arm, he growled, "I thought you knew better than to invite *him.*"

"I didn't invite anyone." She jerked her arm away. Squinting into the sunshine, she tried to see who stood on the top of the bank.

"So he just came uninvited?"

She rubbed her arm and glared at him. "Merrill, how can I know if he came uninvited when I don't know who's up there?"

"You know it's Colton!"

She laughed as the man stepped out of the sun's glare and his silhouette solidified. "Merrill, you're looking for trouble where there isn't any. That's not Wyatt. That man isn't tall enough."

"Then who is it?"

Instead of answering him, she walked through the crowd that seemed frozen in shock. After joining the Community most members had little interaction with anyone outside it.

Kitty Cat rushed after her, for once, silent. Rachel almost wished the youngster was tossing questions at her. It would be better than this preternatural quiet.

She reached the slope of the riverbank just as the man was sliding down the last few feet. In amazement, she said, "Reverend Faulkner, this is a pleasant surprise."

"Good day, Miss Browning." He smiled. "And to you, Miss Mulligan." As Kitty Cat preened at being acknowledged by the minister, he continued, sounding as disconcerted as the residents of River's Haven at his arrival, "Is something going on? I saw the crowd and wasn't sure if you were here. Then, when I shouted your name, I saw you and your brother."

"Merrill just got married." She did not mention that Helga was his third wife, for that would bother the minister.

He looked past her to the people clumped next to the tables. "I didn't mean to intrude on his wedding, Miss Browning."

"You're welcome to join us."

Clearing his throat, he said, "Yes . . . yes, thank you, but I can't stay. What I was coming to ask you can wait."

"You're here. You might as well tell me."

Again he glanced at the wedding guests. "I just wanted to stop by and see if you'd obtained the permission for the children to participate in the Fourth of July celebrations. I can see this isn't the time to discuss that."

"I haven't received an answer from the Assembly of Elders yet, although Mr. Foley has agreed to speak to them on my behalf."

"Mr. Foley is speaking to them on *your* behalf? Well, well. I see." He shook himself and said, "That's excellent, Miss Browning."

It took every ounce of Rachel's will to keep her smile

in place. The minister's first reaction told her that he had heard that Mr. Foley was courting her.

"I'll let you know, Reverend Faulkner, as soon as the Assembly of Elders has made its decision."

He tipped his hat to her. "Thank you, Miss Browning." He glanced once more at the wedding guests, then scampered back up the hill as if he believed the devil was nipping at his heels.

"You were very gracious with that outsider, Miss Browning," said Mr. Carpenter from behind her.

Rachel composed herself before she turned to face the white-haired man. She repeated the conversation in her mind and knew there was nothing that could be construed as a problem for the Community . . . or her.

"Reverend Faulkner is a very nice man," she replied.

"He is, although he was very distressed when we first set up the River's Haven Community here. However, he has always treated us with respect, and it's good to offer him the same, so I'm pleased how you spoke with him."

"Thank you." Should she ask Mr. Carpenter if Mr. Foley had spoken to him about the Centennial celebration? Mr. Carpenter must have heard what she and the minister were discussing, so she should wait for him to bring up the subject.

"I'm glad to see you treat outsiders with the same kindness that you do those within our Community," Mr. Carpenter said. "It was so kind of you and Mr. Foley to invite Miss Turnbull along on your carriage ride. She told me she had a grand time when she went out with you on Thursday."

"Thursday evening?" Rachel gasped before she could halt herself. She had not been with Mr. Foley and Miss Turnbull on Thursday evening.

With an apologetic smile, Mr. Carpenter said, "Perhaps I'm recalling the wrong night. It could have been Wednesday evening. Ah, here they come. Looking for you, no doubt."

Rachel was not certain of that when she saw how close Miss Turnbull stood to Mr. Foley. They had ended their marriage three months ago, as the Community's rules required. Hadn't they? An uneasiness filled her stomach, but she did not want to accuse them of using her as an excuse to allow them to spend an evening together. Mr. Carpenter had been unsure of the evening. Maybe he had been unsure of other details as well.

"Mr. Carpenter," gushed Mr. Foley, "I see you have very charming company."

"As do you." Mr. Carpenter bowed his head politely to Miss Turnbull. "I was just telling Miss Browning about how you enjoyed your carriage ride with her and Mr. Foley last Thursday evening."

Miss Turnbull flinched, her face growing bright red. Mr. Carpenter did not seem to notice. He prattled on a bit longer, then went to speak with Miss Stokes, who was waving rather frantically to him.

As soon as Mr. Carpenter was out of earshot, Miss Turnbull said, "Oh, please forgive me, Miss Browning. I told Mr. Carpenter that I couldn't come to a meeting because I went for a ride with you and Cal—Mr. Foley." She colored again. "It was horrible of me to include you in a lie."

"Lying is wrong," Kitty Cat said sharply.

Miss Turnbull's face grew a deeper red. "I know. Forgive me."

"What sort of meeting was it?" Mr. Foley asked, giving her a sympathetic smile.

"Rewriting the constitution of the Community to include the changes made over the past year."

He laughed. "I can understand why you wished to avoid that meeting."

"As can I," Rachel said. "You're forgiven, Miss Turnbull."

"I assure you that I won't use your name again to slip away from a duty."

"But lying is wrong," Kitty Cat insisted, her arms folded in front of her and her lower lip stuck out.

Rachel knelt in front of the little girl. "We know that, and Miss Turnbull just admitted that she made a mistake. I'm sure she has learned her lesson and won't lie again."

"But you said I should *never* lie."

"Yes, I did. And I meant that." Looking over her shoulder, she saw that Mr. Foley and Miss Turnbull were rejoining the other guests. No doubt Miss Turnbull had wanted to put an end to this embarrassing conversation posthaste, and Mr. Foley was leaving to allow Rachel to deal with the child. "Miss Turnbull won't lie again. You can be sure of that."

"If I hear her lying, I'm going to tell her that it's very, very wrong to lie."

Standing, Rachel smiled. "If you hear what you believe is a lie, you should come to me right away. A child shouldn't correct her elders."

"That's a stupid rule. If she's lying, she should have to tell the truth."

"And she will. Just come to me instead of telling her in front of everyone."

Kitty Cat nodded reluctantly, then turned as one of the children called to her from the slow water in the cove. "Can I go with them, Rachel?"

"Give me your shoes first." She chuckled, knowing that Kitty Cat in her excitement would rush into the water with her shoes on—again.

More quickly than she ever had, Kitty Cat unbuttoned her high shoes and tossed them toward Rachel. She raced off, followed by Rachel's warning not to go in past where the water reached her waist.

Rachel bent to pick up the shoes, brushing pieces of grass off them. As she straightened, she saw another man walking along the top of the riverbank. She could not mistake *this* silhouette. Wyatt! What was he doing here today of all days? She had told him not to come back to River's Haven except to get the parts for his boat. Why didn't he listen to her—just once?

Forcing a smile, Rachel went toward a table in the middle of the crowd. Maybe if she acted as if she had not seen him, he would take note of everyone gathered here and leave. It was a worthless hope, she realized, for, even if she had not heard the rumble of surprised voices from the Community residents, every inch of her was aware of him coming nearer and nearer. The sensation grew so strong that she did not need the puff of his breath against her hair to know that he stood right behind her.

His arms reached around her, and she gasped. Was he out of his mind? To embrace her here when the eyes of the Community must be focused on them?

She released her breath when he picked up a sandwich and took a bite. She was not surprised when she turned and found him smiling. He enjoyed keeping her off-kilter like this and putting the most untoward thoughts in her head.

And I enjoy it, too.

Was she the one losing her mind? This was not the time to wonder about that. This was the time to convince Wyatt to come to his senses and leave.

"You shouldn't be here now. Merrill just got married," Rachel said in a near whisper. Not that it mattered. Every ear on the riverbank was straining to hear their words.

"Well, congratulations are due to him, I suppose." He took another bite before adding, "I could keep on walking along the riverbank, if that would be for the best."

"It would be." Then she would not have to notice how the sunlight burnished his hair with blue highlights, as hot as the desire in his eyes. Her fingers longed to reach up and comb through those strands, for the very touch would set her on fire, too.

"Another guest?" asked Mr. Foley.

She fought not to flinch as Miss Turnbull had earlier. As Mr. Foley rounded the end of the table, she tried not to compare Wyatt's easy strength and undeniable masculinity to Mr. Foley's well-groomed elegance.

She hoped her voice did not tremble as she said, "Mr. Foley, this is Mr. Colton. I believe I've told you that he's repairing his steamboat with parts from River's Haven." She held her breath again, knowing that her future might hang on the very first words either man spoke.

Thirteen

Shaking Foley's hand, Wyatt took care not to glance at Rachel. He had not planned on meeting *this* man when he saw the River's Haven folks clustered on the riverbank and decided to see if Rachel was among them. Of course, if the situation had been reversed, he, like Foley, would be keeping a close eye on the woman he wanted to marry. When Rachel stood beside Foley, they were undeniably a handsome couple.

"Have the parts worked well for you?" Foley asked.

"I can't say. They haven't been finished yet."

"I'm sure Rachel will see that they're delivered as soon as possible so you can continue your business along the river."

Did Rachel recoil at Foley's use of her name or was that just wishful thinking on Wyatt's part? Hadn't Rachel said something about folks using proper names unless they were family? His jaw tightened as he wondered if she had married Foley already.

"I've seen," Wyatt drawled, wiping the back of his neck with a handkerchief, "that she can be very efficient about such matters. A rare talent in a woman."

"We have many women with many skills here at River's Haven." Foley was puffing up like a boiler taking on steam too fast.

Thin arms were thrown around his waist, and Wyatt

swung K. C. up in his arms. Cool water spewed over him. K. C. giggled as he tossed her atop his shoulder. The refreshing water flowed from her feet and from her hair down both sides of him.

"What have you been up to?" he asked as she wiggled on his shoulder.

"Put me down! Put me down!"

He set her on her feet, wiping his hands on her soaked hair. When she beamed a smile up at him, he asked, "Where have you been swimming?"

"In the river, silly!"

"Kit—Katherine," Rachel said in a chiding tone, "remember what we just talked about with speaking to one's elders."

K. C. rolled her eyes. "I remember."

Wyatt chuckled under his breath, then said, "I know this is your brother's wedding, but I'd like an update on those last parts, Rachel."

"Certainly, *Mr.* Colton," she replied with a glance toward Foley who was frowning. "Follow me."

"Of course, *Miss* Browning," he said with the same emphasis she had used. Apparently Foley could use her given name without being dressed down, but no one else could. Again, that piercing sting of jealousy seared through him. If she had married Foley, then Wyatt's plans would be ruined.

"Mr. Colton," Foley snapped as Wyatt stepped aside to allow Rachel to lead the way, "you shouldn't be asking her to do business on her brother's wedding day."

"Why not? It isn't as if this is his one and only wedding day."

"Are you belittling our ways, Mr. Colton?"

Wyatt held up his hands and smiled. He did not want to end up punching Foley in the nose. Well, he would have enjoyed that, but it would upset both Rachel and K. C. "Just stating a fact. Nothing more, nothing less."

"If you'll come with me," Rachel said. "Excuse us, Mr. Foley. This shouldn't take long."

"I'll be glad to go with you." Foley flashed a superior smile at Wyatt.

"That isn't necessary and—"

Another woman interrupted Rachel to say, "You promised this reel to me, Mr. Foley."

Wyatt eyed the voluptuous blonde. She was a beauty, but there was a coldness in her eyes as she glanced at him—appraising him candidly—that did not appeal to him. He had met her along the river. A beautiful woman who knew what she wanted and would do whatever she had to in order to get it. That was a dangerous sort of woman for anyone who got in her way.

Foley must have realized that, too, because he excused himself and went with the blonde.

Wyatt whistled through his teeth. "Put a ring in his nose, and she could lead him around."

"Can't you say something pleasant just once?" Rachel asked.

He smiled. The blonde was stunning, but Rachel was the woman he wanted. Maybe the blonde would waylay Foley from his plans to marry Rachel. He rubbed his hands together. His plan might still be able to work . . . if she would agree to it.

"You sure look pretty today." He winked at K. C. "Is that pleasant enough?"

"Kitty Cat, go and play with your friends," Rachel said, "while I get some information for Wyatt." She glanced at him, frowning. "You know, I told you that I'd get those parts to you as soon as they were ready."

"I'm not a patient man. Haven't you noticed that?" He let his gaze slip along her slender throat to the firm fullness of her breasts, which were accented so perfectly by the velvet strips on her lapels.

"Of course I've noticed that." Her chin was raised in

the pose she always assumed when she did not want him to guess how his words or actions delighted her with his unspoken invitation. "And I don't like to waste time. Maybe *you've* noticed that."

"Sure have, so why are you wasting time jabbering? Are you hoping I'm going to ask you to dance?"

Her eyes widened, and for a moment he thought she would say yes. The very idea of holding her in his arms as they moved to the music was inebriating. His arms were rising toward her before he realized he was letting his thoughts lead him—and her—into trouble. The dance he wanted with her—a most intimate, sensual dance—must wait until they were not being watched by half the residents of River's Haven.

When she walked up the sloping bluff, Wyatt chuckled under his breath. He followed, watching her furious steps. Was she angry at him or at herself for considering his offer? His amusement vanished. If she was upset by a joking invitation to dance, she might be even more distressed by the arrangement he intended to suggest. Maybe today would not be the best time. He would ask her away from River's Haven. All he needed to do was get her away from here. His smile returned as he knew there was one easy way.

He glanced back at the river and the children who were playing in it. His smile broadened.

"Are you coming?" Rachel called, impatience in her voice. "I thought you were in a hurry for the information."

Wyatt walked to where she was regarding him with a vexed expression. Hooking his arm through hers, he said, "You're a bothersome woman."

"Only to you."

"Not to Foley?"

Her steps faltered as she looked away.

Wyatt cursed silently. Pretty Rachel believed she belonged to Foley, even though he knew she did not want to marry the man. If he had thought she truly loved Foley, he would have stepped aside.

Or could he? His senses were filled with the scent, touch, and sight of her. Not only when he was close to her, as he was now, but every breath he took was flavored with the memory of her in his arms.

"Don't say things like that." Rachel stepped away from Wyatt and continued toward the metal shop. Why hadn't she told him to come back tomorrow? By then she would have been able to deal with him professionally. She almost laughed aloud at that thought. Tomorrow or the next day or a thousand days after that would not make any difference in how he thrilled her.

"Why not? It's a legitimate question. Don't you bother Foley?"

"He's bothered that I haven't agreed to marry him yet."

"Not that I noticed. He just went off with another woman to dance."

"Miss Turnbull and he enjoyed dancing when they were married."

"She is his former wife?" He frowned. "They look very cozy still."

"They're friends. It's our way."

He snorted. "A stupid way."

"So you've said before." She opened the door to the unusually quiet metal shop. Heat puffed out, and she had to gird herself to enter the shop that was even hotter than outside. Sweat trickled down her back as she wiped more from her forehead.

"It's hotter than Hades's kitchen in here," Wyatt said.

"Let me see if I can find Mr. Dow's work schedule." She lifted a small board off the wall and sat in the foreman's chair. She tilted the board so she could see the writing in the scanty light coming through the window.

As she ran her finger down the page attached to it, her hand was taken. She looked up to discover Wyatt leaning one hand on the back of the chair. All teasing had vanished from his face.

"Honey, you've got to start seeing things clearly," he said.

"I wish you wouldn't call me that."

"You're lying. You like when I call you honey."

She could not argue with that, because it was the truth. Rather she said, "I know you disagree with the tenets we live by here. You've made your opinion very well known on that. Now, if you want to know when the parts you ordered will be ready, I can—"

"I want to know what you're going to do about Foley. He's already calling you Rachel. He must consider your marriage a done deal."

She put the board on Mr. Dow's desk. "Is that why you asked me to come here with you?"

"No." He gave her a swift grin. "I do want to know when the parts will be finished." He became serious again. "But I also want to know what you're going to do about Foley."

She stood and hung the board back on the wall. "The last few parts should be ready in about a week."

"And Foley?"

"I don't know." She turned to face him. "He's offered to help arrange for the children to go into Haven for preparations for the Centennial celebrations."

"So you'll marry him because of that?"

She yearned to let her fingers explore his rough cheek, but she kept her hands by her side. "I told you that I didn't want to marry him or anyone else. But if I turn down his proposal, I have to offer a reason to show that doing so is in the best interests of River's Haven."

"Forget about River's Haven. What do *you* want to do? Will you marry a man who'll make you miserable for the rest of your life?"

"Rest of my life? The marriage would be for only a year."

"If you don't love him, it'll seem like a lifetime."

"Why do you care?"

He raised his hands, palms up, in a pose of surrender, but she knew he was not going to let this go when he said, "I don't care if Foley is really the man you want. It's just that you could do better than a man who's still sniffing after his onetime wife's skirts."

"Once the Assembly of Elders decides to give their approval to a marriage—"

His laugh was terse. "Will you just do nothing and accede to their edicts?"

"I always have. Now . . . I don't know."

"How long do you think Foley's going to wait?" His hand cupped her elbow as he drew her to him.

"Wyatt, don't!"

"Don't what?" he asked in the same reasonable tone. "Don't mention Foley, or don't hold you?"

She started to step away, but he put his hand on the wall. It blocked her into the corner. Smiling, he moved slowly toward her, backing her against the wall. When she tried to slide away in the other direction, he rested his other hand on the boards.

"You can scream if you want," he murmured, "but I doubt if anyone down by the river will hear you."

"Scream? Why would I scream?" She battled the quiver in her voice. It came from fear, but not for him. She was afraid of herself and how she felt when he stood so close. Time collapsed to when he had held her on the shore and lured her lips into a dangerous obsession for his kisses.

He stepped even nearer and whispered, "Do you react like this when Foley kisses you?"

His mouth on hers was gentle. When her arm curved along his shoulders, he drew her to him. He brightened her skin with kisses until her longing became a need she could not govern. She must stop this right now. He was being his most overbearing self. She should stop him . . . soon. His finger traced the velvet along one lapel, pausing directly over where her heart pounded. She ached with the need careening through her. Boldly she tasted the heat within his mouth in a silent request for him to continue electrifying her with his caresses.

She whispered his name, unable to say anything else as his hand moved along her, revealing the pleasure that awaited them. For a second, he lifted his fingers from her. She clasped her arms more tightly around him, bringing him back to her.

He slowly undid the first button on her coat. She gasped against his mouth when his finger slid along her blouse to reach for the next one. His kiss deepened as he continued to undo her coat. When she trembled with a longing she could not control, he slid it down over her arms. She did not see where he tossed it before he pulled her up to his chest again. His firm muscles pressed against her breasts, each unsteady breath a delicious stroke.

"You feel so sweet," he whispered so close to her lips that his mustache brushed them on every word. "How do you taste, honey?"

"Don't you know by now?"

He grinned. "It's the most blasted thing. As soon as I finish kissing you, I'm eager to find out again every sweet flavor you've got for me."

Knowing that she was being foolish, but unable to deny herself this pleasure, she asked, "So why don't you find out?"

"I think I shall."

She arched her neck as his lips slid along it. When his mouth found hers again, she swept her hands down his back to press his hips to hers. Her dress bunched between them, but she thought only of where his hard body was against hers. His hard body and the need only he could satisfy.

Abruptly Wyatt pulled away. Rachel stared at him, trying to make her eyes focus. She wanted to close them and tug him back into her arms.

Her hands reaching for him froze in midair as he said, "Answer my question, honey. Do you feel like this in Foley's arms?"

Letting her arms drop to her sides, she replied, "Don't ask me that, Wyatt. Don't ask me to choose between you and River's Haven." She reached for the latch on the door. "I must go now. I don't want Mr. Foley to become angry that I've been gone too long with you."

"He has no reason to be angry!"

"Don't you think you'd be upset if the woman you intended to marry was kissing another man?"

Wyatt gripped her shoulders as his furious gaze locked with her eyes. "And what of you? Don't you have a right to happiness? I didn't think Rachel Browning would be willing to settle for just any man, or are you so caught up in River's Haven's dictates that you can't see the truth? If you marry him and then the next man they choose for you and the next, will you ever be happy?"

She bit her lip. Trust Wyatt to see the truth, even when she had tried to deny it. "Wyatt, don't make it worse. Mr. Foley cares for me."

"Does he?"

"He asked for me to be his wife."

"Why wouldn't he? Any man would be lucky to be your first lover, Rachel." He gave her a sudden grin. "I'd gladly volunteer for the task."

She tried to ignore his teasing and her reaction to it. Her heart thudded in anticipation. "Don't pressure me more, Wyatt. That's what Mr. Foley is doing, and look what's happened."

"What has happened?"

"Nothing, but we both know me being here with you like this isn't right, Wyatt. If I kiss anyone, it should be Mr. Foley."

"But you want to kiss me," he said as he framed her face with his broad hands.

"Yes." She could no more imagine lying to him than to Kitty Cat. Coldness seeped into her heart at that thought, for she did not want Wyatt to become as important a part of her life as the little girl was. Then, when she lost him, too . . . She closed her eyes to hold back her tears. "But it's wrong for me to kiss you."

"Why?"

She turned away. Glaring at him over her shoulder, she snapped, "Because I shouldn't feel as I do when you kiss me."

He caught her arm before she could storm out of the shop. "Is it so different from when Foley kisses you?"

"He has never kissed me!" She flushed as she realized she had spoken out of turn. What existed between her and Mr. Foley was not Wyatt's business.

His laughter was cold. "So Foley is content just to court you with pretty words. What kind of man is he?"

"He's a gentleman and a member of the Assembly of Elders! He's not like you!" Jerking her arm away, she raised her chin. "He doesn't go about ravishing reluctant women."

"Ravish?" His eyes widened. "Honey, if that's what you'd like, I'd be more than happy to oblige."

"I'm sure you would."

"And you aren't reluctant."

"I should be."

He laughed humorlessly as he tipped her chin upward again. "Are you trying to remind yourself? For someone who's supposed to be so deeply committed to the ways of this Community, you're amazingly fervent in returning my kisses."

"River's Haven is my home, and I want to belong here. It's just when you kissed me, I—" She stopped, afraid to speak the rebellious thoughts she tried to keep hidden even from herself.

He stroked her cheek tenderly. "You what, Rachel?"

"I don't want you to stop," she whispered. It was useless to try to hide the truth. He had tasted the longing on her mouth. As he smiled and drew her closer, she held up her hands. "No, no more, Wyatt. I have to get back to the wedding celebration." Reaching for the door again, she added, "Good afternoon."

The door exploded open. As she jumped back, she bumped into Wyatt's hard chest. He steadied her, but his eyes were like two rocks glinting in a frozen river as he looked past her.

"What's going on here?" came a shout from the doorway.

Rachel's shoulders shuddered beneath Wyatt's hands. Stepping around her, he faced her brother. Merrill Browning was slipping his hand beneath his coat. For a gun? Wyatt started to shove Rachel aside, but paused when her brother drew his hand away from his coat. Did Browning have a gun, or was he just hoping Wyatt would believe he did? It did not matter. Wyatt was not going to risk Rachel's life to find out.

"I was checking Mr. Colton's order," Rachel replied with a serenity that impressed Wyatt. "He's impatient to get his steamboat fixed."

"Was that all you were checking?" Browning demanded.

"Why would you think I'd be checking anyone else's orders today?"

Browning picked up her coat off the desk. "Because you're half dressed."

Rachel took her coat and folded it over her arm. "If you haven't noticed, Merrill, it's hot in here."

Her brother started to reply, then stepped aside as K. C.

rushed in, exclaiming, "Here you are! Come and see the castle we've built with stones on the shore."

"Rachel will be with you in a minute," Wyatt said, not taking his eyes from Browning's mouth, which was working with rage. Browning grasped his sister's arm and drew her out of the metal shop.

K. C. looked up at Wyatt with large eyes. "What's wrong? Did I do something wrong?"

"You didn't do anything wrong." He held out his hand to the little girl. When K. C. took it, he led her outside. Raising his voice, he called to Rachel, who was several yards away with her brother, "Rachel, one more thing."

As he had expected, Browning stormed back toward him, menace in every step.

"K. C., go with Rachel," Wyatt urged quietly.

She looked at him and nodded, running to where Rachel stood. The little girl gave Browning a wide berth, he noted. K. C. was a smart kid.

Browning stopped an arm's length away. "You've gotten the information you came for. Why don't you leave?"

"As soon as I complete my business with your sister." He strode past Browning, trying not to tense when he had his back to Rachel's brother. He waited for any sound of Browning coming after him.

"You should go." Rachel's face was ashen.

"I will, but I wanted to thank you for the update on the parts."

"You're welcome."

"I'll check back in a few days."

"That would be fine." She glanced past him, then said, "Wyatt, you should speak with Mr. Dow after this."

"And avoid complicating your life further?"

She nodded.

"I get the message," he replied. "And I agree. As long as you're considering Foley's offer of marriage, you can't be mine."

"You make it sound as if he owns me."

"Doesn't he?" When she did not answer, he held out his hand where her brother would not see. "If you've changed your mind about Foley, come with me. We'll be more comfortable in my quarters."

"In your quarters?" she choked. "You're asking me to go there *now?*"

"I guess that pretty much gives me an answer to any invitation I might have offered you." He heard her brother walking toward them. "I'll see you when the parts are done."

"I will let you know as soon as they are ready."

Although he wanted to pull her into his arms and plead with her to leave this crazy place, he simply nodded. He ruffled K. C.'s curls and glanced back at Rachel, who was pulling on her coat to conceal those curves he wanted against him again. She gave him a tentative smile, and he turned to leave, knowing that she believed she would be able to handle her brother's wrath without any help.

Wyatt looked back over his shoulder as he crossed the area in front of the looming common house. When he saw Rachel walking hand in hand with K. C. toward the shore with Browning several paces ahead of them, he headed back toward Haven and *The Ohio Star*. There was nothing else he could do here but cause more trouble for her.

Horace, who was sitting on a bench and whittling, greeted him as Wyatt came aboard. Grumbling something, Wyatt headed for the stairs.

"Whoa there, partner!" Horace called. "Why are you trying to drive your feet right through the deck?" He chuckled. "Or should I ask what has she done now to get you fired up with a full boiler of steam?"

Pausing, Wyatt put his hand on the rail. "Horace, sometimes you are just too blasted nosy."

"Sounds as if you got a cold welcome from pretty Miss Rachel."

"Not from her."

Horace frowned. "Stirring up trouble out there isn't a good idea."

"You don't have to tell me that. Rachel's already mentioned it."

"Figured she had. She's one wise lady." He put down his knife and the piece of wood that was taking the shape of a cat. "Maybe I should go out to River's Haven and get the rest of the parts when they're ready."

"Maybe you should."

"But you're going to go anyhow, aren't you?"

Wyatt arched a brow. "I still have a question I need to ask Rachel."

"A question?" Horace's eyes nearly popped from his head as he grinned. "Are you fixing to ask her to marry you? It'd be great to have her and the kid on *The Ohio Star* with us."

"That isn't what I plan to ask her," Wyatt said quietly. Blast it! Why did Horace have to ask questions like that? He should know better. Yet, Horace's comments had instantly created an image in Wyatt's head—an image of a life on the river with Rachel and K. C.

He shook his head. His plan was better. He could have his free life on the river, and Rachel could have her life at River's Haven doing the work she enjoyed. Each time *The Ohio Star* passed by this way, he could stop and spend a night—or even an afternoon if they were behind schedule—with her. She had said again today that she had no interest in getting married. But she sure was interested in his kisses. The perfect arrangement. All he had to do was ask her when the time was right.

Before Horace could ask another question, Wyatt went up the stairs. He worked in silence the rest of the afternoon, stopping only when it became too dark to see. Then he skipped supper during which he was sure Horace would ask more questions he did not want to answer. He walked along the deck to his quarters and opened the door. The cramped space barely had room for the bed that was built against the wall and the small box that held everything he owned.

He closed the door, on which his best clothes hung on a peg. After stripping off his sweaty shirt, he collapsed into his bed. He closed his eyes. As always, in the twilight world between being awake and asleep, he thought about Rachel and how her sweet body would feel woven with his. Her kisses seared through him, just beyond his reach. He allowed his fantasies free rein. For the first time, his mind led him to the consummation of the yearning. He groaned. His eyes popped open as he ached with the need to love the real woman. If he did not persuade her soon, it was likely never to happen.

As soon as those parts were ready, *The Ohio Star* would be leaving. He had to get an answer from her straightaway. Not just any answer. He needed her to say yes.

Fourteen

Wyatt gave the bolt another turn, then straightened. He pressed his hand to his lower back. It ached as if he had twisted it with the wrench. When he saw starlight drifting across the pilothouse floor, he understood why his back hurt. He had been working here since before dawn.

"Getting old?" asked Horace as he peeked into the pilothouse.

"Just tired." He bent to pick up the tools he had been using. Pain seared his back, and he groaned.

Horace laughed as he leaned on his broom.

"I thought you were my friend," Wyatt said as he placed the tools in the wooden box set on a shelf by the wheel.

"I am. Only your friend would laugh at you like this." He chuckled again.

He pulled off his sweaty shirt and tossed it atop the coat he had taken off earlier when the day had become too hot. "If you were really a friend, you'd have water heating on the stove so I could take a hot bath."

"And have Miss Rachel wash your back?"

"Rachel?" He snorted. "If she were here, she'd be more likely to push my head under the water."

Horace grinned and scratched his side. "She *is* here."

"What?" Wyatt was not sure if he had heard his partner correctly. After the scene with her brother at River's Haven, Wyatt had not guessed that Rachel would come to *The Ohio Star* the very next day.

"K. C. got here about an hour ago."

Wyatt frowned. "You know we were supposed to send her back to River's Haven if she came here."

"You promised Miss Rachel that. Not me." He began to sweep the floor. "Miss Rachel arrived just a few minutes ago. She's down on the deck with K. C."

"Did Rachel come alone?" His mouth twisted as he thought of dealing with Browning again. He would gladly give the fool a few lessons, but not when Rachel was watching. She was upset enough already.

"Her sweetheart is here."

Startled, he blurted, "Foley is here? You let that polecat on our boat?"

Horace chuckled deeply. "I didn't say Foley was here. I said only that Miss Rachel's sweetheart is here." He clapped his hands in amusement.

Wyatt gave him a sheepish grin. Deciding it was time to beat a less than dignified retreat, he said, "Like I said, I think I'll go and talk to Rachel."

"Undressed like that?" Horace laughed again. "You'll get that girl all flustered if you parade around without your shirt on. Girls like that, I understand."

"You understand?" Wyatt shoved his arms into the sleeves of his shirt, then grimaced. Not only did his shirt reek with sweat, but every muscle protested.

Horace chuckled again as Wyatt went out of the pilothouse. A quick stop in his quarters would garner him a cleaner shirt to wear beneath the coat. Then he would find out what had brought K. C. here . . . and Rachel after her.

Rachel tried to restrain her temper. She had been patient with Kitty Cat, but her patience was strained. If Merrill or anyone else at River's Haven discovered where she and the child were tonight, there was sure to be trouble. They were standing on the port side of the boat, facing the far shore, but someone might still be able to see them from Haven.

"Kitty Cat, you promised me that you wouldn't come here without me."

The little girl stubbed her toe against a space between the deck boards as she hugged her rag doll close. "You were upset about having to bring the parts here, so I thought I would."

"Kitty Cat, a promise is a promise."

"And you promised to get the parts to Wyatt and Horace as soon as they were ready."

"*I* would have." She sighed. "Kitty Cat, you can't use an excuse to break a promise."

"But I thought you'd want me to bring the parts to Horace and Wyatt." Kitty Cat stared at the deck, her chin on the rag doll's head. "I thought if I brought the news about the parts here, Mr. Browning and Mr. Foley wouldn't get mad at you."

Rachel put her hand over her mouth to mute her gasp of astonishment. She should not be surprised that Kitty Cat was so attentive to the people around her. The child would have had to develop that skill to survive on the brutal streets where she had lived before being taken to the orphanage and the train west.

She put her hand under the little girl's chin and tilted it up. "Thank you, but you shouldn't worry about Merrill and Mr. Foley."

"You do."

"Yes, I do. Let me worry for both of us."

Kitty Cat's eyes grew luminous with tears. "I don't want you to be unhappy, Rachel. I want you to be happy."

"I am whenever I'm with you." She hugged the little girl.

"Me, too."

"And me as well," said Wyatt as he stepped out of the

shadows beneath the deck. She was surprised to see he was wearing a fringed buckskin coat when the night was still thick with the day's heat.

"Wyatt!" shouted Kitty Cat, rushing to throw her arms around him as if she had not seen him in days.

Rachel smiled as he picked up the little girl and tossed her up in the air, catching her with ease. Kitty Cat giggled when he set her back onto the deck. As he straightened, he grimaced.

"Did you hurt yourself?" asked Rachel.

"If I say yes, will you make it better?" he returned.

Kitty Cat piped up to say, "Rachel's good at making things better."

Wyatt took Rachel's hand and drew her closer. "Are you, honey? Will you make me—and you—feel much better?"

Before she could answer, he enlightened her face with kisses. Her fear for how she would explain this to Kitty Cat vanished into her need for him. She quivered as his lips slipped along her face and his tongue teased her ear. She wanted more of this. Much more. More of the caresses, more of the fire that burned to the tips of her toes, more of the delight that she did not dare to give a name to.

She slipped her hands beneath his coat. Gazing up into his eyes, she longed to cede herself to the blazing promises there. She wanted nothing between her fingers and his skin. To touch . . .

She pulled back as her fingers found cold metal lying against his chest. "Why are you wearing a gun?" she choked.

"I've been hearing things."

"About trouble for you and *The Ohio Star*?"

"Some folks don't like you coming here again and again to retrieve Kitty Cat. I've been hearing things recently." His lips tightened. "Why are you staring at me like that?

Do you think I'm such an idiot that I wouldn't watch out for my boat?"

She shook her head. "You haven't worn a gun before tonight."

"You should know that better than anyone else. You've had the opportunity to check."

A heated flush climbed her face. "But why now?"

"Because of your brother."

"Merrill?" she whispered.

"Do you have another?"

She turned to Kitty Cat, who was listening avidly. "Go and see what Horace is doing."

Kitty Cat nodded and skipped toward the stairs, calling Horace's name with excitement.

Rachel looked back at Wyatt. "Merrill is so busy with his honeymoon now that he won't be thinking of anything else."

"He'll be done with his honeymoon pretty quickly."

"By then . . ." She sighed.

He put his finger beneath her chin as she had to Kitty Cat. Tipping it up, he said, "By then, I'll be gone. That's what you don't want to say, isn't it?"

"Yes."

"You knew right from the beginning that this was just a quick stop . . . this time. The next time we come by—"

"If you're about to say that you'll come and visit Kitty Cat and me, don't. Merrill told Mr. Foley that I've accepted his proposal."

Wyatt swore. "And you aren't going to fight his bully-boy tactics?"

Rachel rubbed her hands together as she walked to the steps leading to the upper decks. Lightning flashed in the distance, and she flinched. "Kitty Cat, we need to go now." She turned to look at Wyatt and said more quietly, "I told Mr. Foley I won't consider getting married until after the Centennial celebration."

"That must not have made your brother very happy." He closed the distance between them, backing her up against the railing.

"What would make *me* happy is for you to step aside."

"And this is what would make *me* happy, honey." When his lips claimed hers, demanding and yet surprisingly tender, she meant to push him away. She intended to shout that she would not be his, but, as lazy thunder sounded in the distance, her arms rose to encircle his shoulders as she answered his fired passion with her own.

Yearning for him was wrong for many reasons, but being in his arms was right for a single one: She loved him.

Rachel gasped when he released her. Why? He ached for more than a single kiss. She could sense that as if his thoughts were her own. And they were, for she craved his eager embrace.

He kissed the tip of her nose and said, "Be careful on your way back to River's Haven. With that thunder and lightning rolling in, it may rain before you get there."

"Wyatt?"

"Yes, honey?"

"I thought—" Swallowing raggedly, she regained control of her voice as Kitty Cat bounced down the stairs. "That is, I wanted to tell you good evening."

"I would have preferred if you'd told me good *night,* Rachel." Wyatt started up the stairs.

She stared after him. Not knowing what she wanted was a peculiar sensation. For so long, she had worked to make a home for herself at River's Haven. Before that, she had focused on her family in Ohio. Now . . . Now she ached for Wyatt's arms around her, but he clearly could not wait to get his boat fixed and back on the river.

A small hand slipped into hers. She looked down at Kitty Cat, who was regarding her with dismay. As she bent to see what was bothering the child, Kitty Cat put her hand up to Rachel's cheek.

Rachel put her hand over Kitty Cat's; then her fingers brushed the little girl's cheek. It was damp, and she knelt, drawing the child into her arms. She wished she could cry, too. When had she last been able to cry? Tears had filled her eyes too often since her father's death, but she had not let them fall. With Wyatt getting ready to leave . . .

She stood and took a single step toward the plank connecting *The Ohio Star* to the shore. She paused and stared at the lights of the village of Haven on the bluff above. Turning, she sought along the river for any hint of River's Haven. Fog was beginning to gather, rolling along the water like an ancient dragon. Its fierce breath was visible in another flash of lightning.

She must not let her own thoughts be caught up in a fog as well. On the morrow, Wyatt would come out to River's Haven and collect the rest of the parts he had ordered. A few days to repair *The Ohio Star*, and he could leave Haven . . . and her to her life at River's Haven.

She stared again in the direction of the Community. There, Mr. Foley was already planning their wedding. No one would heed her protests now that Merrill had spread the story that she had agreed to marry the Elder. If she stayed at River's Haven, she would have to marry Mr. Foley.

Looking down at Kitty Cat, she saw the little girl was also gazing up at the village. Did Kitty Cat wish she had been placed out with a family in Haven? Maybe Rachel should take Kitty Cat and move into the village. Reverend Faulkner would help them until Rachel could find a way to support them. Then . . . It really did not matter what happened then, because she would have lost both Wyatt and her family at River's Haven. She would be alone.

Alone! She hated the very word. And she hated the idea of being alone tonight. She knew what she was risking with these thoughts, but she also knew what she could capture tonight. Even though she would be left with memories of what she wanted every day, she could not turn away from having this night with Wyatt. If she left now, she would lose this single chance to grasp happiness.

She turned and walked up the stairs. Kitty Cat pelted her with questions, but Rachel did not answer. How could she explain to the child that she was letting her heart rule her head?

As she walked along the upper deck, she heard raised voices. Wyatt and Horace! What were they arguing about? Her steps faltered. Maybe she should leave, even though she doubted if she would have the courage—or the opportunity—to come back to *The Ohio Star*.

A string of oaths burst from the saloon, and she was tempted to put her hands over Kitty Cat's ears, although she guessed the little girl had heard much worse in New York City. She froze when the curses were followed by Horace saying, "You're a fool if you let her walk out on you! When are you going to find another like her?"

"Do you want me to hog tie her and make her stay?" Wyatt asked.

"If that's what it takes, then yes. Even the kid can see that you two belong together. Why else did she come here tonight, knowing that Miss Rachel would follow?"

Rachel again looked at Kitty Cat, who seemed anxious to avoid her eyes as she cuddled her doll. Could it be true? Could Kitty Cat be playing matchmaker? She was unsure whether to hug or scold the child.

But one thing she was sure of. Not releasing Kitty Cat's hand, Rachel went to the door of the saloon. She yelped when she was nearly knocked off her feet as Wyatt charged out like a knight riding in a tournament.

"What are you doing here?" he asked as he kept both her and Kitty Cat from falling to the deck.

"I think you and I need to talk." She stepped aside as Kitty Cat ran to sit in a rocking chair beside Horace.

"We've talked and talked, and nothing changes. You intend to ruin your life by marrying a man you don't love."

"What about your life?"

His forehead threaded with confusion. "What about my life?"

She ran her fingers along those furrows as she whispered, "Will it ruin your life if I marry Mr. Foley?"

"It sure wouldn't help anything."

Taking both of his hands in hers, she said, "Then we need to talk. We need to talk somewhere where nobody else will hear."

"This way." He put his arm around her waist, keeping her close as they walked along the narrow deck that was brightened by a bolt of lightning cutting through the fog.

When he opened a door near the stern and motioned for her to enter, Rachel went into the tiny room that was awash with more lightning. It was reflecting off the water and the fog, jeweling them with a shower of diamonds. No lamp was lit, but there was no need.

She turned as Wyatt closed the door and bumped into him. She laughed, the sound as childlike as Kitty Cat's giggle.

"Are you nervous to be here?" he asked in the hushed, husky whisper that sent a tremor of anticipation along her.

"Should I be?"

He chuckled, unhooking the gun and setting it on the windowsill while thunder careened along the river. "This room is my quarters, honey."

"I know."

"Where I want you to stay tonight."

"I know."

"In my bed with me."

She framed his face with her hands and brought his mouth toward hers as she whispered, "You talk too much." She kissed him.

He tilted her head back gently, his thumbs stroking her cheekbones. "I thought you wanted to talk."

"I was lying."

"You? I thought you were always going to be honest."

"I vowed lots of things." Why was he delaying when she wanted him to hold her?

He gave her a leering grin as his arm around her waist swept her to him. "But I want you lying."

"You do?"

"Lying right next to me."

She laughed and sifted her fingers up through his hair as his lips stroked hers. That touch silenced the little voice warning her she was making a huge mistake. It could not be a mistake to have this one night that she would treasure for the rest of her life. Thunder sounded much closer, but she paid it no mind as she lost herself in his exquisite kiss.

He took her hands and drew her to his bed. Sitting, he whispered, "Are you sure about this?"

"Yes," she said as quietly, thrilled that it was the truth.

"Honey, I can't make you any promises—"

"But that you'll delight me tonight." Putting her finger to his lips, she asked, "Will you stop trying to talk me out of this? Or have you changed your mind?"

"On this? Never, honey." With a laugh, he tugged her down to his lap.

Her feet flew up in the air as he reclined her back onto the narrow bed and leaned over her, chuckling along with her. His mouth slanted across hers as he released her hair to scatter down her back and over his pillow. His eyes held hers, promising to bring to life every fantasy she had imagined, as his fingers slid along her hair.

She quivered when a single finger glided along her, grazing her neck and brushing the curve of her breast. When her hair drifted about her, he smoothed it away. She sighed with a longing that was beyond words as he traced a meandering path along her abdomen before his fingers rose to curve around her face. Putting her arms around his shoulders, she drew him down to her. His hungry lips slipped along her neck, sampling each pleasure waiting for him. Teasing the curve of his ear with her tongue, she shivered even though his rapid breath was searing her skin.

He began to undo the hooks down the back of her gown with a patience that amazed her. How could he be going so slow when she yearned to tear his clothes from him so she could touch his bare skin?

As he drew her up to sit, he brushed her sleeve down her arm to reveal her shift. He laughed and reached for the ties holding her skirt in place.

"Stand up!" he ordered. "This thing is too bulky. I never thought I'd say I preferred your other dress, but it has its advantages."

Rising to her knees, she pushed his hand away as she untied her skirt and petticoats. She unbuttoned her shoes. Then she slid to the edge of the bed and kicked the heavy garments and her shoes to the floor to leave her dressed only in her shift and pantalets.

"Better?" she asked.

His voice was raw with passion as he hooked his arm around her and tugged her back to him. "Much better, honey, but it can be better yet."

"I know." She drew his shirt out of his trousers and slipped her hands up beneath it, eager to let her palms learn every inch of his chest. His heart thudded against her fingertips, its speed increasing as she slid her tongue against the rough, bristly skin of his jaw.

He groaned and brought her to lie atop him. Thrilled at how she could please him as he had her, she continued her exploration as she loosened each button on his shirt. When she was undoing the final one, his hands curved up her legs, raising her shift over her knees. She gripped his shoulders, overwhelmed by the sensations battering her.

Then everything vanished into laughter as his hands coursed up her thighs. "No!" she cried. "No! Stop, Wyatt! Please stop!"

"Honey, we haven't even started yet."

"You are tick—You're tickling me!" She collapsed on the bed, unable to stop laughing.

"Tickling you? Where?"

She pointed to her upper leg. "It tickles me when you touch me there."

"It tickles me, too." He pulled off his boots, dropped them on the floor, and then rose onto all fours on the bed to look down at her. "You have no idea how much, honey." He laughed before he silenced her with kisses.

Suddenly, with all her heart, she wanted to know the love that should have been theirs. Locking her fingers together at his nape, she closed her eyes as he drew off her stockings. He took care not to tickle her again, but she did not trust the humor glinting in his eyes. When he entangled his legs with hers, she wondered when he had removed the rest of his clothes. She did not let the thought bother her as she savored the sensation of his skin on hers.

"Better?" he whispered.

"Much better."

He looped one finger over the lace at the very center of her chemise's neckline. "It still can be even better, honey. You need to get rid of this."

She sat, his gaze holding hers while she lifted the hem of her chemise and drew it over her head. When she had tossed it aside, he knelt on either side of her legs and put his hands on her shoulders, leaning her back again into the pillow.

His eyes burned with silver desire as he ran a single finger across her lips and over her chin. When his hand cupped her breast, he bent to caress it with his lips. She writhed when his tongue teased its very tip. His other hand slid along her stomach to curve over her hips. When she moaned his name, he bent forward to taste the heat on her lips. As lightly as his fingers had moved along her, his tongue stroked her lips, then flicked dazzling heat along her, taking the same sensual journey his fingers had.

He raised his head to whisper, "Let's see exactly where you are ticklish, honey."

"Wyatt, don't . . ."

"Trust me."

"I do trust you," she murmured, again elated to know that was true. She trusted him as she had trusted no one else, not just so she could be here like this, but so she could give him her heart.

His hands slipped beneath her bottom as his mouth explored her inner thigh. If it was ticklish, she could not tell because she was consumed by the craving that was beyond anything she had experienced before. Her fingers clutched the blanket beneath her as his tongue laved her with a wave of incredible, intimate ecstasy.

Was that her voice calling out to him in such a desperate tone? She was unsure of anything but the escalating fire erupting through her. Then, she was the fire, untamed and unquenched, scalding away every thought and emotion.

When his arm slipped around her shoulders, shifting her beneath him, she raised trembling fingers to bring his mouth to hers. The musky scents of both him and her surrounded her as he whispered something. She could not understand what it was. She could only see his eyes, his eyes that burned with the same fire that had engulfed her.

She gasped as he pushed deep within her. The glow in his eyes dimmed for a moment, and she knew he feared he had hurt her. How could he when she had waited so long for this moment? She pressed her hands against his hips, bringing him even deeper.

His smile brought forth those uncontrollable feelings again. As he captured her mouth, he moved against her, then with her. So slow was each motion, she panted against his lips in anticipation. She clasped his shoulders and gave herself to the rhythm. As she was enveloped once more in the fiery ecstasy, he shuddered against her. His groan surrounded her as she gave herself to the perfection and to him.

Rachel was unsure what woke her from sleep. The storm must have gone past, for starlight now filtered through the fog. The air remained hot, and no sound of thunder suggested any rain was on the way. If thunder had not intruded on her sleep, then what had?

The bed shifted, and she looked at Wyatt, who was sleeping with his arm around her, his fingers draped across her breast. She smiled. For whatever had woken her, she was grateful, because she could marvel in the memory of his sumptuous seduction before she took them with her into her dreams.

Wyatt had awakened her once to make love with her again. That time had been more exquisite than the first time, for they did not hurry. Her fingers ran along her arm, and she wondered at how his touch made her come alive in a way she had never known.

She closed her eyes. Tonight she had learned many lessons from him. His mouth on her and his body against hers had created a spell of love. A small moan escaped her lips as she fought her need to rejoice in his touch again. Having discovered joy in his arms, she would yearn for it for the rest of her life.

She buried her face in the pillow and breathed in Wyatt's male essence. Had she been a fool to surrender to his spell when she knew this ecstasy could never be hers again once she left the boat? She must go back to River's Haven, and he would return to his life on the river.

No, she would not let any thoughts of the future ruin this night. This one incomparable night. Turning to face him, she was not surprised to see his eyes were open. They crinkled in a grin as he rose far enough to find her lips and draw her into the splendor once more.

Fifteen

A fist pounded on the door.

Wyatt opened his eyes and yawned. The dawn's gray was only beginning to chase away the darkness. Or was that fog or rain? A second storm had ripped along the river valley less than an hour ago. It had been more violent than the first.

He started to swing his feet over the side of the bed, then paused. A smile curved along his lips as he gazed at how his blanket followed Rachel's beguiling body. Her passion had not surprised him, for he had seen her leap to the defense of River's Haven so often, but her eagerness had thrilled him. She might wear puritanical dress when she visited *The Ohio Star*, but she was a wanton who was receptive to every pleasure he had taught her.

And she had taught him, he reminded himself with a silent laugh. He had not guessed that *he* had so much to learn from this sweet innocent.

He forced his hand not to slip along her, for he wanted to watch her sleep a moment longer. Her black hair was spread beneath her, but he could admire the glistening warmth of her cheek and her soft pink lips that had been so luscious beneath his.

He could no longer resist. He ran a single finger along her cheek, and, opening her eyes, she rolled onto her back to smile drowsily up at him. Her hand raised toward him, but she stiffened when someone struck the door again.

"Wait here," Wyatt said, pulling on his trousers as he went to the door. He looked back at the bed. Rachel held the blanket up to her chin, and her hair flowed down over her like melted chocolate. He doubted if he had ever seen a more appealing sight.

The fist hit the door a third time.

Throwing it open, he was astonished to see Horace on the other side. He started to ask his partner why he was bothering him now, but Horace gasped, "Fire!"

"Fire?" He cursed as the unmistakable odor of smoke curled around him. It had not been fog clouding the windows. "Where?"

"At the bow."

"The boiler room—"

"Not there. On this deck and the one above. We've got to get help to put it out."

"K. C.?"

"She's right here." Horace tugged the little girl around him. K. C.'s eyes were heavy with sleep and fear.

"Go! I'll be right behind you."

His partner nodded and raced away.

Wyatt turned. Rachel had pulled on her dress and was buttoning it into place. Taking K. C. by the hand, he drew the little girl into his quarters.

"Honey, the boat's on fire." He stuffed his feet into his boots.

"I heard," Rachel replied. "Do you think lightning hit it?"

"No, I suspect heaven's wrath was less involved than men's fury."

She choked out a denial, then turned to pick his gun up off the windowsill. She handed it to him.

"Thanks," he said. "Finish dressing and head for the stern."

"I can help—"

"Just get to the stairs right away."

"All right. If I can help, call me. Please."

He nodded, caressing her cheek. "Can you swim?"

"Yes." Her eyes widened in horror. "Is the fire that bad?"

"It's at the prow. The planks to shore and the pier are at that end. You need to get off *The Ohio Star* immediately." His voice gentled. "Don't argue with me, Rachel."

Wanting to plead with him to come with her and Kitty Cat, Rachel bit her lower lip as Wyatt rushed out onto the deck.

"Are we going ashore?" Kitty Cat asked.

"It looks like it." Rachel glanced back at her shoes and petticoats on the floor. Drawing on her shoes, she buttoned them only partway. If she had to kick them off, she could. "C'mon. We've got to go."

"Your petticoats!"

Rachel scooped them up. She glanced toward the bow as she hurried Kitty Cat out of Wyatt's quarters and onto the deck. Flames crackled in the predawn darkness, but they did not reach high above the pilothouse as she had feared.

She grabbed a lantern that Wyatt must have left for her, holding it up as she led the little girl to the rear stairs. They were steeper than the ones at the front. More of a ladder than a staircase, so Rachel had to keep Kitty Cat from tumbling down them.

She heard a bell clanging. Something was reeling down the bluff. A trail of men followed behind it. They must be bringing Haven's pumper. She wondered how long it would take to get a head of steam up so they could take water from the river to put out the fire.

Embers floated on the air. Kitty Cat yelped, and Rachel hurried to brush one from the little girl's sleeve. They could not stay here.

"Put this over your head," she ordered, handing Kitty Cat one of her petticoats.

"Why?"

"It will act as a sort of umbrella."

Kitty Cat copied Rachel as she tossed a petticoat over her head. Going to the railing at the stern, Rachel ran her hands along the top. Was there a break in it, so she did not have to clamber over the railing? If so, she could not find it. She glanced to her right. The railing opened there, for that was where Kitty Cat had been fishing. She did not want to swim any farther than she had to.

"Take this." She handed Kitty Cat the lantern, trying not to see the tears on the child's face. From fear or because she had been burned?

Keeping the petticoat over her head, Rachel bunched up her skirt and struggled to climb over the railing. Balancing on the narrow edge of the deck on the other side, she held out her hands to Kitty Cat.

"Put down the lantern," she ordered.

"Rachel, we can't go until—"

"Wyatt and Horace will be fine."

"But, Rachel—"

"Katherine Mulligan! Don't argue! Come now!"

The little girl hurried to obey, and Rachel knew that she had finally convinced Kitty Cat not to linger. Rachel sat on the narrow strip of wood. At her order, Kitty Cat stepped behind her. The little girl clamped her arms around Rachel's shoulders, leaning against her back. Again Rachel looked toward the front of *The Ohio Star*, hoping that she could set Kitty Cat back on the other side of the railing because the fire was under control.

Flames were visible over the upper railing. She scanned the deck but could not see Wyatt. He would be close to the fire, fighting to save the boat. Something snapped, and a shower of embers flew up before raining down on the lower deck and into the river.

"Hold on, Kitty Cat," she called, knowing that she must not wait any longer.

Sliding off the deck, she fought to keep her head—and Kitty Cat's—above water. The little girl squealed and began kicking her feet. Right into Rachel's legs.

"Don't help," Rachel gasped as she began to swim toward shore. Her skirt tried to coil around her legs, keeping her from moving.

Shouts came from the shore, and she heard the clatter of the pumper's steam engine. That strange whoosh must be the pumper spraying water onto the fire.

She stretched her toes toward the bottom, but the water was still too deep. Kitty Cat cried out in terror. Had she gotten water in her face or was it the lightning that sliced across the sky? Another storm?

Rachel wanted to tell the little girl to hold on tightly but Rachel did not waste her energy. They had to get out of the water and to shelter before the storm was over them. Stroking awkwardly, she edged toward shore. She had not realized how far the back end of the boat could drift from the shore while the front was bound to the pier.

This time when she tried to find the bottom, her foot sank into mud. She lifted it quickly before her shoe could be pulled off. Bouncing through the water, not letting her feet linger long on the bottom, she found the stones near the shore. She stood and drew Kitty Cat around her so she could cradle the child in her arms.

Hands came out of the darkness. Someone took Kitty Cat. When she looked up, she saw it was Mr. Sawyer. Sean stood beside him and held out his hand to Rachel. She hesitated, not wanting to pull the boy into the water.

"He's strong enough to help you, Miss Browning," Mr. Sawyer said.

She grasped the boy's hand. Mr. Sawyer had not been jesting. Sean helped her out of the river as if she weighed as little as Kitty Cat. She dropped to her knees on the shore. Mud sucked her down into the dampness. Cool, thick mud. She breathed in its wet scent.

"Thank you," she whispered as she raised her head.

Mr. Sawyer put Kitty Cat in Sean's arms. "Let me help you, Miss Browning."

"Thank you." She was not going to be proud now. She was soaked and scared. Not of being burned, but for Wyatt and Horace. As Mr. Sawyer helped her to her feet, she looked toward *The Ohio Star*.

"They'll take care of it, Miss Browning." Turning her to walk up the hill, he added, "I assume you'd like to get Kitty Cat in and dried off as quickly as possible. No sense anyone seeing the two of you looking like drowned rats."

"Yes, we should get inside right away." She understood what he did not say. No one from River's Haven must learn she had been aboard the boat. She wanted to thank Mr. Sawyer again, but that would ruin the illusion that he was leading her away from the others simply because he wanted her to get to the red house around the corner from the general store without delay. She was not sure how Mr. Sawyer had chanced to see her in the water, but she appreciated his attempt to keep her from being seen by the villagers of Haven.

At the top of the hill, she looked back at *The Ohio Star*. Men swarmed around the pier in the light of the fire on the top decks. An arc of water struck the flames.

"Don't dally, Miss Browning," Mr. Sawyer said. "If someone chances to look in this direction . . ."

Rachel followed him around the back of the livery stable and across the street toward the green. The top of her shoes flapped on every step. Again she glanced behind her. The orange light that had reflected in the river was dimming. The firefighters must be winning their battle with the fire.

Following Mr. Sawyer up onto the porch of the neat red house around the corner from the store, she saw Sean set Kitty Cat on her feet in a comfortable foyer. Mrs. Sawyer threw a blanket over the little girl's shoulders and held out another to Rachel.

"Do come in," Mrs. Sawyer said.

Rachel took the blanket but said, "We should be returning to River's Haven."

Closing the door, Mr. Sawyer said, "You should be dry first. Otherwise . . ."

"Thank you," she murmured. "I appreciate your kindness more than I can say."

Mrs. Sawyer put her hand on Rachel's arm. "We in Haven take care of one another, just as you do at River's Haven. Come in and sit. I'll see if I can find you something to wear."

"I'm soaked. I don't want to drip through your house."

"Come into the kitchen. You can't hurt the chairs out there." She smiled at her husband. "Noah just put extra coats of paint on them so the children can't ruin them after playing outside."

Rachel gratefully followed Mrs. Sawyer into the kitchen. The room barely had enough space for the black stove and the table with six chairs around it. A dry sink was set beneath the window. Beyond the door was another room that was only partially complete, and she guessed Mr. Sawyer was enlarging the house.

Sitting at the table covered with a yellow gingham oilcloth, Rachel reached down and drew off her shoes. "I think I should dump these outside."

"Allow me," Mrs. Sawyer said.

"You shouldn't be doing all this in your condition."

Mrs. Sawyer laughed as she patted her rounding stomach. "My work and my family keep me on my feet most of the day, and it's too early to worry about resting. Doc Bamburger told me that I should do anything I feel comfortable doing."

"But you should take care. Giving birth is so very dangerous." Rachel's hands clenched in her lap. She admired

Mrs. Sawyer and did not want to think of her health and maybe even her life imperiled because of this child.

"I'm not giving birth anytime soon." She chuckled. Taking Rachel's shoes, she went through the unfinished room and opened a door on the far side.

The odor of smoke burst into the house. Rachel stood and went to the door. A heavy, dark cloud hung over the village, blocking the sunrise. Was the fire out, or were they still fighting it?

"Noah has gone back to find out what's going on and to lend a hand," Mrs. Sawyer said as if Rachel had spoken out loud. "He'll come back with news as soon as he can. For now, let me see what I can find you to wear while those clothes dry."

As Mrs. Sawyer went back out of the kitchen, Rachel realized that she had not asked a single question about why Rachel and Kitty Cat had been on the boat. Sinking to the chair again, she leaned her elbow on the table and her cheek against her hand. Mrs. Sawyer did not need to ask questions. Her disheveled state must make it obvious what had kept them aboard the boat last night.

When Mrs. Sawyer returned with an armload of clothing, she dropped them on the table and pulled the thin curtains over the window. Rachel sorted through them and found a skirt and a chemise that would fit her. The skirt would be short, for she was taller than Mrs. Sawyer, but it would be nowhere near as short as the skirts she wore at River's Haven. Only the bottom trio of buttons on her shoes would be seen.

Rachel quickly pulled off her wet clothes and redressed. Mrs. Sawyer dried out Rachel's shoes with a towel. Her steady patter about the upcoming Centennial events seemed to require no answer, and Rachel gave her none.

She needed to concentrate on how she would explain *this* when she returned to River's Haven. Merrill would be furious beyond words, and she had no idea how Mr. Foley would react. He certainly would be outraged to learn that his reluctant bride-to-be had spent the night with Wyatt Colton on *The Ohio Star*.

"Here you go," said Mrs. Sawyer, handing Rachel her shoes. "I figure this is as dry as I can get them. Gladys would have done better, but she's visiting her brother and won't be back for another few days."

"Gladys?"

"Noah's housekeeper. She lives out at the farm to keep an eye on the house there until we decide what to do with it." She laughed. "We don't need two small houses, just one big one."

Rachel put her hand in one shoe, then slipped her foot into it and began buttoning it into place. "The shoe is drier than it's been when I have taken Kitty Cat for a walk along the river and had to fish her out. Thank you so much."

"No need for you to keep saying thanks." She smiled. "I know you'd do the same for my family, for I've seen how much Kitty Cat loves you. Sean tells me that she was mistrustful of others when they were in New York City."

"Mistrustful? Not Kitty Cat!" Rachel laughed, unable to halt herself as she thought of how Kitty Cat had inveigled her way into Rachel's heart with such speed and how the little girl had made friends so quickly with Wyatt and Horace.

"It's clear that living with you has changed her."

"I'm glad to hear that, because she's changed me in so many ways, Mrs. Sawyer."

"Please call me Emma."

"If you'll call me Rachel."

Emma pointed to the dry sink. "You can put your wet clothes there, and we'll tend to Kitty Cat next. She and Sean were running up and down the stairs last time I saw them. At the rate they were going, they might already be dry."

Rachel gathered up her soaked clothes and dropped

them in the dry sink. She followed Emma out into the foyer. No child was in sight.

"Sean!" called Emma.

"Here." He poked his head out of a parlor.

"Where's Kitty Cat?"

He shrugged. "I thought she was out in the kitchen with you."

"Sean, will you check if she's upstairs with the girls?"

He ran up the steps, calling Kitty Cat's name. Two excited little girl voices answered him, but Rachel did not recognize either of them. He rushed back almost throwing himself down the stairs. "She's not up there."

"Sean—"

He interrupted Emma by shouting over his shoulder, "I'll look for her outside."

"No, wait," Rachel said. When Sean paused, she added, "She wouldn't go out in her wet clothes unless she had a reason."

"Would she go without you to see if the boat was all right?" asked Emma.

"Not without me."

"Did she drop something on the way here that she'd want to make sure didn't get burned?"

"Oh! Her doll!" Rachel clenched her hands. "She didn't have her doll when we left *The Ohio Star*. She must be going back to get it."

"She won't get back aboard," Emma said. "There are too many men down on the pier."

Sean rubbed his hands together. "Don't be so certain of that, Emma. Kitty Cat got her name because she could sneak in and out of any place like a cat."

"I'm going to go look for her." Rachel opened the door. "If she comes back here, please send for me down at the river."

"Of course." Emma put her arm around Sean's shoulders. "We'll keep looking for her around the village."

Nodding, Rachel hurried down the steps and along the street. The odd fall of her skirt seemed more determined to tangle in her legs than either of the lengths she was accustomed to. She ran past the railroad station and fought not to tumble down the hill as she had before.

Hot smoke tried to choke her, and she waved it away. To no avail, for more wove in front of her. Reaching the bottom of the hill, she looked along the shore barely lit by the rising sun. No sign of the little girl.

More than a score of men stood on the pier. She looked for Wyatt. She did not see him, but Horace was walking toward the riverbank.

"Have you seen Kitty Cat?" Rachel cried as she rushed up to him.

Horace shook his head as he wiped smoke stains from his face. "I thought Sawyer told us that she went with you up to the village."

"She did, but she's vanished. She may be looking for her doll."

"Doll?"

"She left it on *The Ohio Star*."

"Wyatt!" he shouted.

Rachel pressed her hands over her heart as Wyatt pushed through the crowd. Like Horace, his face and clothes were covered with soot. Holes in his coat must have come from embers. Only now, when she saw him standing undaunted on the pier, did she realize how desperately she had feared for him.

Her feet were carrying her toward him before she could form another thought. Throwing her arms around his shoulders, she pressed her face to his chest. She closed her eyes, thankful for his steady heartbeat beneath her ear.

"You're safe," she whispered.

"What are you doing back here?" he asked as quietly. "I thought you and K. C. would have hightailed it back to River's Haven by now."

She stepped back, although she wanted to remain in his arms. "Kitty Cat has disappeared. I think she may have come back here to get her rag doll."

Wyatt swore before saying, "Stay here. Don't follow us and try to do something stupid."

"But—"

He silenced her with his mouth on hers. Just now, he did not care who saw her with him. Although Sawyer had told him that he had fished Rachel and K. C. out of the river and seen them to his house behind the store, Wyatt had feared that one of them had been hurt.

He released her, not letting the fleeting glow in her eyes beguile him into pulling her to him again. Waving for Horace to follow him, he ran along the pier toward the boat. He wobbled on each step. Smoke and soot filled his lungs, and he was burned in more than a score of places. He ignored it all. They had to find K. C. before she found a hot spot and was hurt worse than he and Horace were.

The lower deck was intact except for where fire had dripped off the upper decks. It was still too hot above to check the extent of damage there. Water dripped down, and sizzles warned that the charred decks remained dangerously hot.

"Where did K. C. sleep?" he shouted to Horace as they pushed through the crowd that had come to help fight the fire. A volley of coughs burst from him. Shouting was not a good idea.

"In a rocking chair in the saloon."

"That's where she's headed then." He leaped aboard *The Ohio Star*, calling back, "Watch your step."

Wyatt was immediately sucked again into the blistering maw of the smoke. Pulling the sleeve of his coat up over his mouth, he tried to run across the deck. The best he could manage was an awkward lope. He heard shouts as he emerged from the smoke. He did not need to listen to the others calling him to come back to the pier. He knew he was being a fool. He did not have a chance of escaping if the fire burst forth again, but he refused to admit that they could not find Kitty Cat.

Where was Horace? He could not see his partner in the smoke. He could not shout again. Not in the midst of this smoke that was already strangling him. Wiping his watering eyes, he hurried at the best pace he could along the deck. Something cracked above, and he threw himself toward the stern. Embers and charred debris fell behind him, smashing into ashes.

He cursed again when his foot slipped on something. He fell to the deck. The indisputable scent of grease came from a cloth that was lying on the boards. Picking it up, he stuffed it in his pocket as he took the stairs two at a time. At the top, he had to stop to catch his breath. More coughs tore out of him until he feared he would vomit up everything inside him.

The upper deck at this end was blackened with smoke and soaked, but the boards had not been scorched. He tested one, then another. They were secure.

He lurched along the deck to the saloon. Peering inside, he saw a shadow.

"K. C.!"

The little girl whirled. "Wyatt! Where's Shirley?"

It took him a moment to realize that she meant her rag doll. Wiping his eyes again, he looked across the room. He saw something under the table. He knelt, grimacing at the burned skin on his knee, and pulled out the doll. Its dress had been singed in several places, but the doll's face and hair were intact. He had been burned worse.

K. C. took the doll and hugged it tightly. "Thank you, Wyatt. This is my only baby until Rachel and I have a real baby."

Wyatt grinned. A real baby? He tried to imagine Rachel growing round with his child, and he chuckled quietly. The thought pleased him more than he had guessed it would.

Thinking of how proud Horace was of his scattered progeny, Wyatt knew he would be boastful of his own child. He *had* to talk to Rachel straightaway and get her to agree to the arrangement he wanted to offer her. Then he could come to visit her and their children whenever *The Ohio Star* passed this way.

"What's so funny, Wyatt?" K. C. asked.

"You!" He tapped her nose, then scooped her up in his arms. He fought not to cough more. If he did, he might drop her. "Let's get out of here."

"Where's Rachel?"

"Worrying about you. You aren't supposed to take off without letting her know where you're going." He walked out of the saloon.

The smoke was beginning to dissipate, and he could see more of the damage. The front railing on both upper decks was gone, and half the boards on this deck were missing or so scorched he guessed they would have to be replaced before he and Horace could walk across them. It was not as bad as he had feared.

"Oh, dear!" K. C. whispered.

"I agree." He turned toward the stairs at the stern. Taking them far more slowly than he had come up, he watched for any debris that might trip him or fall on them.

When he reached the lowest deck, he looked for Horace. He saw his partner on the other side of the boat, gazing up at the bow.

"Got her!" Wyatt called. He began to cough and feared he would never stop. K. C. asked what was wrong, but he could not answer her.

Raising his head as far as he was able, he saw Horace gripping the railing and raising his clenched fist. Cheers came from shore, so Wyatt guessed Horace had devised some signal to let Rachel and everyone else know when K. C. had been found. Those cheers became warning shouts.

A sudden crack was as sharp as a gun firing. Horace swayed before falling with a section of railing into the river.

Wyatt put K. C. on the deck. "Run to the pier and find Rachel." Not waiting to see if she did, he sped to where his partner had fallen overboard. He pressed his hand to his chest as if he could hold back the retching coughs. As he searched the water, he knew he could not be weak now.

Where was his partner?

Sixteen

Wyatt scanned the water, seeing nothing for an endless moment. He would not allow calls from the pier and pointing fingers to distract him.

His partner's head bobbed to the surface. Horace was splashing his arms wildly.

"Keep kicking your feet!" Wyatt shouted before diving into the water.

On the pier, Rachel lifted Kitty Cat off the boat. She silenced the little girl's cries that Horace had fallen into the water. She crossed her arms in front of Kitty Cat and the doll, holding them close. Men surged past them to get to the end of the pier where they could help Wyatt get Horace out of the water. She and Kitty Cat must stay out of the way and let them rescue Horace.

Her plan fell apart when she heard the men shouting to each other to help Horace *and Wyatt*. Holding Kitty Cat by the hand, she squeezed past the men, saying "Excuse me" each time she stepped on someone's toes, until she could see where Mr. Sawyer and a very slight man were bent over the end of the pier, their arms outstretched. Someone caught her before she could rush up to them.

"Wait here, Miss Browning," she heard.

Looking back, she saw Reverend Faulkner's somber face. She nodded. The minister was right, but she wanted to help. Before she could say anything, the two men were dragged up onto the pier. Both were gasping like fish pulled from the river.

"They're alive!" shouted the slender man.

More cheers sounded along the pier before the men began to drift back toward the village. The pumper was shoved ahead of them up the hill.

"Thank you," Rachel said over and over as she went to where Horace had risen as far as his knees. Wyatt was still lying on the pier. "Thank you again, Mr. Sawyer."

He tipped his hat to her. "I hope this is the last time you or the crew here will need our help."

"I do, too." She smiled at the thin man beside him before kneeling next to Wyatt and Horace. "How are you?"

"Alive," Horace said, then coughed. He turned and threw up into the water.

"Barely," added Wyatt. He lifted his head off the pier and looked at her, pain vivid on his face. He began to cough, deep, racking coughs that hurt just to listen to.

"Help him," Horace ordered weakly. "I'll be right as rain once I get all this river water out of my gut."

Rachel slipped her arm around Wyatt's waist. She struggled to get to her feet but she fell back to her knees. His uneven breath struck her cheek.

"Kitty Cat?" he struggled to say as they managed to stand.

"Safe." She glanced back to see a wagon coming down the hill. "You will be, too, as soon as you're tended to."

"I'm fine now," he argued weakly.

"Listen to her, Wyatt," Horace snapped. "She's got a good head on her shoulders."

With Horace's help, she aided Wyatt along the pier. She ignored his protests that he needed to check the boat. When Horace and Wyatt were in the back of the wagon, covered with blankets, she took the reins from a man she recognized as Mr. Anderson, who ran the livery. Mr. Sawyer and Sean were with him.

"I'll bring the wagon and horse back as soon as I can," Rachel said quietly. She did not want either Wyatt or Horace to hear and argue with her more.

"Doc Bamburger—"

"I'll watch over them."

"Out at River's Haven?"

She nodded.

Mr. Sawyer said, "I figured you might say that." He held out a small jar. "Doc Bamburger sent this. He wasn't sure if you'd take it from him directly."

"Thank him, please." She lowered her eyes, embarrassed that River's Haven's ways had stood in the way of a kindness. "Thank everyone for us, please."

He handed her the jar and slapped the side of the wagon. "Sean can go with you and drive the wagon back. He's had plenty of practice with the store's deliveries."

"All right," she replied. "Do you know the way back from River's Haven, Sean?"

"Sure do." The boy raised his chin with pride.

"We have room," Mr. Sawyer said. "You don't need to go all the way out there."

Rachel kept her voice low. "Yes, I do, for many reasons. The most important is that Wyatt will be determined to get back to work right away if he's within view of the boat."

Mr. Anderson's grizzled brows rose. "I guess you know what you're doing."

She gave him no answer as she lifted Kitty Cat up onto the seat, then climbed beside her while Sean scrambled up on the other side of Kitty Cat. It had been a long time since she had driven a wagon, but she doubted if she had forgotten how. With a quick command to the horse, she turned it to follow the river in the direction of River's Haven.

Mr. Anderson's words resonated through her head. *I guess you know what you're doing.* She hoped she did.

* * *

Wyatt woke to pain. Every breath he took ached through his whole body. Fire flickered along his arms and across his chest and down his left leg. His left cheek felt as if every bit of skin had been scoured from it. When he began to cough, he wondered if he was dying. If so, he wished he would do so quickly and be rid of this pain.

Then the coughing eased.

He opened his eyes and frowned. Where in perdition's name was he? The bed did not rock with the motion of *The Rampart*. No, he had left that boat and its useless crew who preferred drinking to making deals for cargo. He could remember him and Horace collecting their final pay—a paltry amount—and leaving to look for other work. There always was plenty for rivermen along the Ohio. It had been less than two hours later that they signed onto *The Ohio Star*. Captain Hancock had appeared to be an astute businessman . . . and he was, but he was no good piloting the boat or overseeing a crew, especially when drunk as he had been when he drove *The Ohio Star* up onto a sandbank.

Wyatt smiled. The captain's bungling had been his and Horace's opportunity to get a boat and find a crew who shared their like for hard work and big profits. They had brought the boat down the river to the first town with a railroad station.

Haven . . . and Rachel.

He looked around and, this time, recognized where he was when he saw the guitar against the wall. Rachel's bedroom in her cottage at River's Haven. He frowned. What was he doing *here*? Not that he minded being in her bedroom and apparently in her bed, but he did not want to be here without her.

Pushing himself up to a seated position, he hung his head as he fought to breathe. Every bit of air teased his throat to explode with more coughs. What had happened? He needed some answers. Now.

It took every bit of his flagging strength to swing his legs out from beneath the covers and put his feet on the floor. He breathed shallowly, concentrating on gaining enough stamina to stand. He could never remember being this weak, not even after joining Horace in a riverside tavern to toast—again and again—the birth of Horace's most recent child.

He pressed his feet to the floor, gripping the headboard to stand. He shuffled toward the door, his hand on the wall to keep himself from tipping over. His knees refused to lock, so he could manage no more than this shuffling toward the door. He wondered where Rachel was.

As if he had spoken her name, he heard Rachel ask in a near whisper, "Are you awake?"

"Yes. Otherwise I'm walking in my sleep." His voice sounded scratchy and crotchety. He dropped to a bench.

"No!" she cried as she rushed forward to put the cup she was carrying on the dresser beside him.

He scowled, and pain swept across his face. "You don't want me sitting here? Rachel, I—"

Settling his arm over her shoulder, she guided him to his feet as she ordered, "You need to be in bed."

When Wyatt did not respond to her provocative comment, Rachel knew he was hurting more than he wanted her to see. He leaned heavily on her as she steered him back to her bed. She stared at the mussed covers. How was she going to help him lie down?

"Just let me go," he murmured close to her ear.

She did, and he sat heavily on the bed.

"I'm sorry," she said as she handed him the cup she had brought in.

"It's not your fault." He downed the water in the cup. "What happened?"

Rachel took the cup and quickly began to explain about the fire. He waved her to silence as a grim expression settled on his face.

"You need to rest now," she added.

"Where's Horace?"

"In Kitty Cat's room. He's sleeping. You should be, too."
She set the cup back on the dresser before he figured out
there had been more than water in it.

She stayed beside him, answering his questions, until he
drifted off to sleep. A tincture of opium in the water was
enough to make sure both men got some healing rest before
they demanded that they go and fix the boat.

Patches of red on Wyatt's left cheek and forehead glistened with the salve she had put on them. His bare fore-
arms were spotted with the same burned blotches and
salve. When he woke, she would find out where else he
might have been burned. She did not want to disturb him
and bring on more coughing spells.

Going out into the cottage's main room, she smiled
when she saw Kitty Cat curled up on the sofa, her rag doll
held tightly against her. She continued on into the kitchen
and rinsed out the cup. As she dried it, the knob on the
front door turned.

Rachel stiffened. She could not halt herself. River's Haven had been hidden in a thick fog, as thick as the smoke
by *The Ohio Star*, when the livery wagon came and left.
She had hoped that no one had taken note of it.

Telling herself not to act as if anything was amiss, she
went to the door. Her eyes widened when she saw, not her
brother or Mr. Foley, but Miss Hanson who oversaw the
small children each day.

"Miss Browning," the gray-haired woman said,
"Katherine didn't show up this morning. When I went
to your office—"

"Katherine is here." Rachel stepped back enough to let
Miss Hanson enter, because her exhausted brain could not
think of an excuse to keep the older woman out.

"I'm glad she's all right. She . . . What are you wearing,
Miss Browning?"

Looking down at herself, Rachel realized that she had been so busy taking care of the others that she had forgotten to change out of her borrowed clothes and into the garments she wore here at River's Haven. She must say something, so she decided on the truth.

"These are clothes that Mrs. Sawyer, who owns the store in Haven, lent me." She forced a smile. "As you can see, Mrs. Sawyer isn't quite as tall as I am."

"Why did you need Mrs. Sawyer's clothes?"

Rachel put her finger to her lips. "Please speak quietly. Katherine is sleeping."

"What were you doing in Haven?"

Rachel knew the cost of hesitation could be astronomical. Quietly, she said, "I went into Haven to get Katherine who had thought I wished her to take a message about the parts Mr. Colton ordered to *The Ohio Star*. When she didn't return right away, I went to get her. Then we were caught there in the storm. Who would have guessed it would last so long?"

"You should have."

"I know. I have to admit that I was thinking only of getting her home safely. Then the fire—"

Miss Hanson sat at the table. "I think you should start from the beginning, Miss Browning."

Rachel gave her an abridged version of what had happened after Horace had discovered the fires on *The Ohio Star*. Miss Hanson's frown lengthened her round face as she listened.

Before Rachel was finished, Miss Hanson gasped, "You ninny! You brought those two men here? If anyone else discovers *him* here, you'll be answering to the Assembly of Elders."

"Be reasonable, Miss Hanson," she argued quietly. She knew *him* meant Wyatt, and she also knew that Miss Hanson was right to be more concerned with what the Assembly of Elders thought about Wyatt being here than they would about Horace. "After all, Mr. Colton is hurt. I couldn't leave him untended."

"They've got a doctor in Haven."

"That's true, but I didn't want them having to live in the hotel there while they recovered. Don't you see that, Miss Hanson?"

The gray-haired woman came to her feet and shook her head. "What I see, Miss Browning, is that your kind heart is going to lead you into trouble. You know that the River's Haven Community doesn't welcome outsiders to live within its bounds."

"I'm not asking them to live here," she answered slowly. Why hadn't she considered this alternative? She and Wyatt could not be together if he was an outsider. Wyatt had denounced the Community over and over, but would he reconsider now that his boat was in need of even more repairs? She knew it was unlikely, but she must ask.

"Take care, Miss Browning." Miss Hanson opened the door.

"You won't tell anyone, will you?"

The older woman paused. "Miss Browning, I've seen all the goodness in you, because you've taken that young rascal into your heart as if she were your own from birth. I don't want you hurt because of your kind heart." Facing Rachel, she raised one finger. "But only this time. If you are so foolish again . . ." She walked out of the cottage, closing the door behind her.

That was one bit of advice that Rachel was glad to accept.

Rachel yawned and rubbed her eyes. It was just barely past dark, but this had been a long day with no chance to rest. Keeping Kitty Cat quiet so she did not disturb Wyatt and Horace had been a full-time task in itself. Finally she had sent the little girl out to play, hoping Kitty Cat would keep her promise not to spill the news that the men were here.

Lightning flashed through the room, and Rachel lit a lamp against the darkness cast by the thick clouds rising up over the river. Maybe this storm would wash the heaviness out of the air.

She went into her bedroom and opened the lowest drawer of the dresser to pull out another blanket. She would use it later when she slept wrapped up in this scratchy blanket beside Kitty Cat. That way if anyone stirred she would be certain to hear. Setting the blanket on the bench, she went to the window.

She froze as a hand caught her arm. Looking back at the bed shadowed by the storm, she said, "I'm sorry to wake you, Wyatt. I was going to close the windows before rain came in."

"Go ahead." Wyatt's voice was husky with sleep.

"How are you doing?"

"Well enough." He drew her down to sit on the edge of the bed. Then, with a laugh, he pulled her toward him. She gasped as she toppled onto him. She wanted to ask him if he was mad, but she had no chance. With a swift motion, he tipped her onto her back. He captured her mouth before she could speak.

She raised her hands to push him away before she succumbed to his easy seduction. It was too late, for her fingers curled along his nape, eager to touch him.

When he raised his mouth from hers and cursed, she asked, "How could you be so foolish? You're hurt!"

"It's not foolish to want what we had last night, honey."

"It is when you're hurt."

He grinned wryly as she started to wiggle out from beneath him. Pinning her shoulders to the pillow, he murmured, "Not too hurt to enjoy that."

"You're a rogue, Wyatt Colton."

"And you're too pretty to resist." He shifted to kiss her, then grimaced.

This time, Rachel did not let him tease her into staying in his arms. She slipped off the bed. "If you don't have the good sense to know when you must take it easy, then you're going to pay with pain."

"I thought you'd have *some* sympathy for me."

"I do. Do you want more salve for your arm?"

"For my leg, honey." When he sat, she saw the scorched marks on the left leg of his denim trousers. How had she missed them before? "I could use some of that salve on them."

"Of course." She went to the dresser to get the jar Doc Bamburger had had Mr. Sawyer deliver to her. When she turned back to the bed, she tightened her grip on the jar and stared as Wyatt peeled off his denims.

Her heart pounded ferociously while she stood, unable to move or speak, as he kicked aside the trousers. Her feet seemed to be stuck as if the floor had become river mud. She had to force them to move . . . at a slow pace instead of running to his side.

She knelt as she opened the jar. Her fingers quivered as she spread the salve along the crimson burns, trying to pay no attention to the strong muscles beneath her fingertips. Her breath came fast and shallow when she tended to one long burn rising along his thigh.

A hand on her hair tilted her face back. He took the jar from her and set it on her dressing table. Then he drew her to her feet.

"Rachel," he whispered with raw yearning.

"You're hurt," she answered as softly. She picked up the jar and took it back to the dresser before she was unable to resist the longing in his gaze.

"I'm hurting more for you, honey."

She faced him. When he held out his arms, she closed

the door. He smiled, and she rushed to slip into his embrace once more.

"Are you sure this won't hurt you worse?" she gasped as his mouth coursed along her neck while he leaned her back beneath him once more.

"If it does, you can massage more of that salve into me."

She laughed before she drew his mouth over hers and surrendered to the storm enveloping them, sweeping away everything but ecstasy.

Seventeen

Wyatt woke as suddenly as if someone had poked him. He slipped out of Rachel's bed, taking care not to wake her. If he did, she would ask him what was wrong. He would explain, and soon her gentle touch would steal him from this sorrow.

He wanted to kill it his own way. Her sweet touch was a delight, but he had to grieve for what had almost been lost in the fire on *The Ohio Star*. Not just his and Horace's dream of owning their own boat, but Rachel and K. C.

If he thought about who had set fire to the boat . . . But that was what he did not want to do. He wanted to drown every thought until it vanished from his head once and for all.

Tiptoeing into the cottage's main room, he found his way to the kitchen. He took down the bottle of wine that Rachel kept there. Seeing the glint of another bottle behind it, he picked up that one and twisted off the top. He poured a large glassful. He downed it. Whiskey! Refilling it, he took it and the bottle to a chair with a view of the river.

"Wyatt?" Astonishment was in Rachel's soft voice.

He smiled as he drank in the sight of her as avidly as he had the whiskey. Her white nightgown became luminous in the light from the crescent moon, and he wondered why she ever wore black. This color was perfect for her. Raising his glass, he asked, "Do you want a drink, honey?"

"No, thank you." She frowned. "Are you all right?"

"I need some time alone to think." *Or not think,* he corrected himself.

"Wyatt, I'd be glad to sit with you."

He took her hand and pressed his mouth to her delicious skin. "I know you hate to be alone, but I need to be just now."

"All right, but if you need anything else other than the whiskey—"

"You'll know because you'll be what I need."

She kissed the top of his head as gently as if he were as young as K. C.

In spite of his words, he stared after her as she went back to her bedroom. He could have gone with her, but tonight he had to think about how to fix *The Ohio Star*. He hoped Horace could dig up some more money from wherever he had found the cash for their food. Looking out the window at the moon-swept river, he smiled. They would repair the boat and get back to their lives on the river. It would be everything he had dreamed of since he was young. An easy life with no ties to the shore. He glanced again at the hallway that led to Rachel's bedroom. Maybe one tie.

When the afternoon sunshine beat on his eyelids, Wyatt groaned. His mouth tasted bad, and his whole body reeked. He forced himself to his feet. No one else seemed to be around. At this hour, K. C. would be playing with the other kids, and Rachel was probably at her office in the big building. He had no idea where Horace might be. Maybe his partner was still asleep.

He lurched to Rachel's bedroom. A quick glance into K. C.'s room revealed that Horace was sprawled on the little girl's bed, snoring loudly.

Wyatt groaned again. Horace's snoring was enough to make his head ache, but today, in the wake of the whiskey he had downed last night, his head threatened to explode like an overworked boiler.

After he washed up, he ran his hand along his cheeks. No wonder Rachel had kissed him on the crown last night. His face was as rough as splintered wood. He would not be able to shave until he got back to *The Ohio Star*.

His steps were a bit steadier as he went back out to the kitchen. He had just reached the table when the door opened.

Rachel was whistling a happy melody as she strolled in, her arms full of flowers. She halted immediately, but her eyes brightened. "Good afternoon, stay-abed!"

K. C. skipped in and put her finger to her lips. "You said to be quiet for Wyatt and Horace."

"So I did." She reached for a vase and put the flowers in it. Then she poured a cup of fragrant coffee and set it on the table in front of him. "How badly does your head hurt, Wyatt?"

He dropped to a chair, then winced as the motion ached through him. "Imagine being run over by a dray drawn by eight draft horses, and you'll have some idea."

Softly, she said, "Go back to bed, and get some more sleep. It's not just the whiskey. Don't forget you got pretty banged up fighting the fire."

"You take good care of me." He tweaked K. C.'s nose, and she giggled. "Both of you."

"Rachel says I need to say thank you for saving Shirley," K. C. said.

"The rag doll," Rachel murmured.

He took a deep drink of the coffee and leaned back with a sigh. "I always try to save damsels in distress."

Rachel sent K. C. back outside to play. As she closed the door, she leaned against it and said, "Kitty Cat isn't the only one who needs to say thank you. We're both grateful for you finding the rag doll, even though it was foolhardy."

"Both?" It took a moment for his befuddled brain to work before he could ask, "Was that your doll before it was K. C.'s?"

"My mother made it for me when I was even younger than Kitty Cat. That and only a few other things here are all I have left from home . . . from Ohio."

He could not miss the wistful sorrow in her eyes. Maybe she had persuaded everyone—even herself—that she was happy here, but there still was a part of her that longed to go back to the sort of life she once had known.

Looking away, he cursed too low for her to hear. She wanted what she had once had. A life he could not give her.

At the knock, Rachel motioned for Kitty Cat to remain at the table and finish her supper along with Wyatt and Horace. Who was knocking? No one knocked at River's Haven, and she had come up with excuses to keep everyone away—even suggesting Kitty Cat was getting sick so no one would call. She opened the door only far enough to look out, not wanting anyone to see Wyatt and Horace. A lanky man she did not know stood on the other side. Then she realized she had seen him on the pier. He had helped Mr. Sawyer fish Wyatt and Horace out of the river.

"Miss Browning?" he asked, tipping his hat.

"Yes. You are . . . ?"

"Sheriff Parker, miss. I understand Mr. Colton and Mr. Appleby are here."

She almost asked who Mr. Appleby was, then realized that must be Horace's last name. Stepping back, she opened the door wider. "Come in."

"Thank you, miss." He smiled at Kitty Cat, who was

regarding him with eager curiosity. "Colton, Appleby," he said with a nod in their direction.

"Have you eaten, Sheriff?" Rachel asked.

"I don't want to intrude on your meal."

"Nonsense." She laughed as she ushered him in and quickly closed the door. "I took a lesson from Horace and cooked extra."

Kitty Cat jumped up to get a chair for Sheriff Parker. When she pushed it across the floor, Wyatt winced and Horace mumbled something under his breath. Before the little girl could push it farther and aggravate the men's aching heads more, Rachel picked up the chair and set it down for the sheriff.

Wyatt pushed aside his plate and folded his arms on the table. "I trust you're here, Sheriff, because you want to know what happened on *The Ohio Star*."

"I'd appreciate you telling me what you heard and saw." He smiled when Rachel put a plate in front of him. Picking up a slice of bread, he took a big bite that suggested he had not had anything to eat all day.

"Heard?" He laughed shortly. "Nothing but the storm. Horace, did you hear or see something?"

"The odor of smoke woke me. When you've been cooking on the river as long as I have, Sheriff, you notice the smell of smoke straightaway. I woke up and saw flames on the upper decks, so I got the young'un here and alerted Wyatt and Miss Rachel."

The sheriff looked back at her. "What of you, Miss Browning? Did you or the child see anything out of the ordinary?"

"No. We were asleep until Horace woke us." She picked up Kitty Cat and set the child on her lap.

"So the fire might have been started by the storm?" asked the sheriff.

"No," Wyatt answered as he scowled. "It was set. I

found a scorched, greasy rag on the lower deck. It must have tumbled down there when the fire was being set."

Sheriff Parker frowned. "Who are your enemies?"

"Horace doesn't have any, and I didn't until I came here to Haven."

Rachel tightened her arms around Kitty Cat until the little girl wiggled out of her grip. "Wyatt, are you saying that you think someone from River's Haven set the fire?"

"Don't you?" he asked sharply.

"I don't know what to think."

Tilting his hat back from his forehead, Sheriff Parker said, "Let's not jump to any conclusions. I take it that the folks here at River's Haven haven't taken a shine to you, Colton."

"No."

"Why?"

Wyatt glanced at Rachel before saying, "These folks don't like outsiders, and I guess I've riled them up with a few of my comments when I came out here to order parts for *The Ohio Star.*"

"Is that all?"

"No," answered Rachel before Wyatt could speak. "They aren't happy about the friendship Kitty Cat and I have with Wyatt and Horace."

"That's still no reason to burn a man's boat." Sheriff Parker stood. "I think I'll knock on a few more doors here and ask some more questions."

"Don't!" She leaped to her feet. "The Assembly of Elders won't allow you to ask questions here."

"I represent the law in this county."

"But not in River's Haven."

Wyatt put his hand on Rachel's shoulder. "Listen to her, Sheriff Parker. She knows what she's talking about. Is there a way the sheriff can get permission to talk to River's Haven folks, honey?"

She saw the sheriff's eyes narrow at Wyatt's endearment,

but answered quickly, "There's only one way. You must present your request personally to the Assembly of Elders, Sheriff Parker."

"Where can I find them?"

"They receive callers from outside the Community only once a month, and that day has already passed this month."

The sheriff muttered something that she did not ask him to repeat.

"Maybe," she added, "if you were to ask Reverend Faulkner to speak with them, they'd be willing to make an exception. They have before because they respect him."

"Just not the laws outside this place?"

"That's right." She was not going to dodge the truth.

"I can see this is going to be more complicated than I had guessed." He turned to Wyatt and Horace. "When will you be returning to *The Ohio Star*? I'd like you to show me around and point out what was damaged in the fire."

"It's pretty obvious." Wyatt scowled. "How about tomorrow, about midmorning?"

"Tomorrow, about midmorning, it'll be." He tipped his hat to Rachel again. "Thank you for your hospitality, Miss Browning. It was, I admit, more than I thought I'd find out here. Good evening." He looked at Wyatt again. "And I hope a much better tomorrow."

Rachel looked up as the cottage door opened, allowing in the moon's glow, which was dimmed by fog. When she saw Wyatt enter, she wanted to jump up and throw her arms around him. Her last caller had been Mr. Foley, who had been quite insistent that she go for a ride with him tomorrow "to talk about the rumors I've been hearing." She had few doubts what he might have heard. By now, everyone in River's Haven must know that Wyatt and Horace had spent last night in her cottage.

Mr. Foley had been polite, as he always was. He had

not interrogated her about her guests or why she had agreed to let them come to stay with her. Instead he had given her hands a kind squeeze and said how he looked forward to their ride tomorrow afternoon.

Merrill had not called, and Rachel was grateful that he was too busy enjoying his new wife to think about his wayward sister. Merrill would not have been as pleasant as Mr. Foley.

"You're up late," Wyatt said, hanging his hat on the peg by her door as if he had done the same thing hundreds of times before. "Where are Horace and K. C.?"

"Kitty Cat is asleep in her own bed. Horace is sleeping on the floor of her room. I told him that he could have the sofa, but he said he didn't mind sleeping in there."

"I guess he thought we might like a little privacy to talk about things."

"Do you want a cup of coffee?"

He nodded. "That might be a good idea. No, don't get up. Just tell me where the cups are."

"On the shelf over the table."

"I'll find them."

When Wyatt came back to the sofa, he was carrying two cups. He handed her one.

Taking it, she asked, "Are you feeling better? You're walking better."

He grinned. "You're about the best medicine any man could wish for, honey."

Setting her cup on the table by the sofa, she said, "We do need to talk, Wyatt."

"And we will." He put his cup right next to hers. "Later."

He pressed her back onto the cushions. While his mouth explored her neck, his breath billowed against her skin, inviting her to open herself to him again. With regret, she looked up at his strong face. He was the realization of her dreams, but she was not sure if he knew that.

"We must stop," she whispered.

"I don't want to, honey, but . . ." He sat and drew her up beside him. His fingers combed through her hair that had tumbled out of its loose bun. "I know you want to hear about *The Ohio Star*."

"Horace told me it's repairable."

"One deck has a hole in it, and the railing is broken in two places. Otherwise, the wood's just charred. It can be scraped down or replaced."

"How will you pay for the materials?"

"Horace tells me he has a few dollars stashed away, and we've got a shipment to deliver down the river. It's coming in on the train, and *The Ohio Star* takes over from there. What we earn should be enough for the wood we'll need. Mrs. Sawyer will advance us the wood, I'm sure, because she gave us the commission to take down the river."

Rachel stared at him. She did not know what to say. She had known that eventually Wyatt would be leaving Haven, but she had not guessed he would tell her this right after they had become lovers. She had hoped—futilely she realized now—he loved her enough to stay.

"When did you know about this?" she asked softly.

"A few days ago. I haven't had a chance to tell you." He curved his hand along her cheek. "Honey, I didn't want to tell you when you were in my arms. I wanted those moments to be perfect."

"When do you leave?"

He lowered his hand. "Some time shortly after the Centennial celebration. It depends on when the shipment arrives on the train." He took her hands. "Honey, I'll be back. Leave River's Haven and find a place to stay in Haven. After all, if you stay here, you'll probably end up married to Foley."

Rachel got up. "Those aren't my only two choices, so why do you keep suggesting that I leave River's Haven?"

"I thought it was obvious."

"If you think this is the way to seduce me—"

"It is." Standing, he put his hands on her shoulders. "To seduce you into being rational and leaving this place. You don't belong here."

"Why do you care?"

"Horace asked me the same thing. He told me I was a fool."

"Listening to you now, I'd have to agree."

"But I've got another solution to this problem."

"What is it?"

"Honey, you want to stay here. I can't stay here. You don't want to get married. Neither do I. If I stay with *The Ohio Star* and stop to see you each time I pass here, we can have what we both want—a life free of commitments and with each other."

"Are you serious?" she gasped. Her head was reeling with all that had happened in the past days.

"Yes, I thought it'd make you happy."

"To be with you only when you have the time to stop by and see me?"

"You know it'd be as often as possible." He arched a brow. "After all, that arrangement has worked well for Horace and his families."

"Wyatt, that won't work for me. I don't want to spend the rest of my life alone, waiting for you to come to see me whenever you decide to." *But I don't want to say good-bye either,* she added silently.

"Rachel—"

She put her fingers to his lips and said, "Maybe you have it backward, Wyatt."

"Backward? How?"

"Instead of me leaving River's Haven, why don't you come and live here?"

He stared at her in astonishment. "What did you say?"

"Kitty Cat and I have enough room in our cottage for another."

"Foley intends to take that spot."

Grasping his sleeve, she said, "Forget about that for now."

"Honey, Foley won't forget that."

"I'm not talking about Mr. Foley. I'm talking about *you*."

"Are you seriously asking me to become a member of the River's Haven Community?"

"Yes."

He laughed so hard that he bent almost in half. He began to cough.

"I didn't mean for it to be a jest," she said, handing him a cup of water.

"But it's funny." He drank the water and set down the cup.

"No, it isn't. I came here because I loved my brother enough not to want to leave him to create a new life alone." She swallowed harshly. "Isn't that what love is? Sacrificing for those you love?"

"Love?" He shook his head. "Don't bring that into this discussion."

"How can I leave it out? You must know that I've fallen in love with you. Otherwise, I wouldn't have stayed with you on *The Ohio Star*."

"Rachel, I thought you wanted to avoid any complications, too."

"Am I just another convenient bit of fluff for you?" Blinking back tears, she kept her voice low. Had Merrill been right? Had Wyatt Colton been using her? "I won't be so convenient any longer, I can assure you."

His jaw tightened. "I thought this was what you wanted. You said you didn't want to get married."

"How lucky for you! You get to tumble me like a cheap whore, and then you can walk away without a care." Her hands clenched at her sides. "I'm no whore! I don't lift my skirts for just any man."

"I never meant to suggest that you did. I didn't mean any of this!"

"I did." Her voice broke as she backed away. "I meant every bit of the love I offered you."

She went into her bedroom, closing the door. She waited for the latch to move . . . and waited and waited until dawn, but it never did.

Eighteen

Rachel adjusted her bonnet as she closed the cottage's red door behind her. Kitty Cat was going to spend the afternoon playing with the other children. Wyatt had gone back to *The Ohio Star* with Horace before dawn. No one was here to ease her anxiety as she went to meet Mr. Foley at the stable for a carriage ride.

It would have been far easier to face Mr. Foley if she had not given herself to Wyatt. What a nincompoop she had been! He had *told* her that he wanted no commitments, even as her heart was pleading to belong to him.

Bugs buzzed along the river, their strident song adding to the tension that made her muscles ache. The sun burned through her bonnet, for the storms had not decreased either the heat or the humidity.

Rachel paused at the door of the stable, waiting for her eyes to adjust from the bright sunshine. She took a deep breath of the aromas of horses and straw and leather polish. When she and Merrill had lived on the farm in Ohio, she had loved helping their father clean his saddle.

As her eyes began to see through the dimness, two forms emerged from the other shadows. She started to call a greeting, but quickly clamped her mouth shut. She stared, unable to believe what was right in front of her. A man and a woman kissing with obvious ardor. Mr. Foley and . . . Miss Turnbull, who was now his ex-wife. She wanted to believe that she was mistaken. When the two drew apart, smiling at each other, she knew she was not.

Miss Turnbull ran her fingers along Mr. Foley's cheek with the gentleness that suggested that they had recently shared far more than this one illicit kiss. Rachel had seen that satisfied expression on Wyatt's face when she was lying beside him in his bed. Had Mr. Foley and Miss Turnbull had a tryst right here in the stable? That was possible, for no one else was in sight.

She must leave, for she could not imagine what she might say to Mr. Foley and his onetime wife. As she shifted to take a step back, her gaze locked with Mr. Foley's. Shock and fury mixed in his eyes before his mouth stretched in a rigid smile.

"Calvin, my love, what's wrong?" asked Miss Turnbull. "You look positively distressed."

Mr. Foley continued to stare at Rachel as he said, "Miss Browning has joined us."

With a tiny squeal of dismay, Miss Turnbull whirled. She jabbed her hair back under her bonnet, but Rachel could see that it was loose and mussed.

"Just as I supposedly joined you," Rachel said quietly, "on a carriage ride. There wasn't any meeting you were trying to avoid, was there, Miss Turnbull?"

As Miss Turnbull's face bleached, Mr. Foley put his hand on his former wife's arm and said, "I'll see you this evening at dinner in the Community room. If you'll excuse Miss Browning and me . . ."

Was he going to pretend that nothing amiss had happened here? Did he think that Rachel would not recognize what had taken place between the two of them? She wanted to ask those questions but bit them back as Miss Turnbull murmured something and vanished into the dusk at the far end of the stable.

Straightening his dark waistcoat, Mr. Foley strode toward Rachel. His smile did not warm as he offered his arm.

She did not put her hand on it as she said, "I believe it'd be better if we canceled *this* carriage ride, Mr. Foley. It appears to be an inopportune time for you."

"Do you believe so?" He moved closer to her.

She pressed back against the wall. Something caught at her skirt as she tried to slide away. His hand on her arm kept her from harboring any ideas of fleeing. She squared her shoulders. She did not want to escape. She wanted him to explain why he had been kissing his ex-wife.

Mr. Foley continued to smile. She said nothing, and his lips fell. He wanted her to beg him to let her go. What an arrogant idiot! Did he think she would forget the rights she had to denounce him to the Assembly of Elders?

She clasped her hands in front of her. Mr. Foley was not the idiot. She was. As a member of the Assembly of Elders, his lies would be believed instead of her truth.

"Come with me, Miss Browning," he said. "Our conversation is more suited for a ride along the river."

"No. I'm going to return to my cottage to do some chores."

"I'll walk you there."

Rachel wanted to decline his company again, but she knew she could not tell him that he was unwelcome to walk anywhere he chose at River's Haven. He said nothing until they reached her cottage. When he opened her door, she wanted to pull it closed behind her.

She faced him as he entered. "If you're intending to explain why you and Miss Turnbull are breaking River's Haven's laws, I—"

"*You* are the one breaking our laws, Rachel." His superior tone returned.

"There's no law against being friendly with our neighbors." She would not pretend not to understand what he meant. There had been too many lies and half-truths already. She untied her bonnet, and set it on the table.

"Neighbors, not outsiders."

She crossed her arms in front of her. "I'll be glad to admit my questionable actions in front of the Assembly of Elders, if you're as willing to admit to yours."

"You know you're to play a special part in my life. What part does that river rat play in yours?"

As she sat on the sofa, Rachel saw rage had come back into his eyes. Until Wyatt had arrived at River's Haven, she had never seen Mr. Foley so angry. She did not like what she was discovering about this man the Assembly of Elders wished her to marry.

"Don't be jealous of Wyatt." She would not be a hypocrite like Mr. Foley and speak of Wyatt as *Mr. Colton.*

"Should I be? Have you been giving him what should be mine alone?"

He sat, pulling her to him. When he kissed her, she shoved him away.

"Mr. Foley, it's clear you and Miss Turnbull are lovers still." She scowled. "Why are you trying to pretend otherwise?"

As if she had remained silent, he went on. "I don't want you giving Colton even a single kiss because you're to be my second wife."

"While you still have a secret affair with your first wife?"

"You'll never speak of that again." His mouth twisted before it pressed over hers.

As he reached to draw her skirt higher along her legs, she cried, "Mr. Foley, stop!" She struggled against him, but he did not release her.

"Why are you resisting?" He smiled. "I can give you everything you want in River's Haven. After all, I obtained permission for anyone, who wished to, to go to Haven for the Centennial celebration." His smile vanished into a threatening scowl. "Prove to me that you want me instead of Colton."

"I don't need to prove anything to you."

"Yes, you do. Prove it to me now." His mouth over hers silenced her protest as he shoved her back onto the cushions, holding her arms tightly.

With a grimace, Rachel exerted every bit of her strength against him. It was not enough to break his grip, but she was able to roll out from beneath him. Sitting on the floor, she pointed to the door and ordered, "Get out! Now!"

"You can't tell me what to do."

"This is my home, and I can ask you to leave. Go, or—"

"Or you'll run to the other Elders with your lies?" He stood and adjusted his waistcoat as he had in the stable. Was that his way of pretending again that nothing out of the ordinary had happened?

"With the truth."

"Go ahead." He gestured toward the door as she had. "Go ahead and spread your filth as you spread your legs for Colton."

Pushing herself to her feet, Rachel paid no attention to the heat on her face at his coarse words. She should not be the one blushing. Mr. Foley was the liar, not her.

With quiet dignity, she said, "I'll spread the *truth,* if you don't leave."

He smiled again, a condescending smile. "It'll be very sad."

"What will be very sad?" She watched him closely, wondering what that smile augured.

"That your river rat is found floating in the river when his half-burned boat goes to the bottom."

"Are you saying if I go to the other Elders with the truth about how you and Miss Turnbull have thumbed your noses at River's Haven's compound marriage doctrine, you'll attack *The Ohio Star* . . . again?"

He patted her arm. "My dear, you're becoming irrational. I believe I'll have to speak to the Assembly of Elders about how you've obviously been overtaxed with taking care of that urchin. It's time we remedied that."

Rachel stepped back, wrapping her arms around herself. He was threatening to hurt both Wyatt and Kitty Cat. Lowering her eyes, she swallowed the bitter taste of defeat.

"There's no need to remedy anything," she said quietly. "I'll concentrate on taking care of Katherine and forget about everything else."

"Save our wedding."

She looked up at him, astounded. "But I thought that you wanted to be with—I mean—"

The door came open as Kitty Cat entered, singing a song that Miss Hanson must have taught the youngsters. The little girl became silent when she looked at Mr. Foley. Hurrying across the room, she grasped Rachel's skirt.

Rachel put her hand on Kitty Cat's shoulder and said, "Good afternoon, Mr. Foley. It's later than I thought, and I must begin preparing supper."

Mr. Foley picked up her bonnet and hung it on the peg by the door. Again he acted as if he had already moved into her house. She banked her shudder as her mind added, *and into my bed.*

"We'll have to have our carriage ride another day," he replied with a cool smile.

As he walked out, Rachel sank to the sofa. Kitty Cat climbed into her lap. Putting her cheek against the child's red curls, Rachel knew she should not have suggested that she would go to the Assembly of Elders about Mr. Foley's liaison with Miss Turnbull. He had so much influence among the Assembly of Elders. She wondered how he would use it to make her comply and which of his threats he would put into action.

One thing was clear: Mr. Foley intended to stay in Miss Turnbull's bed even after he wed her. Miss Turnbull was welcome to Mr. Foley. Rachel would be glad to be rid of him. Yet her heartache did not lessen. Merrill would be horrified, and this could tear at the very soul of River's

Haven. So many trusted Mr. Foley, and he had lied to all of them.

Just as Wyatt warned he would.

Wyatt was always honest with her, even when she did not want to hear what he had to say. He would accept no compromises and expected her to be the same.

If Mr. Foley spread his poisoned tales, all the blame would shift to Rachel. She remembered the family who had been banished from River's Haven because they would not accept the Community's rules. A shudder ached across her shoulders. Mr. Foley had voiced the complaints against them. When they had left, he had been given a seat on the Assembly of Elders. Had he used them to gain himself that prestige?

With a sigh, she knew she must be careful. She no longer knew whom she could trust in River's Haven. She feared it was no one.

Nineteen

When her office door opened, Rachel whirled, her pink striped skirt swirling around her knees. Her eyes widened as Wyatt entered. Despite herself, she could not help admiring the sleek motion of his muscles beneath his cotton shirt and dark trousers. Sweat stained his collar, and she guessed he had been working hard on *The Ohio Star*, even though it was barely past sunrise.

He gave an appreciative whistle. "Very nice. You look like a sweet ready to be opened, honey."

"What are you doing here?" She set down the book she had been looking at by the window. "Weren't all the parts you ordered already picked up?"

"The parts are fine. I came here today to get K. C. to take her into Haven to finish up the decorations for the parade. I promised her that I would when I saw her in town yesterday."

"She didn't mention that she'd seen you."

"No?" He shook his head with exaggerated regret as he sat on the corner of her desk. "And here I was hoping that you were all prettied up because you knew I was calling."

"If you haven't noticed, it's very hot. This is my coolest dress."

His arm slipped around her waist as he drew her to her

feet. "I hear there's a pond out near Jennings's farm where the kids go swimming."

"I don't own a swimming dress."

"You wouldn't need one if it's just you and me."

She closed her eyes to exult in the caress of his mouth against her neck and the image of his sleek body stroking hers in the cool water. His lips were a flame on her. Her arms curved up along his back as his mouth claimed hers. His eager fingers roamed along her when he tilted her back over his arm.

He lifted his mouth away from hers to whisper, "I've missed not seeing you for the past two days, honey, and I missed *this*."

"Me, too." Putting her hands on his cheeks, she brought his mouth down to hers.

He pulled her even closer. His hard body fit along her perfectly. All of her craving to love him again surged through her.

"If you keep doing that, we're going to be late." Kitty Cat's voice was filled with irritation.

Rachel gasped. She had not heard the door opening again. If someone else had seen her in Wyatt's arms . . . She began to laugh at the sight of the little girl standing with her arms crossed in front of her, her toe tapping impatiently. Squatting down, Rachel straightened the white bow at the waist of Kitty Cat's dress. Its green plaid was the perfect complement for her bright red hair.

"Why didn't you tell me you'd asked Wyatt to come and take you into Haven?" Rachel asked. "He's very busy with *The Ohio Star*, you know."

"I told you. I told you during . . ." Kitty Cat giggled. "I *meant* to tell you during dinner last night." She glanced quickly at Wyatt and then away before scurrying out of the office.

"What was that look?" Wyatt asked. "She acted as if she'd let the cat out of the bag."

Rachel sighed as she came to her feet. "Merrill and his new wife ate with us last night."

"And pestered you to explain why you haven't gotten hitched to Foley yet."

"Among other things." She forced a smile. "How's the work coming on *The Ohio Star*?"

"Why don't you come into Haven with us and see for yourself? Don't give me the excuse that you've got too much work to steal a few hours away before the rest of River's Haven is awake."

"It wouldn't be an excuse." Her smile became more genuine. "I do have a lot of work."

"And how are you going to concentrate on it when you're so curious about the boat?"

She glanced out the window. His offer was so tempting. Too tempting. She should walk away. Far away. So far away that this compelling man would no longer be a part of her life or Kitty Cat's. How much farther would she have to go until she could forget the thrill of being in his arms?

Wyatt watched Rachel's face, which revealed every thought. She was going to turn down his invitation. He could tell that by how her smile wavered. What had her brother said to her last night that had pulled her right back into line with River's Haven's laws? Or had it been Browning? Maybe Foley had said something to her.

"If you aren't coming out to *The Ohio Star* today, Rachel," he asked, "will you visit during the Centennial celebration tomorrow?"

She shook her head. "I don't know if we'll be there."

"On the boat or at the Centennial celebration?"

"Either."

As she turned away, he caught her hand. "Rachel . . ."

"I have all this work to do. It's going to take all day, and I want to be done so I can make Kitty Cat a good supper. She always is so hungry. Maybe because she's growing so quickly."

"And what of me?"

"You?"

He closed the door and stepped in front of her. As his fingers swept up along her face to tangle in her hair, he drew her so tightly to him that not even a sunbeam could slip between them. He bent so his eyes were even with hers. Her warm breath brushed his lips.

"I hunger, too," he murmured. "I see you holding K. C. to your breast, and I envy her."

"Wyatt, don't say this. Please don't say anything like that again."

"I thought we were going to be honest with each other."

"I thought we could, but some things need to remain unsaid."

He brushed a strand of hair back from her cheek. The soft silk stirred the craving in his gut. A craving that was as impossible to forget as this lovely woman who had infected his life with a fever for her.

His fingers slipped through her hair and tilted her mouth beneath his. He teased her lips with the tip of his tongue. As they softened, he tasted a hint of her morning coffee within her mouth. That was sweetened by her own dulcet flavors. As her breath pulsed, swift and eager in his mouth, he tightened his arms around her. He ached to sweep aside her pretty dress and hold her silken skin against him.

His hand brushed her breast, and she moaned against his lips. Delighting in her pleasure, which fired his own, he stroked her supple curves until she quivered with a need that tantalized him.

At the sound of footsteps in the corridor, he reluctantly released her. His fingers lingered on her cheek as he said, "I'll make sure K. C. gets home before supper tonight."

He thought she might ask him to join her and K. C. for the evening meal, but she replied only with, "Thank you."

Walking out of her office, he wondered what she was hiding. K. C. must not know, for Rachel would not have allowed the little girl to go with him, knowing how K. C. liked to chatter. This was a mystery he was going to have to unravel on his own.

Rachel was startled to see Wyatt and Kitty Cat waiting in the cottage when she arrived back there at day's end. They had opened all the windows that she had closed, fearing the heavy clouds building to the west meant rain. The clouds had passed overhead without releasing any rain, and now the sky was once again clear.

Kitty Cat ran up to her, prattling about the decorating she had done with the children in Haven and interrupting every sentence to say: "And wait until you see it, Rachel!"

"I can't wait."

"So," Wyatt drawled, "does that mean you're coming into Haven tomorrow for the parade and social?"

"Several people from River's Haven have expressed interest in attending the celebration," Rachel replied, hanging up her bonnet, "and Miss Hanson and the other teachers have decided that the children in River's Haven should have a recitation like the students in Haven will. I don't want to miss Kitty Cat's hard work."

Kitty Cat cheered and danced around the room.

Wyatt watched the little girl. "K. C. tells me that you play the guitar well."

"The guitar?" She had not expected him to change the subject so abruptly.

"How about showing me after dinner?"

Rachel laughed. "You're about as transparent as a handful of water."

"I didn't intend to be mysterious, too."

She picked up a bucket of vegetables that she had asked to have delivered from the Community's garden. Sitting at the table, she began to chop the ends off the onions and early potatoes.

He plucked the knife from her hand. "Let me while you serenade us."

"I thought you wanted to wait until after dinner."

"So am I invited to stay?"

Smiling, she said, "I don't think I have much choice."

"Honey, I've told you over and over that you've got all kinds of choices. You just have to grab the one you want."

When he held out his hand to her, she slipped her fingers through his. Wyatt infuriated her. He was demanding, sure of himself, and yearned to remake the world to meet his expectations. In those ways, he was like her. As he ran a crooked finger along her cheek, she reveled in the thought of how different he was as well, so male and dangerous.

"There are some choices I don't have. I can't keep you here with Kitty Cat and me," she whispered.

"No, but—"

"Don't make your offer to me again."

"Why?" he asked, looking up from the vegetables. "Because you might accept it?"

"Because we might have another argument, and I don't want to quarrel again when you're leaving on *The Ohio Star* so soon."

When Kitty Cat bounced into the kitchen to sit next to Wyatt, she watched as the two of them teased each other during the preparations for their simple supper and throughout the meal. Kitty Cat adored Wyatt, and Rachel could understand why. He treated the little girl with a mixture of tenderness and teasing and with honesty.

As soon as the dishes were done, Wyatt sent Kitty Cat to retrieve Rachel's guitar. The child was barely out of earshot before he asked, "Why didn't you tell me that it was her birthday tomorrow?"

"I don't like to think about it."

"Why not? Don't you celebrate birthdays in River's Haven?"

"Of course we celebrate birthdays. It's just that Kitty Cat is turning seven."

"So?"

She could evade the question as she had before, but Wyatt had to know why Kitty Cat would not be coming to *The Ohio Star* after tomorrow. "When a child turns seven at River's Haven, that child goes to live with the other children in a special section of the common house."

He stared at her. His mouth opened, then closed. With a curse, he strode across the main room to look out the window. "Why didn't you tell me this before?"

"I've been trying to put it out of my mind. I don't want her to go."

"Does she know?"

"She knows the rules, but I don't think she's connected them with herself." She said nothing else as Kitty Cat came into the room, balancing the guitar with care.

"Play my favorite song first," the little girl requested as she sat next to Rachel on the sofa.

Setting the guitar across her lap, Rachel asked, "Wyatt, are you going to join us?"

He nodded and walked back to sit on her other side. Sorrow lengthened his face, just as it had when he had fought the fire on *The Ohio Star*. It startled her, for she had not guessed he would care about Kitty Cat or anything or anyone else as much as he did his boat.

Rachel pretended not to see his expression as she asked quietly, "Are you set to sing?"

"Why don't you warm up your fingers," he replied. "Then we'll sing K. C.'s favorite song."

She tried to respond in a cheerful tone. "You sound as if you don't believe I can play very well."

"I've no doubts that you do everything well." His fingers teased her nape, and she closed her eyes to bask in the fleeting caress.

"C'mon and play, Rachel." Kitty Cat jumped up. "I want to sing and dance."

Rachel chose a piece that required every bit of her concentration. That way, she must think of the notes and not of how Wyatt's leg brushed hers as she bent over the guitar. The music lilted through the room, lingering even after she had played the last note.

"Lovely!" Wyatt clapped.

Kitty Cat giggled. "I told you she played very pretty music."

"So you did." He tapped her on the nose. "I guess I'll have to listen more closely to you from now on, K. C."

"She's going to teach me to play!"

"Is that so?" His expression was somber as he turned back to Rachel. "After your birthday?"

"It's tomorrow!" Kitty Cat spun on her toes again. "My birthday and the country's birthday. Don't you think it is just perfect that we both have the same birthday?"

"I think I'd like to hear you and Rachel sing."

Rachel settled the guitar on her lap and said, "You can sing, too, Wyatt. Do you know 'Greensleeves'?" When he nodded, she picked the first few notes on the guitar. She smiled at Kitty Cat and said, "Now."

Wyatt started to sing, but let his voice drift away as he listened to Rachel sing with the little girl. Rachel let K. C. take the melody while she and the guitar combined to create the harmony for the haunting tune. The sad song in its minor key took on new life as they sang it together. If he had not known before, he could see now how much Rachel needed this little girl and how much K. C. needed her. It would not matter whether they lived in the middle of this silly utopian experiment or in the little village of Haven or in the biggest city in the land. They belonged together.

His arm tightened around Rachel's waist as she swayed with the gentle rhythm her fingers drew from the strings. When she and K. C. finished the first verse, her hands remained on the strings, but she did not continue to play. His breath caught as Rachel raised her eyes to meet his. The rhythms still swirled through him, enticing and urging him to sweep away the song's sorrow as he brought her to the pinnacle of sensation when he was once more a part of her. The subtly passionate words touched him as never before. All he wanted was his arms around her and his mouth on hers.

K. C. throwing her arms around him halted him from giving into that temptation. He looked past her to see Rachel smiling.

When she began to play another song, he was not surprised that it was a lighthearted tune that suggested no illicit pleasures. Her voice and K. C.'s entwined again.

Wyatt looked toward the door as he heard footsteps. Neither Rachel nor K. C., who was skipping about the room in time with the music, seemed to take note of them. They were having too much fun singing.

Foley appeared in the doorway, frowning as he pulled off his hat. He walked in without waiting for an invitation. *As if he already could claim Rachel for his wife.*

Silencing that thought before it burst out of his mouth, Wyatt warned himself to take care. Foley could not hide his growing rage that Rachel was sitting next to another man. When Browning and his new wife appeared behind Foley, Wyatt wondered if they had come along in hopes of forcing Rachel into something she wanted to avoid or just in hopes of seeing the confrontation. They might get more of an eyeful than they had hoped for, because Foley had his arms locked tightly over his chest and wore an expression that suggested he had caught Rachel in a heinous crime.

Something must have alerted Rachel. She looked up

from the guitar and paused in midnote. K. C. gave her a curious glance, then turned. She edged closer to Rachel. Leaning the guitar against the end table, Rachel put her arm around the little girl's shoulders.

"Good evening, Mr. Foley," said Rachel as she rose. "And Merrill! You brought Helga with you to pay a call. This is quite the surprise."

"Apparently," Foley growled.

"Too bad you weren't here to join us for dinner, but you're welcome to join us in singing. It's a wonderful way to forget the day's heat."

Foley did not move. "What is *he* doing here?"

"Wyatt kindly brought Katherine back from Haven after she went to work on the decorations for the Centennial celebration." Rachel's pause was so slight that Wyatt was unsure if he had heard it. "Just as you persuaded the Assembly of Elders to agree to."

"They did not agree for Colton to loiter here." He refocused his glower on Wyatt. "Colton, I trust you'll remember that Rachel is going to marry me, not you. I'd regret having to be forced to remind you of that again."

Wyatt smiled coldly, resisting the temptation to retort that Foley was lying. Foley would be glad to find a way to make him pay for each visit to River's Haven.

He stood and picked up the guitar. Running his fingers along the strings, he did not let his smile waver. "I've never forgotten that. Surely even you can find no sin in singing."

"Just stay away from her!"

"That's enough, Mr. Foley," Rachel retorted. "Wyatt is our guest at River's Haven. Where are your manners, Mr. Foley?"

He swallowed so hard that Wyatt could hear him gulp, but said, "Excuse me, Miss Browning."

"Thank you," she replied with a graciousness Wyatt

knew he would never have been able to summon. "Would you like to join us for some singing?"

Wyatt thought Foley would refuse. Instead Foley glanced at Browning and his wife. Browning's nod was barely perceptible. All three came into the room and Rachel's brother brought chairs from by the kitchen table for himself and his wife. Foley walked toward the sofa, but K. C. squeezed past him and sat on Rachel's left. Wyatt resumed his place on her right.

"You're looking for trouble," Rachel murmured as she bent to retune a string.

"I thought I was trying to halt it," he replied.

"I don't know if anything can."

Those were the last words she addressed to him for the rest of the evening. Each time she started to speak to him, Foley or her brother would interrupt. Browning's wife was silent. At first, Wyatt dismissed her as a well-trained disciple of this Community. That was before he noticed how she fluttered her eyelashes in his direction and gave him a smile he had last seen on a harlot's face in a saloon outside Louisville. He chuckled and wondered if she had started looking for her next husband as soon as she married Browning.

He was not sure how long they would have all sat there with such fake expressions and long silences if Rachel had not said she needed to get Katherine—how strange to hear of K. C. called that formal name!—to bed, because the next day was going to be so exciting. When Foley and her brother rose to bid K. C. and Rachel good night, he did the same because he suspected they would not leave until he did.

As he walked out the door with the others, he caught a glimpse of Rachel's taut face. That was enough for him to be on guard and avoid Foley's attempt to grasp him by the shirt. He sidestepped away from Browning's grip as well. His fist clenched, but he would not swing first.

"Stay away from here, Colton," Foley snarled. "And stay away from *her.*"

"You're not going to have to worry much longer. *The Ohio Star* is going to be on its way as soon as we finish the repairs." He rested one hand on the door frame, so no one could sneak up behind him. "We probably would have been on our way by now if someone hadn't started fires on the upper decks."

Even in the thickening twilight he could see the glances Browning and Foley exchanged. They might not have held lucifer to the greasy rags themselves, but they knew who had.

"It's too bad," Wyatt continued in the same friendly tone. "*The Ohio Star* could have been long gone from Haven by now, and you wouldn't be getting all hot under the collar simply because I did Rachel a favor and brought the kid out here from town." With a smile, he added, "Good evening, gentlemen, Mrs. Browning."

"Miss Page," she corrected in a soft coo. "We keep our maiden names here at River's Haven."

He bowed his head toward her. "Good evening, then, Miss Page."

Wyatt walked away from the cottage, half expecting an attack from behind. Nothing happened. He glanced back to see the two men and Miss Page walking back to the common house. He had won this encounter, but he was not about to fool himself. The battle was far from done, and one mistake would mean Rachel married to Foley.

Twenty

"Happy birthday to you, K. C.," Wyatt said with a smile as he placed a package covered in brown paper in front of the little girl.

Rachel had not felt this uncomfortable on *The Ohio Star* since the first night she had come aboard. It was not simply that her brother and Mr. Foley would be furious to discover her visiting here. This was the first time she had been back to the boat since the fire—since the night she had become Wyatt's lover.

Although both Wyatt and Horace had assured her that the boat was repairable, she had been horrified to see the charred wood at the front of the upper decks. Raw, green planks had been nailed in place in front of the pilothouse. Even the lowest deck was spotted with scorch marks from where embers had fallen.

Was this her fault? More than once Merrill had warned her to stay away from *The Ohio Star* and Wyatt. She did not want to think that her brother had decided to try to ensure that she could not come here again.

Horace put his hand on her arm, and she gave him a tremulous smile.

"Today's a day to enjoy, Miss Rachel," he said. "It ain't every day that we have a birthday party on *The Ohio Star*."

Rachel looked back at Kitty Cat who was giggling as she ripped off the paper. Shreds covered her light blue dress by the time she lifted out a wooden steamboat. She crowed with delight and showed it off to Rachel and Horace before dropping to her knees to run it over the deck.

"What a lovely gift, Wyatt," Rachel said with a genuine smile. "It's just what she wanted. Her own steamboat."

"I know."

"You do, don't you?" She laughed softly.

He took her hand. Rubbing her fingers, he used a single finger to tip her face up so her eyes met his.

She quivered beneath the potent emotions glowing there. Wyatt had never hidden his desire for her. Even when she stood on the deck of his boat that first evening, fearful for Kitty Cat, he had watched her with eager longing. Then he had turned from her, not wanting to get involved with anyone from River's Haven. But the invisible thread of desire that drew them together refused to be cut.

"It's supposed to be *The Ohio Star*," he said while his eyes held an invitation to delight. "I'm afraid my whittling isn't as fancy as Horace's."

"Don't listen to him," his partner retorted. "He's been doing all the carving for the new posts in the rail on the top deck. He's good with a knife. The wheels even move on the side of that little boat." He walked across the deck, calling to Kitty Cat.

Rachel stepped back before she could no longer resist putting her arms around Wyatt. In his fancy silver vest over his white shirt and black trousers, he looked the part of a riverboat gambler instead of riverboat owner. His boots shone in the late-afternoon sunshine like the bright buckle on his belt, and his hair was neatly slicked back. His hat sat on a bench by the boiler room.

All the voices that floated down from the village warned her how easily she and Kitty Cat could be seen here. She knew she was asking for trouble by coming to the boat before going into the village, but she could not deny Kitty Cat—and herself—this visit on the little girl's birthday.

"We should go," Rachel said. "The parade will be starting soon."

"I figured you were about to say that." He smiled grimly. "Did your brother read you the riot act this morning?"

"Pretty much."

"How about Foley? Did he try to browbeat you, too?"

She frowned. "I heard you talking with Merrill and Mr. Foley outside the cottage last night. Did something happen?"

"Not what they'd have liked to have happened. They were right put out when I mentioned *The Ohio Star* might have left Haven by now if someone hadn't set her afire." He chuckled. "I never saw such guilty faces."

Rachel wanted to defend her brother against this accusation, but she could not. All she could think of was how easily Wyatt spoke of leaving. "I didn't think you'd planned to set out until that shipment comes in on the railroad."

"I'm not. That's why I said 'might.' " His smile evaporated like morning fog on the river. "Honey, let's not talk about me leaving today. Let's enjoy the evening."

She started to answer, but the raucous sound of horns interrupted her. The parade must be getting ready to begin. Calling to Kitty Cat, she held her hand out to the little girl.

Kitty Cat grasped her hand and swung it as they crossed the plank to the pier, the little girl bouncing excitedly on every step. She put her boat into her sash and offered her other hand to Wyatt.

As he took it, he gazed over her head to Rachel. She waited for him to say something, not wanting to ruin this moment while they walked up the bluff to the village. To anyone who might glance in their direction, they looked like any other family out for the holiday. She wished it could be more than an illusion.

The little girl pulled away, shattering the fantasy, and ran along the main street to show off her birthday gift. The crackle of firecrackers seemed to burst in her wake.

When Wyatt offered his arm, Rachel put her hand on it. This afternoon, she was not wearing funereal black. She had spent last night adding several bands of fabric to the bottom of her pink-striped dress. She might resemble a crazy quilt, but she would be cool.

The village of Haven was garishly decorated with red, white, and blue. Bunting hung from the store and the livery stable. Flags fluttered fitfully everywhere. The clapboards along the front of the Grange Hall had been painted to make a giant flag with thirty-seven stars. It would have to be changed, in just a few weeks, when Colorado Territory became the newest state.

She saw the few people who had come from River's Haven were bunched together at one side of the green where shadows were already growing under the trees. They watched the villagers uneasily, and the residents of Haven seemed to be as ill at ease to have them in their midst.

"Rachel!" Emma Sawyer was waving to her. "Bring Mr. Colton, and come over and watch the parade with us on the store's porch."

"Shall we?" Wyatt asked. "It looks to be the best seat in Haven."

Rachel hesitated. To sit up there would put her blatantly on view to anyone who passed the store . . . which would be just about everyone. She glanced toward the people from the Community and realized it did not matter. They were already staring in her direction and pointing as if she had suddenly grown another nose.

"Rachel?" The good humor had vanished from Wyatt's voice. "If you'd rather watch the parade somewhere else . . ."

"We would be rude to turn down Emma's invitation."

His smile came back like the sun emerging from behind a cloud. "Now you're being sensible."

"I'm not being the least bit sensible," she said as they crossed the street toward the raised porch at the front of Delancy's General Store. "But Horace is right. We should enjoy this day. I doubt if there will ever be another like it."

"Don't think about that now."

"I'm going to try. I don't want to ruin a bit of Kitty Cat's special day."

Rachel was greeted warmly by Emma and her husband as well as Reverend Faulkner and his wife—an elf of a woman who had the widest smile Rachel had ever seen. Sitting in a rocking chair, Rachel ran her hands along the arms where the paint had been worn off.

"You look as if you've found heaven," Wyatt said, drawing up a straight chair next to her.

"I didn't realize how much I missed having a rocking chair until I saw the ones on *The Ohio Star*." Her voice broke as she added, "Of course, now I won't have a reason to have one."

Putting his finger under her chin, he tipped it up. "Today is a happy day, honey."

"I know." She smiled.

"Here they come!" shouted Mr. Sawyer.

Rachel leaned forward to see past a pole at the end of the porch. Cheers near the railroad station announced that the Haven Centennial parade had begun. Hearing the enthusiastic but slightly off-key version of "Yankee Doodle," she clapped along with everyone else as the band marched by. There were about a dozen musicians, ranging in age from not much older than Emma's son Sean to a gray-haired matron who was the only female in the band. She heard someone say it was the band that usually played at the Grange Hall.

They were followed by the town's pumper, pulled by a

quartet of firemen. She slipped her hand over Wyatt's as it passed. The last time they had seen the pumper was when it lumbered down the hill to fight the fire on *The Ohio Star*.

"Over here!" Wyatt shouted and waved.

She smiled when she saw Horace scurrying across the dusty street between the pumper and four horses decorated with bunting. He climbed up and sat on the edge of the porch, swinging his hat in the air as he cheered for the young riders.

A horse-drawn buggy carried Haven's mayor and his wife. Behind them, a pair of horses drew a flat hay wagon. The wagon had three boys on it. They were as still as statues and dressed in what was supposed to be colonial garb. The two taller boys were Sean and, she guessed from Kitty Cat's description, the Rafferty boy who lived with Mr. Jennings. Another wagon followed that one. This one carried a score of children who were singing the same song the band had been playing.

Rachel waved to Kitty Cat, who was beaming as brightly as the hot sunshine. The little girl raised both hands in the air and wiggled her fingers.

Wyatt laughed. "I do think she believes the whole of this is a party for her birthday."

A few more children following on foot brought up the end of the parade. The spectators fell in line behind them. Horace jumped down and was drawn into the crowd by an elderly woman who talked earnestly to him.

"That's Mrs. Randolph," Emma said with a chuckle. "Do let your friend know that he doesn't need to listen to her all evening, for she'll bend his ear as long as he's willing. If he tires of it, he only needs to excuse himself. She's glad to air her opinions even if nobody is listening."

"I don't think Mrs. Randolph is his target." Wyatt stood and pointed to a slender brunette who seemed to be alone. "I hope I don't need to remind Horace that we'll be around

Haven a while longer, and more trouble isn't something we want." He tipped his hat to Emma and offered his arm again to Rachel. "Thank you for sharing your porch with us."

"Sean made me promise that I'd ask you if you wanted to join us for the picnic at dark," Emma said, putting her hands on the shoulders of two little girls who were younger than Kitty Cat. "Belinda and Maeve want to sit with Kitty Cat, too."

"That sounds lovely." Rachel smiled. "Where shall we meet you?"

Mr. Sawyer said, "The pit to cook the chickens is behind the Grange Hall. Why don't we meet by the Grange's front door when the food is served? I know our children will be first in line for it."

"With Kitty Cat right behind them. We'll meet you there." She walked with Wyatt down the steps and onto the street.

Dust swirled up around them, and for a moment she wished she had one of the dresses she wore at River's Haven, for its hem would not drag in the dirt. Wyatt sneezed, blowing the brown-gray cloud aside. She laughed, and he gave her a mock frown before strolling with her along the street.

"This is a cozy town," he said as they reached the green in the very center.

"I didn't think you liked cozy."

"It's fine as long as I don't have to live with it every day of the year."

Kitty Cat ran up to them before Rachel could reply. "Did you see me? Did you see me?"

"Of course." Rachel laughed. "Didn't you see us waving to you from the store's porch?"

"Oh, that's right." She was deflated for only a second, then tugged on Wyatt's trousers. "Will you?"

"Will I what?" he asked.

"There's a pie-eating contest. Will you enter it, Wyatt?" She grinned. "You could win."

He patted his stomach, then glanced at two of the bulky men who were already standing next to the table on the other side of the green. Pies were stacked on it. "They look as if they can eat much more than I can."

"You can do it, Wyatt. You really can."

"Kitty Cat," Rachel said quietly, but smiled at Wyatt, "you should give Wyatt a chance to decide if he's up to the task of this competition."

"But he can do it." The little girl put her hands on her waist, and Wyatt resisted laughing. The motion brought Rachel immediately to mind.

"What a challenge!" He tapped his chin with one finger. "How does one go about entering?"

"Come with me! Sean said he'd show me what to do."

Wyatt took her hand and grinned at Rachel as he let K. C. lead him toward the tables. When Sean held out his hand for a quarter to donate to the library fund, Wyatt fished a quarter out of his pocket. He wondered if anyone guessed how few coins were left in his pocket.

"I'd better enjoy the taste of this pie if I'm paying two bits for it," he teased.

"You're not supposed to taste it," K. C. said. "You're supposed to *eat* it as fast as you can."

He laughed again and took his seat across from a man who was twice his girth. Several other men found seats around the table, most of them urged to do so by their children. When a man in the somber clothes of River's Haven sat next to Wyatt, a hum of comments raced through the onlookers with the speed of a telegraph message. The man glanced at Wyatt and quickly away.

Was this an attempt to bring the village and the Community closer? Wyatt had no time to ponder that question because the signal was given to get ready. At a shout, the contest began. He reached for the first pie in front of him.

Minutes later, his face was covered with pie filling, and he was barely beginning his third pie. The man across from him was announced the winner for consuming twice that many.

Taking a towel, Wyatt wiped his face. He smiled when K. C. came up to him. "Sorry," he said, "that I didn't win."

"You tried." She patted his arm. "Rachel says that trying is what's important."

"Is that so?" Coming to his feet, he was not surprised to see Rachel behind K. C. She would want to keep a close eye on the kid, especially today when her neighbors at River's Haven were lurking about like vultures. He dropped the towel on the bench and, taking K. C.'s hand, walked over to Rachel. "K. C. tells me you think trying is important. I can guess I've been pretty trying for you, honey."

"More than you can guess." She laughed. "Look at you! You've got mincemeat and cherry-pie filling all down the front of you."

He grinned wryly as he tried to wipe it away. "It's pretty stuck. I guess I should go to the boat and change."

"Walking off some of that pie may help you with eating some dinner, too." Rachel smiled. "We'll wait by the tables over there." She pointed to the middle of the green.

"You could come along with me. If we decide to linger on the boat and are a bit late for dinner, no one would notice."

Her eyes glowed with the longing that he understood so well, but she said, "You're wrong. Every move I make is being watched today."

"By your friends from River's Haven?"

"Yes." She picked a chunk of mincemeat off his waist-coat.

The mere touch of her fingers threatened to shove every bit of his good sense aside, to pull her into his arms, not caring who was watching. He fought that temptation, and said, "I'll be back as quickly as I can."

"Don't be late," K. C. piped up. "I'm hungry, and I want to get the biggest piece of cake before Brendan Rafferty does."

"I'll be back before they begin cutting the first slice of that cake." He winked at her. As he raised his eyes to meet Rachel's, he said, "Later I'll show you—and your friends from River's Haven—a few tricks I've learned about sneaking away when someone is watching."

"I'd like that," Rachel whispered.

He squeezed her hand. "I thought you might."

Wyatt strode across the green toward Haven's main street. He began to whistle. Tricking those nosy fools from River's Haven would be fun, and holding Rachel alone in his quarters later would be heaven.

Twenty-one

Darkness was coming earlier than Rachel had guessed it would. Another bank of clouds was building up in the west. She hoped this rain would hold off until after the fireworks that had been promised for this evening.

Lamps were strung from tree to tree on the green. The light flickered as they rocked in the fitful breeze. Beneath them, the children buzzed about like insects drawn to the radiance.

Kitty Cat ran to join a group of children, from both the village and the Community, playing tag. She was grabbed by a tall boy with carrot-colored hair and squealed with delight as he twirled her about. That was the same boy who had been with Sean on the wagon. Brendan Rafferty, if Rachel was not mistaken. Beside him were two little girls with hair as red as his. The youngest wore glasses that bounced on every step she took. Rachel had not guessed a child that young, she could not be more than three or four years old, would have to wear spectacles.

Rachel saw Mr. Jennings standing beside the cannon set beneath some trees, his glasses that had the same sort of gold rims as the child's catching the light from the lantern. He was watching the children and grinning broadly. He glanced at her and tipped his hat. She smiled back, then turned to look around the green.

She went to a nearby table and sat. Here she would have

a good view of the village's main street, so she would see Wyatt when he returned. That should be any time now. She could also watch Kitty Cat to make sure the little girl did not find too much mischief.

She heard laughter behind her and turned to see a man and woman sitting on the other side of the table from her. She recognized Miss Underhill, Haven's schoolteacher, who would lead the exercises for the Haven children later tonight. The man beside her sat very close to Miss Underhill, so Rachel guessed they were courting.

Miss Underhill stopped in midword and stared at her, then looked away, appearing as uncomfortable as Rachel. Wondering if she should say something or just pretend to be watching the other people, Rachel knew every moment she let pass would make it more difficult to break the silence.

"Good evening, Miss Underhill," she finally said.

The teacher flinched as if Rachel had snarled at her. "Good evening, Miss Browning. This is my fiancé, Mr. Hahn."

"It's nice to meet you, Mr. Hahn. There's quite a crowd here, isn't there?"

"Yes," Miss Underhill replied while her companion remained silent.

Rachel was beginning to wish she had kept her mouth shut, because Miss Underhill obviously would have preferred that. The schoolteacher had a stricken expression as her betrothed was called away. He hesitated, then told her he would be right back.

"I'll move," Rachel said, "if you wish. I don't want to ruin your evening."

Miss Underhill flinched again, then said, "If I gave you the impression that you could ruin my evening, I'm sorry."

"You seem very uneasy speaking to me."

"May I be forthright?" She looked past Rachel to where the children were playing.

"You're curious how Kitty Cat—" She hurriedly corrected herself when Miss Underhill looked baffled. "You are curious how Katherine Mulligan is fitting in at River's Haven."

"Yes. Emma Sawyer has told me how many times the child has fled from River's Haven to come to Haven. I'm not the only one in town who is concerned about her situation."

Rachel met Miss Underhill's eyes steadily. "I'll be as plainspoken as you. She deeply misses her friends from the orphan train, so she likes to come to visit them. However, that doesn't mean that she has been unhappy at River's Haven." Her voice almost cracked on those words, for she did not want to add that she was unsure how happy Kitty Cat would be when she had to go to live with the other children tomorrow. Rather weakly, she said, "She enjoys her friends there as well."

A hand settled on Rachel's shoulder. Through her abruptly thundering pulse, a sure sign of who stood behind her, she heard Wyatt say, "And she knows how lucky she is to have found such a loving home with Rachel."

"Oh," Miss Underhill said.

Rachel introduced Wyatt, who was now dressed in his usual work clothes of a cotton shirt and close-fitting denims, to the schoolteacher. Miss Underhill introduced him to Mr. Hahn, who clearly had hurried back to rescue his fiancée. As Miss Underhill walked away with him, Rachel shook her head.

"I don't think she was any more pleased to talk to you," Rachel said, "than she was to talk to me."

"I suspect she believes me to be an incorrigible rogue and you to be a libertine of the worst sort."

"And she may be half right."

"Ouch!"

Kitty Cat bounced over to them. "Can we get something to eat now? I am *so* hungry."

Rachel wondered if it was possible to be happier than she was while she walked with Wyatt and Kitty Cat to where the food was being served. With her right hand on Wyatt's arm and her left holding Kitty Cat's, she could not imagine anywhere else she would prefer to be. She reluctantly drew her hands away as they reached the tables that were overflowing with food. In the very middle, she saw the basketful of rolls that she had left here on her way to *The Ohio Star*.

Helping Kitty Cat, who seemed eager to try everything but had her heart set on a big piece of cake, Rachel balanced both plates as Wyatt spooned food onto them. She let herself be drawn into the conversations around them, laughing along with the villagers about how many children had crowded onto the wagon and how amazing it was that they all had sat still during the parade.

"There are the Sawyers," Rachel said to Kitty Cat as she placed the plates on an empty table. "Run over and tell Mrs. Sawyer that we'll be sitting here."

Wyatt set his plate next to hers, then walked with her to where a keg of beer was set next to frosty pitchers of lemonade. Pouring a foaming mug of beer, he smiled at Mr. Sawyer who was tilting back his own mug. Handing Rachel two glasses of lemonade, Wyatt said, "The village of Haven sure knows how to celebrate the Centennial."

"It's the only one we'll ever have." Mr. Sawyer chuckled. "But the village has a big party every year on Independence Day. You should stop by next year, Colton."

"I just might do that."

Rachel hoped nobody heard how her heart lurched. The very thought of Wyatt leaving hurt so much she could barely catch her breath. Although she said nothing, he must have understood, for his hand caressed her back in silent commiseration as they walked with Mr. Sawyer to the table where the others were waiting.

Somehow she forced that sorrow deep into her heart

again. She enjoyed the conversation and Kitty Cat and Sean's enthusiasm as they recounted over and over—as if none of the adults had witnessed it—how they played a part in the parade. The two littlest girls listened in obvious awe.

The third repetition of how one of the boys had threatened to jump off the second wagon and throw firecrackers to startle everyone was interrupted by a distant flash of lightning followed lazily by thunder. Rachel looked up to see the stars and the full moon had vanished.

When Emma came to her feet, saying she was going to get the rest of the food into the grange hall before it got rained on, Rachel offered to help. Other women rushed to carry baskets and bowls and pots of food into the building on the edge of the green. Someone lit the lamps inside as the clouds got even thicker, blocking out the last of the moonlight.

Rachel was making her fifth trip to get food when it began to pour. She suddenly understood the term *cloudburst.* The clouds seemed to be ripped apart by the lightning and spilling everything within them onto Haven. Grabbing what she could from the tables, she shouted to Kitty Cat to come inside straightaway. She ran as fast as she could without tumbling in the long dress.

At the Grange Hall door, she had to slow as all the villagers tried to crowd through it at once. She heard a shout and saw Emma signaling her to come around the side of the building. As the wind whipped around her and the dust was obliterated by the rain, she went to where Emma was holding open another door.

Rachel sighed with relief when she stepped inside near where a raised platform that, someone had told her during her only other visit to this place, was used as a dais for meetings of the Grange members and for a stage at other times. She set what she was carrying on the closest table and looked around the hall.

The villagers were shaking water off wet hair and clothes, and laughing. The room was already too over-heated, and a trio of men were throwing open windows on the lee side of the building.

She looked through the crowd for Wyatt, Kitty Cat, and Horace. She found Wyatt's partner first and in quick order the others.

Kitty Cat flung her arms around Rachel and whined, "Can we go now?"

"You want to go?" she asked, startled. "Are you all right, Kitty Cat?"

"My throat hurts."

She smiled. "You probably have been yelling with your friends too much today. Go and get something to drink. It will help, I'm sure."

"It hurts bad."

Glancing at Wyatt, she said, "Maybe I should take her home."

"In this storm?"

As if in response to his question, thunder boomed, shaking the building. Kitty Cat threw her arms around Rachel and clung.

Rachel tried to calm the little girl. It was not like Kitty Cat to act like this. Had someone mentioned to her that in the morning she would have to move in with the other children? Rachel had tried to keep Kitty Cat away from the others who had come from River's Haven to prevent that.

"Here," Wyatt said, handing Kitty Cat a cup. "See if this lemonade helps."

She drank it and then smiled as some of the marching band members began to play what Rachel guessed was supposed to be a waltz. Couples quickly filled the middle of the hall. At the edges, the children paired up, mostly girls dancing with girls and the boys looking as if they would rather be doing chores. Kitty Cat shoved the cup back into Wyatt's hand and ran to join them.

"Shall we, honey?" Wyatt asked as he set the cup on a windowsill.

"You want to dance?"

"Unless you want to suggest something else . . ."

Rachel put her finger to his lips, then jerked them back. "Take care what you say."

"There's no one else here from River's Haven."

Rachel looked around, amazed to see that he was right. She and Kitty Cat were the only ones from the Community in the crowded Grange Hall. "I didn't see when the others left."

"Just as the first lightning started." He hooked a thumb toward where Kitty Cat was now dancing with a friend. "K. C. is having fun. Shall we?"

She put her hand in his. "I don't dance very well."

"Neither do I." He laughed with a low huskiness that scorched her, setting every nerve on fire. "Shall we muddle around the hall together?"

"Take care that you guard your toes from my feet."

He chuckled again as he turned her in to the pattern of the dance. She matched his steps. He had been jesting with her. He moved with the easy grace he brought to everything he did. As he twirled her around the room, she hoped the song would never end.

"Rachel?"

As his breath brushed her hair, she raised her head. Silvery heat blazed in his eyes when he drew her closer. She forgot the music, the other dancers, everyone else in the hall while she stared up into his eyes.

"Yes?" she whispered.

"Come back with me to *The Ohio Star* tonight. You know that you want to be with me as much as I want to be with you."

"Kitty Cat—"

"She can come to the boat with us. You know she'll love to spend the night there."

"No."

He halted in midstep. As the others danced around them, he said, "Rachel—"

"Listen to me." She glanced around, then took his hand and drew him toward the raised platform at the back of the hall. "Wyatt, this is where I first saw Kitty Cat. Right here. Tonight is the last night I'm going to have her all to myself. Don't ask me to give that up, although heaven knows how much I want to be with you."

His smile was a gentle one that thrilled her heart. "I understand why you want to spend time with her tonight, honey." He sighed. "What I don't understand is how you can let her go."

"I don't know if I can."

Shock sharpened his voice. "What?"

"I don't know if I can." She looked toward where Kitty Cat was spinning about on her tiptoes. "I stand here, and I think of the day the orphan train arrived. There were so many children here, but I saw only one. Kitty Cat might as well have been the only child here."

"If you don't give her up, you won't be able to stay at River's Haven."

"I know."

"Then what will you do?"

She took a deep breath before saying, "I honestly don't know."

"Honey, can we talk about this somewhere else?"

"*The Ohio Star*?"

"Yes."

"But if we go there, I don't want to talk." She ran her fingers up his chest. "I want you to hold me and kiss me."

"I thought you didn't want to stay on the boat tonight."

"Maybe a short visit will be all right." She smiled.

"Then I'll take Kitty Cat back to River's Haven and hold her all night."

Wyatt nodded and remained where he was as she went to get the little girl. He understood. Rachel could not bear to say goodbye to both him and K. C. the same night. If they had even a single hour on the boat, they could pretend that he would not be leaving soon. Rachel was usually so honest with him and herself, but this was one falsehood he must afford her.

When they reached the boat, K. C. was happy to curl up in one of the rocking chairs. She mumbled something about not having her doll with her and her throat still hurting, but was asleep almost before Rachel pulled a blanket up over her. Then Rachel slipped her hand in his.

"I do need to talk with you," she said quietly.

As they walked out of the saloon, he waved to Horace, who was sitting at the front of the boat, smoking his pipe. They turned toward his quarters. He was surprised to find a lamp glowing there, then guessed Horace had lit it.

He paused in the doorway. Looking into Rachel's dark eyes, he wondered if she knew how that soft warmth could shred every bit of his self-control.

"Rachel—"

"Please, Wyatt. I need to talk to someone." She closed her eyes. "Wyatt, I need to talk to *you*."

He closed the door behind him. Holding out her fingers, she brought him to sit beside her on his bed. Here she was where he had wanted her to be since the first time he had seen her. In his quarters, on his bed aboard *The Ohio Star*. Slowly he slid his hand along her left arm. The fine material of her dress hid little of the texture of her skin from his questing fingers.

"Talk, Rachel?" he asked as he fought the enchantment of her sweet seductiveness. "Talk about what?"

"I thought I wanted to talk about what I'm going to do when both you and Kitty Cat are out of my life." Her eyes revealed the pain in her heart as she whispered, "I was wrong. I don't need to talk. I need *you*, Wyatt."

He swept her to him. Her hungry lips thrust him into a maelstrom of pleasure. Through her thin dress, her curves were so feminine, so enticing. Her fingers boldly loosened his shirt and slipped up along his chest. Every inch of him reacted to her touch.

When he leaned her back against the pillow, her arms drew him over her. He rolled onto his back, pulling her over him. He captured her lips. He wanted to taste all of her. She arched her neck to give him free rein to pleasure.

He quivered at the very first touch of her tongue against his ear. She was welcoming him again into that netherworld where only the ecstasy he created and his mouth against her skin were real.

"Oh," she breathed against his ear, "you make me feel so wonderful."

"Do I, honey?" he whispered as his fingers curved up her back, pressing her closer.

"Yes. When you hold me, I can forget everything but how splendid this feels."

"Then forget everything now except how much I want you."

He claimed her lips again as he impatiently loosened the hooks along her gown. He pulled her clothes from her and tossed them to the deck. When she was as eager, he helped her rid him of his clothes and leave them atop hers.

With an amused chuckle, he pinned her against the pillows. He gave her no time to say anything as he tasted her skin again. Inside him grew a compulsion to find satiation for this craving that seemed to know no bounds.

He shivered with the uncontrollable sensation of his skin against hers. As her fingers drifted along him, maddening him with this blinding desire, he sought his own fantasies by letting his lips explore her beguiling curves.

The essence of her skin and the silken texture of it against his mouth immersed him in a flood of craving.

When she breathed his name and drew his mouth back to hers, he lifted her over him. Her skin brushed against him, and he knew he could not wait much longer to be inside her. Framing her face, he stared into her eyes. They were glazed with her yearning. Slowly he guided her lips to his as her hands slid along him, firing his skin with their lustrous heat. He grasped her hips as his tongue probed deep into her mouth at the very moment he delved deep within her body.

She gasped as they were melded together by the craving racing around and through them. As she moved over him, the lightning-hot yearning became a desperate need, the ecstasy became torment. It whirled through him, exploding as she quivered against him, lost in the tumult that swirled within them and beyond the bed where they could pretend that they would have this forever.

Twenty-two

Rachel lifted Kitty Cat into her arms and cradled the child against her as she stepped around a puddle in the road between Haven and the River's Haven Community. Bright moonlight sparkled on the wet grass and trees even as a miasma of fog was once again crawling up from the river.

"Do you want me to carry her?" Wyatt asked.

"I have her." She would have gladly handed Kitty Cat to him because they still were almost a mile from River's Haven, but the little girl clung to her and coughed. She hoped Kitty Cat was not sickening with a summer cold. "You didn't have to walk all the way out here with us tonight, Wyatt. I heard Horace saying how early he planned to get to work in the morning."

"I'm like K. C. I don't want this day to end." He mussed the little girl's hair as she gave him a smile.

"My birthday and the country's," murmured Kitty Cat. "Isn't it wonderful that the country has its birthday on mine?"

Rachel laughed softly. "It's just perfect."

"Will they have a party for both of us again next year?"

"Every year, from what Mr. Sawyer told us."

"Good. Next year, I want—"

"Hush!" Wyatt put his hand on Rachel's arm.

Rachel stiffened. "What is it?"

"We aren't the only ones here."

She strained her ears, but she could not hear what he had. Stepping nearer to him, she silenced Kitty Cat as the little girl started to ask a question. The moonlight no longer washed over the countryside, but instead seemed to conceal too much in its sharp shadows.

She never did see where the ambush came from. Suddenly hands were grabbing at her. She kicked at someone and heard Kitty Cat shriek. She tried to hold on to the child, but Kitty Cat was ripped from her arms. She leaped toward the shadowed man who was holding the little girl.

"Run, Rachel!" Wyatt shouted. He groaned, and she heard a fist strike him.

"Wyatt!" she screamed.

If he answered her, she never heard his voice beyond the thump of something against her skull. The moonlight vanished, and the shadows washed out from beneath the trees to sweep over her like a flood.

Water splashed on Rachel's face, then someone slapped her cheek. Not too hard, but enough to make her aching head spin. She heard someone crying. Kitty Cat!

That thought brought her eyes open. She looked around in amazement. She must be lying on the floor of a small chamber off the Community room in the River's Haven's common house.

"If she's awake," came a strident female voice, "get her on her feet, and let's be done with this."

Rachel recognized that voice, too. It belonged to Miss Stokes, the sole woman on the Assembly of Elders.

Hands grasped her arms and pulled her up. Her head spun worse. When Kitty Cat rushed to hug her, Rachel backpedaled, almost falling. The wall behind her kept her from collapsing.

"I'm fine," she whispered, wanting to calm the hysterical child. She wondered what Kitty Cat had witnessed after

Rachel was knocked senseless. Her head jerked up. Where was Wyatt?

Other than her and Kitty Cat, the Assembly of Elders were the only ones in the huge room.

"Where's Wyatt?" Rachel asked. "What have you done to him?"

Miss Stokes motioned to someone who must have been outside the room.

Rachel gasped when Miss Hanson came in, the gray-haired woman's gaze focused on the floor in front of her feet.

Miss Hanson shuffled over to Rachel and said in a whisper, "I warned you, Miss Browning, that you were bringing trouble on yourself."

"Do you know where Wyatt is?"

"Don't ask me anything. I'm just here for the child." She held out her hand and raised her voice. "Come with me, Katherine. I'll show you where you're going to live now that you're a big girl of seven."

Kitty Cat would not be fooled, Rachel realized, when the little girl spat, "I live with Rachel."

"You're seven now," Miss Stokes intoned. "You'll live with the other children. Miss Hanson, if you please."

Miss Hanson pulled Kitty Cat away from Rachel. When Rachel reached out for Kitty Cat, her arms were grasped, keeping her from helping the child.

Kitty Cat screamed and tried to escape. Something hit the floor as she was dragged to the door. The tiny steamboat! Kitty Cat cried out again when Miss Hanson lifted her and went out, closing the door behind her.

Rachel yanked her arms out of Mr. Foley's. She took one step toward the door, but Mr. Carpenter's sharp voice ordered her to stop. She ignored it.

Her shoulders were grasped again. She was whirled to face Mr. Foley. Her hand struck his face before she had a chance to halt it.

He cursed, but did not release her as he pulled her back toward where the others waited. When her skirt brushed Kitty Cat's steamboat, sending it skittering a short distance away, he raised his foot and, with a smile, crushed the toy beneath it.

Rachel raised her chin. If he thought he could squash her will as he had the steamboat, he had something to learn. She pushed past him and walked to the other Elders.

Miss Stokes pointed to a spot directly in front of her. Rachel recognized it as an order, and she went to stand before the Elder in the exact spot Miss Stokes indicated.

"We are very disappointed in you, Miss Browning," Mr. Johnson said, startling Rachel, for she had never heard him speak while with the other Elders.

"Why are you disappointed in *me?* I wasn't the one who arranged an ambush on three innocent people." She frowned at Mr. Foley, whose left cheek bore the bright pink imprint left by her hand. "Where's Wyatt Colton?"

"You know our laws, and we believed you to be willing to follow them."

She did not answer. Anything she said would be used to prove how far she had strayed from the Community's tenets.

Miss Stokes said, "It's time for you to do what you must for the benefit of the Community."

"I'll be glad to listen to what you have to say if you will tell me what has happened to Wyatt."

"Mr. Colton needn't concern you any longer," Miss Stokes replied. "As the wife of Mr. Foley—"

"I won't marry Mr. Foley!" She planted her hands on her hips and scowled.

"And whom will you marry? Colton?"

"If he and I wish. Tell me, someone, please. Where's Wyatt?"

The door opened, and Rachel looked over her shoulder.

Her brother strode into the room. He said nothing as he came to stand beside Mr. Foley.

Mr. Carpenter stepped forward, his eyes as sad as a parent dealing with a naughty child. "Miss Browning, since your arrival, you've faithfully followed the ways of our Community. Until now. Do you want to destroy what we have?"

"I'm not destroying anything." She looked to her brother, then quickly away. Merrill was even more furious than Mr. Foley. "I'll be honest with you as I always have been. River's Haven is my home, and I wouldn't do anything to cause trouble. But you're asking me to marry a man I don't love. No one else has been asked to do that."

"You're wrong," Mr. Carpenter said in his hushed voice. "You aren't the first, nor will you be the last. Miss Browning, you are a great asset to this Community. You've proven your intelligence with your work and have built financial security for River's Haven. That intelligence is something we wish for our future generations." He looked past her. "Mr. Foley also is very smart. Your child will be another asset to the Community."

"You make it sound as if we are beasts to be bred." She looked from one face to the next, wanting one of them to deny her words.

Mr. Carpenter frowned. "You should be as eager as the rest of us to bring the very best to River's Haven. Mr. Foley has agreed to this marriage wholeheartedly."

"That's no surprise." She turned to face Mr. Foley as she asked, "Has he told you that he has agreed wholeheartedly to sleep with Miss Turnbull as well as me?"

The Elders, save for Mr. Foley, gasped.

Mr. Foley's face bleached for a moment; then he smiled coolly. "Really, Miss Browning," he said in his most condescending tone, "I expected better of you than these groundless accusations."

"Groundless? I saw the two of you kissing in the stables only days ago."

He laughed as he shook his head. "I believe you're mistaking your sins for mine." His face grew hard. "How many saw you kissing Colton on his steamboat this afternoon? What more have you shared with him?"

"That, Mr. Foley, is none of your business."

"It is when I'm your husband."

"But you aren't my husband, and I don't wish to marry you . . . not ever!"

Merrill pinched her face between his hands as he growled, "That's enough, Rachel. You'll do as you are told, and you'll do it without any more mewling." He released her.

She put her hand up to her right cheek and stared at him in disbelief. "Merrill—"

"I'm her brother," he said, looking past her, "and I give you permission, Mr. Carpenter, to wed her to Mr. Foley now."

She shouted, "I won't—"

He put his hand over her mouth. "Go ahead." Lowering his voice, he growled, "Cooperate, Rachel, if you value Colton's life."

She froze. What did Merrill know about Wyatt's whereabouts? She could not ask when his hand silenced her.

Mr. Carpenter looked troubled, but opened the book that contained the wedding service used at River's Haven. Again and again, he hesitated as he glanced at Rachel. Each time, Mr. Foley urged him on.

"Will you take Calvin Foley for your husband," asked Mr. Carpenter, "to have and to hold, through sickness and health, through richer or poorer, for the next year?" He frowned. "Mr. Browning, you must allow her to speak."

"Take care what you say," whispered Merrill close to her ear. He withdrew his hand from her mouth.

Rachel looked back at her brother. So many things she

wanted to ask him. Why had he brought her here? To remain a family or to benefit this Community he wanted to belong to by using her skill with numbers? Why was he forcing her to marry Mr. Foley? What was Merrill hoping to gain from this? A chance to marry more young women and have them in his bed for a year? Her stomach cramped with disgust.

"Miss Browning," Mr. Carpenter said, looking more and more unsettled, "you must answer the question."

The door crashed open.

Mr. Foley glanced over his shoulder and ordered, "Keep going!"

When Mr. Carpenter looked past her, Rachel tried to turn to discover what had caused the Elder's face to grow ashen. Merrill gripped her arm, holding her in place.

"Stop this travesty!" came a shout.

Wyatt!

She was not sure if she had shouted that or cried out only in her thoughts. Jerking her arm away from her brother, she saw Wyatt shove his way past two men who were trying to halt him. She winced when she heard a fist drive into a man. Which one? Was Wyatt the one struck or the one hitting someone else? If he had been hurt during the attack on them, he might be injured worse now. She could not let that happen.

With a screech, she drove her elbow back into Merrill's stomach. She had wrestled with him often when they were children, but this was the first time she had struck him in anger. His breath exploded out in a cough. As his grip loosened, she pulled away and ran to where Wyatt was standing over two men who were lying facedown. He wiped blood from his cracked lip, and she saw his left sleeve was ripped and bloody.

"Wyatt, are you badly hurt?" she gasped.

"I've been worse off." He put his arm around her shoulders. "Who's in charge here?"

Miss Stokes answered, because Mr. Carpenter was slowly lowering himself to a chair by the wall. "The Assembly of Elders is in charge of everything within the River's Haven Community. What's the meaning of this intrusion?"

"I'm here to stop this absurd wedding."

"Who are you?" Miss Stokes asked. When Mr. Johnson hastily whispered in her ear, she said, "Mr. Colton, your business with River's Haven was completed some days ago."

"Not as long as Rachel and the child are here. I wish to arrange for them to leave River's Haven."

"Impossible," Miss Stokes announced.

"Why?" Wyatt's voice was as frigid as the Elder's, and Miss Stokes's lips tightened. No doubt in exasperation because she could not order him to follow the Community's rules. Wyatt followed only his own.

"You're an outsider. You dictate nothing here."

He turned to Rachel, taking her hand. "Honey, you aren't an outsider." He gave her a fleeting grin as he added, "Yet. Do you want to marry Foley?"

She did not hesitate. "No."

"Your marriage has been approved by the Assembly of Elders, Miss Browning," Miss Stokes said. "You've agreed to abide by the tenets of River's Haven and the ruling of the Assembly of Elders. You must do so now."

"Or you could come with me, Rachel," Wyatt added.

"With you?" she whispered, wondering how much joy her heart could hold before it burst.

"If you stay here, you'll have to marry this hypocrite who's going to do more damage to River's Haven with his lusts for his former wife than you could ever do."

Mr. Foley took a step forward but stopped when Wyatt drew a gun from his belt.

"The decision is hers, Foley, not yours." Wyatt asked, "What's your decision, honey?"

"Kitty Cat and I will leave, and go with you."

His eyes widened before he looked past her to the Elders. "You heard what she has decided."

"Yes." Mr. Carpenter shoved himself to his feet. "You're banished from River's Haven Community, Rachel Browning. You must leave now."

She trembled, overwhelmed with how she had changed her future with one moment of rebellion. "As soon as I get Kitty Cat . . . Katherine."

"You are banished. She's still a member of this Community!"

"No!" she cried. "You can't take her away from me."

Wyatt said quietly, "Let's go now, honey."

"But, Kitty Cat . . ."

"You first, honey." He gave her a bolstering smile. "If you stay here, you'll end up married to Foley. You've got to leave now. We'll get K. C. later."

She knew he was right, but every instinct told her to keep arguing. If she left Kitty Cat here . . . No, she must not panic. Miss Hanson was kindhearted, and Kitty Cat had always adored her.

Turning, she squared her shoulders as she said, "Goodbye, Merrill."

"If you leave with him," her brother retorted, "don't think you'll be welcomed back. Spend the rest of your life alone!"

Wyatt herded her out of the Community room before her resolve could crack. Her brother had known the exact words to say to wound her and make her reconsider her rash actions.

"Ignore him, honey," Wyatt said as he led her onto the grass of the common area. "Stop worrying about what your brother thinks! You should be ecstatic that Foley can now remarry his Miss Turnbull instead of making you miserable!"

"You would think so, wouldn't you?"

"But you aren't."

"No, for this could—"

"Make trouble for Merrill. Why don't you think of yourself for once?"

"He's my brother. I love him."

"Does he still love you?"

"I don't know." Rachel paused on the wet grass and looked back at the windows of the children's dormitory. If Kitty Cat happened to peek out, what would the child think to see Rachel leaving without her?

"K. C. knows you love *her.*"

She rested her head on his shoulder, so glad he understood what would be too painful to speak. "Thank you, Wyatt. Let's get my things."

"Leave them for now."

"All right. Let's go . . . wherever."

Wyatt nodded, putting his arm around Rachel. He had not said anything about the tearstains on her face or how her voice quivered on each word. As she leaned more heavily on him with every step they took away from the dark heart of River's Haven, he lifted her into his arms and against his chest.

He grimaced, hoping that she had not seen it. A foolish hope, for she immediately asked if he was all right. He gave her a brief and very expunged version of what he had endured during the scuffle along this very road. He did not want her to guess how only luck and quick reflexes had kept him from being killed. As it was, blood was dripping down his arm, which burned as if someone had stuffed a torch into it.

He was unsure if Rachel was asleep or had lost consciousness when she did not reply to his tale. Rage gave a boost to his flagging strength. When he had seen one of the men strike her with the butt of a knife, his fury had blinded him . . . and betrayed him. He had tried to get to her to protect her and found himself surrounded by a half-

dozen men who seemed at first just determined to teach
him a lesson. Then he had seen the flash of steel in the
moonlight and had known that scaring him off was not
their intention. They had tried that—and failed—by setting
fire to *The Ohio Star*. Now their methods were growing
more deadly.

The lamps still hung, wet and unlit, around the green.
Only a few people remained to watch sky rockets being
fired off.

At the first dull boom, Rachel shuddered in Wyatt's
arms. He set her on her feet, knowing that she would not
want to create a scene by being toted across the village
green. Putting his arm around her waist to steady her, he
peered through the darkness.

"This way, honey," he said.

"All right."

That she was so compliant warned him that those River's
Haven bullyboys had hurt her worse than she had let him
guess. She wobbled against him while he led her to where
Sawyer and his family were cheering as more rockets deto-
nated.

"We need to speak with you, Sawyer," he said quietly.

In the glare from the explosions overhead, he saw Sawyer's smile fade at their sorry state.

"Come with me," Sawyer said. He glanced at his wife
and motioned with his head toward their house.

Mrs. Sawyer gathered the children, who protested sleep-
ily. No one said anything while they went to the red house
around the corner from the store.

Helping Rachel up the steps, Wyatt winced as his bloody
arm brushed an upright on the porch. He heard Mrs. Sawyer's sharp intake of breath when they stepped into the
light of the lamp Sawyer had lit. She sent the children
upstairs to bed before they could see the blood.

Sean paused on the stairs and said, "Emma, my throat's
still really sore."

"I'll bring you a posset," Mrs. Sawyer replied. "As soon as I can."

The boy went up the stairs while Mrs. Sawyer went through a door at the end of the foyer.

"Rachel needs a place to stay." Wyatt sat her in a chair in the parlor. "She can't go back to River's Haven, and *The Ohio Star* is already a target."

Sawyer nodded, although curiosity filled his eyes. "We don't have room here, but out at our farm—"

"Where is it?" When Sawyer began to give him directions, Wyatt added, "No. It's closer to River's Haven, and I think she'd be better off here in the village."

Mrs. Sawyer returned and placed a damp cloth on Rachel's head before handing another one to Wyatt. "We'll find a place for her here in Haven. That's no problem."

Dabbing at the blood on his sleeve and grimacing, he said, "It has to be some place where she wouldn't be expected to be. Tempers are pretty high right now, and I don't know what foolish thing they'll do next."

"We'll find a place," Mrs. Sawyer repeated. "Does that arm need to be stitched up?"

"I'll have Horace bandage it when I get back to the boat." He wondered if he could have refrained from asking questions about what had happened. Then he realized that they must have a very good idea of what exactly had happened.

That was confirmed when Mrs. Sawyer asked, "Where's Kitty Cat? Was she hurt, too, in this attack on you?"

Rachel stood and came back out into the foyer. She measured each step with care. When Wyatt put his arm around her again, she gave him a grateful smile. Quietly she said, "Emma, Kitty Cat is still at River's Haven. They took her away from me before . . ." Wyatt's fingers dug into her shoulder, and she patted his hand. "They sent her to the children's dormitory. We thought it best to go back and get her later."

"They won't welcome you back."

"They won't stop me." She closed her eyes and clutched the banister to keep herself from collapsing. "But I've got to be able to take more than a few steps on my own before I go for her."

Emma took her arm. "I know the perfect place for you. Noah, get one of my nightgowns for Rachel to use and send it to Alice's house. Wyatt, you're welcome to join us for breakfast when we can talk about this more."

"I'll be here," he said. Tilting Rachel's face toward his, he added, "Honey, don't worry about K. C. tonight. They aren't angry at *her,* and you know Miss Hanson will keep a close eye on her."

"I know, but I'll still worry."

A smile warmed his face, which was hard with fury. "Why am I not surprised at that answer?"

When he drew her to him, she took care not to touch his bloodstained sleeve. His lips caressed hers, and she wanted to lose herself completely in his kisses. Lose herself and never have to return to the pain surrounding them. As she rested her head against him, while he stroked her back, she knew that was impossible. They had to think of Kitty Cat, too.

"Be careful," she whispered.

"We will be. Horace has been standing guard on the boat since sundown, and I need to go and give him a chance to get some sleep so he can take the watch again on the morrow."

"But you both were here at the Centennial celebration."

He laughed without humor. "No one, not even the zealots at River's Haven, are stupid enough to cause trouble when everyone had a good view of the river from the green."

"I haven't told you thank you."

"No need, honey." His eyes began to sparkle. "I'll figure out a way later for you to show me your gratitude."

"Good." Rachel kissed him again, a lingering kiss that she hoped said all she wanted to say, then went with an obviously distressed Emma out the door. "Where are we going?"

"Across the street to Alice Underhill's house."

"Miss Underhill?" Rachel halted in the middle of the street. "She won't want me there. She despises everything about River's Haven, including me. Everyone knows that."

Emma opened the gate in front of the neat white house. "True. Everyone *does* know that, including the folks at River's Haven."

"But will Miss Underhill let me stay with her?"

"Alice is a warmhearted woman. If you two had met under different circumstances, I believe you'd have been the very best of friends."

Rachel did not want to contradict her, so she said nothing as they went to the door. When Miss Underhill answered Emma's knock, the schoolteacher's eyes grew so wide they almost bulged from her face.

"May we come in, Alice?" Emma asked.

"Yes . . . Yes, come in." Miss Underhill stepped back, but continued to stare at Rachel. "Sweet heavens, is that blood on your dress, Miss Browning?"

Looking down, she saw a swath of dark red where Wyatt's arm must have been against her skirt. She met Miss Underhill's shocked gaze evenly as she replied, "Yes, it is."

"Alice," Emma said, "I think it'd be best if we discussed this inside where we won't be overheard."

"Come in." She motioned to a wooden chair just inside the parlor door. "Sit down, Miss Browning."

Rachel did, folding her hands in her lap. This room with its overstuffed furniture, worn rugs, and books scattered about reminded her of the minister's house . . . and the house that had been home in Ohio. Her fingers tightened until her knuckles were white. She had left that home to be with Merrill. Now they were separated for what she feared would be the rest of their lives.

As Emma outlined the need for Rachel to have a sanctuary that would not be discovered by anyone from River's Haven, Miss Underhill dropped to the sofa covered by a crocheted blanket. The schoolteacher asked, "But why? She's one of *them*."

"Not any longer," Rachel said, lifting her chin with what fragments of pride she had remaining. "When I refused to marry the man they insisted I wed in an effort to breed the next generation they wanted, I had no choice but to leave."

"They did what?" Miss Underhill jumped to her feet. "That's outrageous!"

Emma nodded. "Now you understand why we and Mr. Colton wish to keep Rachel out of sight for a few days. No one will think she's with you, Alice, for you've been outspoken in your distaste for River's Haven from the moment it was established."

"Miss Browning," the schoolteacher said, "you must stay here. I won't hear of you going anywhere else."

"Alice, I knew we could depend on you." Emma gave her friend a quick hug. "And her name is Rachel." Embracing Rachel, she said, "Don't despair. Kitty Cat is a resourceful little girl. If she could survive in New York City's worst slums, she'll be able to handle another night at River's Haven."

Rachel whispered, "Thank you. You've been a good friend."

"I know what it's like to worry about a child's welfare. Just believe that all will come to rights. Mr. Colton is, I have seen, a most determined man and very attached to Kitty Cat and you." Emma went to the door. "I need to get home. Sean was complaining of a sore throat."

"So was Kitty Cat."

She grimaced. "I suspect by this time any sickness they

might have has been shared with every child in Haven. I'd best make a big batch of my posset because Belinda and Maeve may need it as well." She hurried out the door.

Silence filled the room; then Alice said, "Come this way, Miss—Rachel. I'll take you up to the guest room, and you can rest. You look as if you've had a truly harrowing night."

Rachel had to agree with that estimation when she caught her reflection in the looking glass over the small table in the cozy bedroom. Her hair hung loose over her shoulders. When she had been struck, blood had glued some of her hair together. Dirt covered her face and clothes, left by the attack on them.

But she was safe now. She looked around the small room. The ceiling slanted over the far side of the iron bed, but there was still enough room on the far side of the small woodstove for the table that held an ewer and a bowl. Towels and cloths waited for her to clean her face that was almost hidden by her snarled hair. As she dressed in the borrowed nightgown, she knew she would need to buy a comb and brush in the morning. She was not sure how she would pay for it, but she guessed Emma would let her pay when she got some money.

But how would she do that? Beyond River's Haven, no one was interested in a woman with her skills. She had to hope someone in Haven would know of work she could do.

Sitting on the edge of the bed, she looked through the window with its thin curtains that fluttered in the breeze left behind by the storm. She blew out the candle, but the room was almost as bright with the light from the full moon. If she closed her eyes, she could imagine how it would reflect on the river. Were Wyatt and Kitty Cat thinking the same? She would never know unless they were together again . . . which she hoped would happen before she had to say goodbye to Wyatt and *The Ohio Star*.

Twenty-three

The word spread swiftly through Haven in the days following the Centennial celebration. In almost every house, someone was very sick. Sore throats, stiff necks, and high fevers, and a name of the sickness that was whispered because no one wanted to say it aloud.

Diphtheria.

Rachel spent hours each day working beside Emma Sawyer as they tended to Sean and Belinda. This morning, Noah had taken Maeve to their farm outside of the village, hoping to protect her from sickening as well. He returned within an hour with the news that the farm was no safer because it was said that the people at River's Haven were taking ill, too.

"Go. Take the store's wagon," Emma said as Rachel listened in horror. "You know you won't be able to rest unless you have Kitty Cat back here with you."

Rachel did not hesitate. Tying her straw bonnet under her chin, she lifted her borrowed blue skirt as she raced down the front steps and along the oddly silent street toward the river. She saw Doc Bamburger coming out of a house near the shore. The woman in the doorway had her apron to her face, weeping. The very sight spurred Rachel's feet faster.

She shouted Wyatt's name as she ran aboard *The Ohio Star*. Slowing to a stop, she called his name again. When she got no answer, she rushed up the stairs to the saloon. Either Wyatt or Horace must be here. They would not leave the boat unguarded.

"Wyatt!" she cried. She did not care who heard her desperation. "Wyatt! Where are you?"

The saloon door swung open, almost knocking her to the deck. Strong hands caught her. Not Wyatt's, but Horace's.

"Miss Rachel, what's wrong?" Horace asked. "Is it the young'un?"

"Where's Wyatt?" she panted.

"Up at the railroad station. He—"

She threw her thanks over her shoulder and raced back toward the stairs and the pier. Pain stitched in her side, but she ignored it as she scrambled on all fours up the hill and toward the building that served as both Haven's station and its telegraph office.

Flinging open the door, she cried, "Wyatt!"

He turned from where he was talking to a neatly dressed young man. "Rachel, what is it?"

"The sickness is out at River's Haven, too." She dropped to a bench, pressing her hand to her aching side. "Will you go with me out there to find Kitty Cat and bring her here?"

Thrusting a stack of papers at the dark-haired man, he said, "Kenny, *The Ohio Star* is ready for the supplies to be loaded. Horace is on board, and he'll oversee the delivery and loading if you can send a couple of lads down with the dray."

Rachel bit her lip. The shipment that Wyatt had been waiting for, his first shipment as a partner in the boat, must have arrived in Haven. Her stomach cramped more, but she came back to her feet and put her hand on his arm.

"Wyatt?" she asked. "Will you go with me out to River's Haven?"

"Let's go, honey."

As they went back out onto the deserted street, she said, "Emma offered me the use of the store's wagon."

He nodded and hurried with her to the barn between the store and the Sawyer house. While he hitched the horse to the black wagon with its white lettering that announced it was from Delancy's General Store, she went into the house. A stack of blankets waited on the kitchen table, and she gathered them up, knowing that Emma had left them there for her.

Wyatt threw the blankets in the back of the wagon. Then he handed her onto the high seat. She had barely enough time to draw in her skirt before he leaped up next to her and slapped the reins on the horse.

"About the shipment," he began.

"Not now." She blinked to keep her frightened tears in her eyes. "Let me think only about taking care of Kitty Cat just now."

"You know they aren't going to let us walk in the door and see how she's faring."

"I know."

"When I tried to sneak in there the day after the Centennial celebration, it was so well guarded I couldn't get to the children's rooms."

She stared at him in amazement. "You went out to River's Haven? Why didn't you tell me?"

"Because I wasn't able to sneak K. C. out of there, and then diphtheria struck in Haven. I thought she'd be better off out there away from the sickness." He put his hand over her fist clenched on her lap. "Honey, if she's sick, she might be better off staying there even now. Moving her if she's got diphtheria is very dangerous."

"I know." She gripped his hand on hers. "But, Wyatt, you don't understand about River's Haven."

"That's the truest thing anyone has ever said."

"They won't call in a doctor," she continued as if he

had said nothing. "No outsider will be allowed to tend to anyone who's sick."

He swore. "How can they be so stupid? Don't bother to answer. I know you're going to say it's just their way."

"It is."

"Is it your way still?"

"I don't know." She looked at the road that followed the river. "I know I don't belong there any longer, but I'm not sure where I belong now."

"With K. C."

Her smile returned. *"That* I know."

"How are the Sawyer kids doing?"

As she began to speak about helping Emma with her sick children, he listened intently. She explained how she and Emma and Noah and the housekeeper who returned to Haven in time to help took turns heating warm cloths and baths for Sean and Belinda. Possets of catnip were given every two hours, and it was important to check in the children's mouths for the membrane that could grow across their throat, suffocating them. They tried to get the youngsters to drink thin broth, for anything else might cause vomiting and further injure the children's throats.

"How are other families handling it?" he asked, amazed.

"Everyone who isn't sick is helping those who are."

"Why haven't you sent for me to help?"

She laughed. "Wyatt, I can't imagine you in a sickroom with the windows and draperies closed. You prefer the sunshine and fresh air."

"I could help, if you need me."

"Yes, you could." She grew serious. "I just hope you don't have to."

Rachel drew in her breath as she saw the common house appearing over the hills along the river. Less than a week ago, this had been home. Although she had questioned the rules and even the Assembly of Elders, she had been proud of the part she played in the River's Haven Community.

When Wyatt drove the wagon into the common area, she was surprised when nobody halted them. Emma often brought supplies out from the village, but she was not allowed to come this close to the center of the Community. He drew in the reins in front of her cottage and jumped down. Coming around the wagon, he held his hands up to her.

"Before we get thrown out of here," he murmured as he scanned the common area that was as empty as Haven's streets, "why don't you get your things?"

"Forget them. Kitty Cat—"

"Will never forgive me if I let you leave your guitar and her doll here."

"All right, but we must be quick."

He smiled grimly. "My thoughts exactly."

Rachel put her hands on his shoulders as he lifted her down from the seat. His fingers brushed her cheek, and she tried to smile. Wanting to thank him, she nodded when he urged her to hurry and collect what she wanted.

The red door opened easily, and Rachel walked into the cottage. Her fear that it had been stripped of everything was eased. It looked as if she still lived there.

"What do you want me to get?" Wyatt asked, and she flinched. "Did I startle you?"

"Yes . . . No. I was lost in memory." She asked him to get some of Kitty Cat's clothes and the rag doll if it was on the little girl's bed.

He set a wooden box in the middle of the parlor floor. "Put whatever you want in this. I'm sure Emma won't mind if you use it."

Rachel emptied the stones from the metal pitcher onto the floor. She set it in the box. Pulling the linens she and her mother had embroidered off the tables, she dropped them in. She rushed into her bedroom and got her two dresses that were suitable to be worn outside River's Haven.

She faltered as she stared at the bed. Some of her most cherished memories of River's Haven had taken place here. She had sung with Kitty Cat here and told the little girl stories while they sat together on the bed. And, here, Wyatt had captivated her with his bewitching touch.

Turning, she saw him standing in the doorway. His gaze slipped from the bed to her, and the passion in his eyes lured her to step into his embrace once more. She looked away while she still could resist that invitation.

"I have your guitar, honey," he said, his words rasping past his lips that she wanted to taste. "Anything else?"

She swallowed the answer she wanted to give him and said, "No, I have everything that is mine. Did you find K. C.'s doll?"

"It's already in the box."

Rachel went with him into the main room. He picked up the box and they walked out of the cottage. She leaned the guitar against the back of the wagon's seat, then reached into the box he had put in the wagon and drew out the rag doll. She held it close to her heart as they walked across the common area.

"Where is everyone?" Wyatt asked.

She wanted to ask the same thing. Even when they entered the common house, no one came forward to meet them. An outsider should never have been able to walk about here without being challenged.

Her pace increased as she climbed the stairs and went along the hallway in the direction of the children's rooms. The sounds of crying echoed toward her. She halted at the door, shocked to see several obviously sick children lying on beds. Other children were on the floor. Babies were sitting in filthy diapers, and what could have been the remnants of food had been scattered on tables in the middle of the room.

But she saw no adults.

A little boy toddled toward her, his thumb in his mouth.

She knelt and brushed aside his hair that was sticky with something. He threw his arms around her. She held him for a moment, then asked, "Where's Miss Hanson?"

He popped his thumb back in his mouth and shrugged.

She tried again. "Do you know where Katherine Mulligan is?"

He pointed toward the far end of the room with the thumb he was not sucking.

Rachel wove among the children, who stared at her with curiosity. She wondered if the youngest ones had ever seen a woman dressed as she was. Most of the children seemed healthy. Maybe Kitty Cat . . . She moaned when she saw Kitty Cat lying on a low cot, her red curls soaked with feverish sweat.

She touched the little girl's arm, which was frighteningly hot. Although she should not feel guilty, she did as she recalled the lies she had told when she tried to keep Wyatt and Horace hidden in her cottage. She had spoken of Kitty Cat being sick. Now her lie had become the truth.

Kneeling next to her, she whispered, "Kitty Cat, can you hear me?"

The child's eyes opened slightly. Her lips formed Rachel's name, but no sound came out. Rachel handed her the rag doll. Kitty Cat struggled to smile as she hugged her doll. Then the little girl's eyes rolled up, and Rachel opened Kitty Cat's mouth. The light was dim, but she could see the milky membrane already forming on the sides of the little girl's throat.

Bundling a blanket around Kitty Cat and her doll, Rachel lifted her. She turned to see Wyatt behind her, the little boy in his arms.

Wyatt asked, "How is she?"

"She needs to be seen by Doc Bamburger right away." She looked around the room. "We can't leave the other children here like this. The ones who aren't sick may starve if no one comes to take care of them."

"Where do you expect to take them?" He arched a brow as his lips tilted in a wry grin. "Why do I even ask? You want me to take them aboard *The Ohio Star*, don't you?"

"Only until I can get Reverend Faulkner to arrange for them to stay somewhere. Maybe the Grange Hall can be opened as a shelter for them." She paused. "It shouldn't take Reverend Faulkner long to find them a place to stay. How long before you have to leave Haven?"

"We can stay long enough to help these kids." Putting down the little boy, he stuck his fingers in his mouth and whistled sharply.

Every child, even the sick ones, looked at him. He gave orders with the ease of a general commanding a battlefield, but in a tone that did not intimidate the youngsters. The older ones who were healthy enough carried the sick children or helped the littlest ones. Over each shoulder, he put a sick child who was too big for another child to carry.

He bent to pick up a third, then swore.

Rachel bit her lip to hold back her own curses as she realized the youngster was dead. She drew a sheet over the child's head as Wyatt herded the other children out of the room. Then she peered into the rest of the rooms, glancing around to make sure no child was being left behind. She called out, but no one answered. The only sounds came from the hallway and Kitty Cat's struggling breaths.

As she emerged from the dormitory, she saw Wyatt was halfway to the stairs with the children. A weak voice called from the other direction. She turned and choked back a moan as she stared at Mr. Atlee. His brown hair was straggling down into his eyes, which were blurred with fever. His skin had the chalky pallor of a corpse.

"Where are you taking the children?" Mr. Atlee wheezed, fighting for every word.

She put her hand on his arm, then drew it back when she felt how it shook. When she began to explain how they were taking the children where they could be tended to, she was unsure if he understood anything she was saying. He swayed, and she caught his arm as he slowly slid to the floor. His head fell forward onto his chest.

"Leave him," Wyatt ordered from by the stairs.

"But he's so sick."

"We'll look for someone to take care of him on the way out. If we can't find anybody, we'll send the doctor out here."

She hurried to catch up with him, keeping Kitty Cat's head close to her chest. "Doc Bamburger barely has time for all the calls he's making now."

"Everyone here can't be sick."

"Then where are they? Why isn't someone taking care of the children?"

"I can't answer that. All I want to do is get out of here."

Rachel walked down the stairs slowly, watching that none of the littlest children fell. Some were so young that they sat and bumped down the steps on their bottoms. Against her breast, Kitty Cat's forehead was so hot that the heat burned through Rachel's dress. The rag doll was pinned in the blanket between the child and Rachel, but she watched to make sure it did not fall either. She wanted every possible ally to help in the fight to get Kitty Cat better.

The children were clambering into the back of the wagon by the time she reached it. Wyatt must have moved her guitar before they could bump it, because it now was on the seat. He tossed the bigger kids up, and their laughter rang across the eerily empty common area. The little children pressed up to him, their arms raised, wanting to be the next.

She said nothing as Wyatt listened with rare patience to each child. He never showed such forbearance with Rachel. His gaze caught hers, and she knew he could not be as patient with her because his longing for her refused to let him. Her heart wanted to dance with joy at that thought.

She was being silly. When was she going to accept that falling in love with this man who loved his boat and the river was bound to ruin her life? But she did not want to listen to good sense. She wanted to relish the need that brought her into his arms again and again.

"Careful," he called to the children. "Watch out for the sick ones." He put the last one in and closed the back of the wagon. Coming to Rachel, he said, "Hand K. C. to me, if you can get up there yourself."

"I used to do it all the time back in Ohio." She bunched up her skirt and climbed into the front of the wagon. When Wyatt gently placed Kitty Cat in her arms, she whispered, "Thank you."

"We'll get back to Haven as quickly as I can drive without bouncing some of those kids in the back out onto the road." He squeezed her hand and turned to walk to his side of the wagon.

Rachel tightened her arms around Kitty Cat when she heard a shout. Her brother ran toward them, waving his arms as if he thought he could take off and fly. She almost smiled, then saw his furious face.

"Get out of here!" Merrill shouted.

"Browning, this is no time—" Wyatt began.

"I told you to leave!"

"Or?" He rolled back one sleeve to reveal the brawny muscles of his forearm that was crossed by the healing wound left by a knife. "I already owe you and your friends for ambushing me and Rachel and K. C."

Merrill scowled. "If you're talking about the night my sister was banished, then you're making a big mistake. I didn't have anything to do with that. Rachel is my sister. Do you think I'd hurt her?"

"I think you'd do whatever you had to in order to curry favor with Foley and the other Elders."

"You don't know our ways, Colton."

"Maybe not, but I know what's right and what's wrong. Letting a child die because of your bigotry is wrong."

Merrill seemed to notice the children for the first time. "What are you doing with them?"

"We're taking them into Haven," Rachel said, "to make sure they get taken care of. No one was upstairs but Mr. Atlee, who is sick by the main stairs." When Merrill lost his bluster and fear filled his eyes, she asked, "Can you send someone to help him?"

"You can't take these children."

"Merrill, for the love of heaven, think of someone other than yourself. Mr. Atlee is ailing, and I've got no idea where Miss Hanson is. We didn't see anyone else in the house."

"A lot left after you . . ." He scowled, and she knew he had not wanted to admit that the forced marriage had opened many eyes along with hers. "More are gone, scared of becoming sick."

"Then you need to help those who are still here while you can."

He grasped her arm. "Rachel, how can I help everyone who's here?"

"I don't know! But I'm going to help these children. You figure out a way to help their parents." She pointed to the common house. "There's a key in my office to the safe in the Assembly of Elders's conference room. Open it, and you'll find several thousand dollars. Use it to get some help out here. I don't know if Doc Bamburger will come from Haven, because he's so busy there with this sickness."

"Do you expect me to bring an outsider—"

"There won't be any *insiders* if you don't do something!" When Merrill continued to stare at her, obviously shocked at what he had not considered, she urged, "Do something! Otherwise, you'll be the only one here."

Wyatt swung up into the wagon and sat beside her. He

picked up the reins and asked, "Are you ready to go, honey?"

"Yes." She saw her brother's stricken face as Wyatt turned the wagon toward Haven. Had Merrill ever considered having to be on his own and having to make his own decisions about something more important than whom he would marry next?

He must now, because she had to focus on getting Kitty Cat better . . . and saying goodbye to Wyatt.

Twenty-four

Miss Underhill smiled when Wyatt entered her house as he had each day at this time since they had brought the children from River's Haven. "Good evening, Mr. Colton. I'm glad you're having dinner with us tonight."

"I'm not here for dinner."

"Oh? That's a shame. I have a lovely chicken roasting."

"More than one, I suspect, from what Rachel's told me. She says you're really helping with the River's Haven children over at the Grange Hall. Not just with food, but teaching them lessons and games to keep them busy."

The schoolteacher's smile was dim with sorrow. "It keeps me busy, too, so I don't have to think about those who are dying. Two more this morning."

"Kitty Cat?"

"She's still alive." Miss Underhill glanced at the ceiling. "Go up. Rachel will be wondering what's keeping you."

Wyatt climbed the narrow stairs that opened into a sunwashed hallway. He barely took note of the immaculate furniture as he went to a door that was partly ajar. From the room came the aroma of peppermint, but it was not a comforting smell. Rachel must have dropped more oil of peppermint into the pot boiling on the stove. She alternated it with a mixture containing alcohol that burned his throat. He did not want to think what it did to K. C.'s.

He knocked quietly.

"Come in," came Rachel's voice.

She stood as he entered. Her eyes were shadowed by gray arcs, and he wondered if she had slept at all in the past three nights. She moved as if struggling through molasses.

"Good afternoon, honey." He brushed her lips with a light kiss, fearing if he did more, he would knock her from her unsteady feet. She looked as fragile as the child, but he knew that was not so. "How's K. C.?"

"No worse, but no better." Her voice was lifeless with fatigue.

He went to the bed where the little girl was gasping for each breath. Her eyes were closed. She might have been asleep or senseless. He could not tell which. Bending down, he touched her cheek. It was still dangerously hot. He picked up her rag doll that had fallen away across the bed. Placing it next to her on the pillow, he turned to look at Rachel.

"Honey, can you spare a moment to talk?" he asked.

"A moment. Soon I need to swab her throat with the mixture Doc Bamburger had me make up."

He lifted the glass jar from the night table and sniffed. Choking, he lowered it. "What in perdition is that?"

"Carbolic acid, glycerine, and water. It helps combat the membrane trying to close her throat." She rubbed her hands on her wrinkled apron. "Any medicine he had to fight diphtheria is long gone. Emma has ordered more, but it hasn't arrived yet."

"Does he think K. C. will recover?"

She walked with him out into the hallway and sat on the top stair. Resting her head against the wall, she said, "I've asked him that every day. The answer is always the same—we must wait and see. If she can survive the disease's symptoms, it'll be obvious, for the first recovery is almost as quick as the onset."

He sat beside Rachel and took her hand. Her skin

was raw from the constant wringing of cloths to put around K. C.'s throat to keep the little girl from taking a chill. He cupped her cheek with his other hand. She sighed and closed her eyes as she leaned against it.

Looking past her, he could see out the window at the far end of the hallway. The sun's glitter on the Ohio River held a siren song for him, urging him to return to the free life that was his. Everything he had dreamed of since he was K. C.'s age awaited him there.

He took a deep breath and said, "Honey, I've got to leave. *The Ohio Star* is already more than a week overdue with its very first shipment. I don't want to leave you when K. C. is still ailing, but—"

"You must go." She sat straighter and met his eyes. The anger or disappointment he had feared he would see was not there. Only fatigue that must be weighing on her eyelashes because her eyes were only half open.

"Rachel, I want to stay and help with K. C."

"I know that." She stroked his cheek. "I also know that if you don't deliver that shipment, you and Horace will lose *The Ohio Star*."

"K. C.—"

She interrupted him again. "Doc Bamburger and I are taking care of her as best we can. There's so little we can do." She sighed. "I hope whoever's left out at River's Haven will change their minds and allow him to go there to help."

"Even if they did, would he have time? There are so many ill in Haven. I heard what you said to your brother out there. Doc Bamburger can't tend to everyone who's sick in Haven *and* in River's Haven."

"I don't know what we'll do if he sickens." She took his face in her hands. "I know why you need to go, but I wish you could stay."

"You've found a home in Haven. I can't do the same.

My life is the river. I'm glad I was here to help you bring the children from River's Haven."

"You always seem to be around when I need you to save me from my own stupidity."

"It wasn't stupid to save those children."

"No, it wasn't, and it wasn't stupid to fall in love with you."

He smiled sadly. *"That* was stupid."

"I don't care. I love you."

Her lips welcomed his, and he wanted to lose himself in her warmth. As he teased her ear with the tip of his tongue, she whispered his name. His fingers slipped along her, rediscovering every delight that awaited him. He brightened her skin with kisses until the longing for her became a need.

It took every bit of his willpower to release her as a clock downstairs chimed three times.

She rose and straightened her dress. "I must tend to Kitty Cat. The doctor said it's important not to miss a single time of clearing out her throat."

He stood more slowly. With his feet on a lower riser, his eyes were even with hers. His arm around her waist brought her back to him as he asked, "Will you be all right?" He shook his head. "I don't know how many times I've asked you, and your answer's the same. You'll be fine."

"I *will* be."

He tipped her chin toward him. "I know how you hate to be alone."

"I'm not alone. I have Kitty Cat in there." She pointed to the bedroom, then put her hand over her heart. "And I have you here."

"I'll be back as soon as I can."

"I know."

"Are you going to stay in Haven?"

"For now. I really can't make any plans." She glanced at the bedroom door.

He tilted her face toward him again. "If, after she's better, you want to go somewhere else, *The Ohio Star* will take you any place along the river where you want to settle."

"Thank you," she said, her voice suddenly as cold as it had been when she bade her brother goodbye. Was that what she was telling *him* now?

He had thought now—when she had no more connections to River's Haven—she would reconsider his offer for the life that would make them both happy. They would have each other and the lives they wanted. Or so he had thought. He had been wrong again.

As she turned to go back into the room, he opened his mouth to call after her. He closed it. Anything he said now would only hurt her more.

Wyatt walked down the stairs, halting when he heard a weak cry. K. C.! That concoction that Rachel was using must burn her already ravaged throat. His hand tightened on the banister; then he strode out to the street. As he reached the gate, he saw Sawyer on his porch.

He was about to call to Sawyer and ask about the children, but paused when Mrs. Sawyer opened the door and held out her hand to her husband. The look they exchanged was so intimate that Wyatt felt like a voyeur. It linked them together, and it was made up of a tenderness that could not be described and a love that did not need to be.

Walking along the street, he stared at *The Ohio Star*. The fingers of smoke coming from the twin smokestacks announced that Horace had the boiler going, just as Wyatt had asked. The cargo was no longer on the deck, so it must have been put in the storage room, just as Wyatt had asked. The planks had been pulled in, disconnecting the boat with the land, just as Wyatt had asked.

He looked back at the village as he went down the hill to the river. Then he turned toward the river. He was a riverman, and he had a chance that few others got. *The Ohio Star* would make him and Horace rich men.

"How is K. C.?" Horace asked as Wyatt strode down the pier.

"Just the same." Loosening one of the thick ropes from the post holding the boat in place, he tossed it onto the deck. He walked to the other.

"We're really leaving today?" Horace walked along the prow of the boat, matching Wyatt's steps. "You're leaving them when the young'un is so sick?"

"Rachel told me to go so we didn't lose *The Ohio Star*." He jumped aboard, sensing the eagerness of the boat to take to the current in the middle of the river. He waited for the answering anticipation to fill him.

"This shipment can wait," Horace argued.

"We're more than a week late."

"Who cares? There isn't anything perishable in the storerooms."

"Perishable . . ." He grabbed the railing on the stairs and started up them. "C'mon, Horace. You need to get the boiler sending some pressure to the wheels before we drift out into the river."

"I can't believe you're abandoning her after you seduced her."

Wyatt climbed to the uppermost deck with Horace trailing after him. Throwing open the door to the pilothouse, he faced his partner and asked, "And why can't you believe that, Horace? Haven't you abandoned every woman you've bedded up and down the Ohio?"

"You ain't me, and Miss Rachel *loves* you!" Horace stayed outside the pilothouse, his hands fisted. He hit one against the other in frustration. "And you love *her!* That's the difference!"

"We can't talk about this now." He glanced out the window. "The boat's drifting away from the pier. Will you get the wheels turning?"

He thought Horace would say something more, but his partner stamped away. Wyatt was sure he could hear every step between the upper deck and the boiler room.

Resting his arms on the wheel, Wyatt waited for the whistle that would tell him the boat was ready to get underway. He started to look downriver, but his eyes were drawn back to the little town huddled beside the Ohio. When he and Horace had first come here, seeking a haven to repair *The Ohio Star*, he had not guessed that he would leave with his mind on a woman who had given him every reason to stay. Every reason, but then she had asked him to go to seek his dreams upon the river.

The whistle squealed up the tube beside the wheel. He reached for the controls for the paddlewheels. This would be the first time he had piloted *The Ohio Star* with both her paddlewheels working. A dream come true was now his. He steered the boat out into the river, this time not looking at anything but the water.

"Easy, easy," Rachel said as she put her arm around Kitty Cat. Rearranging the little girl's hands on the neck of the guitar, she added, "I told you that you could play it only if you didn't sing. You can't strain your throat now."

"But, Rachel—"

She put her finger to the child's lips. "No unnecessary talking either, Kitty Cat. You must rest your throat so you don't get sick again. That's the C chord. Now show me that G chord."

As Kitty Cat stretched her short fingers to place them in the proper place among the frets, Rachel smiled. She had almost given up on miracles, but Kitty Cat was alive. As the doctor had told her, once the little girl passed the most crucial moment of the disease's progress, the first signs of recovery would come swiftly.

Across the street, both Sean and Belinda were slowly

recovering. Others had not been so lucky. Many houses still had new cases, and more than a dozen people had died. Four of those were children from River's Haven, but they had been beyond help when they arrived in the village.

Somewhere amid all the work and the prayers, she had been cured, too. She had committed her life to River's Haven because she had been afraid of death, which had taken all her family except Merrill. As she had fought to save Kitty Cat, she realized that she had to accept death as she had learned with Wyatt's help to accept life. She had to let go of what had been and not regret its loss, but relish the memories she would never lose.

She looked in the direction of River's Haven. In the past two days, all sorts of rumors had come along the river, and she had no idea which ones might be true. There were whispers that everyone in the Community was gone or dead. Other stories suggested that the River's Haven folks had found a surefire cure for diphtheria but would not share it. That rumor she did not believe, because the River's Haven children would not still be here if that was true. She hoped the other tale was as inaccurate.

A whistle blew, and Kitty Cat tried to move to look out the window toward the railroad tracks.

With a laugh, Rachel kept her in place. "Young lady, you need to rest. Doc Bamburger told me the last time he was here that you must stay away from drafts."

Rachel's smile evaporated as she picked up the guitar and put it in a corner of the small bedroom. Doc Bamburger was now sick with the disease he had tried to halt. The villagers were left on their own without the doctor's gentle care or any medicine. Telegrams sent seeking help had not been answered. No one, not even doctors, wanted to risk death by coming to Haven.

Had that whistle announced the train arriving from Chicago with the medicine the village so desperately needed? She hoped so.

What her heart yearned for could not be relieved that easily. She lowered her eyes before Kitty Cat could see her sorrow. How odd that she now had what she had always hoped for—a family—but the dream was hollow without Wyatt.

"Are we done with my lesson?" whispered Kitty Cat. "Will you read me a story?"

"The one from Miss Underhill's fairy tale book?" She smiled weakly.

"Yes! The one about the princess on a glass mountain and the prince who rescued her."

Picking up the book, Rachel sat on the bed. She started to page through it. When Kitty Cat took it and balanced it on her lap, the little girl quickly found the story she wanted.

" 'Once upon a time,' " Rachel began, " 'there was a king with a daughter so beautiful that he placed her on a glass mountain. Only the bravest, most worthy knight would be able to scale it and win her heart. So she sat there, day after day, year after—' "

"Rachel!" Alice came running up the stairs.

Putting down the book, Rachel called, "We're in here."

"Rachel, Emma just stopped by to say that medicine *and* doctors have arrived in Haven!" She smiled at Kitty Cat. "Maybe everyone else can be saved."

"Doctors?" asked Rachel. "How did anyone convince them to come here?"

"I can be very persuasive," said a deeper voice from the hallway. "Or so I've been told."

"Wyatt!" She jumped up from the bed.

He scooped her up into his arms and twirled her about. As he lowered her back to her feet, his mouth slanted across hers, eager and demanding and offering her everything she had feared was lost forever. She locked her fingers behind his nape and clung to him, fearing if she let him go she would open her eyes to find he was only the fantasy created by a broken heart.

When he raised his mouth from hers, his heart beat against her and his breath warmed her face. He was real!

"What are you doing back here?" she asked, combing her fingers up through his hair. She wanted to touch every inch of him to convince herself that he was really here holding her. "Your shipment was going to take you at least a week down the river."

"I couldn't worry about delivering some dry goods down the river. My most important delivery was right back here to Haven."

"You? *You* brought doctors and medicine?"

His thumb coursed along her cheekbones as he smiled. "They really didn't need much persuading. The doctors want to stop this outbreak of diphtheria before it goes beyond Haven and River's Haven."

"River's Haven? You took doctors there, too?"

"Our first stop once we had a full cargo of help to bring here." He smiled. "Your brother's alive and well and just as ornery as ever, but even he had to see the sense of getting assistance from outsiders."

She closed her eyes, but could not halt her tears. Covering her face with her hands, she sobbed as she had not dared to since before her father died. She had been determined to be strong, first for Merrill and then for both Wyatt and Kitty Cat.

He put his arms around her and let her weep against his chest.

"Wyatt!" called Kitty Cat.

Rachel stepped away and chided, "Kitty Cat, you *must* not shout."

Taking Rachel's hand, he led her into the bedroom. Alice smiled and stepped out, closing the door. He sat on the bed and smiled.

"How are you doing, K. C.?" When she opened her mouth to answer, he added, "Quietly."

"Better," the little girl whispered. "Rachel's teaching me to play the guitar, and she reads me stories, and she tells me about how Sean and his sister are doing."

"Pretty boring, huh?"

Kitty Cat dimpled and nodded.

Ruffling her hair, he said, "You'll be better soon. You'd better be. I'm going to need you to help me."

"On *The Ohio Star*?"

Although his answer was for the child, he looked up at Rachel as he said, "No, not on *The Ohio Star*. I sold my share of it to Horace just before I came ashore."

"You did what?" Rachel gasped.

He stood and folded her hands between his. "Honey, I couldn't endure having you be let down again by someone you love . . . by someone who loves you."

She repeated his last words silently, then asked, no louder than Kitty Cat's whisper, "But, Wyatt, owning that boat with Horace was what you've always wanted."

"It was, but it's not what I want from this point forward. What Horace was able to give me now will be enough to buy a few acres of land. I hear those left at River's Haven are going to be selling off everything there. I've been thinking of buying a small cottage like one I saw from the river. A small cottage with a red door that will be perfect for you and me and Kitty Cat." He chuckled. "And anyone else who comes along."

"You want to live at River's Haven?" She could not believe she was hearing him correctly.

"No!" He laughed again. "But we can build a replica of your cottage on some land near the river. There, we'll also build our own pier, and I can repair boats. I'm very good at it, you know."

"So Horace told me." If this was a dream, it was the sweetest one she had ever had.

"My agreement with Horace is that he'll pay me a small percentage of the profits from the boat, which will help me buy the machinery I need from River's Haven's metal shop. Horace intends to gather up some of his kids along the river to help him on *The Ohio Star*. So what do you say, honey? I've admitted that I can change my mind. Will you tell me that you've changed your mind, too, and give up the notion that you never want to get married? Will you marry me?"

"Yes, she will," piped up Kitty Cat from the bed.

Rachel hugged the little girl, then looked back at Wyatt. Softly she said, "Yes, I will."

Epilogue

The guests were gone. The cake was now crumbs among the other emptied dishes on the table. The music and laughter had faded away, leaving only the songs of the insects and the river to swirl through the night. A soft breeze barely moved the leaves in the tall trees that stretched their branches over the small cottage in a verdant blanket. In the cottage, a single lamp burned in the larger bedroom, for the one in the smaller room had been extinguished nearly an hour ago. Above the trees, the stars could not challenge the brilliant glow of the half-moon. Its light danced atop the ripples in the river.

Rachel drew her gaze from the water as she heard footfalls behind her. Standing from where she had been sitting on one of the pair of rocking chairs on the porch, she held out her hand to Wyatt—to her husband.

He wove his fingers through hers. "That was the best housewarming party I've ever attended, honey."

"Was it the only housewarming party you've attended?"

He laughed and spun her into his arms. "You're never going to stop being so honest, are you?"

"No, because I want you to know how happy I am to be with you and Kitty Cat here. Our own house and our own family. It seems incredible."

"You're incredible, honey." Even in the moonlight, she could see that roguish sparkle come into his eyes. "Now that everyone is gone, but us, I think it's time to warm up our house in the very best way."

"I like how you think." She kissed him quickly, then stepped back, holding out her fingers to him.

Again, he clasped her hand, and they walked hand in hand through the door that in the daylight would be a brilliant red.

If you liked MOONLIGHT ON WATER, be sure to look for Jo Ann Ferguson's next release in the heartwarming Haven series, AFTER THE RAIN, available in bookstores everywhere September 2002.

For Irish immigrant Cailin Rafferty, America is the land of *broken* promises. Her husband's betrayal and his family's cruel lies might have separated her from her three beloved children, but Cailin will stop at nothing to find them. Penniless and alone, her journey brings her to the sleepy town of Haven, Indiana, where gentle Samuel Jennings rescued them from the orphan train that carried them west. A solitary farmer with painful secrets of his own, Samuel is more of a father to the children than their own was—and wrenching them from the peaceful comfort of his home is nearly as difficult as the realization that Cailin feels something for the quiet, warmhearted man. Risking her heart again is a chance Cailin isn't willing to take—unless Samuel can convince her that his love will provide shelter from every storm. . . .

Readers can write to the author at: P.O. Box 575, Rehoboth, MA 02769 or visit her Website at: www.joannferguson.com.

COMING IN AUGUST 2002 FROM
ZEBRA BALLAD ROMANCES

__A FALLEN WOMAN: The Brides of Bath
by Cheryl Bolen   0-8217-7249-X $5.99US/$7.99CAN
Since her husband's tragic death, Carlotta Ennis had hoped to attract a
wealthy husband in Bath. Instead she made the ruinous mistake of loving a
rake who was willing to seduce her, but not to marry her. Now she is certain
no decent gentleman will ever marry her . . . until James Rutledge returns
home from the war and offers his hand . . .

__A DANGEROUS FANCY: American Heiresses
by Tracy Cozzens   0-8217-7351-8 $5.99US/$7.99CAN
Lily Carrington's ambitious mother had set her sights on a titled marriage
for Lily. As honorable as she was beautiful, Lily vowed not to disappoint
her family—even as she became the pawn in a sordid plot of seduction by
the Prince of Wales himself . . . and found herself falling in love with a most
unlikely hero.

__KING OF HEARTS: The Gamblers
by Pat Pritchard   0-8217-7255-4 $5.99US/$7.99CAN
Wade McCord, a U.S. Marshall, poses as a gambler at a stagecoach stop to
smoke out a notorious outlaw gang. But he never counted on his burning
desire for Lottie Hammond, a woman who may be in league with the outlaws.
Wade knows Lottie has secrets, but he also knows that the time has come
for him to gamble his heart on the promise of love.

__ON MY LADY'S HONOR: . . . And One for All
by Kate Silver   0-8217-7386-0 $5.99US/$7.99CAN
Sophie Delamanse envisiones a dull marriage to Count Lamotte, one of her
twin brother's Musketeer friends. Her life took a tragic turn when the plague
consumed her family. Her brother promised that Lamotte would come for
her, but when he never arrived, Sophie vowed to go to *him*—disguised as
her brother—and make him pay for his dishonor.

Call toll free **1-888-345-BOOK** to order by phone or use this cou-
pon to order by mail. *ALL BOOKS AVAILABLE AUGUST 01, 2002.*
Name _____
Address _____
City _____ State _____ Zip _____
Please send me the books that I have checked above.
I am enclosing $_____
Plus postage and handling* $_____
Sales tax (in NY and TN) $_____
Total amount enclosed $_____
*Add $2.50 for the first book and $.50 for each additional book. Send
check or money order (no cash or CODs) to: **Kensington Publishing
Corp., Dept. C.O., 850 Third Avenue, New York, NY 10022**
Prices and numbers subject to change without notice. Valid only in the
U.S. All orders subject to availability. **NO ADVANCE ORDERS.**
Visit our website at **www.kensingtonbooks.com.**

Celebrate Romance with one of Today's Hottest Authors
Meagan McKinney

__**In the Dark** $6.99US/$8.99CAN
  0-8217-6341-5

__**The Fortune Hunter** $6.50US/$8.00CAN
  0-8217-6037-8

__**Gentle From the Night** $5.99US/$7.50CAN
  0-8217-5803-9

__**Merry Widow** $6.50US/$8.50CAN
  0-8217-6707-0

__**My Wicked Enchantress** $5.99US/$7.50CAN
  0-8217-5661-3

__**No Choice But Surrender** $5.99US/$7.50CAN
  0-8217-5859-4

Call toll free **1-888-345-BOOK** to order by phone or use this coupon to order by mail.
Name_____
Address _____
City_____ State_____ Zip_____
Please send me the books that I have checked above.
I am enclosing $_____
Plus postage and handling* $_____
Sales tax (in New York and Tennessee) $_____
Total amount enclosed $_____
*Add $2.50 for the first book and $.50 for each additional book.
Send check or money order (no cash or CODs) to:
Kensington Publishing Corp., 850 Third Avenue, New York, NY 10022
Prices and numbers subject to change without notice.
All orders subject to availability.
Check out our website at www.kensingtonbooks.com.

The Queen of
Romance

Cassie Edwards

__Desire's Blossom $5.99US/$7.99CAN
   0-8217-6405-5

__Exclusive Ecstasy $5.99US/$7.99CAN
   0-8217-6597-3

__Passion's Web $5.99US/$7.50CAN
   0-8217-5726-1

__Portrait of Desire $5.99US/$7.50CAN
   0-8217-5862-4

__Savage Obsession $5.99US/$7.50CAN
   0-8217-5554-4

__Silken Rapture $5.99US/$7.50CAN
   0-8217-5999-X

__Rapture's Rendezvous $5.99US/$7.50CAN
   0-8217-6115-3

Call toll free **1-888-345-BOOK** to order by phone or use this coupon to order by mail.

Name_____

Address_____

City_____ State _____ Zip _____

Please send me the books that I have checked above.

I am enclosing	$_____
Plus postage and handling*	$_____
Sales tax (in New York and Tennessee)	$_____
Total amount enclosed	$_____

*Add $2.50 for the first book and $.50 for each additional book. Send check or money order (no cash or CODs) to:

Kensington Publishing Corp., 850 Third Avenue, New York, NY 10022

Prices and numbers subject to change without notice.

All orders subject to availability.

Check out our website at **www.kensingtonbooks.com**.

DO YOU HAVE THE
HOHL COLLECTION?

Call toll free **1-888-345-BOOK** to order by phone or use this coupon
to order by mail. ALL BOOKS AVAILABLE DECEMBER 1, 2000.

Name_____

Address_____

City_____ State _____ Zip _____

Please send me the books that I have checked above.

I am enclosing $_____

Plus postage and handling* $_____

Sales tax (in New York and Tennessee) $_____

Total amount enclosed $_____

*Add $2.50 for the first book and $.50 for each additional book. Send check
or money order (no cash or CODs) to:

Kensington Publishing Corp., 850 Third Avenue, New York, NY 10022
Prices and numbers subject to change without notice. Valid only in the U.S.
All orders subject to availability. **NO ADVANCE ORDERS.**
Visit out our website at **www.kensingtonbooks.com.**

Put a Little Romance in Your Life With

Betina Krahn

__Hidden Fire $5.99US/$7.50CAN
0-8217-5793-8

__Love's Brazen Fire $5.99US/$7.50CAN
0-8217-5691-5

__Luck Be a Lady $5.99US/$6.99CAN
0-8217-7313-5

__Passion's Ransom $5.99US/$6.99CAN
0-8217-5130-1

Call toll free **1-888-345-BOOK** to order by phone or use this coupon
to order by mail.
Name _____
Address _____
City _____ State_____ Zip_____
Please send me the books that I checked above.
I am enclosing $_____
Plus postage and handling* $_____
Sales tax (in NY and TN) $_____
Total amount enclosed $_____
*Add $2.50 for the first book and $.50 for each additional book.
Send check or money order (no cash or CODs) to: **Kensington Publishing Corp., 850 Third Avenue, New York, NY 10022**
Prices and numbers subject to change without notice.
All orders subject to availability.
Visit our website at **www.kensingtonbooks.com**.